PRAISE FOR *The New and Improved Romie Futch*

"*The New and Improved Romie Futch* not only marks the arrival of one of the funniest, smartest, and most unnerving novels you'll read this year, but also a vision for Southern literature that could only have sprung from Julia Elliott's wild, devastating, and wholly original imagination. Consider me a fan for life."

—LAURA VAN DEN BERG, author of *Find Me*

"This novel reminds the cynical, seen-it-all reader [that] sometimes strangeness is enough. Elliott's work, in its own snarling and unruly way, contains brilliance."

—*Kirkus*

PRAISE FOR *The Wilds*

Named a BEST BOOK of 2014 by

Kirkus
BuzzFeed Books
Book Riot
Electric Literature

And a *New York Times* Editors' Choice

"Elliott makes us hear contemporary English in a new way."

—*New York Times Book Review*

"Remarkable . . . [Elliott's] dark, modern spin on Southern Gothic creates tales that surprise, shock, and sharply depict vice and virtue."

—*Publishers Weekly*, starred review

"Robots may search for love, but there's nothing wilder than human nature in this genre-bending short story collection from debut writer Elliott . . . This book will take you to places you never dreamed of going and aren't quite sure you want to stay, but you won't regret the journey."

—*Kirkus*

"Humans, robots, and humans with robotic limbs pine for carnal satisfaction in Elliott's impressively inventive, often macabre collection, animated by her characters' outsize appetites for sex, knowledge, faith, and kindness."

—*Booklist*

"This is wacky, bizarre content, but with a nice dose of realism even in the most absurd points. If you like Karen Russell, this is a good choice for you."

—*Book Riot*

"[Elliott's] work is unique and haunting, often drifting into apocalyptic and dystopian territory, but in many ways rooted in reality. I could not turn away from her tales. At the end of my time with *The Wilds*, I was completely devoted to Elliott's dark depictions of the world."

—*The Rumpus*

"Elliott's inventive first collection is replete with robotic limbs and levitation—but also grit and force. A dark piece of magic that glows in the reading."

—*Flavorwire*

"Julia Elliott's stories—which thrive beautifully somewhere between the lyrically haunting works of Barry Hannah and the retrospective works of Lewis Nordan—offer nothing but the great, beautiful, dark regions of the human heart. These are stories to be cherished, taught, and brooded upon. These are stories in which to bathe oneself."

—GEORGE SINGLETON, author of *Stray Decorum*

"Julia Elliott's stories are an endangered species—vital, poignant, and rare. Readers should send themselves recklessly into *The Wilds*, for they will emerge spellbound, all the better for it."

—KATE BERNHEIMER, author of *How a Mother Weaned Her Girl from Fairy Tales*

"*The Wilds* [is] a very well-written book of short stories that are creepy and weird in the good way. In the title story, a girl wearing a homemade crown of bird skulls tells of getting taken prisoner by a feral pack of boys, known as the Wilds, who live nearby. 'Their chests glowed with firefly juice. They had steak knives strapped to their belts and some of them wore goggles.' How can you go wrong with that setup?"

—ARTHUR BRADFORD, author of *Turtleface and Beyond*

THE NEW AND IMPROVED

ROMIE FUTCH

THE NEW AND IMPROVED
ROMIE FUTCH

JULIA ELLIOTT

 TIN HOUSE BOOKS / Portland, Oregon & Brooklyn, New York

Published by Tin House Books, Portland, Oregon and Brooklyn, New York

Distributed by W. W. Norton and Company.

Library of Congress Cataloging-in-Publication Data

Elliott, Julia 1968-
    The new and improved Romie Futch : a novel / Julia Elliott. -- First U.S. edition.
        pages cm
    ISBN 978-1-941040-15-7 (alk. paper)
    I. Title.
    PS3605.L4477N49 2015
    813'.6--dc23
                            2015016030

COVER IMAGE CREDIT:
Illustration from *Greek Myths*. Illustration copyright © 2010 by Sarah Young. Reproduced by permission of the publisher, Candlewick Press, on behalf of Walker Books, London.

First US edition 2015
Printed in the USA
Interior design by Diane Chonette
www.tinhouse.com

For Eva

By the late twentieth century, our time, a mythic time, we are all chimeras, theorized and fabricated hybrids of machine and organism; in short, we are cyborgs.

—DONNA HARAWAY, *Simians, Cyborgs, and Women: The Reinvention of Nature*

PART ONE

ONE

On a Friday evening in June, stoked by the awesome weather, Chip, Lee, and I were doing tequila shots on the patio of Noah's Ark Taxidermy. Out on the blood-spattered bricks, we talked about old times—when we'd skip biology and get baked in the parking lot of Swamp Fox High.

"Back when I turned you two dorks on to metal," said Chip.

"You got it backwards," I said.

"Yeah," said Lee. "Romie had that Rush tape."

"Rush is for pussies," said Chip.

"Rush wasn't the only one," I said, wanting to hash out the differences between King Crimson's metal moments and the lameness of he-hussies like Mötley Crüe, but, as usual, I found my tongue paralyzed by weed.

"As I recall"—Chip grinned like a donkey—"old Romie was into the Moody Blues."

When Chip started bellowing "Nights in White Satin," we all had a decent laugh.

There we were, three bachelors of a certain age, none of us remotely successful. I was a year into my divorce, a fortyish animal stuffer, balding and childless, though pregnant with a beer belly. The heavy-metal mane I used to flaunt had dwindled to a puny ponytail. Bank of America was threatening to seize my house. AAA Financial, who'd "bought my debt," had, just that morning, offered to "renegotiate" my payment plan. And three irked customers wanted to know when I'd have their specimens stuffed—buck head, mallard, coon—each animal currently chopped and scattered, hides in pickle baths, organs rotting in thirty-gallon Hefty SteelSaks.

Chip Watts, an ex-jock turned pothead turned drunk, had long since flunked out of Clemson and returned to Hampton to marry several festival queens (Watermelon, Okra, Cooter), divorcing one for the other before running to fat and losing his mojo. But that summer he was on Atkins. He'd lost twenty pounds. He popped testosterone supplements like Tic Tacs. Hiding his sagging gut under the pleats of his Duck Head khakis, he pranced around, bragging about how much poon he was pulling, how many ATVs he'd unloaded that week, how many touchdowns he'd scored back in high school, when his body was still a beefcake and he sported a mullet with a body wave.

Chip had always been a talker. He knew how to bait the ladies, how to floor them with tales that featured him wrestling grizzly bears, tracking wild boars over rough terrain, grabbling sixty-pound catfish from their nests and dragging the thrashing monsters to shore with his bare hands.

Lee Decker was a much chiller dude. An aspiring surrealist painter in high school who now painted houses, he was skinny and still had enough hair to show off. An inch or two of sun-streaked shag casually brushed the collar of those olive shirts he ordered from camping catalogs. His smiles came quick, without nervous tics. He slept like a NyQuil-dosed baby and never fussed much over life.

We were in high spirits that evening, just because it was June. The grass was thick, the fruit trees were starting to put out, and a million cicadas buzzed in the pines. I thought I might call my ex-wife, Helen, just to catch up, or at least whip out my phone and check her E-Live status, gawk at her latest round of photos, even though I knew she had certain settings in force to keep my nose out of her butt.

Her relationship status still taunted me: DIVORCED. She still worked at the Technomatic Quick Lab (doing mostly paternity testing, which she hated with all her soul). The girl still enjoyed swimming, moonlit walks, Art with a capital *A*, and deep-sea creatures (watching them on the Internet, at least). In fact, her latest profile pic was of a vampire squid blinking three thousand feet below sea level, its weird arms covered with threatening spikes. When I first saw it, I choked out a bitter laugh. That was Helen all over: too prickly to hug, sulking in the dark, making herself invisible, but then *bam*—a burst of light so beautiful it knocked the wind out of your lungs.

"Stop thinking about Helen," said bastard Chip.

"What makes you think I was?"

Chip raised a wild eyebrow. That day his face seemed to droop from his sticky hairdo. Unlike me, whose hairline receded in a heart formation, exaggerating my widow's peak with a Dracula vibe more comic than sexy, Chip had a low hairline and was balding from the crown down. His take on the comb-over involved gelling the fuck out of his auburn hair and finger-brushing the clumped bristles straight up, like Billy Idol circa 1983, but with scalp patches galore. He also sported a hick-van-dyke, the facial hair that aging country singers and motorcycle dudes often cultivate to downplay their jowls.

"Y'all ready to rumble?" said Chip, who was already walking crooked—half due to tipsiness and half to a ruptured disc. We

piled into his monster Escalade, RATT blaring on the stereo—
"Round and Round" mocking me with its stupid lyrics.

. .

We were being digested by the Power Bar, sucked down into its
pumping intestines, its thick press of shimmying bodies, flashing
wide-screens, and vintage poker machines. The sound system was
blasting the latest teen skank, that Brit with a blue beehive who
yodeled through a pitch corrector to pounding synths.

Chip had cornered three data processors in day-to-night mode.
Their office duds were sparked up with costume jewels. They
looked hopeful. And I felt tired already.

"What do you do?" said the prettiest of the three.

"I sell dreams," yelled Chip.

Watching Chip bellow over the music made me feel sleepier.
For some reason, I craved the sunken den of my childhood, with
its shag carpet the color of algae and its lumpy plaid couch that
smelled of gravy, the residue from countless suppers cooked by my
mother. I wanted to curl up there and watch our old TV, its rab-
bit ears lumpy with tinfoil. I wanted to smell country-fried-steak
fumes wafting down the linoleum stairs, hear my daddy washing
up in the half bath, hear my mother crooning some dreamy 1950s
tune, her pitch-perfect voice full of eerie longing as she tended the
sputtering beef. I wanted to slip into a nap, calmed by the pleasant feeling of having *the future* light-years ahead of me, not even
hounded by hormones yet, penis curled in soft innocence like a
dozing baby gerbil.

But I was smack-dab in a meat market, in a fantasy cave at the
end of Magnolia Plaza strip mall, listening to Chip tell a dumb
joke to three half-attractive ladies worn out from paper pushing

and ready to call it a night. Everybody seemed run-down all of a sudden, despite the loud music and spastic light. It was like the vents oozed some sort of gas and we'd all soon collapse into a strobe-spattered heap.

"I say we repair to the VIP," yelled Chip, pointing toward the VIP lounge, so we relocated to this over-air-conditioned nook furnished with armless couches, plastic coffee tables, and a beer clock that featured blondes in fur bikinis.

I ended up knee-to-knee with a girl named Renee—midthirties, dyed red hair, her skin freaky from too many cosmetic procedures and crusted with an inch of makeup. She had a degree in administrative office technology. She owned a blond Labrador named Ace. And I could tell by the way she narrowed her eyes that she thought taxidermy was a redneck thing, that all it took to escape her own hick origins was a slick haircut, designer footwear, and mobile uploads of her lunches at quirky "indie" joints like the Chuckling Newt Café.

Every time I spoke, Renee crinkled her nose and cast a lusty glance Chip's way. He'd started up with his outdoorsman routine, describing the time he'd tracked a two-hundred-pound cougar through thirty miles of swamp and shot it with his bow and arrow.

"It was like an outer body experience," said Chip, "like *I* was the arrow, flying through the air."

"Thought cougars were extinct," said Lee.

"Making a comeback," said Chip.

"Course, it ain't legal to shoot 'em," I said.

"What about when a wild beast tries to *kill you*?" Chip bugged his eyes at me. "You got a right to protect your life."

"Thought you chased it." I smiled.

"That motherfucker *chased me* for ten miles," said Chip, switching stories midstream, backtracking through his own bloody footprints. I pictured the cougar flying backward from its death sprawl, running in reverse through the swamp, all the way back to the pine forest where Chip had first spotted it. I saw it pounce on Chip, who'd been innocently target shooting, knocking beer cans off a hickory stump while whistling "Sweet Child o' Mine."

"Whatever." I rolled my eyes.

Renee duck-faced at Chip and slipped off to the powder room. The other two women had their eyes firmly planted on the aging athlete as well. I sat sulking as Chip ordered yet another gin and tonic and amped up his courtship spiel with the prettiest of the trio. His girl inched closer. Their booze breaths mingled. Soon they'd be calling it a night: her first, in a nervous flutter; him five minutes later, his smirk unbearable, his pants crooked, his splotched cheeks the color of pepperoni.

I sighed, exhausted, suddenly, to the bone. I was hatching an escape plan when I saw Helen.

Dear Lord. She fluttered in the flashing light, not dressed in designer-slut mode as I'd feared but wearing a simple green sundress, a red zinnia tucked behind her ear. Her hair was braided in some old-timey fashion that had yet to grace this shit town. In the dimness of the Power Bar, through my beer goggles, she looked fifteen years younger. Hell, she looked almost like her high school self. I wondered if she'd hit the jackpot and hired some clever plastic surgeon who could make a woman look dewy, not pinched and raw, straining to look young, fillers and nips doing peculiar things you couldn't quite put your finger on.

When she stepped under a strobe, I got a better look and saw the age on her, more like thirty-one than eighteen. But she still looked good. My heart was split into two pieces. One part felt certain that she was my destiny, that we'd just hit a glitch, that this woman was truly mine and would be again. The other part whispered that she was out in the world making her own life.

When I saw a man cruise up behind her and paw at her zinnia hair accessory, I drifted toward the second feeling. She was already romping in a meadow of wildflowers with this linen-pants-wearing twerp. He looked sharp and overironed, trim with a slight gut, beyond fifty for sure, his silver-blond hair blow-dried just so. He had that *professional* quality. At first I thought *lawyer*, then *insurance*, then *entrepreneur*, which could mean anything these days—pharmaceutical mogul or putt-putt profiteer.

I was ready to slither into a gash in the ground, lie in my hole and let the soil fall over me, when Helen spotted me. She looked half-horrified, half-amused. We had no choice but to wave and trudge through the crazy disco lights toward each other.

"Hey, you look great," I said, sounding too chirpy.

"How are you?" She looked me over (brief pause, like a hiccup, as she inspected my gut).

"Fine."

"How's the stuffed animal business?"

"Same old, same old." I shrugged.

The corners of her mouth twitched downward. I recognized her pity-tainted frown from the old days.

"This is Boykin." She turned to her friend.

Boykin? Are you serious?

"His mother was a Boykin," Helen explained, "and a breeder of the infamous spaniel, our state dog."

Boykin was indeed what he called an *attorney*, and he'd recently *invested in* a gallery on Azalea Street, that teeny-tiny nook of artsy-fartsiness supported by rich dabblers in this town, mostly trophy wives with liberal arts degrees. There was a lunch spot or two, a brewpub, a pet boutique, a coffee place, a designer clothing shop, a salon/day spa, and what have you. Though the establishments in this so-called historic district tended to display lame paintings of flowers, pet portraits, and the occasional "abstract" smears a monkey could paint, Hampton had yet to open a bona fide art gallery. And here was Boykin on the forefront of the art scene, looking sleepy and a bit jowly.

I didn't feel the pain until they'd danced off into the night. I imagined them hopping into a convertible Jaguar or some other pimpin' geezer ride. Lee was right behind me, saying, "Let me buy you a drink, buddy." The office ladies had skedaddled. Some other party had settled into the VIP room. So Lee and I sat at the bar doing tequila shots—I can't remember how many—until the whole joint glowed darkly like a video-game dungeon. The black lights were doing freaky things with Lee's freckles. He grinned like a ghoulish Opie Taylor and offered me another shot. Like a fool, I took it, longing for fresh air, longing for those lazy summer nights Helen and I'd once spent on our front porch, chilling in fold-out lounge chairs, watching clouds skim over the moon. One night she told me that shadows were darker on the moon than on Earth, yet another fascinating factoid she'd pulled from the Internet, and we got lost in endless speculation, sipping Millers, our hands moving into the one-foot space between our chairs to touch idly, to punc-tuate the wonder we felt—for the moon and the universe and the endless casual mystery of our love.

"You got to give it a rest, Romie," said Lee.

"What?"

"Helen." He whispered her name.

"I thought you meant the shots." I choked out a laugh.

"That too."

I was about to call it a night when in walked a girl with a pan-da face and a heart of gold—a sweet, maternal, somewhat flaky, slightly pudgy girl who'd once saved my ass.

Crystal Flemming was a mess. Her fake snakeskin purse rat-tled with pill bottles. Her bleach job had not been maintained, and dark roots sprouted from her scalp. She smoked Marlboro Reds, guzzled gin like it was Dasani, dipped generously into God-knows-what kind of pharmaceutical helpers, but somehow looked half-decent. Haggard, yes, with crow's-feet and lines around her mouth. But her lips were still luscious, her eyes still big and dreamy and shiny as crystals. She could still rock a pair of jeans from the juniors department, despite her muffin top and bubble butt, an inch or two south of where it used to be.

I know I sound like a sexist ass. But actually, Crystal's imperfections were what comforted me, making me less self-conscious about my potbelly and thinning hair, which I refused to cut and which I gathered into a pathetic snake of a ponytail and fastened with a cheap rubber band.

"Roman Morrison Futch," she said, using the full name that only relatives and ex-girlfriends were in on, wagging her finger like a grandma while licking pink gloss from her lips. "What you been up to?"

"Same old, same old."

I ordered a bourbon on the rocks. Lee flashed me a thumbs-up and stumbled out into the night. Within thirty minutes, Crystal Flemming and I were right back where we used to be: me thinking about Helen as Crystal shit-talked her ex, Chad Hutto, a former fullback nicknamed Chewbacca who had recently struck gold in the life insurance racket.

"Of course he was running around on me," Crystal said. "You remember Chris Gooding's little sister Carla? Dumb as mud but thinks she's hot to trot? I used to babysit her. Changed her diaper. One night after I put her to bed, Chewy and me were making out on the couch and suddenly she was just standing there, hugging her Care Bear and watching. I think she's had a thing for him ever since."

"Warped," I said.

"And if that ain't bad enough, State Farm's got a billboard with his face on it, right behind Kmart, which is on my way to the unemployment office. Thank you, Universe. Just in case I forget that bastard for one second, there he is, larger than life and grinning at me."

I'd recently spotted the billboard in question on my way back from Yoda's Toyota Salvage Yard, noting the *Star Wars*–themed coincidence at the time. I was hungover as usual, and the sight of Chewbacca Hutto's puffy orange face rising like the sun over Kmart was too much to take. A fringe of chest hair peeked from his collar, hinting at the sweaty Wookiee hidden under the starched dress shirt. His green eyes still had that wolf-man glow.

"Are you friends with him on E-Live?" I asked.

"Hell no," said Crystal. "You friends with Helen?"

"I'm a dumb-ass," I said, and Crystal Flemming did not disagree.

• •

I woke in a panic attack, naked and tangled in sweaty sheets. A foot above my head, crystal unicorns frolicked on a particleboard shelf. Crystal suncatchers shimmered in every window. Assorted new age crystals were set out in mystical arrangements on the dresser, right under a framed *Excalibur* poster. And Crystal herself, looking like Stevie Nicks in a whispery robe with batwing sleeves, fluttered into the room, an amethyst amulet dangling between her boobs. Her eyes were huge and glossy and bloodshot. She kissed my forehead and placed a Xanax on my tongue. I eased back down into a pile of satin pillows and waited for the pill to calm me.

"I had a weird feeling when I drove up to the Power Bar last night," she said. "I was wondering what the old universe had in store. I walk in, and who do I see? Roman Morrison Futch."

"Last night was off the chain," I said, accepting the goblet of spiked orange juice that had magically appeared in her hand, straining to remember what, exactly, had happened.

I vaguely recalled Crystal veering into the parking lot of Druid Forest, an apartment complex on Highway 21. Vaguely recalled stumbling through a dark studio apartment that smelled of Nag Champa, crashing onto the bed, falling off several times due to an insane number of tiny, slippery pillows. And then I was washed in purple light, hunched over a three-foot Day-Glo bong, Pink Floyd on the stereo. Crystal was naked, wreathed in cigarette smoke. I had a raging erection. And then I didn't. I think there was some rolling around at some point in between these two states.

"And I had a dream about you last week, Romie," she said. "Dreamed we were doing acid like we did twenty years ago, except we were in a hot-air balloon, floating over the mall. Your hair looked just like Robert Plant's, except not as blond."

"Robert Plant now or Robert Plant way back?"

"Way back." Crystal smiled, that small, slightly sad bending of the lips that made her look like a panda, especially when she'd gobbed on too much eye shadow. "And Helen had moved to Mexico. What do you think the universe is trying to say with that one?"

Crystal shot me a smirk. Then she grabbed a glass pipe from her wicker nightstand, stuffed a fat bud into it, took a long hit, and handed it to me.

"It's too early for the bong." She winked.

"What time is it?"

"Twelve thirty."

I took the pipe.

The Xanax was working its magic. My mad-dog heart began to chill. Shame over the general failure of my life and feelings of nameless dread melted away as Fleetwood Mac flowed from dusty stereo speakers and Crystal poured me another mimosa. Sunlight gushed through the sliding glass doors that led out to her tiny balcony, which boasted a dying geranium and overlooked the back of Patriot Self-Storage.

Three drinks and two bong hits later, I found myself entwined with her on the bed, breathing in the familiar swimming-pool smell of her hair and the Poison perfume she'd worn back in 1994, when Helen left me for an art student named Adrian and sweet Crystal had saved my life.

· ·

Crystal's son, Sam, was off at a Surf City time-share with his daddy, so I camped at Crystal's place, not setting foot out of her magical cave for a solid week. We smoked weed, drank booze, popped Adderall at midnight, and took Morpheus to sleep. We buffered our hangovers with Crystal's precious Xanax, which she fed me as a mother would Skittles to a diabetic child. And then we'd repeat the whole deal the next day, starting around one.

Bands sometimes practiced down at Patriot Self-Storage. Our favorite was a cover band whose half-decent "Stairway to Heaven," along with a half tab of Soma, soothed our stoned brains. We'd kiss, grope, stumble to her bed, with its avalanche of accent pillows. We'd fuck so lazily that sometimes I'd pass out on top of her, then I'd wake up, go to town like a jackrabbit on crank, feel myself go numb, and lose myself in a dream of Helen, at which point I'd surge back to life. I'd charge forward with tears dripping down my cheeks.

Each day at four, just as her second beer began to melt her angst about her employment situation, Crystal spoke to Sam on the phone. She'd be quiet for a spell after she hung up. Then we'd pack the bong, switch from beer to liquor, and stream something trippy on Netflix—*A Clockwork Orange, The Wall.*

"It's different," Crystal would say. "What do you think the universe is trying to tell us?"

"I can't exactly describe it."

"Me neither, but I know it's something important."

She'd look at me with those eyes. I'd note a little flower of feeling that was sweet enough, but then I'd remember Helen. Sometimes the memory would be dramatic: Helen renting a hotel room for our tenth anniversary and filling it with wisteria. But mostly I'd recall everyday moments: Helen squatting over a flower bed, yelling at me to come check out this weird beetle she'd found, smiling slyly, treasuring the brilliant blue creature like a jewel in the bowl of her palms. Just like in the old days, my feelings for Crystal would shrivel. By the time her son was due back from Surf City, I was ready to go home. I was not prepared to face life—lapsed mortgage, Visa bills, failing taxidermy business—but I did need a break from the constant partying, the hangovers that grew more bottomless each day, each trap door leading to another trap door, and so on, over and over, until my brain was free-falling at the speed of light.

So I went home, stripped the dingy sheets off my bed, and passed out on the naked mattress. With the help of two Morpheuses, I slept for twenty hours straight, the last stretch spotted with nightmares involving my mother during her final days, shrunk down to seventy-five pounds, her body wreathed in the plastic tubing that kept it going. I woke up with cotton mouth and tremors, only six pills left in my stockpile, a departing care package from sweet Crystal.

· ·

I allowed myself a half Xanax to survive that first morning, fortifying myself for a slew of voice-mail messages from the irate customers I'd ignored during my stay at Druid Forest. Timmy Dennis wanted to know where the fuck his mallards were (slumped in the fridge, skin rancidity threatening their plumage quality). Duval Elliott had finally taken his kill, a prize buck with a Boone and Crockett antler spread of 143.6, "elsewheres." Ben Horton didn't want to pester me much but thought he should check on the status of his coon. Though I'd finally got that sucker in just the right pose, playfully pawing the air where a varnished bream would soon be gasping for its life, I hadn't stuffed the fish—didn't remember what I'd done with the carcass, in fact—plus the raccoon itself had no eyes.

I made some calls, cleaned Timmy's birds, and picked out a set of rotating glass eyeballs for Ben Horton's coon. By the time I finished up, it was 6:00 PM. My stomach was growling. So I microwaved a burrito, sat down in front of my laptop, and settled back into the slump of my bachelor ways. I checked my e-mail (more static from irate customers), checked E-Live (twenty-seven notifications and all of them bullshit), and, idling over Helen's profile out of mindless compulsion, nearly fell out of my chair when I saw the words IN A RELATIONSHIP.

This sent me straight to the liquor store, where I bought a pint of Jack, a forty-ounce bottle of vodka, and two cases of Schlitz with ginseng and ginkgo biloba.

By midnight I was wasted, had gobbled half my precious Xanax reserve, had wrung myself dry over YouPorn. At 1:00 AM I was still staring at the screen—eyeballs dry, dick sore, face radiation-burned. I'd hunkered down to watch "She Blinded Me with Science" on YouTube, a nostalgic jolt from my middle-school era, when I noticed an ad in the upper-right-hand corner of my screen, that spot where Google dangled bait generated by my own e-mail content and pathetic surfing habits, taunting me with taxidermy-supply sales, penis-enlargement pills, and memberships to cut-rate gyms. But this was something different.

HAVE YOU EVER DREAMED OF BEING A GENIUS?

I could almost hear Crystal's husky voice whispering into my ear: *What's the universe trying to tell you, Romie?*

I clicked and read with a crazy sense of fate:

Males between the ages of thirty-five and fifty-five, without course-work or degrees from four-year colleges or universities, are invited to participate in an intelligence enhancement study at the Center for Cybernetic Neuroscience in Atlanta, GA. Testing period starts on June 30 and ends on August 15. Subjects will undergo a series of pedagogical downloads via direct brain–computer interface. Subjects will receive $6,000 compensation—$4,000 upon finishing a series of bioengineered artificial intelligence transmissions and $2,000 upon completing follow-up tests. Travel expenses paid. Room and board provided. Serious inquiries only. Contact Matthew Morrow, MD, PhD, 404.879.4857, drmorro@cybercenter.com.

TWO

Four days later, I was standing in the lobby of the Center for Cybernetic Neuroscience in Atlanta, a fuckup among fuckups, because, apparently, I was the only one arriving way past the official check-in time. The sun was setting beyond the row of sickly palmettos that fringed the mostly empty parking lot. The floor-to-ceiling windows were all fired up from the setting sun. Light beams bounced on the shiny white floor tiles and ricocheted off the metallic walls, right through my aviators and into my bloodshot eyes. The receptionist, in the process of packing up glossy pocket folders, turned with a huff. She was tall and skinny and middle-aged pretty, like a woman in a detergent commercial, the kind of down-to-business babe who's serious about stain control.

"You almost missed me," she said, patting her bobbed hair. "You've got five minutes to look over the paperwork, which I presume you've already perused."

She sat me down on a couch shaped like a tadpole, placed my packet on the funky plastic coffee table, and handed me a pen. Inside the folder was a map of the building, questionnaires about my medical history, pamphlets containing rules and regulations, and consent forms galore. The consent forms had been e-mailed to me as PDF attachments, but of course I hadn't looked them over as carefully as I should've, busy as I was getting hammered each night, wondering if I should answer Crystal's booty-call texts. Score a few Xanax for the road. Feel the sweaty warmth of her motherly palm on my forehead one more time.

I had a single Xanax left, stashed between two Trojans in a balled-up sock and stuffed into a pocket of my duffel bag. It had taken every ounce of self-control I'd had to save this last ticket to Peace of Mind. I knew that night would be hell—first night sober in months, the strange locale, my brain on the verge of an over-haul. Over the last few days, I'd lifted the pill to my trembling lips countless times, but I'd somehow refrained from popping it.

"Are you ready yet?" said the receptionist. "Carl's here for the night shift and I've got to get home."

Carl, the elf-like security guard stationed at the front desk, waved at me.

"He'll take you through the tunnel," said the receptionist.

"Say what?"

"You'll see. Now, how about signing a form or ten?"

Halfway through the first paragraph of the first consent form, I'd already come up for air, scientific mumbo jumbo swirling in my head. My reading comprehension skills, never the best, were not up to par that evening. So I said fuck it, scrawled my signature at least a dozen times, and handed the receptionist a sloppy bundle of paper. Then I traveled through the security tunnel, a contraption straight out of *Star Wars* that highlighted every bone and organ in my body, every tooth in my mouth, every dirty piece of underwear in my duf-fel bag, every last mint in my box of Tic Tacs, but which, via some miracle, did not detect my precious last Xanax.

.. .

I could tell my roommate was a haunted motherfucker the second I walked into the room and caught him in tighty-whities, spinning around to throw karate moves at his mirror image. But what did I expect? Though I figured the Center for Cybernetic Neuroscience might be packed with down-and-out SOBs, I hadn't given it much thought until I was face-to-face with a man who looked like the love child of Steven Tyler and one of those lizard creatures from the miniseries *V*. Regarding his spastic, frog-eyed face, I got the sense that a green reptile hid under his scabby human skin. I got the sense it might bust out any minute with a sputter of slime. I got the sense this creature might gnaw my head off while I was sleeping. Still, I introduced myself, politely offering my hand as my mother had taught me, remembering her advice: *No need to break anybody's fingers, Roman, but you don't want to hand them a dead fish.*

"Romie Futch."

Last time I checked, I had a normal human hand—though my nails were bitten to the quick and my palms were stained from the epoxies and varnishes of my trade. But my new roommate backed toward the wall as though I'd offered him a rabid bat.

"Needle," he muttered.

"That your nickname?" I said.

"That's my name." Needle spun around to demonstrate a David Lee Roth karate kick. "Ask me again and I'll tell you the same. I'm from Cairo, Georgia. Got a black belt. Don't take shit from nobody."

There was a strange shadow on his sunburned chest—a faded tattoo that was too murky to make out.

"I'm from South Carolina," I said, trying to play it cool.

"South Carolina?" He winced and pretended to spit. "Look." He grinned, revealing a case of meth mouth that gave me the serious creeps. "It's all good. What you got in that there bag?" He crept closer and I caught a whiff off him, rotting leaves and a stab of perfumed laundry detergent.

"You know, the usual—clothes and shit."

"I was hoping you might have you some Scooby Snacks, maybe some Get Nekkid."

He flashed his ghoul grin again. A special-effects artist could not have done better.

"What?"

"Nothin'. You got a smoke?"

"No."

Needle started jogging in place like a cartoon spazz ready to rocket over a cliff, steam shooting from his ears. He was at least six feet tall and couldn't have weighed more than a hundred and ten.

"You got five dollars?"

"Why?"

"Vending machines." He leapt toward the door and then jerked back like a leashed dog.

So I doled out five dollars, just to have a minute's peace. Needle, after peering left and right several times, dashed down the hallway in his underwear. I took a look around, grooving on the college-dorm vibe, which reminded me of the time I'd visited Helen at the University of South Carolina at least two decades ago. I recalled the two of us, entwined on her twin bed, waiting for her super-dork roommate to skedaddle. In particular, I remembered how, when the roommate finally heaved off with her enormous back-pack, we didn't pounce on each other like starved leopards. We stared at each other, electricity zinging back and forth between our eyeballs so intensely you could almost hear a crackle in the air. We gulped. We eased into it slowly. But soon, we almost fell off her ridiculously narrow bed.

These beds weren't much bigger. A twin with a headboard that doubled as a desk hugged each wall. Teeny closets flanked the entryway. The cinder-block walls were painted the strange orange beige of prosthetic limbs. I put my duffel on my dresser, sat down on the cheap mattress, and attempted to study the map the receptionist had given me.

But there was my roommate, stomping back in with two Dr. Peppers, a tube of Oreos, and a pack of Marlboro Reds. Fortunately, he ignored me: plugged himself into his MP3 player and zoned out to some death-metal filth—Nightrage or Fleshcrawl—tracks that make Metallica's darkest jams sound like Disney tunes. Guzzling Dr. Pepper and smoking an illegal cigarette (according to the map, there was a smoking patio downstairs with ionic smokeless ashtrays), Needle rocked to his dismal music, releasing a tortured moan every five minutes. His bed was about three feet from mine. A plastic BI-LO bag jammed with clothes sat on his dresser. We had a sliding glass door with a cramped balcony that overlooked the parking lot, and even though it was open wide to the summer night, the tiny room was filled with smoke. At the rate he was going, Needle would work through that pack of Reds in a few hours.

And then what?

I shuddered to think.

I unpacked my duffel and went to check out the Richard Feynman Nanotechnology Lounge, which, according to my map, was just at the end of our hall beyond the reading room. Vending machines glowed eerily in the dim lounge. Not a single human being was relaxing on the IKEA sectional. Not one down-and-out bastard was milling around in the hallway outside. And I wondered if

Needle and I were the only poor fools desperate enough to let mad scientists tinker with our brains.

When I returned with my supper (Diet Coke, Snickers, a pack of Nip Chee crackers), Needle looked a bit more relaxed. His long body sprawled over his bed, troll feet dangling off the end. His smile was not what I'd call peaceful, though it was way less manic than the grin he'd first greeted me with.

I inserted my earbuds and scarfed down my pathetic supper while listening to *Aqualung*. Thank Jesus for Xanax, I thought as I fumbled for my green socks. I might have been a sorry son of a bitch who hadn't quite managed to get his shit together, but I had a thing about balling my socks just so. So when I found my green socks with the toes sticking out, I knew something was up. The Trojans were still there, just not taped together like they had been. And my ticket to relaxation was gone. Needle, a bloodhound for substance of any sort, had sniffed out my last yellow bus and gobbled it up.

I slumped on my bed, feeling my balls deflate at the thought of confronting a meth head who dabbled in the martial arts. I wondered if I should just hightail it—gun it down I-20 and be back in Hampton by midnight. But the thought of spending one more minute as the old Romie Futch was enough to keep me cramming tasteless crackers into my mouth, listening to the faint hum of the fluorescent overheads as my lizard-faced roommate lapsed into twitchy sleep.

When I got back to Hampton, I'd have 6K in my pocket. I'd have a brand-new brain. Maybe I'd have the get-up-and-go to do something with my life. Chip would turn hot pink with hypertension and envy. Helen would take one look at the New and Improved Romie Futch and dump her stuffed shirt of a boyfriend. My retired father would get off my case for once in his life about running *his* taxidermy shop into the ground. And my dead mother would look down from whatever limbo she inhabited and, seeing that her son had finally grown up, ascend to the fourth dimension or merge with a thousand other shining souls on some distant astral plane. I could envision her up there, some kind of lavender ectoplasm, hovering, all-knowing, shooting beams of love down at her lost son.

It'll be okay, Romie. You'll make good in the end.

THREE

Chloe, a pretty female technician not much older than twenty, leaned over me, warming my face with her minty breath. She wore a blue paper cap that matched her eyes and made her look like a Mennonite.

"Are you comfortable, Mr. Futch?"

"Yes, ma'am. I'm just glad y'all didn't shave my head."

"No." She smiled, revealing beautiful teeth, except for one weird yellow fang, which was kind of sexy. "That won't be necessary."

"Thank God. I mean, that would've sucked."

Despite the framed paintings of flowering meadows and a potted tree, the room had a hospital vibe—blue walls, rolling shelves of medical equipment, a disinfectant funk. The technicians, hip variations on the chess-club types I remembered from high school, explained everything to me in patient Mr. Rogers voices. There was Chloe, with her pale blue eyes. There was Josh, with his hipster 'stache. I could see Chip dork-baiting both of them—dissing Josh's piddly facial hair, mimicking Chloe's Yankee accent while checking out her ass. There was also Dr. Morrow—the head honcho—but he was busy with another *subject* (a word that basically meant *guinea pig*).

"We're going to implant your wet chips today." Chloe clapped her hands like a kindergarten teacher. "A simple procedure involving the insertion of five biocomputer transmitters just beneath the skin—one on each temple, three on the crown of your head."

They'd already burned the bald spots with a laser—just a bleep of pain, and then it was over. But, Chloe explained, they'd knock me out for the *intracerebroventricular injections*, when they'd drill tiny holes into my skull just behind my ears and pump serum into my brain. She went on as though my brain were some hatchback they were souping up with a badass turbocharger and platinum hubcap spinners.

She lifted the vial of violet serum, which glowed like something out of *Frankenstein*. An army of nanobots swarmed in the fluid. These microscopic creatures, she explained, concocted from *N. fowleri* amoeba genes, would revamp my brain, whipping it into shape for the downloads.

"Creating the neurological infrastructure necessary for nanobiotic data transmission," Chloe said. "Now we're going to administer a premedication."

"That's cool." I turned to avoid the sight of the needle.

"Five cc of clonidine, an alpha-two-adrenergic agonist," said Josh.

"There," said Chloe. "One more to go."

"And now a hit of propofol," said Josh. "Ouch. Yikes. That's it."

Just as the walls turned to sky and I felt myself dissolving, Dr. Morrow strolled in—long and lean, with thick gray hair, his face blandly handsome, his voice a mellow mix of God and game-show host.

"You must be Roman Futch," he said. "How are you?"

"Frine," I said. And then I couldn't speak, my tongue a lump of dead meat, though I could still hear every word they said about me.

"What did you gas him with?" Dr. Morrow asked.

"P," said Chloe.

"LOBNH." Dr. Morrow waved his hand over my face. "How did his tox screen look?"

"About like you'd expect," said Josh. "AOB, benzos, cannabinoids."

Dr. Morrow loomed over me, his smile endless, whitened teeth multiplying, tombstones extending into infinity.

He commented on my decreased heart rate as I drifted into a dream about cleaning fish. Dad kept finding hundred-dollar bills in the guts of bass, and Mom was hanging slimy money on the clothesline to dry. Brisk and efficient, she focused on the task of making us filthy rich. The woods had grown thick again. We could feel animals watching, big-eyed and growling in a forest that went on and on, dense and green and stretching past Main Street and City Hall, past the Palmetto Shopping Center, all the way out past Dixie City Fashion Mall—the world as I knew it covered in trees.

"We finally got some money, but there's nowhere to spend it," Mom said. "That's what my English teacher used to call 'irony.'" She chuckled as I settled into the crook of her arm, which seemed designed to hold my small body. And I basked in the safe warmth of her laughter—the everyday joy that held darkness at bay.

When I woke up, my brain felt like a lathered sponge. A few floaters bobbed in my peripheral vision. Chloe assured me they'd be gone within hours, and so would that fizzy brain feeling, which she asked me to describe. I spoke into a microphone attached to an Oracle micropad that automatically put my words into text.

"It's kind of like a mental Alka-Seltzer," I said. "A zillion little bubbles and pops. I can feel them and hear them. Know what I mean?"

Chloe nodded and patted my arm. "All we've got to do now is fill those holes with some bioengineered epoxy," she said.

"A dab or two of clotting agent," said Josh, "and you'll be ready to rock."

"I trust you remember the details of the confidentiality statement you signed," said Chloe.

"Refresh my memory?"

"You're not supposed to discuss your treatments with other subjects"—there was that word again. "Nothing too complicated."

"No prob, right?" Josh gave me a thumbs-up.

"No prob," I said.

• •

I picked up a cold burger from the cafeteria, which was in shutdown mode, overturned chairs on the tables, the whole place reeking of ammonia, and headed back toward my room. I found it odd that the halls were still empty, not one fellow subject ambling in clueless limbo, his brain on the verge of a major transformation. The elevator was empty. The Richard Feynman Nanotechnology Lounge was empty. But, unfortunately, my room was not empty. There was Needle, snoring away, wearing a pair of see-through jogging shorts without underwear. Now I could see the crappy cartoon on his chest: a dragon with the freakishly small head of a furious Chihuahua. His tattoo motto—FUCK THE WORLD—was spelled out in a cursive so fancy that I could barely read it.

I flicked off the overheads and sat in the dark, eating my grade-D burger, listening to the snap-crackle-pop of my transforming brain.

• •

The Biological Artificial Intelligence Transmission (BAIT) Lab was in the Right Lobe of the complex, behind the cafeteria and the infirmary, beyond a twisty series of hallways named after parts of the brain (Cerebellum Boulevard, Medulla Lane, Amygdala Street). The master computer was basically a floor-to-ceiling fish tank with a row of lava lamps pulsing on top. Inside the tank, strange-looking creatures—or parts of creatures—floated in water the color of a blue raspberry Slurpee. Some of the parts looked like mollusks. Some looked like eels. Others looked like slugs or leeches, tentacles or bundles of worms. According to Chloe, this computer was made out of bioengineered microorganisms and animal components: leech neurons, strings of bacteria, bat ribosomes, and assorted amino acids.

"The nanobiotic components should harmonize with your own gray matter," she said, motioning for me to go ahead and hop into the space-age lounge chair that sat in front of the glowing tank. "This will make your downloads a lot more seamless." She left me lying there, getting increasingly creeped out by the creature parts, which, I noticed, would occasionally jerk as though in pain.

At last, Dr. Morrow strolled into the room with his fresh face and perfect hair, tailed by Chloe and Josh.

"How are you feeling, Mr. Futch?" he asked me.

"Not so bad," I said.

"Any uncomfortable cerebral sensations?"

"Say what?"

"Headaches?" said Chloe.

"Not really."

"What do you mean?"

"Maybe a little sinus trouble, like I'm fixing to get a headache."

With latex-gloved hands, Dr. Morrow fingered my BC transmitters. He pulled a tiny plastic wand from an instrument tray and stuck its nipple-like tip into each transmitter. Through a metal gadget that resembled a toy telescope, he took a look at the epoxy fillers that clogged the holes behind my ears.

"Very good," he said. "I think we're ready, as you kids say, to rock and roll."

"*Ready to rock* suffices," said Josh, shuffling over with a tube of ointment. He rubbed cold slime onto my BC transmitters.

"This stuff kicks ass," he said. "You won't feel a thing."

Chloe hooked five wireless electrodes up to my scalp. Dr. Morrow typed something into a micropad, and then *bam*—a 3-D hologram of my brain popped up two feet from my face, each section a different color.

"Neato?" said Chloe.

"Cool," I answered.

"Just relax," said Dr. Morrow. "This won't hurt at all. You won't feel the transmission of data. You'll probably experience a random memory or a series of stray thoughts. And then you'll fall into something that resembles a pleasant nap as your VPL signals are interrupted."

"Which refers to your *ventral posterior lateral nucleus of the thalamus*," Chloe said very slowly while patting my arm.

Funny thing was, I could actually *see* her voice whirling like feathers up there in the light as I sank into some sort of well. But then, flooded by a sudden vision of Helen, I left the BAIT Lab behind.

There we were one May night in the late '80s, cruising the Hardee's drive-through, grooving to a King Crimson cassette. A late bloomer, I'd finally filled out. I'd shed my pimpled skin and grown my hair into a lush, heavy-metal mane. At last, after years of lusting on the sidelines, I'd lured Helen Honeycutt into my Camaro.

We bought Big Gulps and jumbo fries. We spiked our Cokes with my dad's Jim Beam and drove out past Sky City Discount store. I gunned it past Whitmire's Sand and Gravel, past the SPCA, past the juvenile correction facility and the wastewater treatment plant, refusing to stop until I found a setting that lived up to Helen's beauty. When I finally yanked up my emergency brake, we were a half mile into Caw Caw Swamp, windows rolled down, the funk of black water in our nostrils. The frogs were belting it out. The moon floated above the cypress trees. And just as our whiskey buzz came on and "I Talk to the Wind" slipped into its flute solo, lightning bugs rose up from the swamp, glittering in weird patterns.

We could not help but kiss at that moment. Like a humming-bird sticking its beak into a flower, I crammed my tongue into the sweet pinkness of Helen Honeycutt. I had no idea what I was doing. I'd kissed three other girls. She pulled away from me, wiped my mouth, and smiled. Ever so gently prying my lips apart with the slippery dart of her tongue, she taught me how to kiss.

I'd seen a show on *Nature* about a zoo seal that was released into the sea. The animal knew *exactly* what to do. What to eat. How to find a mate.

That's what it was like for me after five minutes of kissing Helen.

We kissed, and the lightning bugs kept coming. Turned out it was their season. They'd just hatched from the worm state and were rising en masse to mate, something scientists and photographers traveled to the swamp to see. Helen explained the whole thing to me that night. She'd read about it in the *Hampton Herald*. We kissed again as fireflies coupled in luminous clouds.

I woke with the word *luminous* in my head, Dr. Morrow's soap-opera face coming into gauzy focus. Chloe hovered angelically behind him. My brain had that fizzy feeling again.

"Hi there." Chloe waved at me.

"Um, like, salutations," I said, using a word I didn't know I knew.

"Subject showing verbal signs of cerebral optimization immediately upon gaining consciousness," Dr. Morrow enunciated into a wireless mic. "New activity in the superior and middle temporal gyri confirms this."

I sort of understood what he meant for once. He was talking about specific parts of my multicolored brain. There it was, twirling before my eyes, lit up like a psychedelic novelty toy from Spencer Gifts. As Chloe turned to retrieve her micropad, it occurred to me that she was a callipygian nymph with pulchritude to burn, and that Josh, the pathetic ectomorphic dork, was smitten with her. His desire, however, was unrequited. Every time I thought about something, SAT words popped into my head. The computer was bioluminescent, for example, palpitating with neural tissues. Dr. Morrow was unctuous and virile and subtly malodorous. My ergonomic medical recliner was so well designed I felt like I was in utero.

"Holy shit!" I said. Josh chuckled and rubbed his hands like a mantis.

"Why don't you say a few words for the record?" He thrust a mic into my personal space.

"Like what?"

"Absolutely anything. It's all good."

"I'm, um, like, ravenous," I said. "Um, um, like, um, famished, um—what the fuck—rapacious. I could eat a hecatomb of hamburgers."

"What's a hecatomb?" Josh looked amused.

"Says here." Chloe typed into her micropad. "A Grecian sacrifice to the gods."

"I don't get it," said Josh.

"Oh," said Chloe. "A sacrifice of *one hundred cattle*. That makes sense."

"That's awesome!" exclaimed Josh. "After one *OED* download and *Roget's Thesaurus*, Roman's a poet. Watch out, Shakespeare."

I engaged in a high five with the affable hobbledehoy. I saw myself stumping Chip and dazzling Helen with my newfound gift of gab. I saw Helen snorting like she used to when I said something clever.

"For a while you'll feel verbally overwhelmed," said Dr. Morrow. "But your mind will settle after a good night's sleep. Here's a Sophiquel sample to help quiet your thoughts."

The good doctor handed me a capsule packet (nine pills), which I promptly pocketed.

"Now you'd better get down to the cafeteria before it closes. Try to eat some green leafy vegetables and berries if you can. Avoid hydrogenated oils, as they are horrible for your neurons. And remember, you must not discuss your treatments with anyone."

"Don't worry," I said. "I won't. Not that I've had an opportunity to anyway."

"You will tonight." Dr. Morrow smirked like a jaded god. "And I ask you to please remember section 2, clause 6.5 of contract 3 if you feel the urge to share your experiences with another subject."

• •

Sure enough, the cafeteria was buzzing that night, some thirty-odd men grabbing grub or clustering at the laminate tables—crackheads, meth heads, potheads, and speed freaks, pill-popping maniacs and bloated alcoholics, aging heshers and ramshackle players, washed-up men on the down side of life. It was as though Dr. Morrow had snapped his fingers and—behold—a crowd of male human specimens had materialized in the cafeteria, each one modeling a particular flourish of middle-aged decrepitude. I noted all manner of potbellies, diverse patterns of baldness, various shades and stages of graying hair. Though there were some solid working-class types who must've been suffering bad patches, most of the subjects were clearly of the debauched variety.

Debauched.

Now, there was a useful word. From the Middle French *débaucher*, which meant *to turn away from one's duty.*

Debauched creatures lurked in the fluorescent light with their molded plastic trays. Debauched creatures hunched over classic cafeteria food—burgers, fries, corn dogs, tater tots, and victuals of that ilk. Debauched creatures grumbled and brooded. Debauched creatures stared sullenly. Just about all of these debauched creatures (including me) were in withdrawal mode and, hence, not in the best of spirits. They seemed to avoid one another, each withdrawing into his own bubble of personal space and staring out at the world with shell-shocked eyes. I wondered if the Center was providing heavy-duty pharmaceutical assistance to the more drug-addled among them.

Addled.

There was another useful word. From the Old English noun *adela (liquid filth)*, *addled* was synonymous with *spoiled, corrupted, rotten, putrescent.*

Mephitic, loathsome, fetid, foul.

Tainted, noisome, moldering, putrid.

I felt vaguely nauseated, as though the words themselves were festering in my head, lodged like parasites in the slimy tissues of my brain. Still, I made it through the grub line, collected a plate of lo mein, and absconded to a remote table at the edge of the room, where I could endure the streams of verbiage in peace.

Feculent, noxious, rancid, fecal.

Like the birds in that Hitchcock movie, the words kept coming. I'd be sitting there, eating my noodles, trying to have a normal thought about something. And then *bleep*—after a mental hiccup, a new word, shiny and strange, would fly into my head. The skinny fucker sitting at the table on my right was lupine, for example, hirsute in the extreme, downright lycanthropic. He was eating french fries with a fork and muttering to himself. Another dude, sulking over a bowl of soup, looked ursine and melancholic. Another had this clammy ecclesiastic quality, plump, pallid, and dank, like he'd been dwelling indoors from day one of his life.

I couldn't decide if all these words were *helping* me think or *preventing* me from thinking. Maybe they were just hijacking my thoughts, taking them in new directions. According to Dr. Morrow, I wouldn't retain every single info unit from each download, though it usually took a night or two of sleep to sort it all out. In the meantime, I felt uncomfortable, mentally constipated, like I needed to express (*squeeze out; convey by words or gesture*) something.

Bespeak, broach, communicate, convey.

Pontificate. Proclaim. Vent.

That's why I was talking to myself, I guess. That's why this older hepcat with hoary dreadlocks backtracked with his tray of sushi and sat down at my table.

"What it is?" he said. "You got the dog, or the dog got you?"

"The dog's got me," I said. "Most definitely."

"Irvin Mood," he said, extending his hand. "Elloree, South Carolina."

"Romie Futch." We shook. "Hampton."

"I'll get right to the skinny," he said. "Reason I sat down here is because I heard you using some polysyllabic diction, some, uh, I mean, uh, lofty lingo, some, uh, uh, uh, I mean, crusty academese. Do you copy?"

"I certainly do."

"Now, I'm hip to the confidentiality statement, don't get me wrong."

"As long as we don't talk directly about the procedure, the, um, agenda, um, um, like, goddammit, modus operandi," I said, "it's all good."

"Your dome feel kind of effervescent, uh, carbonated, uh, uh, I mean, uh, spumous?"

"If by dome you mean cranium, um, like, you know, brainpan, um, skull, man, then that's about right. Kind of fizzy."

"Right on, youngblood. Ought to call it *the fizz*. Kind of like the mental equivalent of the fuzz. You copy?"

"I do."

"In addition to the fizz, my brain's too zippy, too jiggy, but not in a funky way. Can't think without some Latinate polysyllable, or, uh, I mean, some bone-jacked Chaucerism jumping my dome."

"Hey, Irvin, you've hijacked my lexicon, my palaver, um, like, you know, um, um—shit won't stop. My motherfucking word hoard. Talking real fast is the only way to beat it."

"Dr. Whodunit said a decent night of slumber would mellow the manic logorrhea," Irvin muttered briskly.

"Yeah, but the problem is, how do you achieve, uh, fuck, dormancy, um, um, you know, fucking quiescence, like, alleviation when your brain won't chill the fuck out?"

"Don't know," Irvin said.

"You didn't get any, um, like, medicinal, I mean, pharmacological helpers? Shit, I wasn't supposed to say that."

"I was psyching you out." Irvin spoke quickly. "I got the dope."

We laughed. We did a high-five gesture but did not slap skin. And then Irvin went to work on his sushi for a minute or two.

"So," he said rapidly, "what brings you to this questionable institution?"

"Divorce," I spat. "Financial difficulties, chronic intoxication."

"I dig. I dig."

"How 'bout you?"

"Credit-card debt, doobie saturation point, my band of a decade folded."

"You a musician?"

"Trumpet."

"That's cool. What kind of music you play?"

"Fusion, uh, uh, amalgam, uh, I mean, uh, alloy, shit, uh, jazz, jive, bop, boogie-woogie. What the fuck? That's wacked, man. Didn't mean to say that cheesy scat."

Irvin clutched his cranium and worked his feral eyebrows up and down.

"See you on the flip side." Irvin stood up. "Got to take refuge, uh, uh, I mean, abscond, uh, crash in my, my, uh, pad, I mean cubicle, uh, chamber. Damn. So, uh, yeah."

Irvin picked up his tray and hustled toward the Rubenesque woman who rinsed off our filthy trays. She toiled in a gloomy room behind a window—plump and swathed in steam. I looked away from her, but the words would not stop. Nurturing, fecund, maternal, fructiferous. Voluptuous, lactiferous, primeval, rich. I could not stop verbally wallowing in her roseate fleshiness, rollicking in her succulence. I longed to slither into the humid room and nestle my head between her mammaries, bask in sensation like an infant, drinking in the synesthetic riot of sight-smell-sound-touch. But I hurried over and dropped off my tray. Averting my gaze, I fled to my room.

• •

My room, of course, was no place of refuge. There was Needle, smoking a cigarette, pacing to the final throes of some death-metal paroxysm, packing the tiny space with smoke and his signature odor of rotted leaves and laundry perfume. And there was another weird olfactory undernote, something chemical that, I theorized, issued from his meth-addled flesh. The Center had provided him with pills to ease the withdrawal pangs, thank God, and a plastic bottle lay overturned on his dresser, surrounded by Dr. Pepper cans and crushed Marlboro packs.

He regarded me with a sneer.

"Shit ain't workin'!" He waved his clenched fist. "I done took at least ten pills."

"Probably, um, like, an excessive, I mean, extravagant dosage," I offered.

"What?"

"Too many pills!" I shouted.

"I can't hear you!" he shrieked.

Of course he couldn't. His MP3 volume was so amped that I could decipher some of the lyrics spurting out (*I'll drink your blood and eat your bones and shit you out when you are gone*). Needle shot me a lewd, cannibalistic grin and turned off his player.

"Fuckin' vocabinary words," he muttered. "I'll ream them up your asses."

"Vocabulary words?" I asked him. "What do you mean?"

"Vocapilary." He eased closer to me, his zombie maw gaping. "I ain't supposed to talk about it if I'm gonna get my cash. But they got some pip-squeak college dork teaching me how to talk."

"That's cool." I backed toward my bed. "It's all good, um, commendable, um, like, goddammit, exceptional."

Needle scowled and seemed on the verge of jumping me. But then his eyes went wonky and he sat on his bed.

"Hey, I think this shit's working now. Ah yeah."

He stripped off his shirt (the poor fucker was perpetually over-heated, despite the excessive air-conditioning), tossed it onto the floor, and sprawled out on his bed.

I walked down to the communal restroom to pop my Sophiquel in peace. When I returned, the reptilian cretin had fallen into something like slumber, though Needle never ceased to fidget and mutter.

I lay down on my bed. I closed my eyes. As I scanned the day's events in my head, words continued to assault me from every angle. I recalled Josh leaning over me to adjust one of my BC transmitters, his ephebic mustache shining like angelic down. I envisioned Chloe, nubile and fecund, dewy as a damn daisy, caressing my cranium with her soft hands. I dallied with visions of her opalescent thighs, her delectable neck, her red, nectarous mouth. I would have resorted to onanism had Needle not been three feet away, a handy anaphrodisiac. And the Sophiquel seemed to be working, subduing the swarms of words.

I reviewed my experience in the laboratory, trying to remember when, exactly, I'd felt language stirring in the depths of my soul like a vast flock of birds in a dark forest. I remembered the dream I'd had just before going under—not simply a dream but a bona fide flashback of Helen—vibrant, animated, pulsating with life.

I could still recall the elusive smell of my Camaro's moldy interior. I could hear the frogs singing. I could almost taste Helen—booze and Bubblicious and a faint hint of snot. I remembered how shame over my relative inexperience had melted away as I'd gotten lost in that endless first kiss, which brought on a whole new heap of memories about the best summer of my life.

Helen had lost her virginity to a ferret-faced asshole named Farrell Sims, but I became her first true lover. Within a month after first hooking up, we'd fallen deep into the spasmodic throes of teen coitus. Every second of every minute we dreamed of the raptures we'd taste during our free hours, in the back of my car, in forests and swamps, in air-conditioned bedrooms whenever we were lucky enough to find ourselves in an empty house. No matter what we were doing, our minds remained fixed on the bliss we'd snatch, like the crosshairs of a rifle poised brutally on a flower, some delicate concoction of dew and scent that we'd blast to sodden mash.

We fucked in graveyards, under bleachers, in the plywood-smelling skeletons of houses half-built. We fucked in patches of woods too scant to host a squirrel, in toolsheds reeking of motor oil, on the roofs of our own houses as our parents sat narcotized before televisions. No place was too humble or too gross to house the portable Eden of our mutual desire. We could not refrain from touching each other, no matter where we were—buying condoms at Revco, caught up in a Fritos-or-Cheetos dilemma at the Piggly Wiggly, or, while attending the visitation of Helen's dear Aunt Doody, stealing a few caresses in the janitor's closet of Shives Funeral Home.

Our bodies brimmed with the sap of adolescence, the same stuff that dripped from pimples and shot through veins to bring on sudden fits of angst. Sometimes we seemed as helpless as coupling rabbits, guided by pheromones and neurochemicals, robotically seeking that exquisite brain burst of oxytocin, dopamine, and adrenaline that obliterates the universe for a few seconds, or makes you *one* with the universe, or makes you *become* the universe as you behold the entire whirling cosmos in that sweet warbling vortex that blooms from a pesky genital itch.

So, yes, we were addicted to each other biochemically, like the musky young animal machines we were. But we were careful. I shot my spunk into countless tubes of latex. Zillions of sperm, each one endowed with its own mysterious genetic cachet, bit the dust. And each month Helen's hopeful egg dissolved into goo and passed from her body.

Our ceaseless carnal acrobatics were accompanied by declarations of eternal love. Our love was so huge that only tumid ballads like "Nights in White Satin" could halfway express the swooniness of it all. Our love was so formidable that we felt confident it would conquer everything in its path, like a horde of Visigoths sweeping over the globe, obliterating villages, cities, entire civilizations.

Our love outlasted our senior year. Our love continued when Helen went off to Columbia to attend USC while I piddled at Trident Tech. Our love survived her dalliance with an art student and my trysts with sweet, laughing Crystal Flemming, a girl with innocent panda eyes and sparkly nail polish. Our love flourished through the madness of my mother and the suicide of Helen's father and her bitter return home, marine biology degree half-finished. Our love burned on as I dropped out of Tech and took on my father's trade. Our love prospered as Helen earned a phlebotomy certificate and began her tedious employment at Palmetto Blood Plasma Donation Center. Our love thrived into our late thirties, prevailing in the wake of Helen's miscarriages and fertility treatments, my alcoholism and Xanax addiction, the clusterfuck of the twenty-first century, with its terrorists and nanobots, its chat rooms and dark matter, cyber wars and wikis and genetically modified meats.

Our love kept on ticking, like a fluffy, robotic bunny trudging in circles in an empty room, until one ashen afternoon in January, when I was taking inventory in my shop, reviewing unpaid accounts, assessing the buck heads and mallards that Hampton County's poor fuckups could not afford to pay off, Helen walked in with her job-interview face on and announced that she had leased an apartment. She would be moving out in a week. She hoped our disentanglement (she did not use this word) would not be too *messy* (her word, precisely).

I took three Xanax, drank a pint of Beam, and slept in the lobby of my shop, without a pillow, on the ancient vinyl couch. I spent the next year in a drunken dream, trudging from freezer to microwave, from TV to shitter, from living room couch to the bedroom, and, after gazing at the bed that Helen and I had once shared, I'd trudge back to the couch and crash there because I couldn't tolerate the thought of smelling a ghostly trace of her scent on the sheets, nor could I muster the energy to wash said sheets, nor buy new ones, nor locate an alternate set in the house. So I crashed on the sofa, sans covers in the summer, under an ancient electric blanket when winter reared its fugly albino head.

Which is why I was now in the clutches of a mad scientist, my brain souped up with nanobots, trying to fall asleep three feet from a muttering meth head. When I finally nodded off, the words were still coming, clustered around images of Helen.

From the Greek Ελένη, *Helene*, her name went way back, was probably the appellation of an ancient vegetation goddess and symbolic of fertility and life. I could picture her, verdant and fructiferous, asprawl in some lush, emerald valley, bedecked with flowers and offering her melons to the sky.

But as I slipped into sleep, I saw her popping a beer, pulling a pan of home fries from the oven, filling our tattered kitchen with life. I saw her squirming closer to me on the couch, snorting over the lies of some talking-head politician on TV.

"Listen to this idiot, pretending like he's human," she said, conspiring with me, mindlessly massaging my arm—her love ordinary, reflexive, miraculous.

FOUR

I was back in the BAIT Lab, waiting for Dr. Morrow, surrounded by pulsing, luminescent ectoplasm. I sat in the hot seat, watching the organic components of the biocomputer undulate and twitch. Although the liquid was an electric blue, the biotech organisms steeped in it were distinctly fleshy, fraught with nervous tissue, covered in veiny rinds and wavering a thousand cilia. They reminded me of those obscure ocean animals Helen once dreamed of studying, those alien creatures that gathered around deep-sea vents to suck sulfur, strange organisms that manufactured their own light. We spent many a night watching documentaries on the deepest part of the ocean, those depths where the sun did not penetrate, where the pressure was insane, the water unfathomably cold and isothermal. We'd drink beer and sink into mysteries of the deep, Helen speaking quietly about the reclusive animals, almost whispering, as though she didn't want to disturb them. And then she'd go silent and sad, thinking about her unfinished marine biology degree, the different life she could've had. Back then she'd still sink into me, nuzzle my neck with her wet-eyed face, letting me know without saying it that I was enough for her.

I was trying to remember the last time this had happened when Dr. Morrow strolled in wiping crumbs from his perfect chin. Chloe and Josh were hot on his tail.

"How are we doing this morning?" the doctor asked.

Chloe flicked on my brain hologram.

I watched my multicolored brain rotate.

"I don't know," I said. "Guess I'm feeling kind of uncanny."

"Uncanny, eh?" said Dr. Morrow. "That's it? Not mystified or preternatural or anything else?"

"Those aren't bad words, but uncanny seems more apt."

"You're not feeling overwhelmed by verbiage this morning?"

"Not really."

"Any conceptual delays or gaps in your thinking?"

"Nah. I'm actually having trouble distinguishing between the old and new diction."

"That's a good thing. Headaches?"

"Not at the moment. I had one last night, briefly, though it might've been the MSG in my lo mein."

"Dissociative identity or cognitive dissonance?" Dr. Morrow tested my BC transmitters with his little wand.

"Actually, now that you mention it."

"Don't worry, a little DI and CD are both perfectly normal as you adjust to the BAIT downloads. Now, Chloe, let's have the phase one verbal."

"Just a little test," said Chloe, placing a micropad before me, the screen displaying a series of multiple-choice questions. "You scroll through like this and touch your answers."

She fingered the screen.

"I know how to work it." I huffed, feeling a familiar sense of dread, the desire to flee a high school classroom, take refuge in my Camaro, and cower in a cloud of weed smoke.

"Good for you." She clapped her hands and retreated, pausing at the door to give me an encouraging smile.

"Just press the red SUBMIT button at the end." She slipped out of the room.

I stared down at the first question, my panic subsiding as I read through it with ease:

Forced into familiarity, then, with such prodigies as these; and knowing that after repeated, intrepid assaults, the White Whale had escaped alive; it cannot be much matter of surprise that some whalemen should go still further in their superstitions; declaring Moby Dick not only ubiquitous, but immortal (for immortality is but ubiquity in time); that though groves of spears should be planted in his flanks, he would still swim away unharmed; or if indeed he should ever be made to spout thick blood, such a sight would be but a ghastly deception; for again in unensanguined billows hundreds of leagues away, his unsullied jet would once more be seen.

1. The passage implies which of the following about the White Whale?

A) The White Whale is dead, for its sides have been impaled with numerous spears, and the animal has spurted gallons of blood into the ocean.

B) The White Whale is the name of a slow cruise ship, and it is far quicker to travel by airplane.

C) The White Whale is unkillable, and even if the animal appeared to be gravely wounded, filling the ocean with blood, it would pop up alive and happy in some other part of the sea, its spume clean and healthy.

D) The White Whale is a magical island, and fruit trees have been planted on its body.

I zipped through the test in thirty minutes, answering reading-comprehension, fill-in-the-blank, and sentence-equivalence questions. When I pressed the red button, Chloe breezed in, beaming. She plucked up the micropad.

"Very good," she said.

"How many did I get?"

"Dude," said Josh, rushing out from Dr. Morrow's lair. "You aced it!"

"Not a bad start," said Dr. Morrow, cruising in with his own personal micropad, a model I'd never seen. "Though the numerical aspect is confidential. Just know that you are doing well. And now I do believe we are ready to rock and roll."

"What's on the docket today?" asked Josh.

Dr. Morrow read the titles listed on his screen. "*The Art of Rhetoric, Bulfinch's Mythology,* and *Rhetorica ad Herennium.*"

"Cool," replied the hobbledehoy.

Josh smeared my BC transmitters with gel. As Chloe leaned over to install my electrodes, Dr. Morrow typed something onto his keypad, and I sank into a well of darkness again, the three of them peering down at me over a distant circle of light.

Then I was in the Swamp Fox High art room, an airy space with a darkroom and special alcoves for artists deemed gifted—not officially by BSAPs or IQ tests but by Mrs. Breen, our art teacher, an aging hippie who wore paint-spattered wraparound denim skirts with suede boots. Mrs. Breen coddled my talent, gave me free rein of the kilns and darkroom, the glazes and oil paints. Each school day between two and three I sat in Advanced Art, in a small room sequestered from the dabblers and hacks, with two other students:

a hot Goth named Alexandra Cunningham, who'd been accepted to Duke on a full scholarship, and my fellow stoner Lee Decker. (Mrs. Breen, bless her heart, had a soft spot for stoners.)

While Alexandra painted brutal abstract images that looked like mangled and dripping bits of flesh, Lee attempted the epic task of representing every song on *Led Zeppelin IV* in oil paints. Meanwhile, I fashioned hand-built clay sculptures of grotesque hybrid beings—part human, part animal, part mythological entity.

I could see myself, the young artist at work, my dark Byronic mullet flowing over the collar of my King Crimson T-shirt as my hands caressed a lump of wet porcelain clay. I pinched it into the likeness of a voluptuous female nude with a fish's lower body and hair cascading past her ass. She resembled Helen, with her sly simper. I spent hours stippling her fish parts with a pipette to produce scales, which I glazed a deep black green and brushed with a shimmer of gold. I adorned her hair with actual hummingbird feathers and glued a set of epoxied luna-moth wings to her delicate shoulder blades. I created a magical diorama in which she dwelt with chubby octopus men and leering sea monsters. I even installed black lights, a tiny fan that made Mylar ribbons waver like psychedelic seaweed, and, upon the recommendation of Lee Decker, a cassette player (secreted in the display's hollow wood base) that submerged the whole scene in the ambience of "The Ocean."

"I'm not stealing your thunder by using Zeppelin?" I asked him.

"Naw, man," he said. "It's like a movement, you know? Like the Dadaists or the abstract expressionists."

"Totally."

We went out to the student parking lot to burn one in my Camaro. We relished a Yes cassette and strolled back into the prison-like building to groove on our creations. Lee's giant painting of a red medieval castle taking off like a rocket looked kinetic as all get-out, though I told him he needed a touch of yellow to make the vapor trail truly fiery. He agreed.

I queued my forty-minute loop of "The Ocean" and dimmed the overheads. We stood before my diorama, steeped in its otherworldliness, bewitched by the beauty of the mermaid, the oily grotesquery of the sea mutants swarming lasciviously in her midst.

"Killer," Lee whispered.

"If only the creatures *moved*," I said, trying to think of the right word (which was *undulate*, though I didn't know it back then).

"Surreal," said Mrs. Breen, who'd slipped from her office to admire my creation. "Are you still thinking about majoring in art?"

I nodded. I swallowed. We were talking about something more ethereal than my diorama, something that made my stomach knot up, something that brought the taste of pennies to the back of my throat. We were talking about *the future*. At that moment, I still had one. I could feel *the future* squirming larva-like inside my chest as Mrs. Breen admired my diorama. Alexandra Cunningham muttered the words "naïve redneck art," but I didn't let that bother me. Especially when Helen cut calculus and came whirring into the art studio, her permed hair bouncing in a thousand chestnut ringlets, cleavage spilling from her décolleté top like a double scoop of butter pecan. Checking out my sculpture, she smiled with pride.

Poor Lee trembled in her presence. I didn't begrudge him his crush and wished sincerely that he'd find his own portal to the more ineffable pleasures of life, some pretty, multifaceted female who understood his vision as Helen did mine.

I snatched an envelope of negatives I'd developed (of Helen frolicking naked in the strange blue waters of the kaolin mine pond) and led my beloved to the darkroom. I held her hand as we leaned over the chemical trays, relishing each moment she'd emerge from the murk, my beaming muse.

There she was, twinkling in images, emanations from my visionary brain. And there she was, standing beside me in the safelight, her breath warming my earlobe.

I peeled down her acid-washed jeans and unbuckled mine and we coupled on the floor in a narcissistic teenage frenzy, surrounded by images that not only immortalized her at the height of her nubile beauty but also attested to my own manly artistic genius, something that, if I played my cards right, would land me a *future*. I concentrated on *the future* to stall those initial convulsions that prick a man on toward melting oblivion. I closed my eyes and saw *the future*, a red, fleshy blob pupating in dark fluid like something in a mad scientist's incubator. I saw strange organs throbbing beneath its translucent shell. Saw *the future* bust from its chrysalis in scattering blazes of diamond light, winged and glistening, already flitting out the window, darting off toward the horizon before I could get a good look at it.

Helen lay on the linoleum, her face flushed. Alexandra Cunningham was pounding on the door. We scrambled into our jeans, slipped our soft porn into a manila file, and stumbled from wombish darkness into stark fluorescence. Strolling from the institutional air-conditioning into the tropical freedom of spring, we hopped into my Camaro and gunned it. *The future* lay dormant within us, protozoan in our cells.

I woke up with the taste of Helen in my mouth, aware now of the highfalutin aspect of her name, the Helen of Troy allusion bestowed unknowingly by her mother, a certified medical assistant, and her father, a melancholy Monsanto sales rep who trafficked in poisons.

O Helen, Helen, Helen!

Sunbeam.

Zeus's mortal daughter.

The face that launched a thousand ships.

"Roman," said a voice.

The goofy grin of Josh materialized before my eyes. And there was Dr. Morrow, probing the mysteries of his left ear with a paper clip. And Chloe, beautiful Chloe, not as beautiful as Helen in her prime, but very pretty, with a luscious bottom and an unnerving habit of brushing against me as she performed her scientific chores.

"Describe this paper clip," said Dr. Morrow, thrusting forth the implement with which he'd just been picking his ear.

"Poor paper clip," I joked. "How rudely you have been used. Forged by Vulcan to serve some noble purpose, like securing a ream of poetry, you have been forced to retrieve detritus from this man's ear canal."

Dr. Morrow smiled and muttered into his micropad mic. "Evidence of cerebral enhancement immediately apparent in verbal communication. Fanciful rhetorical tropes, if I'm not mistaken. References to what must be a mythological figure. Chloe? Did you get the data on that ref?"

"Vulcan," said Chloe. "Roman god of fire. Depicted as a blacksmith."

"Awesome," said Josh, grinning like a lowly adolescent satyr at Pan's loveliest nymph.

• •

Despite its excessive brightness, the cafeteria, with its garish orange walls, was the lowest vale in Hades—Tartarus, to be exact. Wretched shades trudged to and fro. Muttering to themselves, trembling with DTs and more sinister withdrawal spasms, they toted trays of slop. A loner by nature, I took up my usual spot at the edge of the action, thinking of Sisyphus as I watched the imprisoned souls grub up in the food line. But not all was gloom and doom. A lively crew at the table to my left was chatting about sports. I thought I heard the word *serendipity* pop out of one dude's mouth, and I wondered if he was on the same BAIT track as me. I was about to break character, walk over, and initiate a convo when I spotted Irvin cruising my way, sacred fruits of Demeter piled up on his plastic tray.

"What it is?" He sat down. "You got Cerberus, or Cerberus got you?"

"Freaky," I said. "I was just thinking I was in Tartarus. Every time I think I got the dog underfoot, that hellhound bastard pops another head."

"I feel you." Irvin picked a green olive from his salad and set it aside. "Don't know about you, but the flashbacks have been a bugout to an otherwise groovy ride. Mnemosyne's a bitch. Don't much feel like tripping down particular memory lanes, if you copy."

"I copy. Being reacquainted with the glorious teenage flesh of my ex-wife is kind of like groping after Persephone in the dark."

"Right on. Just when you pinch her ass, she vanishes into mist."

"Like that SOB Tantalus, with his water and grapes. Though it's not all bad. I'd forgotten how awesome high school art class was. I reckon I used to be a sculptor."

"Thought you still were. Didn't you say you were a taxidermist?"

"That's a whole 'nother animal, pun intended."

"Why? What is sculpture?" Irvin shot me a sly, Socratic smile.

"I don't know. The creation of three-dimensional art forms, I guess."

"And what is taxidermy?"

"The preservation of animals."

"Are you preserving the actual flesh-and-blood animal as it is?"

"No, I'm basically re-creating a facsimile of the creature with molds and hide scraps and fake parts."

"A two-dimensional facsimile?"

"You got me there. A three-dimensional facsimile."

"Same skills, man. Funkabilly, hep hop, zamrock jazz. What-ever. Never did like labels. Fusion's the only genre that works for me on a semantic level."

"I reckon there's something to that."

"Damn straight there is."

Caught up in a hermetic reverie, Irvin went to work on his salad. It occurred to me that his dreadlocks were vaguely Medusan. It oc-curred to me that his goatee made him look like the quintessential philosopher king. There had been a time in my life when I'd briefly considered the artistic possibilities of taxidermy, though I'd always characterized anything falling outside the naturalistic tradition as a novelty stunt, and hence, not Art with a capital *A*. And this di-chotomy had stifled the kind of artistic expression that might've saved my ass from the clutches of Bacchus.

"Well," said Irvin, tossing one last crouton into his mouth, "I'll catch you on the flip side. Got to close the shades. Got an early date with Hypnos tonight. Phantasos, you trippy old head, please be kind to me during this round of slumber!"

Irvin shook my hand. And then the gray-haired senex strolled off with his tray, leaving me alone in Tartarus, a place so low that a bronze anvil dropped from Earth would fall for nine days before reaching the cursed realm.

• •

"Congrats," said Josh as he scanned my multiple-choice rhetoric test. "You killed it, dude."

"What was my score?"

"Classified." Chloe winked like a Bond villainess and then test-ed my BC transmitters with her fairy wand.

"One more download, and you'll be ready for phase two," she said.

"Where's Dr. Morrow?"

"With another subject," said Josh, "but he'll be here ASAP."

Although Dr. Morrow was often *with another subject*, I hadn't yet run into anybody in the tiny waiting room of the BAIT Lab, the retro vibe of which evoked the subtly funky 1970s office of my childhood pediatrician (olive plastic chairs; pumpkin vinyl couch; macramé owls that gazed into my soul with huge wooden eyes)—an association that made me envision the '70s incarnation of my mother with her sleek, long hair, bell-bottom jeans, and loud-print, neo-peasant blouses fabricated from petroleum products. She kept it real, never lied about what would happen in the depths of the doctor's office.

"Yes, you'll get a shot today," she'd say, "but it'll be over quick. Just a bee sting, nothing you can't handle." She looked away when I got the shot, bit her bottom lip as though she could feel the needle prick. She'd take me out for a Happy Meal afterward.

"Pure-T trash," she'd say, "but you earned it."

Now, as I waited in the BAIT Lab, I got the feeling that I'd traveled, à la *Fantastic Voyage*, into some psychedelic chamber of a dreaming giant's brain. In the windowless room, which had that ineffable hospital disinfectant smell, I felt the beginnings of a panic attack. I hoped that Dr. Morrow would soon appear like Hermes to reconfigure my mortal brain, and then I'd be distracted by some random memory tugged from an obscure fold of my temporal lobe.

I recalled a game Helen and I used to play, in which we'd vow to remember a particular incident for the rest of our lives—like the time an ancient woman had appeared in the park, a tiny silky monkey perched on her shoulder, its fur iridescent in the summer sun.

"Gremlin," Helen whispered, taking my hand. When the woman vanished into the rose garden, we vowed to remember her and her monkey for the rest of our lives. So far, none of the set pieces had appeared, and I began to wonder if the originals were stashed in my head after all, or even copies of copies from all the forced remembering that Helen and I had done over the years, a process that I'd once seen a show about on the Discovery Channel. Now I couldn't remember how it all worked. The room felt cold. And the hospital smell was filling my system with mild dread, the fear that my body would be cut open, that some essential organ would be removed.

"Roman Futch," said Dr. Morrow, looking even taller than usual. "Sorry you had to wait."

Chloe was back too, this time without Josh, looking like a priestess in her pale blue smock. She fiddled with her micropad.

"How do you feel?" the doctor asked.

"A touch of anxiety."

"To be expected. Any depersonalization? Derealization?"

"A little of both, I reckon."

"Do you ever regard yourself from a distance, as though you are outside of your body and watching a movie of yourself?"

"Every time I get a BAIT download." I pointed at the hologram of my brain, which rotated in its usual spot.

"Naturally, but otherwise?"

"Only when dreaming."

"Have you had any trouble recognizing yourself in the mirror?"

"Unfortunately not."

Dr. Morrow chuckled politely, a kind of fake musical cough. He regarded the floating image of my brain, studying it from several angles and typing notes.

"Have you experienced any garbled speech, spoonerisms in particular?"

"Like, *the Lord is a shoving leopard?*"

"Exactly."

"Not that I can remember."

"Josh says you *aced* this morning's test."

"Yes, but he was rather hazy about the numbers."

"I do believe we are ready to rock and roll," Dr. Morrow said, ignoring my comment.

Quick as Hermes, the doctor fingered his sacred tablet. And I sank, bracing myself for whatever image would materialize in the darkness.

Two seconds later, I was at Concrete Pond, a feed warehouse transformed into a magical skating rink in 1984. I could smell corn dogs and popcorn, the limbic alchemy of polyurethane floor shellac and nylon utility carpeting. I could hear the cheesy DJ Dr. Funk, tucked mysteriously behind his window of smoked Plexiglas, calling all foxy ladies to the rink for Ladies' Special Skate.

I sweated adrenaline. A drop of testosterone trembled upon each of my myriad zits, the pustules themselves aflame with purple triumph. After strutting my stuff to "Mr. Roboto," I'd been declared champion of Guys' Special Skate. I'd ended my routine with a bold jump over the fallen toad-shaped body of Brent Stein, a clammy math whiz with a cryptic smile and Coke-bottle glasses. I'd earned not only a three-dollar snack-bar tab but also the privilege of taking the hand of the Ladies' Skate Queen during Couples Only.

And now Helen, aka Hell on Wheels, was gliding onto the floor for Ladies' Special. She froze, closed her eyes, waited for the beat to rouse her from her mannequin pose. Clad in a pair of painted-on Gloria Vanderbilts, sporting a flimsy top the color of Gatorade that highlighted her incipient breasts, she pumped her narrow hips as the intoxicating bass riff of "Maneater" began. In the flashing disco light, she twirled and leapt and thrust her delicate pelvis, interspersing *Solid Gold* moves with elegant ballet. Embodying all that was sexy and feline, she became the quintessential man-eater.

Dr. Funk declared Helen the Queen of Friday Night. Following the DJ's instructions, I rolled bashfully forth, took her sweaty hand into my own sweaty hand, and led her to the proverbial dance floor. Dr. Funk dimmed the lights and slowed the strobe. He immersed the rink in a rosy glow. Round and round we rolled, hands clasped, as Lionel Richie and Diana Ross sang ecstatically of "Endless Love." I had problems looking directly at Helen. Her profile hovered just to my left, hazy and angelic. And then the song ended.

"Later, alligator." Helen pivoted on her back left heel and skated away. Eviscerated with emotion, I rolled to the boys room (its door marked with a sparkly sign that read STUDS) and almost threw up. I'd eaten two hot dogs and three Butterfingers. I'd tossed back shots of Mountain Dew with sizzling jolts of Space Dust on my tongue.

Sneering at my stupid face in the mirror, I adjusted a crunchy strand of gelled hair, took a deep breath, and went out to find Helen. What I'd say to her was anybody's guess.

The lights on the rink had deepened to an eerie purple black. Skeezy older guys with mustaches were milling around the video games. "Hungry Like the Wolf" was on, Simon Le Bon panting as he chased a sleek panther woman through the jungle of his desire. I spotted Helen, hunched over the Ms. Pac-Man game, caught up in a maze, eating dots. To her right, slumping with sexy ennui in black jeans and a jacket of fringed suede, his blond hair resembling the crest of a cotton-top tamarin, was Farrell Sims. Reputed to smoke weed, sip from a flask, and bang married women, he was a bad boy par excellence. He drove a Trans Am as black as Satan's goatee. And there he was, eyeing Helen's taut little ass. She was thirteen. He was seventeen. She was likely a virgin, while he, according to rumor, had spent the afternoon dallying with a plumber's wife, taking bong hits while listening to Fleetwood Mac.

I'd seen such movies as *The Karate Kid*, however, in which the Macchio men of the world prevailed over the macho—those confident assholes with pectoral muscles and fancy cars. So I maneuvered toward them. Stood on the other side of Helen. Watched her squeal as her fourth Pac-woman got melted by a ghost. And then she, without even glancing my way, rolled off with Farrell Sims.

I watched them share a plate of nachos. Watched her mock slap him when he put his hand on her knee. Watched them roll out onto the rink for the next Couples Only, Farrell skating backward with the effortless aplomb of a pro while stooping to receive Helen's embrace. My girl laced her slender arms around his manly neck as "Love Lifts Us Up Where We Belong" caressed them with gentle melodies. Sitting on a rink-side bench, I took in the whole sickening spectacle. After the song reached its soaring climax, eagles crying from mountain cliffs as poor wretches watched in awe from the earth below, I saw them leave together.

I imagined him whisking her off in his Trans Am, deflowering her in some seedy parking lot. As soft porn flickered inside my skull, I watched Brent Stein skate alone, hands clasped behind his back, a look of intellectual constipation on his face as he rolled around in the gloom. I fought back tears as "Total Eclipse of the Heart" plunged me into exquisite depths of degradation and despair. Dr. Funk knew what he was doing. Now I can see him for what he was, a washed-up disco duck from the funkalicious '70s, a demented Oz figure chuckling behind his Plexiglas screen, pulling the heartstrings of overwrought teens with the latest Top 40 schmaltz. After the final Couples Only, knowing that tortured souls skulked in the shadows, racked with envy as lovers came together in bliss, Dr. Funk always played a song of heartbroken despair.

Feeling a total eclipse of the heart, I staggered toward the snack bar with my three-dollar prize coupon. There was Larry, awash in eerie light like the ghost bartender in *The Shining*. Larry, with his puffy worn face and devil-may-care feathered hair.

"What's yer poison?" Larry drawled, as though we were in some badass movie together.

Attempting an expression of infinite existential boredom, I slapped my coupon on the counter.

"Suicide," I said.

As Larry filled my paper cup with Mountain Dew, Coke, Dr. Pepper, Diet Coke, Sprite, and orange Crush, the stinging fluorescent lights popped on, which meant that it was almost eleven, that hour when the skating rink shut down for the night. "I Will Survive" was still playing (Dr. Funk, merciful after all, always queued a rallying song for the jilted before tossing them out into the cold). I blinked like a mole and scowled. Suicide in hand, I rolled off toward the front desk, where my shoes were stowed.

Out in the night my sleepy father waited in his idling truck, the radio set on oldies. His clothes smelled of tanning agents and formaldehyde. The creases on his face were deep. As the ice in my Suicide melted, my paper cup went limp, dissolving as we drove in silence through the empty streets of Hampton. It was January. We didn't speak. I pressed my cheek against the cold glass and gazed up at the swarm of winter stars.

That's where that particular memory ended—neat as a vignette—and darkness shrouded my mind. My third BAIT download was *The Bedford Anthology of World Literature*, and I lay stunned as incandescent pulses of knowledge flowed through my unconscious mind. I don't recall any sensation of data transmission, only waking up with lines from *The Iliad* dancing through my brain:

> *With these words the goddess set in Helen's heart*
> *sweet longing for her former husband, city, parents.*
> *Covering herself with a white shawl,*
> *she left the house, shedding tears.*

FIVE

Three weeks and a hundred downloads later, I sat in the Richard Feynman Nanotechnology Lounge drinking fermented Dr. Pepper with Trippy J, my brain exploding with newfangled thoughts. We were discussing Thomas Bernhard's tendency to assume privileged academic personas in his novels, while his memoir, *Gathering Evidence*, evoked his impoverished upbringing with an emotional intensity that his fiction tended to shy away from.

"Except maybe *Wittgenstein's Nephew*, which keeps it real, but with significantly more game," said Trippy, whose real name was Ernest Jeffords.

Trippy rubbed his temples, which were still crusted with BC gel. In keeping with the bio nature of the technology, Chloe had proudly informed me, the goop was composed of slug slime and some enzyme from a GM goat's gut.

"Nasty-ass, postindustrial, trans-bio ectoplasm," Trippy said, scratching at his brow with a fingernail.

Trippy was an aging player with ripped arms and a slight gut that he hid under voluminous sports jerseys. He perpetually donned a do-rag to cover his receding hairline. Neck and neck in the same

BAIT schedule, we'd met during our first week at the Center, when we'd run into each other in a rare moment of unscheduled overlap between sessions. Since week two we'd been hanging in the Nano Lounge, hashing out our learning in lively scholarly debate, our tongues going full throttle like outboard motors.

Bernhard's entire oeuvre had just been uploaded into our brains. And we were digging the dude. In addition to laughing our asses off at his dark humor, we enjoyed his musical verbal motifs and antinationalist rants. We thought Bernhard kicked Thomas Mann's pretentious swollen ass up and down the street.

"Knocks his fuckin' bourgeois mustache off," I said.

"Wanted to haul off and slap that old dithering bitch in *Death in Venice*," said Trippy. "And not 'cause I'm homophobic either, dog. *Lolita* did the whole obsession-with-youth thing much better, went way beyond flirting with taboo. Homie can spit. *Probed* the whole titillating nightmare. Got down into the pink throbbing horror with black humor and spasms of genuine despair."

"Yeah, but *Lolita* ain't homoerotic."

"True that. If the nymphet had been a catamite, that shit would have never flown."

In addition to the Bernhard, our brains were swimming from the slew of more theoretical "texts" covered in that day's BAIT downloads: *Gender Trouble* by Judith Butler; *Of Grammatology* by Jacques Derrida; *Postmodernism: The Cultural Logic of Late Capitalism* by Fredric Jameson; *Simulacra and Simulation* by Jean Baudrillard; *Discipline and Punish: The Birth of the Prison* by Michel Foucault; and *Simians, Cyborgs, and Women: The Reinvention of Nature* by Donna Haraway.

We had shit to talk. Our brains were on fire. And we still had at least a hundred downloads to go before reaching full cognitive capacity (FCC).

"Fuck that punk Derrida," said Trippy. "Got game in his flow but no heat."

"He had a few moments," I said, "but, yeah, fuck that noise."

Moreover, this was the first night that Trippy and I tapped into our vat of Pep. We'd dumped a whole box of Dixie Crystals packets into a hundred-quart cooler of Dr. Pepper, added Robitussin and herbs, yeasting the elixir with a wild growth Trippy'd cultured in a quick-noodles cup. At last, the yeast cells had gone to town, and we had booze to swill. We were keeping it on the down low for obvious reasons, discreetly enjoying our heady swill in the Nano Lounge. Nothing stronger than ibuprofen was allowed at the Center, with the exception of the pharmaceuticals prescribed by Dr. Morrow, who'd recently weaned me off Sophiquel.

We'd stashed the cooler in my dorm room in spite of Needle's drug-hound nose. We could totally see that tweaking freak sticking his head into our vat hog-fashion to swill up our precious Pep. Nevertheless, we also intuited that the Center for Cybernetic Neuroscience, despite its progressive lip service, would be more likely to ferret our vino in a black ex-con's room. So we hid our cooler under my dirty laundry, careful to block the security camera with a piece of paper. Plus, we crowned the laundry pile with some Fruit of the Looms we'd smeared with chocolate ice cream. Trippy had learned this trick at Georgia State—not the university but the maximum-security prison in Tattnall County, where he'd done a few stints since his late teens for weed-related escapades: bullshit like intent to distribute, possession within one hundred feet of a park (a barren lot featuring an unused jungle gym that he didn't know existed), and distributing to a minor (some seventeen-year-old at a party who he never even *saw* that night).

"Ain't nobody gonna touch your unmentionables if they think they're smeared in feces," Trippy advised. "The most taboo, most abject biological substance in the human catalog of thou shalt nots."

So far, Needle had stayed clear of that area, avoiding it as he would a biohazard-stickered waste bin.

Trippy had also mastered the ancient art of alcohol fermentation at the clink. He could manufacture all kinds of intoxicating substances out of common household chemicals, food scraps, human biological effluvia, and herbs of the field gathered from the prison yard. That's why peeps called him Trippy J. He was famous for a brew called Cobra—concocted from various pain-relief pills, gasoline, powdered lightbulb tungsten, and red phosphorous scratched from matchbox strikes, mellowed with dandelion root and a dash of lemon balm. The recipe had come to him at Georgia State, when he'd discovered a moldy nineteenth-century edition of *Culpeper's Complete Herbal* in the library and Christmas lights started blinking in his head. He remembered his grandmother, who'd spent her life on Daufuskie Island bent over a hoe. She seemed to know all kinds of shit without the aid of books.

"You think I absorbed one word of her bumpin' herbal knowledge?" he asked me. I shook my head and smiled sadly, remembering my own freckled Meemaw fussing with her okra patch. She used to point out clumps of peckerweed in the woods, told me it was good for arthritis and male potency.

"Course I didn't get in on my grandma's game," said Trippy. "Thought myself too fly, missed out on a wealth of lore that might've kept my ass from supersliding down into the River Styx."

We chatted into the night, sprawled on the Nano Lounge's endless IKEA sectional, sipping Pep as our cerebral networks sizzled with the electric blurps and neuro-alchemy of our most recent downloads. A plasma TV, mounted over the vending machines, presented the talking head of our president. A fake hick Tea Party jackass with an Ivy League degree, he spit out sound bites about the war in Syria. Halfway into our second cups of Pep, the fluorescent overheads started to throb. So we switched them off, turned on the floor lamps, enveloped the room in a mellower mood.

Test subjects drifted in and out, defeated males every one. While we figured there were at least thirty mortal men at the Center (judging by the cafeteria crowd), there were only six of us BAITs, as far as we knew, our heads on fire with enlightenment. Since the downloads were glaringly obvious in our speech, we could tell the difference between us and the others right after the phase-one BAIT downloads began. Plus, you could recognize a BAIT learner by the perfectly symmetrical bald spots on our cranial crowns, our subdermal transmitters spaced exactly like finger holes on bowling balls. By week two we'd all broken our confidentiality contracts, comparing notes about our experiences.

We each got between four and six downloads a day, depending on our Cognitive Capacity levels and state of neuronal health. Meanwhile, we had learned, the other dudes from the various control groups (whom we called slow learners) digested a negligible percentage of the shit they pored over for eight hours a day, suffering a boredom-shame combo they hadn't felt since taking rudimentary high school courses in rural ghettos and backwater towns. By eavesdropping in the cafeteria, we figured out that the non-BAITs either (1) received no lessons whatsoever but had access to a reading room full of old-school hard-copy texts, (2) sat through eight hours of tedious computer tutorials (CTs) daily, or (3) endured excruciating sessions with so-called licensed pedagogical practitioners (LPPs), i.e., male PhD-track students from Emory who already had master's degrees. After less than a week, most of the LPP learners (including my dear roommate Needle) hated the fuck out of their tutors, breaching their contracts to shit-talk the young bastards from Emory. Their hostility only grew as they watched us BAITs blossom into brains.

The living arrangements enhanced the dichotomy, pairing BAIT learners with slow learners, so that each of us BAITs had a sulky roommate, some poor loser who struggled daily with a more archaic form of pedagogy. The powers that be also coupled black dudes with black and white with white, expecting redneck racists and brothers seething with black rage, a potentially volatile mix, and they weren't completely wrong. Needle, for example, liked to hiss the word *nigger*, as though, borne on a sputter of his acid spittle, the slur might burn any black face that got too close. And Charles Jasmine, a CT learner and crackhead from Cope, South Carolina, did threaten to "cut any cracker" who passed through the force field of his personal proxemics bubble. A couple of black–white altercations had escalated into fistfights, but so far, only two perpetrators had been removed from the facility.

Most of the tension was not of the racial variety, however, but between BAITs and slow learners. As soon as they heard us talking our fancy talk in the cafeteria or Nano Lounge, they seethed with resentment and bonded together against us.

By the end of week two, we six BAITs were clumped at our own elite table, gibbering spastically, our speech peppered with polysyllables and arcane academic cant. We started off simple, imagining professional wrestling matches between Aristotle and Plato, for example, or tallying up the number of atrocities in Shakespeare's *Titus Andronicus*. Words like *Machiavellian* and *sprezzatura* were bandied about. By week three, we'd worked our way through classical antiquity, the Middle Ages, the whole kit and caboodle of European Renaissances, Reformation, Enlightenment, yada yada yada, zipping up through the nineteenth century to the false climax of high modernism, where, right after we got our bearings, our minds were promptly blown with all the posts (-modernism, -structuralism, -humanism, -colonialism). Thereupon, our Babel towers began to buzz with cacophonous tongues, mortar crumbling, brick chunks hurtling miles downward from heights beyond the stratosphere. The whole concept of a tower, of progress, is always already undermined by its own aporia, and that night we were reeling.

After 9:00 PM, the rest of the BAITs began to pop in.

"How's your hammer hanging?" said Skeeter Rabin.

A miniature hesher with long stringy hair and the enormous spooked eyes of a nocturnal monkey, Skeeter had also done time for weed-related shenanigans, which had derailed his career as a vinyl siding installation consultant and led him to the halls of this hallowed institution. Alvin Gooding, aka Al, was a Desert Storm vet and unemployed security guard from Goose Creek. With his horn-rimmed specs, stiff posture, and impeccably trimmed beard, Al looked like he could be on the cover of *Black Enterprise* magazine. Just like all of us, he had a history of substance abuse, though he was mostly into prescription meds (being a vet with chronic pain issues gave him a better excuse).

After securing their eternal secrecy, Trippy whipped out our milk jug of Pep, which we'd stashed behind the sectional. Al took a hesitant sip.

"Now we're talking," he said. "Trippy here has engineered a pretty decent bug juice—just what I need to clean the fizz out of my neuronal networks."

But who knew what went on within our actual neural tissue? Though we were getting "smarter" by the minute, we didn't have much training in physiology. The technicians never gave us scientific downloads, mostly stuffing our heads with highfalutin humanities data. The closest we got to the hard sciences was through philosophy of science or cultural materialist critiques.

"Y'all get *Discipline and Punish* yet?" asked Skeeter, his huge eyes aglow with enlightenment.

"Aw hell," said Trippy. "Don't get me started on the Panopticon, the perfect metaphor for my punked state of subjection, my socially constructed soul bugging under the weight of hierarchical observation, the prison guard internalized. The Man inside of the man, man. Just watch any male of color walking down the street, eyes on the lookout for the hobgoblin Man, frequently materializing in the form of an armed cop. The prison guard's inside you, dog."

"Pair that text with Angela Davis," said Al, "and it's a brain barrage. Makes me reevaluate my ordeal with Gulf War syndrome. Getting ganked by the gov and the medical bureaucracy. Had a boil on my leg the size of a tennis ball. What boil? they said. Took me six months, reams of paperwork, and eighty-five calls to the VA to get access to a doctor who didn't know his ass from a hole in the wall."

"Word," said Trippy. "I can tell you from personal experience that Davis nailed it: the prison-industrial complex, the punitive corporatization, the commodification of punishment. The police force is there to keep the underclass down. Prisons need warm human bodies to make bank. Brutal combo if there ever was."

Skeeter and I stared at our shoes—we were wretches, yes, and Skeeter had even done time, but we still enjoyed some of the perks of white privilege, particularly the luxury of growing up without constantly watching our backs. Plus, there was no telling what kind of deeply embedded racist societal shit tainted our unconscious minds.

"Yeah, bo." Skeeter shifted the subject, glancing up at the security camera we'd blocked with a potted plant. "Try adding microsurveillance to the mix. The electronic trail any poor fucker leaves every time he surfs the net, uses a credit card, or calls somebody."

"And here we sit in an institution par excellence, punked subjects," said Trippy, "our fucktard brains commodified."

"What you talkin' 'bout, Willis?" said Skeeter.

"What I mean is . . ."

"I know: *I am Ironic Man.*"

Skeeter always spoke this phrase in a Black Sabbath robot voice whenever we failed to detect his sarcasm. He was up out of his knockoff egg chair, pacing like a terrier, his Styrofoam cup sloshing with Pep.

"Killer buzz," he said. "I haven't experienced this kind of killer upper-downer combo since my Tussin-weed-Adderall trio in the spring of 1999."

"You party like it was Y2K? Who with?" asked Al.

"Girl named Rocky Revels."

"That's a fake name if I ever heard one," I said.

"Swear on my mama's grave."

"She ain't got no grave," said Trippy.

"Actually, she does, bo, though her body ain't in it yet: *pre-need*—Newspeak coined by the funeral industry. Mama ponied up for a two-for-one double plot at Sunset Memory Gardens in Stuckey."

"And you swear on this hallowed square footage that the girl's name was Rocky Revels?" I said.

"Cross my heart and hope to die. Her name was Rocky Revels. She had a wondrous ass, bleached hair the color of polar bear fur, the pallor of which was heightened by her orange suntan. We were groovin' to Steve Miller out on her trailer porch, watching a meteor shower."

"Aw shit, dogs," said Trippy, for we'd started up on women again, our longing heightened by the late evening hour and our delightful reintroduction to inebriation.

Each of us had, stashed in the sacred cabinet of his chest like a nesting doll, some Laura, some Beatrice, some Lady Dulcinea del Toboso, beauteous beyond compare. I had my Helen, the face that launched a thousand ships. Skeeter had Rocky Revels, a girl he did drugs with during the late '90s, who eventually left him to rot on a sagging sofa while she got her shit together and earned a paralegal degree. Trippy had Lady L, a DJ from Atlanta who'd interviewed Prince, a club hopper too sophisticated for the Trippy of that era, three shades lighter on the color caste hierarchy, suburb-bred and college-educated. He was a small-town hustler three weeks off a Greyhound when he'd first laid eyes on her dazzling form. He still carried her pic in his wallet. Would pull it out and raptly gaze. Showed it to me once and only once: a 1980s shopping-mall glam shot, immortalizing Lady L in a teal blazer.

He let me gawk for two seconds before snatching it from my hand.

"Part of the reason I subjected my sorry brain to this overhaul," Trippy said quietly.

Al was more cryptic about his true love, shrouding her nebulous image in dry-ice fog. For weeks he'd kept her cloaked in the mists of abstraction—*pulchritudinous, incandescent, ethereal*—wispy as a succubus, until, tongue loosened by Pep, he finally revealed that his succubus was an incubus, one special air-bear named Will Jones.

"Your boo's a bo?" said Skeeter. "You gay? It's all good."

"Not exactly," said Al, who adhered to Foucault's formulation of homosexuality as a medicalized identity invented during the nineteenth century. "There's no such thing as a homosexual, only homosexual acts."

"Bisexual, queer, trans?" said Trippy.

"I'm done with binaries, though I don't want to reaffirm their dichotomies with some lame attempt at deconstruction either," said Al. "I'm just me."

We were discussing whether or not maintaining straight identification while dabbling on the do-lo was heterosexist when in

walked Vernon Lafayette Hooper III, ne'er-do-well and squan-
derer of trust funds. A debauched prep from Beaufort, South
Carolina, Vernon had spent a year at Wofford partying but never
managed to grace a classroom with his presence, or even officially
enroll. He'd blown his daddy's money on intoxicants instead.

"Greetings," said Vernon.

Man boobs pressed voluptuously against the fabric of his lime
polo. His plaid shorts boasted a chartreuse element. Like a broiled
ham freshly removed from the oven and glossy with grease, his face
burned above his green attire. Vernon's DTs were still in force, long
after the rest of the BAIT crew's had subsided. He was still twitching, still had that clammy quality of a dude sweating out poisons.

I gave Trippy a look that said, *Should we share our Pep with this
booze fiend?* And Trippy gave me one that said, *Let's keep cool and
play it by ear at this present point in time.* So I smiled a fake smile
and took a discreet sip of my drink.

"What's up, Vern?" said Skeeter.

Now, Vernon's replies were often long-winded, going above
and beyond in the purple-prose department, intentionally cryptic,
somewhat incoherent, but, for the most part, decipherable. Tonight was a different story.

"Gouty sniffles," said Vernon. "Always already impervious,
gleety, sleety, and bloated with testicular quintessence."

"Say what?" said Trippy.

Vernon plopped down on the red egg chair with a sigh that seemed
to go on and on, air leaking slowly from his puffed physique. He
snorted. Crossed his legs. Squeezed them together and uncrossed
them again, spreading his knees wide as though to air his genitals.

"The existential ylem of evil eely voles," he attested. "Midnight
precipitation of chthonic swagger. Hark! Mine bladder. Hark!
Mine bonnets. Oozing into the Pleistocene."

"I feel you, man," I said, going along with Vernon's coy new game, thinking he was highlighting the uselessness of verbal communication, the slippage between signifier and signified. Which was cool. But still.

"Gerbilisms," Vernon hissed. "Difficult to parse. Dirigible oblong peasant follicles in blooming obscene granite."

"What's with the jabberwocky, bo?" inquired Skeeter.

Vernon didn't even glance Skeeter's way. He groaned with Shakespearean theatricality and pounced to his feet.

"Trollish and ecclesiastical!" he cried. "Tumid as rain! Geiger gravy in herniated perpendicularity!"

Strolling out of the lounge, Vernon mumbled something about the "ectoparasitism of baroque unshaven cantaloupes" while shuffling his strangely tiny feet, which were shod in ancient, tattered Top-Siders.

• •

The next night at supper, Vernon didn't sit with the BAIT crew in the cafeteria as he usually did but, after piling his plate with nothing but salad bar carrots and croutons, plopped down randomly at a table of touchy roughnecks, which happened to include my dear roommate Needle, plus a few other meth-corroded bastards of his ilk. We could hear Vernon going at it two tables over—"the silly hegemonic dentistry of bioluminescent hominids"—in a breathless rasp. Meanwhile, Needle scowled, consuming his cheeseburger in grim silence while a couple of his fellow troglodytes tittered.

"Pantomimic regurgitations and pre-Copernican vicissitudes of elephantiasic lace," said Vernon.

Needle actually growled, squashing a french fry with his fork.

"Zoological farthingales discombobulated by poontang," opined Vernon.

One of Vernon's tablemates, finally recognizing a word he knew, hooted in appreciation.

"Phallogocentric gorgons of diabolical hirsutism," argued Vernon, "silurid and whiskery with malicious obfuscation."

"Shut the fuck up," said Needle, who, I'm almost sure, assumed that Vernon was taunting him with scholarly riddles beyond his ken.

Language had become a touchy subject with Needle. When forced to spend time with him, I was careful to use the simplest diction possible—the syntax of toddlers, the grunts of Neanderthals—so as not to set him off.

"The quiddity of quidnuncs and squid," ejaculated Vernon. Speaking louder, he went on: "Bamboozled by syphilitic logodaedalians."

Seemingly unaware of his surroundings, he spewed words, mostly obscure Latinate polysyllables. His voice grew louder, more annoyingly rhythmic, a tad more high-pitched. By this point, Needle was clutching a plastic fork in his white-knuckled fist. Al and Skeeter had both risen tentatively from their chairs, sensing that some violence was afoot but not committed to thwarting it just yet. In the blink of an eye, Needle's fork prongs were impaled in Vernon's neck. French fries were flying through the air. The cafeteria echoed with Vernon's shrieks, the clatter of falling trays, the buzz of male voices crying out in what-the-fuck bewilderment.

There were guards, of course, haunting the shadowy margins of our cheerful cafeteria. And they rushed into the light, darkly uniformed, reminding us that this was no vacation, no summer-camp jaunt, but an institutional operation, hierarchically structured, equipped with surveillance cameras and a well-trained security staff in keeping with that of a correctional facility. And we were just a bunch of thugs. We were low-life losers prone to violent episodes, each of us gridlocked into his particular subject position—race, class, gender, sexuality—squirming like some pathetic pinned insect. Kingdom, phylum, class, order, family, genus, species—the archeology of knowledge pressed heavily upon our socially constructed souls.

One of the guards put Needle in a headlock. Two others took Vernon's arms, gently lifting him as they guided him toward the exit. Although his stab wound trickled enthusiastically, it didn't appear to be in a fatal place.

And still he muttered, swiping absently at his gory neck. "Heliotropic hamadryas hurtling toward heinous hootenannies," I thought I heard him say as he was escorted from the premises.

• •

After supper, Vernon didn't drop by the Nano Lounge as he usually did. It was the same gang of four as the previous night, until Irvin Mood arrived to make it a quintet.

"What it is, youngbloods?" he said. "Who's got the skinny on Vernon?"

Irvin had been AWOL the previous night and all day that day. He was over a decade older than the rest of us—fifty-four—and occasionally spent mealtimes and evenings noodling some reggae-funk fusion on his horn, a process that had not been significantly enriched by his downloads, because, according to Irvin, the kind of bullshit lollygagging they stuffed our heads with didn't have jack to do with real art.

"My roommate was at that table with Needle and his jiggy crew," Irvin said. "Told me Vernon got shanked with a plastic fork. Said he was jive-talking too much grandiose bull."

"I'm pretty sure it was just gibberish," said Al.

"I don't know, bo," said Skeeter. "Maybe he's in deeper than Derrida, or James Joyce during his *Finnegans Wake* stage. Maybe we ain't advanced enough to decipher his shit—not on the first read, at least. Dude needs footnotes, marginal annotations, exegetical appendices."

"Or maybe his brain just busted out," said Trippy. "Stuffed beyond his cognitive capacity."

"Jelly brain," said Irvin.

"Maybe he caught a virus," I joked. "And some kind of bug lacing one of the downloads is fucking with his hard drive, wiping out data, sabotaging the language centers of his brain."

Every man in the room turned a shade lighter.

"Wack," said Trippy. He glanced toward the security camera. He whispered, "How the fuck is it that with all the nights we spend in here tripping on dialectic, the concept of a brain virus has not *once* entered our discourse?"

"Maybe we been engineered *not* to think of it," I said.

"But where would a virus come from?" said Skeeter. "If the Center rigs its own downloads like the contract says."

"That's no safeguard," said Irvin. "And not necessarily straight either. Even if they *are* using in-house bio components for everything, the actual data has to come from someplace, right? E-books, electronic indices, even the lawless World Wild West of the Internet, all of it converted from old-school digital into wetware."

"Vernon was a freak to begin with, though," said Al. "Never been good at a two-way convo of the collaborative sort. Thinks he's smarter than the rest of us because he almost went to college. Wears his white privilege on his oxford sleeve."

"Totally," I said. "Maybe his brain was always already too fried; no infrastructure for the data to stick to."

There we sat, sipping our Pep like medicine, our buzz deeply spooked. I was pretty sure that, just like me, the others were imagining rogue nanobots wreaking havoc in their brains, GM amoebae running renegade, munching through neurons like Pac-men. I was pretty sure they also imagined microscopic parasites mutating, changing their function, releasing terrorist electric signals, and slurping up neurochemicals. Maybe, as we sat there in the Nano Lounge drinking our crunk Dr. Pepper, we were changing into new creatures: posthuman cyborgs with no self-reflexivity, dupes of the Power Structure, thoughtless patsies of the Matrix.

"Mucho wackoid," said Irvin. "We got to find Vernon. See what they're doing with him. See if he's got anything solid to say."

· ·

First, we swung by Vernon's room, where a poker game was in progress. Vernon's roommate, Frankie, held court, chewing a cinnamon toothpick into splintery goo.

"Haven't seen him since supper," he said. "Didn't come back after he got shanked."

"When did you start noticing his peculiar behavior?" asked Skeeter.

"From day one." Frankie squinted over his cards, his lazy right eye caught in a mild tic. "Always been a weirdo. But two days ago is when he started up with the nonsense. Sounds like he's reading the dictionary."

Next, we hit the infirmary, where Big Eduardo, a sprinkler-installation consultant from Vienna, Georgia, was getting an ingrown toenail looked at.

"I seen nobody," he said. We checked the laundry facilities, the reading room, every nook and cranny where ice or vending machines were stashed. We roved the dorm halls, knocking on the door of every last room, eighteen total, and asked questions. Nobody had laid eyes on Vernon Lafayette Hooper III since he got shanked.

"Should we hit up Barney Fife?" asked Skeeter, referring to the residence hall monitor who manned the dorm security desk, a fellow who vaguely resembled Don Knotts (a hint of comic panic in his bulging eyes).

"You know he'll just be evasive," said Trippy. "And immediately inform Dr. M that we're sniffing around."

"You think they took him to the hospital?" said Al.

"How about the BAIT Lab?" asked Trippy. "We haven't scoped that."

So we headed downstairs, skirted past the cafeteria, and made our way through the eerie, empty halls toward the business end of the Center, the so-called Right Lobe, that warren of labs and cubicles where Dr. Morrow crammed our brains like sausages each day. The main door was locked. But when we pressed our ears against the reinforced stainless steel, we thought we heard rumblings, officious shuffling, muffled tech speak. We sensed the animal presence of human bodies. Huddled in an unlocked janitorial closet, we waited for almost two hours, slumped on the floor, breathing in disinfectant cleaner fumes. We whispered witticisms, sputtered with laughter, and devolved into scatological humor as we lost our Pep buzz, until, at last, we heard someone emerge from the lab complex and walk right past our door.

"I don't know if this guy Vernon is competent enough for release," said Chloe, "given the state of his dendrites and those horrifying arachnoid cysts."

"Pretty gross," said Josh. "Dude was competent enough to sign a release form, though, so the scan must've done something."

"Not exactly a state-of-the art program," said Chloe. "And Dr. Morrow expects us to finish the new scans by next week?"

"We can knock it out with a few all-nighters." Josh sighed. "Got any Adderall?"

"For a price," Chloe said, her feminine contralto fluting upward into singsong before erupting with a terse giggle.

We waited in the dark until we heard the pneumatic groan of the heavy exit door, a brief surge of crickets, and then: thick institutional silence, the hum of vents and pumps, fans and motors, obscure machinery tucked away above the ceiling and below ground, behind walls, going about its preprogrammed business in dark, utilitarian labyrinths.

SIX

That night, Needle didn't retire to our dorm room to sleep in that fitful way of his, his skinny legs bedeviled by cramps, mouth sputtering with groans and threats (like, *I'll break your fucking neck*). Though I was concerned about his sudden departure, I didn't miss his harrowed ass.

The next morning, when I appeared in the BAIT Lab for my nine o'clock session, I had my excuse ready. According to Irvin, our consent form had advised us to inform the technicians should we experience any unceasing headaches, seizures, blackouts, tremors, involuntary movements, and/or uncharacteristic nervous tics. There was no way in hell I was about to risk a brain virus, even if my poor noodle had already been stuffed like ravioli with dangerous organisms that, at that very minute, were reorganizing my gray matter according to their evil designs.

I was about to tell Chloe I'd been racked with a migraine all night, the kind of vomit-inducing nightmare headache that reduces you to a pure blob of pain burrowing through endless minutes like a maggot through shit. But before I could speak, she disarmed me with her best kindergarten-teacher smile, though her eyes were bloodshot, encased in puffy, discolored flesh.

"No BAITs today!" she sang. "After your test, you'll be good to go."

"No downloads?"

"Nope. Just an old-fashioned computer essay exam, the kind you took in high school."

"When I was in high school, we still scribbled with archaic ap- parati like ballpoint Bics."

"Cool," she said, motioning for me to follow her. "Retro chic."

She led me into a gray grid of soft-wall cubicles, each one equipped with a desk, a chair, a tablet. After pointing out the micropad's touch- sensitive keypad attachment, she shut the FiberCore door behind her. And there I sat until lunch, typing my poor heart out, pathetically longing to dumbfound whatever faceless authority figure would be reading the streams of words I wrung from my guts.

The essay question that I chose from a lame list of five options was probably written by one of the grad students who toiled daily with the slow-witted subjects of the LPP control group:

> *According to postmodernists, there's no such thing as a stable, coher-*
> *ent identity, only socially constructed subjects whose realities are con-*
> *text bound and subject to change. Using the interconnected categories*
> *of race, class, gender, and sexuality, consider how Frankenstein (Mary*
> *Shelley), "Bloodchild" (Octavia Butler), and "St. Lucy's Home for Girls*
> *Raised by Wolves" (Karen Russell) each explore the concept of socially*
> *constructed, alienated identities.*

Upon first reading this question, I laughed—the feverish, what- the-fuck laugh of a ruined king at the beginning of act 5, two scenes before his spectacular decapitation. Each of the fictional works in question described subjected creatures brainwashed by authority figures of questionable objectivity. There were power struggles involved: hierarchies, class wars, bitter clashes of ideology. The binary of civilized and uncivilized was questioned in each work and, to different degrees, tragically reaffirmed.

I loved all three of these rich, dark narratives and was eager to strut my stuff. Realizing that the test designers were mocking my own recently acquired sense of postmodern self-reflexivity, however, I sneered bitterly. Those smug little bastards! They didn't know who they were messing with!

I could see them, sniggering as they dreamed up their trifling essay questions, positioning us as savages, cheerfully aligning themselves with the oppressive institutions that filled us poor beasts with specious educational light. I could see them, crammed three to an office at Emory, fussing with their computers as nubile undergraduates drifted in to shoot the shit. I could see them in nerdish dishabille, clothed by catalogs, bespectacled and suburb reared, strolling across swaths of campus green, oases of order and fertility amid the honking, dingy clusterfuck of Atlanta. I could see them as adolescents, talking smack to their poorly paid private-school teachers—these privileged bastards who could afford to blow two hundred thou of parental funds on fucking humanities degrees. These coddled creatures who dabbled in Marxism. These dog-walking brunch eaters who piddled with essays on *the alterity of the colonized*.

And so I wrote. With slavering gusts of animal rage, I wrote—howling like a wolf, bellowing like a patchwork creature composed of stinking corpse parts, my monster face distorted with fury, my skin straining against the crude black stitches that affixed it to the pulsing musculature beneath. I was alive! Every nerve within me sparked with rage.

Thankfully, I'd taken Basic Keyboarding at Swamp Fox High and could type seventy words a minute. By the time my three-hour allotment had ended and I lay my poor spent noggin upon the desk, just as I used to do during Miss Bussy's fourth-period study hall, I had written a twenty-page essay. And it was good, especially the chilling conclusion:

> *Unlike Frankenstein's monster, I'll never waste my time dithering over sophomoric Oedipal ontologies, the kind dreamed up by dinky-souled pseudointellectuals with balls like pellets of dirty, industrial ice. I'll bolt this hellhole, leave you to a lifetime of Sisyphean institutional (and I use this signifier with full Foucauldian force) hoop-jumping. As Beckett put it, "Habit is the ballast that chains the dog to his vomit."*

I e-mailed the essay to myself for posterity.

• •

At lunch I discovered that the rest of the BAIT crew had also spent the morning writing essays. Everybody but Al (who'd wanted to write about queer theory) had selected the same question I had, and had also erupted into angry passion over the ironic connections to our own pitiful states of subjectivity, with the exception of Irvin, who usually maintained an aura of Zen-like calm. We spent most of our lunch break rabidly discussing our essays, until Irvin rapped his plastic knife against his Coke can to silence us.

"Why's everybody ignoring the mastodon in the room?" he said. "Big hairy son of a bitch up on its hind legs roaring. They suddenly decide to forgo the usual download schedule and fake us out with an essay test the morning after Vernon's brain blows a fuse and he checks out of Dodge, supposedly on his own volition? WTF? Do you copy?"

"Roger," said Al. "Let's just wait and see what they do after lunch."

"And tomorrow's Sunday," said Skeeter. "A whole 'nother day download-free."

"No way Vernon had the competency to sign a release form," I said.

"He's out on the street for all we know," said Al.

"Something's rotten in the state of Denmark, dogs," said Trippy, drawing a piece of sushi to his nostrils and taking a good whiff.

• •

Sure enough, our postlunch sessions involved nothing but multiple-choice tests, featuring such tedious brainteasers as the following:

Women, LGBTQ people, people of color, people with disabilities, and _____ are often defined in binary opposition to dominant groups.

A) Other others

B) othered others

C) other Others

D) each Other's other

E) each other's Other

On and on the idiotic questioning went, entrapping me in busywork for nearly three hours before I was released—brain numbed, fingers cramped, left foot prickling with pins and needles. I stumbled down the empty hallway to the pisser. There I ran into Trippy, and we strolled toward the Nano Lounge for a quick cup of pre-prandial Pep.

• •

It was Hawaiian night in the dining hall, 1950s exotica on the sound system, elderly cafeteria ladies wearing plastic leis and grass skirts as they dished out huli huli chicken and loco moco. The powers that be, who lacked imagination, tried to spice things up with predictable Saturday-night theme meals (like Disco Daze!), which most of us ignored. Over by the grub line, the head dietician stood grimly with an armful of plastic hibiscus garlands. Every now and then, she'd catch the eye of some ghoul-faced wretch and attempt to bedeck his neck with flowers. But most of the men steered clear of her, or else tossed their leis into the trash. They reviled the lame Muzak. They picked chunks of canned pine-apple from their pre-grilled frozen chicken breasts and defiantly thumped them onto the floor.

To our left, a table of compulsive gamblers discussed a recent cockroach race, their yet-to-be-cashed stipend checks already div-vied up in an intricate array of IOUs. To our right, various druggies gathered around Big Eduardo, who supposedly had a line on some generic OC.

"Despite the potency of our beloved Pep," I said, "I wouldn't mind a short jaunt to Ocean City—just a weekend in some swank time-share."

"Word." Trippy sighed. "Except Big Eduardo's punking their asses."

Al walked up, followed by Irvin and Skeeter. They sat down and started hacking at their leathery chicken breasts with plastic knives.

"Hey, Trippy," said Skeeter, "we still on for cocktails tonight?"

"Sure thing. Got that cask of amontillado chilling in my wine cellar."

"Hey, anybody get Percival Everett yet?" said Trippy.

"*Erasure*," I said. "Holy fucking shit. Brilliant."

"You get *Glyph* too?"

"Yep," I said. "Kind of a philosophical echo of our particular situation, relationship with the power structure, I mean."

"Exactly," said Trippy, "with the deconstructionist infant writing smack to his pedantic parents and all. You'd think that—"

"My fellow carnivores," said Al, "your chicken taste like jerky too?"

"Frankenfood, bo," said Skeeter. "Pretty damn depressing."

Al dropped his plastic knife. His hand crimped into a raptor claw from some kind of palsy. His eyes rolled back into their sockets demon-possession-style. He belched out a few guttural bullfrog croaks. But then he recovered, smiled politely, and dabbed at his lips with a paper napkin.

In a posh New England accent he said, "Do you ever feel the weight of sadness bearing down upon your meaningless existence?"

"Wait 'til you're my age, youngblood," said Irvin.

"Do you ever feel an overwhelming sense of hopeless despair, as though your flabby body contains no soul, as though your life is a tedious series of meaningless reps: eating processed food, shitting processed food, fucking on automatic pilot, shuffling data in an office cube? You may no longer enjoy activities that used to give you joy—like watching television, walking your dog, or playing Zombie Babe Attack on Xbox One. These are some symptoms of depression, my friends, a serious medical condition afflicting over twenty million Americans."

"What the hell?" said Skeeter.

"Depression may be caused by an imbalance of natural chemicals between nerve cells of the brain," Al continued. "And prescription Nepenthe works to correct this imbalance. Side effects may include urethral aplasia, sleep paralysis, hirsutism of the eye, and anal hemorrhaging. Nepenthe is not habit-forming. Call 1-800-N-E-P-E-N-T-H for more information. Get ready to strap on your parachute and jump back into life!"

Al flashed a twitchy smile. His glasses were crooked. His buzz cut was looking a little bushy. His beard, usually fastidiously trimmed and groomed, was losing its shape. A convulsion shook his broad shoulders. He stared into space for a few seconds, his lower lip drooping. Then he snapped out of it. Swallowed. Shook his head and plucked a tater tot from his plate.

We all smiled uneasily.

"You all right, Al?" said Trippy. "That was, like, a parody, right?"

"What you talkin' 'bout, Willis?" said Al.

Chewing a cube of processed potato product, Al glanced around at our flushed faces.

"Seriously," he said, "what?"

He shrugged, then squirted another blob of Heinz 57 onto his plate.

· ·

That night in the Nano Lounge, we were all dishing about our friend's odd dinner theater, hoping his quirks were an intentional parody but fearing some delayed manifestation of Gulf War syndrome.

"Some kind of biological warfare bugging," said Trippy.

"Maybe the biowarfare is a bad mix with the BAIT downloads," I said, "like mixing liquor and beer."

"Y'all don't think he's joshing us?" said Skeeter.

"Don't know," said Irvin. "Maybe."

Just then, Al came striding into the room sporting a plastic lei.

"You got *leid*, bo?" Skeeter quipped, and we all groaned like Inquisition victims on the rack.

"What?" Al blinked.

"That garland of plastic orchids around your neck," I said.

"Orchid means *testicle* in Latin," said Trippy. "You got plastic bollocks round your neck, dog."

"What you talkin' 'bout, Willis?" said Al, whereupon Irvin rose from his chair to tug on Al's floral wreath.

"This thing right here is known as a *lei*," Irvin said gently. "The Hawaiian word for *garland*."

Al removed his lei, bunched it up in his hands, studied the lilac plastic mass, and tossed it into the garbage. He sat down on the edge of the sectional.

"How about a cup of Pep?" he said to Trippy.

"Sure thing." Trippy pulled out the sacred milk jug, gave it a brisk shake, and then sloshed a few inches of hooch into a Styrofoam cup and handed it to Al.

"I've been thinking about your theory, Irvin," said Skeeter, charging into a new subject to clear the air.

"Which one?" said Irvin.

"About the different eras of porn and the ineluctable modality of the visual—"

"Gentlemen," interrupted Al, and then he rose from the couch, strolled to the center of the floor, and held his drink aloft like a chap with a crystal tumbler in a Chivas Regal ad.

"Let's be frank," he said in a New England accent with a detectable midwestern undertow—vaguely academic, the television voice of scientific reason.

"Every man worries about the size of his member." Al winked. "So let's be honest. Even if you're John Holmes, you still feel inadequate, still want that extra inch of prowess, that erection of triplealloyed tungsten that makes the ladies howl."

Al winked.

"Take my penis, for example. The pitiful appendage used to be about two inches long, a Napoleonic cocktail weenie that was downright cherubic—until I started using Priapus. Priapus is a state-of-the-art gene-therapy program bioengineered by scientists from MIT. In a revolutionary new process, nanobots deliver gene therapy through the patient's bloodstream, using RNA interference to block growth inhibitors. As microscopic polymer robots reprogram penile building blocks on a subatomic level, stem cells recalibrate to pubertal levels that lead to rapid genital growth in less than thirty days! Guaranteed! Or your money back. Call 1-866-P-R-I-A-P-U-S, and you'll be a ballin' lothario in no time!"

And then, as though nothing had happened, Al returned to his chair and took a slurp of Pep.

"You feel okay, man?" said Skeeter. "You joshing, right?"

Al frowned, glanced from face to face.

"I get it." Trippy flashed a fake smile. "Pop-up-like random commercials, a postmodern parody of spam, yeah?"

"What are you talking about, Willis?" Al tried to smile, but a tremor overtook him, crumpling his face. He dropped his cup, clutched his head, and groaned.

"What's the matter, man?" said Irvin.

"Headache," growled Al. "Motherfucking übermigraine." Al whimpered and rubbed his temples.

Skeeter stood up, his enormous eyes swimming with sympathy, and patted him on the back. "Want to go to the infirmary, bo?" he said.

"Uggrh," said Al.

Then he straightened himself, blinked at us. "It's gone," he said. "Just like that. *Poof.*"

SEVEN

Later in my room I fell into a strange half sleep as traffic from the interstate beeped and droned outside the sliding glass door. Needle was still gone, but I kept sensing him there, looming over me with his invisible samurai sword.

I flicked on the light, glanced around.

Nothing.

It must be the Pep, I thought.

I got out of bed, walked to the window, and looked out at the corporate landscaping: fountain, Bradford pear trees, sickle moon hanging over the parking lot. I had a headache. I took two Advils and lay down again.

First thing next morning I'd ask them point-blank what the hell was going on. I'd tell them we knew about Vernon's suspicious release. Ask them what the deal was with Al. I'd refuse any more downloads until they gave me a satisfying answer. I'd even go home if I had to—screw the six thousand dollars I so desperately needed. I'd called my dad a few times since arriving to stave off suspicion but otherwise hadn't communicated with anybody. I'd sent out a volley of cryptic e-mails predeparture, hinting at a retreat to some

remote detox facility, telling people not to worry about my incom-
municado state, and now I wondered if I ought to tell someone
exactly where I was just in case I needed an emergency escape plan.
I pictured my little vinyl-sided house, ninety-eight percent of it
owned by Bank of America after my ruinous postdivorce refinance.
I could see Helen cutting zinnias out in the yard, waving at me,
eager to give me a second chance. Ten years ago we were happy,
though I didn't know it then: happy enough to be ingrates about
our happiness, happy enough to spend long Saturdays working in
the yard together, planting a vegetable garden, working our bodies
until felled by delicious fatigue. We'd collapse into lawn chairs as
the sun sank, buzzed but not drunk, discussing heirloom toma-
toes. One summer Helen was trying to track down this species her
grandfather used to plant, the perfect tomato, according to her: not
too big, not too little, not too firm, not too squishy, somewhere
on the spectrum between Cherokee Purple and Black Prince. She
wanted to plant a "Goth garden," all deep purple and dusky blooms,
and she pulled me into her obsession, made me her coconspirator.

"Black Lace elderberry," she said one evening, licking her lovely lips, passing the sweat-crimped catalog from her lap to mine.
"Black Lightning iris and eggplant calla lilies. And you could do
some kind of wacked-out garden sculpture, Romie, just to freak
the neighbors out."

With this peaceful domestic vision, I drifted off again, into a
dream.

I was playing an instrument—a trumpet, I think, which I've never
picked up in my life. In a high school band room, surrounded by
white and black dorks, most of them dressed in ornate polyester
'70s shirts and bell-bottom jeans, I blasted away with mad skill. Under the direction of a spastic, clammy honky, we rocked that room.
We filled it with glorious tunes, pumped it with the heady musk of

adolescence—twenty sweaty bodies of different shapes, sizes, hues, and genders, creating a synesthetic miasma of hormones and noise.

I caught the eye of a pretty girl with glinting specs, her demure Afro as perfectly round as a vinyl LP. She raised her eyebrows while tootling her flute, traipsed through a delicate solo that left me weak-kneed. Next it was my turn to cut a figure in phallic brass. I darted with ease like a metallic dragonfly. I glittered and soared, the instrument fused to my respiratory system. And then it was over. I pulled the horn from my mouth, felt the pull of a slobber strand. Wiping drool from my lips, I noted the deep chestnut tone of my arm. I was a black dude in the final stretches of a crazy growth spurt, shedding the last of my baby fat. I liked to slouch in corners and watch the world's ado with an air of contrived nonchalance. I could see the reflection of my Afro in the golden luster of my horn, my face too distorted to recognize.

"One more time," said the band director, his wet mustache gleaming like a centipede.

And we went at it again, played until the bell rang. Then we slapped our instruments into their coffin-like cases and pressed out into the hall. The flautist strode in front of me, a slender reed of a girl decked in autumnal plaid, gold hoops in her delicate earlobes. When she smiled at me, I noted braces on her teeth—thought *rich girl*. But I had to ask her something.

I could feel the question burning in my chest.

"Hey, Linda," I coughed. She spun around, smirked like my zipper was down. I checked it. Shit was cool.

I said, with affected huskiness, "You want to hit that cheesy dance together?"

I was talking about some Halloween carnival, some hell-themed disco inferno that was going down in the school gym that Friday night.

"That would be nice," she said. "I'm in the phone book," she said. "Check ya later," she said, before flouncing off toward the chemistry lab.

My heart pattered fast as a jackrabbit's. I needed a smoke. So I slipped into the bathroom and lit up, regarding my face in the mirror as my nostrils tusked smoke, noting something familiar about my eyebrows, the way they flared in surprise. And then the dream shifted, and I was *outside* my body, looking down at Irvin—for it was Irvin—half rake, half nerd, sixteen years old, perfecting his exhalation before the mirror.

• •

Touched by weird dreams, I slept on and off past noon, then scrambled into my pants to catch lunch. The BAIT crew, all assembled save for Al and Vernon, looked pretty zombified. *Must be the Pep*, I thought as we ate in sulky silence, wondering where the hell Al was, fearing that he, too, had been forced to sign a release form and now wandered the streets in a robotic daze.

"Anybody seen Al today?" I asked.

"Saw him in the Nano Lounge," said Irvin. "Greeted me rather formally but otherwise seemed okay."

"That's a relief," said Trippy. "Need to keep an eye on the man."

Skeeter glanced up from his pizza and said, "Romie, bo, I had a weird dream about you last night."

"Yeah?"

"I dreamt I *was* you, man—like, total immersion in your identity."

"And what happened, exactly?"

"Well, you were with your daddy in his taxidermy shop, and he was teaching you how to mount a boar's head. Made you do the work while he leaned over you in coach mode, talking into your left ear, so close I could smell the pickles on his breath. I could smell formaldehyde and rancid carcass. Plus, the Speed Stick you'd just started smearing your hairless pits with, even though you didn't need it. And I could hear the radio whining out mellow '70s tunes your father dug, songs you deemed too pussified for your burgeoning badassery."

At this point the whole crew had stopped stuffing their faces, each man swallowing a last mouthful with an uncomfortable gulp and leaning forward on tensed forearms.

"Lord Tusky the Second," I whispered.

"Who?" said Skeeter.

Lord Tusky the Second was the wild boar I helped my daddy stuff in 1984, the year I first fell for Helen at Concrete Pond, the year Reagan trumped Mondale, that year of Orwellian foreboding when the new wave crested and some psychopath opened fire in a McDonald's, slaughtering twenty-one innocent fast-food consumers—a banner year for DNA fingerprinting, Macintosh computers, and the AIDS virus.

"That really happened," I said. "That's an actual memory, Skeeter. What the fuck?"

As I told them about my dream, Irvin shook his head, creased his forehead in puzzlement, and worked his feral eyebrows up and down.

"Also a memory," he said. "Right down to the braces on Linda Green's teeth."

We all started babbling at once about our night of strange dreams, until Irvin yelled, "Be still!"

"One at a time," he said. "You next, Trippy."

Trippy had dreamed of Skeeter, while Irvin had dreamed of Trippy, a perfect shuffling of identities as though we were enmeshed in some parlor game, some pomo variation on telephone or musical chairs. Again, we erupted into panicked babble. Again, Irvin, who often played the elder Socrates in our symposia, commanded our silence. Despite our rising panic, he managed to ref an orderly debate that yielded the following theories:

1. During our BAIT downloads, we each left residual memories in the system, contagious memories that others could pick up. In that case, the transfer of memories probably reflected the order of our BAIT sessions.

2. Our identities were fusing into a network, a form of file sharing that formed a kind of collective consciousness.

3. The memory swap was evidence of a virus, perhaps even an intentional aspect of the BAIT program, and our brains were in the process of being hijacked to disastrous results, just as Al's and Vernon's had been.

"I wouldn't put anything past BioFutures Incorporated," said Irvin.

"What the hell is Biofutures Incorporated?" asked Skeeter.

"The contract research organization funding this study, man. Guarantee you they don't give a rat's ass about our personal well-being."

"How you know who's funding the study?" asked Trippy.

"It's right there in the contract if you got eyes in your head," said Irvin, "though it is in the fine print, so I had to pull out my bifocals to read it."

"I'm still a bit fuzzy as to the nature of the so-called research organization," said Skeeter.

"According to Google," said Irvin, "BioFutures is a jack-of-all-trades outsourced mega-conglomerate, with money as the bottom line and no central authority in line to regulate. They dabble in all kinds of shit: neuropharmaceuticals, biotechnology, even telecommunications. At least that's what I gather from the Internet, which is out there for the world to see. Nothing but your own apathy and laziness stopping you from digging it up. No telling what kind of dark shenanigans go on behind the scenes."

"Bet you they sell their research to the highest bidder too," said Trippy, "decontextualized and repackaged."

"You got it, youngblood. Some sinister jive," said Irvin. "Can't help but think about the Tuskegee syphilis experiment or the MK-ULTRA LSD research. They could be yanking our chains. Tearing our brains up just to put them back together, y'all copy? I say we go to our cribs and examine our consent forms. I say we read the fine print. See how much they got us by the balls."

• •

I sat in my overchilled room, sliding glass door open to let some balmy air in. The summer breeze was tainted with car exhaust. Sighing, sipping Mountain Dew, I turned to the dismal task of contract reading. I snorted at the statement *This consent form may contain words with which you are unfamiliar. Please ask a member of the staff to explain any terminology you do not understand.*

I read through an explanation of the purpose of the BAIT study. I read through a jargony description of the download prep process, installation of transmitters, injection of nanobot serums, yada yada yada, and then on through an exhaustive account of the procedures I'd been undergoing for the past four weeks—water under the fucking bridge. I briefly gave pause over the possible administration of *random drug and alcohol tests*, which I had not noticed upon my first attempt at reading the contract. At last, I reached a juicy section titled "Risks and Discomforts," a bulleted list of over fifty side effects suffered by one in forty subjects from similar tests, ranging from *mild headaches* and *feelings of dissociation* to *intracranial hemorrhaging, anomic aphasia, and atonic seizures.*

I vaguely remembered chuckling dismissively over this list when I'd scanned portions of the contract in the lobby of the Center, a seasoned ironist even before my brain overhaul. Like most twenty-first-century Americans, I was used to drug commercials featuring beautiful women frolicking through fields of sunflowers, high on the latest antidepressant, beatific and radiant despite warnings of blurred vision, decreased libido, and spastic colon. I ate GM Frankenfood bled of nutrients and "fortified" with vitamins, synthetic grub chock-full of pesticides, artificial compounds, and carcinogens. Nuclear power plants surrounded me on all sides, pulsing with toxic radiation. Ever since the ozone had been shot to hell, sunshine itself had turned evil, blighting my skin with dark, precancerous spots.

Even if I were to sequester myself in a cabin deep in the Blue Ridge Mountains, live off game, wild plants, and creek water, I couldn't escape the poisons of civilization. As *National Geographic* had recently informed me, even the most remote tributary of the Amazon River contained *twenty-nine contaminants of various chemical groups.*

Our oceans were dying. Ice caps melting. Rain forests shrinking. A new species went extinct every 9.3 seconds. You could drive yourself crazy tallying them up. During the time I'd been reading this particular consent form, sipping Mountain Dew, and scratching my poor harrowed balls (the sperm counts of American men had declined by forty-five percent since 1950), 96.7 species had bitten the dust. I imagined the last kipunji monkey staggering through brush, coughing up blood, falling into death throes on the jungle floor as the sounds of chain saws droned in the distance, and jumbo jets roared through the sky, and cell phone towers rose upon Mount Kilimanjaro.

I felt weak and scared. I wanted to call Helen. I wanted to hear her rich laugh veer into nasal tones. But she was probably enjoying the summer day with Boykin: picnicking, skinny-dipping in his pool, or worse—lounging in a postcoital torpor in a tank top and panties, eating Thai noodles while streaming Netflix.

I could not call Helen.

I turned back to my dismal contract:

Because these procedures are experimental, their full range of side effects may be unknown. Some may be life threatening. Please inform the staff about any side effects you may experience.

The staff had access to my medical records. The Center was equipped with surveillance equipment. There was a chance that our behavior *might be monitored.* The head doctor and his staff had the right to distribute information about us *to research sponsors, employees, and/or owners of research sponsors as well as governmental agencies.*

I had a headache already and still hadn't reached the section I was looking for. I wanted a drink. I kept glancing anxiously toward the Pep cooler, then around at various spots where microcameras might be stashed. At last, I found the section in question, titled "Compensation for Injury," which explained that the study's principal investigator would treat us *as needed* and dismiss us from the study if it was in our *best interest.* If we chose to leave the study early, we would be *partially compensated on a prorated pay scale* unless we *violated any of the rules or regulations listed in clause 7.5*, and finally, *receipt of total stipend is dependent on full completion of download procedures and participation in follow-up tests.* This hazy section concluded with a particularly ominous tidbit: *research subjects will submit to any end-of-study procedures deemed necessary.*

Whatever the fuck that meant.

I whipped out my phone, logged on to E-Live, and pulled up Helen's profile. She was still IN A RELATIONSHIP. She still dug freaky marine life and *Art*. But she'd updated her profile pic. Gone was the vampire squid floating in a solipsistic dream at the bottom of the sea, its skin radiant with self-made light. Now my Helen was leaning against what looked like the porch railing of a fancy beach house. The ocean seethed behind her. The ancient, boiling sun sank with a hackneyed burst of gaudy flamingo light.

I suspected that Boykin had snapped the picture. I feared that Boykin owned the oceanfront property at which my ex-wife dallied in such casual elegance like a lady of means. I recalled a morsel of wisdom from that dumpy womanizer and war criminal Henry Kissinger, who looked like a bloated proboscis monkey but still got bookoo pussy: *power is the ultimate aphrodisiac.*

Power is *money*. Power is *positional*. Power is *rooted in hierarchical observation*.

As I gazed at the snapshot of Helen, her sun-kissed body hazed in a nostalgic glow by some retro phone app, I felt the power draining from my body. I needed a drink. In a fit of paranoia, I went around the room affixing strips of masking tape to suspicious units of hardware and electronics—ceiling-mounted sprinkler heads, the blinking smoke alarm, the digital thermostat box—anything that might conceal a security camera. I removed my soiled undergarments from the top of our secret cooler, and dipped my plastic cup into the vat of Pep. I lay on my depressing twin bed, in my tiny cube, staring at the cinder-block wall and drinking Trippy's prison swill.

I could feel eyes upon me: the bulging, deadpan eyes of the nighttime residence hall monitor, the beautiful young eyes of the tech assistants, the green eyes of Dr. Morrow, which sparkled with childish curiosity despite their crow's-feet, and finally, the eyes of the nameless suits from BioFutures Incorporated who'd financed this study. I could feel them staring at me, their eyes huge and opaque, without depth or irises—the blank reptilian eyes of Sleestaks.

I toyed with the idea of heading down to the Nano Lounge for some company but decided to wallow in the cozy pigsty of my misery while shuffling through Helen's pics and scanning her Wall for evidence of her new life. Rifling through her roster of 256 "friends," I couldn't find Boykin, whose last name I didn't know and whose first could be some form of sobriquet. So I image-Googled *Hampton County attorneys*, alighting, at last, upon his headshot. The fucker was wearing a bow tie with a sweater vest. He smiled like a possum.

Boykin Wallace Hagman had graduated from Furman University and Charleston School of Law. He was in real estate, naturally, and belonged to a firm called Hagman and Banes. He had a weak chin. A thin, long nose. His eyes were squinty, rodential, and scheming. An unwholesome, fleshy growth dangled from his left lower eyelid. He looked vaguely clammy, sun-damaged, and pink. He had to be at least fifty-five when this pic was snapped, despite his suspiciously thick gray mane, which looked like it had been cosmetically enhanced with silver-fox highlights.

He was a member of the Edisto Island Historic Preservation Society. He owned an Irish setter and loved sailing. He supported *the Arts*.

This was all I could gather from his short bio.

I downed another cup of Pep. Glared at his image until it started to vibrate demonically. When I finally stood up, I felt the drunkenness fluttering inside my body like plastic flakes in a shaken snow globe. I stumbled down the hall to call Helen.

• •

At the end of the hall, the reading room got decent reception, so I hunkered down in a fake Barcelona chair for the task at hand. My heart sputtered as I shuffled through my contacts, located Helen Honeycutt, and pressed DIAL.

"Romie!" she answered, ambushing me with her deceptively intimate voice—a big surprise since she usually banished me to the limbo of voice mail. "Where the hell are you?"

"In an undisclosed location."

"Romie," she said gently, reminding me a little of Chloe, "are you in rehab?"

"Something like that."

"I think that's a wonderful thing, and so does Lee. I talked to him the other day. He and Chip were worried—thought you might be doing time at a mental hospital someplace."

"All institutions—rehab, mental hospitals, public schools—pretty much follow the prison model, using hierarchical observation to socially construct docile bodies."

"Excuse me? What are you talking about?"

"Never mind. Just wanted to ask you a few things."

"Wait a minute. Are you drunk?"

"Not really. Why?"

"You're slurring. You said *Jush wanted to ash you a few tings.*"

"I am Ironic Man, referencing drunkenness to create a deceptively comic subtext for our extremely sober conversation and thereby deconstruct the binary opposition between drunk and sober."

"You are definitely inebriated."

"Listen. Remember when you used to say that most real estate lawyers you knew were either glorified accountants or hustlers?"

"Romie."

"Well, do you remember saying that?"

"I said *most*, not all. I know what you're driving at, buster, and I don't appreciate it."

"Buster. That's funny. But listen, just listen to me."

I paused, hoping to be calmed by the whispery metronome of her breathing, lulled into a state of pseudo-comfort by the illusion of intimacy. Of all people on this shit-ball planet, Helen was the only one I felt close to, and I still sensed that we functioned as a unit, telepathically intermeshed on some subcellular level—despite her budding relationship with Boykin Wallace Hagman.

"I was wondering why," I said, "after upholding more or less feminist ideologies your entire life, unselfconsciously, which is a beautiful thing, you now submit to an old-school paternalistic, perhaps even mercenary, sexual relationship?"

"Mercenary? What the hell? Look, Romie. You're drunk. I'm worried about you. But this is bullshit. I hope you're okay. I've got to go."

"Wait, Helen. I may be in trouble."

I hated to use this hackneyed cinematic line, felt disgusted when I heard my voice going all squeaky on the word *trouble*, quivering with emotion and dropping dramatically into a void of silence. But it worked. And maybe it was true. Maybe I was in trouble.

"Romie?"

Her voice softened. I heard movement. Perhaps she was relocating to a place out of Boykin's earshot. I could picture him in the background, quivering his snout while feigning nonchalance, pretending to be absorbed in a TV commercial or riveted to his laptop, flipping idly through his stock portfolio, basking in the warmth of his assets.

"Romie, what's going on? You can talk to me."

I felt conned by the familiar conspiratorial dip of her voice, the lapse into throatiness—her private voice, her domestic voice, the voice she'd used when we had serious talks on the couch and she'd wriggle close, entwining her limbs with mine, sending waves of heat from her flesh to my flesh. Like the time when my mother's diagnosis finally came in, MRI scans featuring dark spots on key areas of her brain, *blighted tissue, atrophy of the frontal and temporal lobes.* In my parents' living room, Mom had smiled nervously, her mouth smeared with thick, bright lipstick, as Dad broke the news.

"I'm having some memory problems," Mom kept saying, still able to talk then, still able to balance a checkbook, still able to drive.

At home, afterward, I drank three beers that might as well have been water and paced around the house until Helen sat me down.

"We'll get through this, Romie," she'd said, reminding me of those dark months after her father killed himself by eating all of the pesticide samples in his Monsanto kit—a messy end—and the ordeal had taken us to a darker, closer place.

"Romie," Helen said now, sounding sterner, "are you still there?"

And then I had another savage headache, same as last time, as though my brain wanted to break free, to burst out with a sputtering of gore like the larval creature from *Alien.* "My brain wants to jump out of its—I mean *my*, goddammit—skull."

"What? Stop groaning, Romie. Talk to me, please. Tell me where you are."

And then I saw, clear as day, my father sitting grimly at the kitchen table as my mother served him a raw pork chop. A raw pork chop also sat on my plate, stark and pink beside a mound of undercooked rice, and on Helen's as well.

By this point, Mom's Pick's disease had progressed, but my father's coping tactic was to act as though everything were normal, letting her do her thing. She could no longer drive and her cooking had grown strange. Her vocabulary was dwindling rapidly, and she forgot who people were. Though she'd always been a conservative dresser, she became an eccentric fashionista that summer, sporting, that evening, a 1980s purple power blazer with coral warm-up pants. Her penciled-on eyebrows gave her face a Kabuki vibe. The sight of her, shuffling around the kitchen in clownish clothes, this woman who'd once snorted at dolled-up women, hurt, because I knew she was gone. Her smoking habit, once a secret vice, had grown fierce. A butt fumed in her ashtray, and yet she held a freshly lit Camel in her hand. She took a drag and winked at me.

"Is it delicious?" Mom said.

"Betsy," said my father, "this meat's raw."

"It's delicious," Mom said.

"You need to *cook* it," said Dad.

"It's delicious."

"Raw," Dad pronounced, taking his meat slab up with a fork. "Not cooked. We could get salmonella poisoning, trichinosis, yersiniosis."

Leave it to Dad, who owned three different medical dictionaries, to name a disease we'd never heard of. He pinched his thin lips into a line, intensifying his iguanoid features. It was not so much his slightly bulging eyes and burgeoning neck wattle that made him resemble the lizard as the horny emotional husk that separated him from the rest of the world.

As Dad gathered our pork chops on a plate, Mom shuffled around him in an anxious jig.

"It's delicious," she said.

"I've got to cook it, Betsy," Dad said, "or we could get sick."

Mom lunged for the plate, attempted to snatch it out of his hand. When Dad lifted the pork chops high over his head, she jumped like a terrier for a Milk-Bone. Giggling, she dropped her cigarette, which sprayed sparks as it bounced across the butter-yellow linoleum.

Helen gritted her teeth, something she did when she was upset but wanted to hide her feelings. She fussed with her fork. She reached for my hand. Our sadness fused into a mutual mood.

And then a gust of blackness swept through the bright kitchen, obliterating the scene.

EIGHT

When I emerged from this oblivion, I was in the BAIT Lab, strapped into the familiar ergonomic medical lounger of blue Naugahyde, a sheet of wax paper crackling under my damp body. Dr. Morrow plucked wireless electrodes from my scalp. He frowned at each slimy unit as though it were an engorged tick before dropping it into a metal bowl.

"What the fuck?" I squawked. "You strapped me down?"

"In case of convulsions." Dr. Morrow gave me a stern frown. "Chloe will unstrap you in just a minute."

"Convulsions?"

"Petit mal seizures caused by temporary electrical disturbances in the brain."

"What kind of electrical disturbances?"

Before Dr. Morrow could swindle me with another stream of jargon, Chloe breezed into the lab, her face marred with a black eye.

"See why we had to restrain you?" Dr. Morrow shook his head.

"God," I said. "I'm sorry, but— "

"No prob." Chloe smiled—a strained simper. "Part of the job description."

"But it's not my fault," I said. "I'm just a powerless guinea pig and these so-called electrical disturbances are side effects of the BAIT downloads. I wasn't even conscious when I kicked you."

"Actually," said Dr. Morrow, "you were."

"Only partially." Chloe unfastened my Velcro leg straps. "And we're ironing everything out. You should be fit as a fiddle now."

"What the fuck did you do to me?"

As I struggled against the straps, Dr. Morrow eased away from me.

"We installed a program that will block any unsolicited signals and microprograms," he said sternly, "for your own good."

"Unsolicited signals? What the hell do you mean by unsolicited signals and microprograms?"

"Some of the downloads may have contained residual data from previous digital models," said Dr. Morrow. "No biggie."

"You mean viruses?"

I said it. The nasty word festered in the silent room like an Ebola strain in a petri dish. As Dr. Morrow rubbed his nose and picked a dot of invisible lint from his lab coat, I felt my stomach liquefy and ooze into my large intestine.

"Not exactly," he said.

"Very encouraging."

"Ha, ha," said Dr. Morrow. "I am Ironic Man."

He even attempted to do the robot voice, very badly, which made me think he was unfamiliar with the Sabbath song. He grinned like a fox.

Of course they'd been watching us all along.

"We know about your little chemistry experiment, Mr. Futch," said Dr. Morrow. "We detected alarming rates of alcohol, dextromethorphan, and toxic tropane alkaloids in your blood sample, which we have in cryogenic storage should we find ourselves in a legal suit. We trust you have read the consent form. We assume you are aware that we may nullify your participation in this study without compensation for consuming unapproved medications and/or intoxicants."

"But we'd love for you to stay on board," chirped Chloe.

"Look," I said. "I know something funny was going on with Al and Vernon. I don't think either of their conditions is listed under 'Risks and Discomforts.'"

"I think the unknown-side-effects clause has them covered," said Chloe. "Though you should know that Al is feeling *much* better now after his scan."

"Also," said Dr. Morrow, "since substance abuse increases the likelihood of suffering unknown side effects, *you* are the one who has put yourself at risk, as the consent form clearly indicates."

"This wouldn't have happened if you hadn't been abusing intoxicants." Chloe actually wagged a finger at me.

"What about Vernon? He wasn't drinking anything, and look—"

"Vernon had other issues," said Dr. Morrow.

"Had?"

"Still does, as far as we know," said Chloe.

"Where is he?"

"Unfortunately, he opted not to continue the experiments," said Dr. Morrow.

"Sounds like a smart decision to me, though I have my doubts that this was a conscious choice on his part," I said. "What if I choose to stop this madness now? Will I get any compensation at all?"

"Well"—Chloe smiled brightly—"you're only a dozen BAITs away from phase three testing. So you're almost there! Why not finish the last sprint and collect your six grand?"

"I thought I still had hundreds to go before reaching FCC?"

"Change of plans," Chloe said tightly. "We're going to get you out of here earlier than planned."

"And we'll throw in an extra thousand to compensate for your, um, setback," said Dr. Morrow.

"Just think about it," said Chloe.

"We can assure you," said Dr. Morrow, "that after today, all unsolicited signals and microprograms will be blocked."

"The awesome thing about the final series," said Chloe, who looked pretty pitiful with that black eye, "is that *you* get to choose among a number of arts-related subjects: dance, music, painting, sculpture. We'll show you the program tomorrow. You should be able to knock them out in two days."

"And then what?"

"A few days for the downloads, a few for testing, and you'll be good to go. You'll even get out of here a week before planned, with seven thou jangling in your pocket."

"As a taxidermist whose career has reached a rough patch," said Dr. Morrow, "I think you would benefit from the visual arts modules. But don't answer now. Take a night to think it over."

"Can you fucking unstrap me now?"

"In just a minute."

He popped on my brain hologram. I watched it twirl in the empty air.

"Everything's pretty much back to normal!" said Chloe.

Dr. Morrow pressed a few buttons on his micropad and I felt the waning of adrenaline, the fight leaking out of me. Cautiously, Dr. Morrow unfastened my straps.

· ·

I stood beside the railing of my budget balcony, watching dark clouds roil over the parking lot as I checked my messages: texts galore from Helen, a few semiurgent lines from both Crystal and

Lee, an assortment of irate taxidermy customer e-mails, a terse voice-mail blip from Dad, and one sarcastic voice mail from Chip Watts, who—clearly wasted and shouting in a crowded bar—said he'd buy me a round of Jäger the second I busted out.

In several redundant messages, Helen declared that our friendship was important to her: *You'll always be a formative influence in my life no matter what.* She accused me of being *unfairly judgmental* toward Boykin. Begged me to please call, text, e-mail, E-Live poke—show some sign of life, some indication that I was breathing, still on this planet, still the same old Romie Futch she'd always known and . . .

No, she did not complete the sentence with the tender word *loved,* or use ellipses to imply it. She ended this message abruptly, probably in a fluster of furious emotion, and started on another harangue, raving about my *potential,* about the *dark path* I'd taken in life, about the countless ways I needed to *grow up.* Clichés, all, from the realm of romantic comedy.

While she worked part time at Technomatic Quick Lab, sucking the flabby man boob of a sugar daddy, she had the nerve to talk about *my* immaturity and potential—as though *she* need not aspire to the same standards due to her gender.

You've internalized your status as Other, I wanted to write. *What the hell happened to your dreams of becoming a marine biologist?* I wanted to write. *Why do you succumb to the socially prescribed role of cheerleader to a privileged white male?* I wanted to write. *At least I try to express my artistic vision in my own humble way*—I actually did type this into my phone—*though you probably look down your nose at taxidermists now that you're dating a possum-faced pen pusher and patron of the arts who wouldn't know real art if it crawled up his butthole and painted Sistine Chapel frescoes on the inside of his rectum.*

I deleted this message, however, and opted to maintain a state of mysterious, sulky silence. Prodded by the Imp of the Perverse, a nihilistic jolt of self-destruction, I decided to go ahead with the fucking downloads—give my brain one final dose of High Art before heading back to Hampton. I needed a drink, badly. But our Pep cooler had been confiscated. It was almost six o'clock. I realized I was starving, so I walked down to the cafeteria to see what the BAIT boys were up to.

. .

Sans Vernon, they were huddled around Irvin. Even Al was there, looking mildly concerned, and I hoped against hope that the virus scan had restored him. Sprawled in a chair, Irvin pressed a bloody tissue to his nose.

"What the hell?" I said.

"Dude just kicked Dr. Morrow's ass," piped Skeeter.

"Hyperbole," said Irvin, his voice a nasal croak.

Irvin sat up, removed the tissue, gave us a full look-see at his battered nose, which was swollen and oozing a rivulet of blood.

"Told them I wanted out," said Irvin, reapplying his Kleenex, "fuck their stipend. According to the contract, I could still split with a piddly two grand after their vampiric prorate. But Morrow said any BAITs conducted after our foray with substance abuse were bogus, that I'd get nada if I didn't *submit*. Can you believe he actually used that loaded term?"

"But then you wupped his ass," said Skeeter.

"Not exactly. Of course they offered me an inky backroom deal, promising a full return with an extra thou if I'd agree to a couple more sessions and some tests. Said they'd forget they had a damning DNA sample stashed in cryogenic deep freeze. So I let that sink in—tried to figure out how they got that off me—if they crept into my room while I was slumbering. Naturally, this pissed me off, so I jumped up out of my chair, and Dr. Morrow tried to push me down. Then *bam*—I got him in a crippler crossface, but he's stronger than he looks. Elbowed me in the nose. At least I got in an uppercut to his jaw before the security guard materialized to put me in a headlock."

Everybody let out a whoop in unison and raised clenched fists.

"When did this happen?" I asked.

"Maybe twenty minutes ago?" said Irvin.

"Can you even detect intoxicants in a DNA sample?" asked Trippy. "Sounds like a hustle to me."

"Only way to find out would be to blow my stipend on some low-rent lawyer," said Irvin, "probably end up paying the monthly on his Porsche with nothing to show."

"Totally," I said.

"Chloe had the audacity to start rubbing my arm," said Irvin. "Tried to sweet-talk me into staying on."

"What did you say?"

"Said I had to think about it, but only so they'd give me some space, give me the opportunity to cut out. Wanted to let y'all know what happened. See how everybody else was doing first."

We compared notes: everybody else had been coerced into submitting to the same scans I'd received in a state of unconscious innocence. Al stated that he had "undergone the procedures," but would reveal nothing more about it. Skeeter had done so reluctantly, only after Morrow mentioned the extra bucks, while Trippy had managed to bargain for an extra two grand, which pissed the rest of us off. Irvin, ever the levelheaded patriarch, decided he was going to refuse any more procedures.

"Cutting my losses, youngbloods," he said. "Prorate or no prorate, seizures or no, I'm out of here."

"Where you going, Irv?" asked Skeeter.

"Gonna toot in a square beach band for a few months, hit retirement communities in the Myrtle Beach area. I'll be revitalizing the sluggish blood of elderly shaggers with my golden horn. After that, maybe Florida; depends on what this cat Turtle's got lined up. Swears the geriatric dance scene is ripe for plundering. A couple thou per gig, plus tips if there's booze involved, divided six ways after overhead, grub and lodging not provided."

Irvin said he'd be departing ASAP, before those bastards tried to stop him, and he advised us to think hard about our next move.

"Don't let that money blind you," he said, unstanching his nose to give us a fatherly stare before reapplying pressure. At this point everybody but Al looked down at the floor, and I knew that Skeeter and Trippy would go on with the last round, just as I would.

"I figure the damage is already done." Trippy sighed. "So why not reap what's mine?"

"Exactly," said Skeeter. "They already revamped our brains from the bottom up. What more can they do?"

"That's the thing," said Irvin. "No telling. But I see I'm the odd man out; call me old-fashioned. Here's my digits."

Irvin passed around an actual card—*Irvin Mood, Trumpeter, The Fifth Dementia*—e-mail and phone number inscribed.

"Alas, the band's defunct," he said. "But the contact info's good. We ought to keep in touch, compare notes. No telling what'll go down years hence. And I want to see how it all shakes out."

We sent Irvin off with a round of handshakes and gruff hugs. I felt like a coward as I watched him walk away, the only one among us with the integrity to resist the pull of Mammon. And then we sat down to a grim institutional supper of deep-fried nuggets and assorted potato products.

"What do you think's up with Vernon?" asked Trippy, breaking a round of silence.

"Probably wallowing in a ditch someplace," I said. "Still spitting out endless streams of verbiage."

"We all know the official story," said Trippy. "Signed a release form, yada yada."

"I smell a rat," said Skeeter.

"Who knows?" said Trippy. "Maybe Vernon did have the balls to skip out."

"Vernon doesn't strike me as particularly blessed in the testicle department," said Skeeter, a lame attempt at levity. "I see his junk as mouse-like and bald, with a webbing of veins and reeking of baby powder."

Everybody forced out a laugh except Al, who'd been strangely silent the whole time, and who now started sputtering as though a speech impediment was preventing the delivery of some urgent bit of information.

"Dtho, dtho, dtho," he spat, bobbing his head like a chicken and clenching his fists in frustration. And then he went silent, leaned back in his chair, and gazed down at his last french fry, a twisted, burnt mutant that looked like some undead witch's pinkie. He plucked up the morsel. Took a rodent nibble. Swallowed. Frowned. Gingerly placed the remainder on the edge of his plastic plate.

"What's the matter, Al?" said Skeeter.

"What?" Al blinked.

"How you feeling, man?" said Trippy.

"Never been better," Al replied, without enthusiasm.

"You being Ironic Man?" asked Skeeter.

"I am speaking in earnest," said Al.

"What kind of download you scoping for tomorrow?" asked Trippy, trying to get us back into play.

"I have not yet perused the options," said Al, taking a careful sip of Sprite.

"I'll prolly go with music," said Trippy, giving me a covert what-the-fuck look. "Ever since I saw that Eurhythmics video in 1983—'Sweet Dreams Are Made of This'—I always wanted to rock a cello, though back then I was too tough to admit it."

"Talking 'bout that masked neo-romantic babe in the eerie cow pasture?" I said.

"Word," said Trippy.

"I know what you mean, man."

"Funny you should say that, bo," said Skeeter. "I feel the same way about the violin, but it was 'The Devil Went Down to Georgia' that put the fire under my ass. I've still got some postcolonial lit to get through, a half day at most, they said, and then I'll have my pick of arts modules."

"Gnu, gnu, gnu," said Al. "Gnu."

"What's happening, man?" asked Trippy.

"Nothing." Al stood up, scooped up his tray. "Now, if you'll please excuse me, gentlemen, I shall be returning to my room forthwith."

Balancing an imaginary pile of books on his head, Al strode stiffly from the cafeteria.

• •

"Yay!" squealed Chloe, looking even younger as she clapped her hands. "You decided to go for it! You won't be sorry."

"What's up?" said Josh. "You ready to make your selection? It's all pretty cut-and-dried."

He handed me yet another form, the usual consent sleaze, coupled with a list of BAIT categories: *Music: History, Theory, and Practice*; *Visual Arts: History, Theory, and Practice*; *Theater: History, Theory, and Practice*; and *Dance: History, Theory, and Practice*. After selecting visual arts, I had to choose among *Graphics and*

Computing, 3-D Design, and *Illustration and Painting.* Without hesitation I went for 3-D design, scrawled my John Hancock beneath several dense blocks of fine print, and, with a devil-may-care toss of my thinning ponytail, climbed into the hot seat.

Josh initiated a high-five and pounded my tentatively raised palm. Chloe daubed my temples and cranial bald spots with especial gentleness. Brushing bagel crumbs from his chin, Dr. Morrow emerged from his sanctified office to do the honors of applying my electrodes. I still wanted to smash his chiseled jaw, but I pulled myself together.

Orbed in a halo of light, the neurologist receded as I began the familiar descent into the dark well that always preceded the onset of a BAIT session. I braced myself for whatever random memory would soon come swirling up from the obscure convolutions of my frontal cortex.

Nine years old, shirtless, I padded down the hallway of our old ranch house, the algae-green carpet spongy beneath my bare feet, my head stuffed with unsettling dreams. My mother was at the end of the hall in her sewing room, bent over a chugging Singer, her hair a glossy spill, the deep auburn of dry pine needles. She looked up at me, smiled slyly, and held up a tiny pair of trousers for Dad's new novelty line. The bookcase behind her displayed a variety of miniature squirrel athletes: a gray squirrel hurling a football, a brown squirrel shooting hoops, a rare white squirrel from the North Carolina mountains teeing off with a tiny club. Mom pressed the fairy-size britches against Dad's golfer squirrel and chuckled.

Her laughter filled the room like a cloud of furry moths. I was still coltish, silk-skinned, could still press myself against her mammalian warmth without shame. When she hugged me, I got a deep whiff of lavender talc, plus obscure pheromones that calmed me. She never rushed me back to bed. Never complained about the insomnia that'd started to torture her after she hit thirty-five.

I curled up on the floor beside the window, crickets throbbing behind the dark screen, paean to the endless summer night. The *chug, chug* of her sewing machine started up again. She laughed softly, then sang one of her nonsense songs in perfect pitch, dark treacle that soothed me back to sleep:

> *Poor old Mister Lizard,*
> *Who had cancer of the gizzard,*
> *Stumbled through a blizzard,*
> *To meet the local wizard.*

I fell asleep marveling at the craftsmanship of Mom and Dad's most elaborate diorama—a bucolic scene with rodents playing croquet and enjoying picnics on blankets. The animals' tails shimmered with vitality. Their eyes gleamed like warm molasses. And I was bowled over by the clothes Mom had sewn in her sleepless delirium: frock coats and brocade vests, Gibson girl skirts and velvet riding jackets.

And then I woke up, a thousand years of Art with a capital *A* weighing heavily upon my brain. My occipital cortex, hippocampus, and amygdala crackled with visionary electricity as I imagined a taxidermy diorama as elaborate as an Elizabethan masque. I saw animatronic animals created from a variety of artistic media. I saw a wide-screen backdrop employing elements of stop-motion animation, film, music, sound effects—you name it. I saw a diorama that the viewer could actually step into.

I'd display my work at some fancy gallery that knew what was what in terms of obsolete highbrow/lowbrow dichotomies. Fuck Hampton County—I was talking Columbia, Charleston, maybe even Hotlanta. Down in the dingy dollar cinema of my mind, I saw Helen walk into the gallery. Saw her drop the clammy hand of her lame boyfriend as she, overwhelmed by my talent, stumbled around in a daze of delight.

I'd create the most ass-kicking diorama in the history of taxidermy.

NINE

We were in the Nano Lounge, overhead fluorescents deadened, the room enveloped in a Rembrandtian glow via strategically placed floor lamps. Somehow, the air smelled of rosewater and old ivory. Skeeter, small and wizened, clad in an ancient Danzig tee, held a beautiful chestnut violin under his chin. He summoned bewitching melodies with his bow. Trippy, his head swathed in a nylon do-rag reminiscent of Renaissance piratical adventure, his ripped arms pulsing, sawed at a mahogany cello.

After administering their BAIT downloads in *Music: History, Theory, and Practice*, the Center had provided them with rental instruments, which were necessary for their post-BAIT tests. And every night since, they'd filled the Richard Feynman Nanotechnology Lounge with gentle concertos, études, and stately waltzes from days of yore.

That night I sat at the snack table, basking in their music as I sculpted mythological creatures out of a microwavable polymer clay product. The Center was not equipped with glazes, clay, and a kiln, so I made do with Sculpey and a box of acrylic paints. Lulled by the gentle rhythms of Alexander Bakshi's "Winter in Moscow,"

I shaped exquisite miniatures for a neo-baroque surrealist diorama that I envisioned as a kind of 3-D Rubens on acid, painted in pop-art colors and set into motion by basic animatronics.

Transformation was my theme: men and women caught in the agonizing ecstasies of morphing into magical beasts. A satyr with hairy goat thighs thrust his massive caprine cock toward the heavens. A nightingale bobbed heavily through the air, burdened by human boobs that swelled pornographically from her rich plumage.

I laughed at the ease of it all, how nimbly my fingers pinched out each creature and etched it with makeshift carving tools.

Al twirled shyly in, his buzz cut sleek, his beard impeccably trimmed, his eyes flashing alertly behind glasses as though he were ready to swing a real-estate deal or argue a case in court. But he wore a leotard, a nylon bodysuit the sickly prosthetic pink of "Crayola Flesh." He performed a series of strange contortions only vaguely recognizable as dance. He'd opted for *Dance: History, Theory, and Practice* (or perhaps, guided by racial and sexual stereotypes, the powers that be had made this decision for him), and his routines were baffling. He jumped in place for a solid minute, got down on all fours and skittered like a crab, and then wrenched his shoulders in a series of micromovements. His motions were strangely arrhythmic, as though his brain didn't register the tunes Skeeter and Trippy pumped out, as though he marched to the beat of some demented Lilliputian drummer who pounded skins inside the soundproof chamber of his brain. As far as we knew, Al was busting modern moves too complex for our untrained sensibilities. Or perhaps his BAITs hadn't taken, and his dancing was the equivalent of choreographic stuttering.

"How's it going, Al?" said Skeeter, pausing between tunes.

"Fine," he replied with icy formality. "Your concern is appreciated."

And then he bounded out into the hallway with a twitchy fouetté jeté.

This is how we had passed our final week. Though Dr. Morrow kept us busy with tedious tests until noon, afternoons were designated studio time. Even though we knew our efforts were being monitored, even though we could feel institutional eyes upon us, we couldn't help ourselves: our brains bristled with new skills. We itched to strut our stuff. As I sat before my grotesque yet strangely beautiful little Sculpey figures, I thought about the creations I'd fashion upon returning to my shop. For the first time in twenty years I could feel *the future*, curled in pupal expectation inside my heart, pumping charged chemicals into my bloodstream.

I'd return home, clean up my act, buckle down, and get to work. I'd rise at six, meditate, go jogging, then eat a bowl of oatmeal with fresh fruit. Sipping green tea, I'd tend to the demands of what clients I had left, expanding my customer base through word of mouth. After supper each night, my humble taxidermy shop would transform into an atelier. I'd invest what was left of my seven thousand dollars on supplies and tools, including animatronic parts, a whole new fleet of Quick Pupil digital eyeballs, plus paints, epoxies, dyes, and finishing powders that would enable me to turn ordinary game animals into mythic beasts of wonder.

In my mind's eye I could see them inhabiting Boschian worlds that bloomed in the fertile darkness of my imagination. I caught glimmers of their sleek odd bodies scampering through forests unknown. I saw their robotic eyes twinkling in the black void. I heard the ghostly buzz of their electronic hearts. Saw their teeth, lustrous with fixative. Saw their latex tongues, pink and dewy with polyurethane spit.

I saw them roaring and flapping in a giant terrarium, bounding through velveteen foliage, nibbling at plastic fruit. They sat on their haunches, leonine and golden, under an artificial moon the color of Mello Yello.

• •

Our last breakfast together was a melancholy affair—remnants of a summer thunderstorm trickling down the floor-to-ceiling windows, the light outside a seasick green. Four middle-aged men slumped over scrambled eggs and toaster pastries, bracing our asses for return to the draconian whims of reality. The cafeteria was half-empty, most of the subjects having left already. Vernon was gone. Irvin was gone. Al was gone in spirit, inhabiting his chair with impeccable posture, forking eggs into his mouth with Victorian fussiness, spitting out robotic tidbits of polite conversation. But his pupils were dilated, his eyes filmed with an unwholesome sheen, hinting at some secret distress. And now his body was seizing up again, caught in a tremor. His hands trembled. His fingers crimped. He dropped his fork.

We all stared at the fork, its leftmost prong lancing a gobbet of greasy egg, an abject morsel that made me turn my eyes toward the window. I thought of Kristeva's *Powers of Horror* and its catalog of abject fluids: blood, pus, snot, piss, and shit—flowing and clotting, oozing and crusting. Remembering her obsessive description of the coagulated skin of proteins that forms on the surface of warm milk, I wondered if it was true that all of these things brought us in touch with our semiotic mothers, those prelinguistic, milk-bearing women whom we'd attempted to banish from our minds.

I thought of my own mother, tried to remember the nubile version who'd suckled me, the one I'd greedily clung to as an infant and toddler, snuffling and licking, pinching and groping. But all I could envision was a pair of tanned legs clad in olive Bermudas, a set of pretty feet with wriggling simian toes.

A plastic kiddie pool glowed aqua behind her. Flowers swayed in warm wind. A lost world.

"You all right, dog?" Trippy finally said.

"I guess so," I said.

"Talking about Al." Trippy chuckled.

Al recovered himself, plucked up his fork, removed the egg bit with his napkin, and discarded the tiny bundle of filth. He spread a fresh napkin and resumed eating.

"So," I said, "we ought to get each other's digits, stay in touch, you know."

"Right," said Trippy, who immediately scrawled his number and e-mail on napkins for each of us. I did the same.

"I'm kind of between phones right now," said Skeeter, "and can't seem to remember my e-mail password, but I'll be in touch when I get that shit settled."

"Al?" I said.

But he was already out of his chair, striding with his tray toward that window beyond which a plump, maternal woman toiled in steam, scraping abject substances from our plates before inserting them into the orderly symbolic grid of an industrial dishwasher, a machine that obliterated every last trace of flesh and grease.

PART TWO

ONE

The parking lot was mostly empty, just as it had been when I'd arrived. Looking up at the Center for Cybernetic Neuroscience, a faux brutalist monolith of precast concrete inset with greenish glass, I wondered if the whole ordeal had been a hallucination, the people I'd met figments, with no fleshy presence out in the world. I slipped on my aviators, stood listening to the tangled howl of traffic, and climbed into my truck.

I cranked the engine, heard its familiar rumble, clutched the worn phallic gearshift, and breathed in smells of musty velour. I watched two seagulls spin above a dumpster only partially concealed by sculpted shrubs. And then I pulled out into the sprawl of Atlanta, a hodgepodge of medical parks and chain restaurants, and found my on-ramp. Though it was a straight shot down I-20, the sun was in my eyes most of the way home, and I felt like a man in a desert, squinting at a ball of fire, adjusting my car visor to no avail while cursing the broken mirror flap that forced me into existential battle with my own ugly face.

Wincing at an onslaught of classic-rock clichés, I drove four hours without stopping, back to the little vinyl-sided house Helen and I had bought ten years before, now brutally refinanced in my name, mildew-speckled and in need of a new roof. I sat in my truck, not quite ready to jump back into my old life again.

At last, as dusk came on, I hauled my old body out into the muggy air of my yard. Mosquitoes veered in to suck my blood. They bred in a drainage ditch that didn't drain, its pipe clogged with detritus and slime—one of the problems I'd put on hold when flying off to revamp my brain. But there it was now: something I'd have to deal with.

I walked up the pea-gravel drive, unlocked my door, took a deep breath, and stepped into my house. I smelled mold, leaking refrigerator chemicals, and lingering traces of Helen—the tropical tang of her waterproof sunscreen, the crisp lemon scent of her laundry soap, stubborn fragrances whose molecules had once stuck to her warm body, now empty of life—fruity chimera of the twenty-first-century olfactory-industrial complex, dead and haunting the dusty air.

· ·

The next day, after cashing my check, I decided to drop by Emerald City Retirement Village and surprise my father by coolly slipping him five hundred dollars—a drop in the bucket of what I owed him but a sign of my new and improved life.

Dad opened his back door cautiously, even though he'd gotten a good scan of me through the peephole. He'd taken to wearing suspenders on account of his stubborn potbelly and thinning frame, completing the jaunty look with midnight-blue cutoff Rustlers and Reebok EasyTones, puffy silver clodhoppers that made it look like he had robot feet.

"Well, well, well," he said. "Look who finally rose from the dead. Where have you been, son?"

"Out of town," I said.

"Stopped by your place last week and the week before."

"Sorry you didn't catch me at home."

"Shut the door quick. The AC's running."

"Marble heavy, a bag full of God, ghastly statue with one gray toe."

"What was that, son?" Dad tilted his head like a hen. "This hearing aid is crap."

And then he ushered me into the deep interior of his prefab Cape Cod—seventy degrees, forty percent humidity, the draped windows sealed with caulk and insulated foam. I stepped into the ineffable miasma of his indoor lifestyle: the outgassing carpet, obscure air-conditioning molds, microwave-cooking effluvia, and scores of artificially scented products. In the blinding light of their kitchen, my stepmother, Marlene, a retired hairdresser, was thawing chicken in the microwave, adding a gamy tang of meat. Beyond the gleaming kitchen was the darker fluorescence of the living room. And Dad stood poised between the two realms, listening to the siren song of his wide-screen.

"Romie! Long time no see." Marlene enveloped me in a perfumed embrace. "He's on nerve pills," she whispered. "So his mind's all over."

"What did you say, woman?" barked Dad, but then the TV pulled him back in. He stepped into the dimness of the living room, gravitating toward his futuristic La-Z-Boy. Because he had a guest, he did not sit down.

"It's that spot he had removed," whispered Marlene.

"What spot?"

"He didn't tell you? On his arm. Dark in the middle, uneven edges with a strange shape. The girl at the dermatologist said it might take a week for the tests to come back, and he's a nervous wreck, swears it's a melanoma that's spread to his blood—so we got him on nerve pills."

Marlene resembled Robert Smith, the Cure's lead singer, during his post-glam pudgy years when his cockatoo hair became a crunchy mess, his eyeliner perpetually smeared. She even favored tunics bordering on Goth—black lacy numbers with sequins and bows—which she wore with stretch pants and bedazzled sneakers.

"Maybe you can help take his mind off it all," she said.

"I doubt it," I said. "You know he's a committed hypochondriac."

Marlene added a layer of frozen broccoli to a tier of chicken niblets, sprinkled on some grated cheddar, and swung around dramatically, eyes full of water, to clutch my arm.

"It's good to see you, Romie. You seem different. What you been up to?"

"*I have sailed this way and come to the holy city of Byzantium.*"

"Excuse me?"

"Nothing." I shrugged.

"I wish we could all go out to supper tonight," she said. "There's this new place out by the mall called Chuckling Newt Café. It's different. Slow food fast. But you know how he is about his routine."

"I'm sure whatever you're making will be delicious."

"Sweetheart." Marlene cupped my chin with her hand and gazed soulfully into my eyes. Just when I feared she'd kiss me, she let me go. "Get your butt in here, Bob," she yelled.

· ·

At supper, the elders enjoyed mugs of Metamucil with their casserole, which was plated with whole-wheat pasta and crinkle-cut frozen carrots glazed with margarine.

"So what's new, Dad?" I said.

"Did Marlene tell you about my melanoma?"

"I doubt it's an actual melanoma," I said.

Dad pointed at me with his fork, a carrot lanced upon it. "Melanoma's no joke," he said.

In the bright kitchen light, Dad looked ancient as Tiresias. I could see green veins in the craterous flesh of his enormous nose. His eyes looked panicky, the pupils dilated, the bags beneath them heavy. His teeth were huge and yellow, darkening to umber near the receding gums. But his hair was thick, an iron-gray buzz cut Marlene kept impeccably trimmed.

"Were you aware that you can get melanomas on your eyeballs?" Dad said. He speared a few fusilli with his fork, dragged the pasta through the casserole's cheesy ooze, ate the morsel, chewed slowly, swallowed, and took a cautious sip of Metamucil.

"I dreamed it got down into my lymph nodes, son. Turned my blood black as motor oil. I cut my finger: out dripped something that looked like molasses."

"Have you seen that show," said Marlene, "where dogs do karaoke?"

"In the dream I hovered above my body," said Dad, "watched them cut me open. Just like the surgery channel."

"But the dogs aren't really singing," said Marlene. "It just looks like they are."

"I saw tumors all over my heart," said Dad. "Looked like smoked oysters."

"The dogs wear clothes and wigs," said Marlene. "It's the cutest thing I've ever seen."

The fluorescent strip lights flickered. The stainless-steel kitchen appliances cast sparks. The ceiling fan shot shadows onto the walls.

I felt dizzy. I took a swig of iced tea sweetened with some chemical that had a bite. Dad's skin glistened. The light was a strange blue white.

"Some of the dogs can sing real good," said Marlene, "but some of them are horrible."

Dad stood up. "You never know what's inside you," he said. "Where's my flaxseed?"

"Same place it always is," said Marlene. "But I'll get it. You sit down."

Dad refused to sit until Marlene had fetched his flaxseed. He shifted his weight from leg to leg and rubbed his ornery coccyx.

"The largest tumor on record weighed over three hundred pounds," he said.

As Dad described the monster tumor, removed from the ovary of a thirty-year-old woman in 2010, I saw lightning flash in the kitchen. It shot from the refrigerator to the stove.

And then I saw an image from the past: my father dressed in Carhartt coveralls, donning protective gloves, a helmet, boots. Lips pinched into a line, he descended into the gorge beyond our backyard, chain saw in hand. He'd be out there until dusk, fighting the jungle that, he insisted, threatened to encroach our house.

My father battled that jungle for decades, hacking through the malarial green with haunted Sisyphean eyes. He thought it would improve the ventilation around the house. But the vegetation always grew back, overnight, it seemed, feeding the mold and rot.

When Mom got sick, he gave up. His chain saw grew rusty. As my mother regressed into an infantile state, my father struggled to care for her—initiated, suddenly, into the domestic arts, the daily drudge, the endless buildup of toilet scum, dust, and crusty dishes. And the jungle crawled over the azalea hedge. Vines snaked across the grass, coiled up the patio rails. Dad turned the air-conditioning down to sixty-eight degrees. It was the only way to fight the moisture that fed the mold, he claimed. In her last days, longing to escape their freezing house, my mother took refuge in the Florida room with her pack of cards, playing solitaire as the summer days waxed and waned, cicadas screaming outside in the green blur of the yard. She smoked cigarette after cigarette and smiled.

"Are you my son," she'd ask me every time I visited, "or my brother?"

Her mind was gone, but the earthy part of her longed for the feel of unprocessed air, the smell of grass and trees. She'd leave the sliding glass door open, but my father didn't scold her. He'd stand alone in his dim, freezing den, looking out at the bright air where the husk of his wife played cards, slapping them down on the wicker table, laughing at the sight of carpenter bees drilling holes in the eaves.

I saw my father as an old man hunched at the door, but then a Technicolor memory flared in my skull like an old-fashioned camera flash: Dad as a younger man, decked out in gear like an action hero, his shoulders broad, his hair thick and dark as a mink's pelt. My mother was at the sink, smiling and lovely as Penelope, standing upon golden linoleum.

•   •

When I came to, my mother was fingering the wisps around my receding hairline, humming "Hotel California" out of key.

"Mom?" I said.

"Bless your heart," she said. "That's so sweet."

I noted the crunchy mass of her Robert Smith hair, backlit by a lamp—Marlene, not Mom. I recognized the dozens of taxidermic sculptures mounted on the walls—bobcats, coons, mallards—staring at me with glass eyes. I saw my father lurking behind Marlene, working his gums over with a vibrating massager that emitted a soft hum.

"Honey," Marlene said, "you passed out."

"We woulda taken you to the emergency room"—Dad removed the plastic wand from his mouth—"but I know you don't have health insurance. One hospital stay and *bam*! You'd be wiped out."

"Don't start up on that," said Marlene. "Give him a chance to wake up."

"I kept an eye on your vitals," said Dad. "The blackout lasted for about five minutes."

"When you came to," said Marlene, "we walked you to the bedroom."

"Slept for about thirty minutes after that," said Dad.

"I'll be okay," I said. But when I tried to sit up, I felt my discombobulated brain undulating like wax globs in a lava lamp. I lay back down.

"You hungry, baby?" said Marlene. "You didn't finish your supper."

"Not really."

Dad scooted a chair up next to the bed. "Go fix him something," he said. "I'll keep an eye on the boy."

Dad massaged his gums as woodland creatures snarled behind him. With the exception of the buck that hung over their faux fireplace, Marlene had crammed Dad's entire taxidermic oeuvre back here in the guest room, along with one piece by my grandfather Roman: a half-pint primate with mischievous eyes. I could still remember the taxidermic wonders on display in my grandfather's house. There, I first smelled the uterine brine of the sea, patted the belly of a shaggy black bear, and inspected the miraculous ears of bats, the diverse patterns of snakes, the creepy feet of a three-toed sloth.

Mom had loved Grandpa Roman's monkey and displayed it on our dining room buffet. She'd spread Dad's creatures throughout the house: boar head snarling over the fireplace, bobcats crouching on end tables, armadillo perched on the toilet tank. She'd had a sense of humor that'd kept Dad's darkness in check.

"You never know," Dad said now. "You might have a brain tumor. I read an article the other day about the correlation between mold and brain tumors."

And then he started up on toxic mold. He took me deep into the labyrinth of their HVAC system, where mold lurked like a restless Minotaur in ducts and tubes and evaporator coils. Frowning like Tiresias, he described damp dust coagulating on cooling fins, mold colonies thriving deep in zone dampers, airborne spores blasting from vents to contaminate carpets and furniture.

I felt suffocated by Dad's voice, which, slurred by the nerve pills, plodded on in a sleepy murmur.

"You never know what kind of filth is down in ductwork," he said, "until you pull it out and look."

I had to get out of his dark maze. I tried to sit up again. Though my head ached, my brain felt firmly moored.

"I feel better," I said. "I'd best get home."

"What?" Dad blinked, pulling himself out of his bleak reverie.

Marlene appeared in the doorway with my old *Dukes of Hazzard* TV tray, the one with the racist rebel flag backdrop, the major characters grinning with aw-shucks innocence, the General Lee hovering right under Daisy's cleavage. Mom used to prop it on my lap when I was sofa bound with a stomach virus. I could hardly bear to look at it now. I could almost hear Mom singing, chiding me with her special adaptation of the theme song: *Been in trouble with the law since the day you were born.*

"Can't you just eat a sandwich?" said Marlene.

"I'm really not hungry," I said. "And I've got stuff to do."

"Ought to see a doctor at least," said Dad, following me into the living room. "Though it'll cost you, it won't be as bad as the emergency room."

..

We stood on my father's mouthwash-green lawn, saying our good-byes, the sun sinking behind the tiny patch of forest that skirted Emerald City Retirement Village's fake pond.

"This isn't much, but it's a start," I said, pulling five one-hundred-dollar bills from my wallet and offering them to my father.

His eyes widened. His mouth wavered between sneer and smirk.

"I must be dreaming." He rubbed his eyes for effect.

After examining each bill to check for authenticity, Dad folded the money and tucked it into his breast pocket. And then, trembling with wrath, he stooped to inspect a yellow spot left by a dis-solving dog turd. I left him there, surveying the blank expanse of his territory like a general. The jungle was far from him now, but he still feared it—vines slithering from some wild fertile place, weeds sprouting, pods swelling and discharging like bomber planes, fill-ing the air with hosts of seeds, each genome drifting like an enemy parachutist.

I drove home through the partially revived downtown, noting a new antique store that would fail within a month. I passed the iconic drugstore that was somehow still hanging on, its pharmacist so ancient he'd probably sold patent opiates in his heyday. I passed through a fancy block of nineteenth-century houses and headed down into my neighborhood, a half-"gentrified" grid of bungalows poised between the historic district and a flood zone where poor black people lived.

I pulled into my drive, which snaked between my house and Noah's Ark Taxidermy, which was basically a glorified shed, not-ing, for the umpteenth time, that my sign needed painting, that the whole building gave off a derelict air. Who could blame a hunter for not entrusting his specimens to such an establishment? But I didn't have the energy to deal with that yet.

I walked inside and texted Trippy about my blackout, wondering if Skeeter would get in touch when he secured a phone. I e-mailed the Center to inquire about *the seriously disturbing side effect of lost fucking consciousness* and received an *out of the office* automated reply. I called the help desk and was directed to an elaborate voice-mail menu. I spent ten frustrating minutes in a maze of robots before finally squawking my frustrations into a voice-mail echo chamber until I was hoarse.

TWO

The first two weeks, I bucked up and cleaned out all traces of my former love: sheets and blankets, beach towels that still smelled of her waterproof sunscreen. I hauled off boxes to Goodwill and reorganized my taxidermy studio. I paid my lapsed mortgage. Stoked, I browsed my favorite websites and dropped a third of my stipend on state-of-the-art supplies: eyes, animatronic joints and jaws, a fancy airbrush kit, and a dozen new casting products. I limited myself to one or two beers per night. Filled my fridge with fruits and vegetables. Did crunches and pull-ups and went jogging in the woods each morning at dawn, when the air was damp and birds trilled softly at the newborn sun.

I studied the SC Department of Natural Resources website, hunting seasons and harvest regulations. I dusted off my old crossbow and polished the vintage rifles that once belonged to my Grandpa Roman. I read *Poison Arrows: North American Indian Hunting and Warfare.* I read *Zen in the Art of Archery.* I read *The Hound and the Hawk: The Art of Medieval Hunting.* I pored over various small-game hunting message boards, learning that mutagenic squirrels inhabited the forests near the Safety-Kleen waste-disposal plant, which got me thinking about their symbolic significance, the postmodern poignancy of mutants.

I pressure-washed my shop and refurbished the sign from my father's golden era, a teal rectangle of plastic with NOAH'S ARK TAXIDERMY in black Industria font.

I e-mailed all my clients a twenty-percent-off coupon.

Diverted all thoughts of Helen.

Thwarted all invitations to binge drink with Lee and Chip.

Allowed myself only brief, utilitarian forays into the labyrinth of Internet porn.

Delighted in the shrinkage of my potbelly.

Took pleasure in the flexing of new muscle tone.

Snacked on baby carrots.

Learned to appreciate the slow crawl of the sun over my patio as I gingerly sipped a Miller Lite.

I chose not to ponder my blackout. I tried not to worry over Trippy's lack of reply to my friendly texts. Tried not to let panic creep into my heart when night settled upon my backyard and I rose from my lawn chair, crushed my beer can, and opened the rusty-hinged screen door.

..

Three weeks into my new-and-improved life, I woke at dawn, ate a monkish bowl of oatmeal, and performed a sun salutation on my front porch, bathing my limbs in Ra's healing rays. I strode into the bathroom with my chest bravely puffed. With the assistance of a hand mirror, I chopped off my sad ponytail. I preserved the mangy relic in a Baggie for posterity and clipped my hair into a Roman coiffure. I no longer looked like an aging hesher. I looked clean and sleek and ready for business.

I slipped into fatigues and a camo tee. I loaded up my grandfather's old Remington with a .17 HM2 cartridge, hopped into my truck, and headed toward that toxic waste dump with the Orwellian nomenclature of Safety-Kleen. I aimed to bag a brace of mutant squirrels, which I planned to mount in a grotesque wedding diorama that would reflect my jaded vision of the world, a satirical dissing of the kind of romanticized dioramas that dominated the Wildlife Artist Supply Company convention. Hearkening back to a mythologized past, WASCO tended to feature Disnified animals from some fictional paradise of pristine nature uncorrupted by human filth. I planned to underscore the ironies contained in the farce of "lifelike" mounting styles. I'd highlight the dead stiffness of my specimens with jerky animatronic movements. My mounts would critique the run-of-the-mill naïveté while also bursting the confines of parody with fantastic flourishes to highlight the dire situation of all species on our depleted planet.

I imagined myself growing famous, being interviewed on NPR. When Matt Bland asked me if my work fell into the genre of rogue taxidermy, I'd explain the difference between the concoction of imaginary animals versus the hunting and conceptual mounting of postnatural specimens. I'd speak eloquently about the cyborgian predicament, the trans-human ecology, and the deconstruction of the nature-culture binary, noting the ironies of naturalistic taxidermy, the denial of our degraded ecological state. I'd quote Donna Haraway and reconfigure taxidermy into cybernetic code.

Of course Helen would happen to catch my radio interview, as would Boykin Wallace Hagman, who'd wince as my voice emanated from stereo speakers, mellow and confident, shooting the shit about my opening at the Columbia Museum of Art. Helen would insist on seeing my show. Boykin would sulk but man up. Disguising his insecurity with fake bonhomie, he'd sport a cheesy bow tie at the opening.

I could see them strolling into the museum, marveling at the combo of craftsmanship and vision that characterized my dioramas. Boykin would scurry off to chug wine in a corner, cowering like a rodent, a quicksand feeling in his gut. Helen would spot me, surrounded by tedious arts journalists. I'd wave, smile modestly as she approached. She'd run her eyes over my sleek new body. Nod approvingly at my understated haircut.

"Wow," she'd say. "Just, um, wow."

· ·

I moved through the monotonous geometry of second-growth slash pines, making my way toward a primeval patch of woods that thrived near the Safety-Kleen security fence. I remembered this spot from my boyhood. Deep in the throat of a cypress hollow, I'd once stashed a *Hustler*. I used to trek there with fear in my heart, a spring in my step, a ruttish tingle in my groin. I associated the soughing sweet gums, the chortling birds and insect thrum, with desire. Safely tucked within an Edenic thicket of myrtle oaks, I'd turn rain-crinkled pages, feeling faintly squeamish as I ogled folds of vulval pink.

But then Safety-Kleen set up their hazardous waste management operation in the late 1980s, installing a high, barb-tipped fence that cut right through my *locus amoenus*. I was surprised to see that my myrtle oaks were still there, loaded with acorns that resembled the testicles of wood goblins. Just beyond my haven, bifurcating a patch of sweet gum, was the fence, emblazoned with hornet-yellow hazardous waste signs. Judging by the broken nuts scattered on the forest floor, squirrels had recently fed there.

So I secreted myself behind a gallberry bush and waited for the high twitter of hungry rodents. Around nine thirty, they began to appear, scampering on the ground and twitching in the trees. The air crackled with the industrious chomping of sciurine teeth. The beasts barked and chattered, squealed and screeched. They chased each other through the branches, pausing to crack almost-ripe acorns and nibble the bitter meat.

Through my field glasses I scoped them, noting, with disappointment, the healthy shimmer of tails; the soundness of their eyes, noses, and ears; the ho-hum quartet of normal limbs. Though one of the animals was missing a hind leg, the scabbiness of its stump bespoke an incident with a predator. Another had a seam of dried blood where its left eye should've been. A few had bald spots or patchy tails. But I saw no signs of environmental mutagenesis. So I lazed in the thickening heat, settling into the soporific hum of the season's last cicadas. I was half-asleep when I spotted a runty squirrel with an enormous head making its nervous way through the woodland throng.

Pausing to pick at a nut, the creature turned toward me, revealing a plum-size canker on its left cheek, its mouth drawn up into a wry snarl. It had fat, furry testicles—the perfect groom for my wedding diorama.

I lifted my rifle, emptied my mind to focus on the square inch of chest beneath which its grape-size heart throbbed. My rifle melded with my body as I took aim. My 17-grain bullet found its target and knocked the beast off its hind feet.

The squirrel toppled onto its side, jerked once, and fell still.

I decided not to bag my kill just yet. I lay low to see what other oddities the day had to offer. Waiting for the feeding frenzy to reach its peak, I slumped in the oblivion of late morning. Birds tweeted drowsily. Mosquitoes swarmed around my force field of Deep Woods OFF! And gradually, my woodland friends left the scene. A few of them inspected their fallen brother. They nosed him over with quivering snouts before scampering away.

I put down my rifle, reached for my father's old game bag, felt a crick in my back as I pushed myself up with my hands. But then I eased myself back down, for there, perched like a fairy in the magical green, was a bald squirrel. Asquat on a myrtle oak branch, it eyed me as it noshed a nut. Its skin had the yellowed patina of a white vinyl sofa long aged in the smoky fug of a dive bar. Its fur-less paws resembled gargoyle claws. It had a snub-nosed face and bulging eyes.

I groped for my gun. Took clumsy aim. Fired in a nervous spasm.

I hit the poor monster just where its belly met its upper groin, a tender spot, but not instantly fatal. It fell from its perch and con-vulsed in the dead leaves, and I felt sick-hearted from my sloppy shot. But it was dead by the time I reached it. The squirrel was female, the perfect pale bride for my wedding diorama.

I put on my field gloves. I encased both bodies in a plastic Baggie before dropping them into my game bag. The air turned a strange sulfuric gold. A mourning dove moaned. The slow hiss of drizzle pushed through the forest as I headed back to my truck.

• •

I was in the studio at the back of my shop, into my second beer, windows yanked wide, crickets strumming silvery songs in the moon-bright night. *Larks' Tongues in Aspic* flowed from my old boom box, the cassette player still working its magic. The room stank of varnish and epoxies, the waxy taint of animal hide. My half-finished mutant-squirrel diorama sat on my worktable, the creatures upholstered but eyeless, their dark gaping sockets giving them a Munchian air.

I'd disassembled traditional Flex Foam squirrel forms and put them back together with Neuro-Touch wiring and Smooth Moves

animatronic joints. I'd concealed a crankshaft motor beneath a ure-
thane rock, upon which my little couple cavorted. Now I picked
through my assortment of Quick Pupil digital eyeballs, looking
for just the right set for each animal, finally settling on a pair of
oversize red ones for the lady and tiny emeralds for the gent. I
pinned their eyelids, tucked their ducts, and behold: the animals
had souls, personalities, desires, and whims. The groom was an old
curmudgeon, the bride a smart-mouthed firecracker.

I dressed the lovers for nuptials, in Victorian doll clothes I'd
won on eBay. The canker-cheeked groom sported a coat with tails,
an ascot, a top hat. The bald bride wore a diaphanous gown of
dry-rotted lace that matched her sallow skin tone. I coated their
mounting rock with Quick-Stick snow and encased the couple in
a glass dome, installing a miniature blower to keep sparkling flecks
of hydrophilic polymer whirling in the air. A black light added to
the eeriness.

At last, just before midnight, I was ready to activate the motor
that put them in motion. After an anxious sip of beer, I pressed
the button on the back of their platform. The lovers jerked toward each other, rubbed their snouts together, and then groom
embraced bride. Tilting his beloved back to feast upon her lips,
he let his eager mouth travel down her throat into her delightful
décolletage. The wedding march, piped from a microspeaker and
rendered spookily in electronic cello, played on an endless loop.

The bride's hyperthyroid eyes glittered like rubies, matching her
lips, which I'd dabbed with a touch of crimson. The groom's cheek
canker gave him the air of an old statesman, à la John McCain.

It looked pretty killer for my first attempt at an absurdist animatronic taxidermic diorama.

When I stood back to inspect my handiwork, I could feel my
mother's presence in the room, congratulating me on my artistic

vision. I could almost hear her taking nervous sucks off her cigarette as she sized up my work, offering constructive criticism, just as she used to for my high school masterpieces.

"Sure is ambitious," she'd said about one of my sculptures, "which is wonderful. But I think you need to work on those hands some more. Take a look at some actual hands. Hands are pretty strange, you know."

I could see her kind, sly smile, her tousled hair, her beautiful eyes pouched from a sleepless night. She bore her insomnia stoically, hiding an undertow of anxiety and depression with bright chitchat.

I grew teary-eyed, popped another Miller, and felt a chemical headache coming on, so I walked out back onto the patio to get some fresh air. I gazed down at the gulch where the primordial jungle grew. I could see the stained roof of our old ranch house, the house I'd dwelled in from birth to age twenty-two. It was now inhabited by a crew of Trident Tech students, the rotting deck littered with beer bottles.

When Dad had decided to sell the house, he'd asked me if I wanted it. Said he'd let me have it dirt cheap. But the thought of dwelling in my boyhood home, spooked by ghosts from the past, particularly the phantasm of my mother, who'd eked out her last demented days there, had made me balk. When Midge Silverfield died of chronic obstructive lung disease, and the bungalow on the other side of Noah's Ark Taxidermy came up for sale, Helen and I snatched it up. We refinished the oak floors and painted the rooms "interesting" colors. We retiled the bathroom and half updated the '70s kitchen. For about six years our domestic enterprise was imbued with the mellow rose light of casual optimism. We were building a nest, hunkering down for the arrival of a tender being, a repository for our combined DNA, our love rendered into flesh. We actually talked about the hypothetical child back then.

"If we have a girl, I won't paint this room pink," Helen said about our then-computer room. "Green would be a good neutral color for a girl or a boy. I won't let Walt Disney raise my child."

"But a kid's got to have a little bit of toxic culture," I said. "For immunity, right? Isn't that how vaccines work?"

Helen trotted out her science know-how, explaining how vaccines were manufactured from a weaker or dead form of the microbe in question, her voice upbeat, not yet bilious with defeat.

We never decided on a color for the computer room, which was still a dingy yellow, still littered with outmoded equipment, including a fat Dell from the turn of the century that contained thousands of digital photographs I'd never transferred to my laptop.

"We need to print some of these up," Helen insisted one night, "in case of a nuclear holocaust."

"Like you'd be comforted by old pics in a nuclear aftermath?" I said.

"I don't know. In a warped way, maybe."

She'd even burned the pics onto a disc (perhaps she still had it?), but as far as I knew, she'd never printed up one picture. Now the old computer seemed like a plastic sarcophagus, chock-full of dead memories.

I gazed down at Helen's flower garden, currently lit by a fat white moon.

Things rank and gross in nature possessed it merely.

I felt a headache creeping up from the base of my skull, a throbbing affliction that spread from my ears to my widow's peak. It seemed to intensify around those spots where my BC transmitters had once been installed. Tracing red webs of pain in my mind's eye, I still saw my brain as a hologram. Saw blobs of crimson diffusing as the pain grew fierce. I rubbed my temples and groaned. I hightailed it into my house, made a beeline toward the medicine cabinet, tossed three Advils into my mouth, and stretched my wretched body out on the couch.

THREE

By the time my boys Lee and Chip came over to catch up, September was pretty much spent. I'd finished three of my mutant dioramas: the squirrel wedding, an Odysseus versus Cyclops battle enacted by a one-eyed possum and an albino bullfrog, and, to celebrate my brand-new life, a Phoenix diorama featuring a three-legged blue jay rising from a pile of ashes. I displayed the pieces on a marble-topped pedestal table I'd scored on Craigslist for a hundred bucks. I'd also installed a mini fridge in the lobby of Noah's Ark Taxidermy, plus a fancy speaker for my MP3 player, which resembled a 1920s radio. I'd painted the walls a dusky color Home Depot called Mad Monk and repaired Lord Tusky the Second's bashed snout, restoring the boar to his former glory above the old vinyl sofa. I'd also garnered a modest customer base of late, had made it through the day headache-free, and was feeling pretty damn good when I heard the buzzer announcing the arrival of my old friends.

Almost two months had passed since my return from the Center. I'd seen Lee but once (tanking up on Sun Drop at the BP station) and Chip not at all. We greeted one another with hearty slaps upon the back, those bearish bursts of manly affection that can sometimes knock a little wind out of your chest.

"You look great, Romie," said Lee. "And the shop does too."

"Yeah." Chip ran his eyes up and down my physique. "What you been doing to stay in shape?"

"Mostly jogging. Been dabbling in Ashtanga yoga this past week, mastering some pretty wicked Indian wrestling moves."

"Yoga." Chip drew his leg up into the tree pose and chuckled. "My ex-wife used to mess with that Chinese shit."

"Which one?" quipped Lee.

"The Cooter Queen," said Chip.

"Actually," I said, "yoga's an ancient Indian discipline, though a Taoist tradition does exist."

There was a blip of awkward silence as both men blinked at me.

"Good to have you back, Romie," said Lee. "We brought you a case of O'Doul's."

"We didn't know what was up in the drinking department," said Chip. "So we thought, well, you know."

"And we don't want to be, what's it called?"

"Enablers," said Chip.

"Don't worry," I said. "I still indulge in spirituous beverages. Got me some Miller Lite in the mini fridge, in fact."

Relief washed over their faces as we fell into old ritual, popping our brews, settling down for a round of shit talk.

"What the hell are those?" Chip pointed at my dioramas.

So I gave the boys a guided tour, activating each unit with a remote control, discoursing on the ironies of postnatural specimens. I fell smoothly into a stream of pomo clichés as my magical animals danced. My squirrels kissed. My froggish Odysseus crept up to the sleeping Cyclops and poked out his eye with a stick. And most inspiring of all, my three-legged Phoenix rose from a pile of ashes to spread its cerulean wings just as "Voices in the Sky" by the Moody Blues kicked in.

"You talk different, Romie," said Lee.

"Yeah," said Chip. "What's up with the SAT words?"

"Nothing much," I said. "Had lots of time to read while I was in the clink. Speaking of which, let me show y'all my Panopticon."

"What the hell's a Panopticon?" said Lee.

"You shall see."

I took them back to the studio to see my work in progress. I flicked on the overheads, hand-pounded a mock drumroll on the table, and whisked aside a poly tarp to reveal my pet project: a four-foot reproduction of Jeremy Bentham's eighteenth-century prison. I explained how its central "inspection house" enabled guards to potentially check in on any given prisoner at any minute of the day or night, thereby instilling a compulsive fear of perpetual observation.

"An obsessive motif," I said, "of the French philosopher Michel Foucault."

"Jibber-jabber," said Chip, who'd rather skinny-dip in the fecal lagoon of an industrial hog farm than admit he doesn't know something. I longed fiercely for the company of the BAIT crew, the ideal audience for my work, men who understood the psychological fallout of hierarchical surveillance on more than one level.

"It's all good," said Lee.

I'd stationed a squirrel guard in the central tower, and I was still working on the inmates. Each cell was a mini diorama containing one or two prisoners doing their thing: reading the Bible, pumping iron, checking a hidden stash of Jack, or slitting his wrist with a shank. So far, all of the prisoners were mutant frogs, mostly albinos, one-eyeds, and amphibians with stunted flippers, though I'd lucked out on two rarities: one poor fucker with three eyes, another with an extra leg.

"Damn," said Lee. "That's pretty genius. I'll never forget that piece you did in high school. The one with the mermaid."

"Preesh," I said. "I'm trying to get back to my roots as a sculptor."

"That mermaid looked just like Helen," said Chip, smiling malevolently, well aware that mentioning my ex was bound to tamp down my exuberant mood.

"Yup," I said.

"Where'd you get your specimens?" said Chip.

"Shot 'em myself."

"Didn't think you hunted that much." Chip drowned his frown with a gulp of beer.

"When the situation calls for it."

"What kind of ammo you been utilizing?"

"My grandfather's Remington .22, mostly. Good luck charm. Been practicing with a target out back."

"For real? Want to try a few rounds?"

"Why not?"

Chip pulled forth a Baggie of weed and smirked. "Y'all wanna burn one before playing with dangerous firearms?"

"Sounds like a plan," said Lee, but his grin petered out when he looked at me.

"Why not?" I shrugged.

"You sure?" said Lee. "We don't want to be—what's it called again?"

"Enablers," Chip and I said in unison. And then I took Chip's little one-hitter, a metal cylinder cleverly disguised as a Camel cigarette.

"This is not a pipe," I said.

The boys blinked at me.

"That s'pose to be a joke or something?" said Chip.

"Inside one, I guess," I said, longing for the rich, troubled laughter of the BAIT crew.

"Well, ha-ha," Chip said. "Even though it ain't funny."

• •

Stoned, we stepped out into the evening. The world was still green, a few blighted leaves spotting the trees. Birds twitted fussily, winding down, hustling toward their nests. I'd set up a few targets at the edge of my yard, just where the lawn tumbled into the jungly ravine that overlooked the roof of my old familial home. On a pine trunk I'd nailed a cardboard cutout of our buffoonish president, his Baptist bulldog face already pocked with bullet holes. Lee couldn't stop laughing. But Chip, shrimp pink with hypertension and chagrin, clutched at his collar.

"I will not shoot the president of the United States," he said.

"It's a cardboard facsimile," I said. "One of many in the house of images pumped out by the media-industrial complex."

"It's illegal to threaten the commander in chief's life." Chip pressed his lips into a line.

"That's not what we're doing here," I said.

"Whatever," said Chip. "You could've put up Sahib Omar Rashid or Pee Wee Gaskins. Why you got to shoot the president?"

"*You* don't have to shoot him," said Lee. "Just stick with the bull's-eye, Chip."

"We gonna shoot this firearm or just talk about it?" said Chip.

So commenced our target practice, which quickly morphed into a competitive sport, with a score scratched in the dirt and shots of Jäger between each blast. While Chip and I were stuck neck and neck, Lee lagged good-naturedly behind. The sun sank behind my ancestral ranch house. My neighbor's blinding security lamp popped on, and his hound dog barked. When our game finally ended in a stalemate, we relocated to the patio and opened fresh beers. Discussed hunting seasons, coyote migrations, the mysterious habits of interdimensional deer.

"Never knew you were such a gung-ho hunter, Romie." Chip sneered.

"Didn't used to be," I said.

"You're such a good shot, Romie," said Lee. "You ought to try to bag Hogzilla."

"Hogzilla?"

"You ain't heard of Hogzilla?" said Lee.

Chip emitted a groan of disdain. "I don't think that hog exists," he said. But his eyes looked shifty. He scratched his nose.

"The feral hog that's been raising hell in Hampton County," said Lee. "Started up a few months ago."

Right then I knew I had to bag that fucker. A sacred feeling washed over me, akin to the time Ahab got wind of that legendary albino Moby-Dick, before the sperm whale destroyed his boat, chomped off his leg, sent him spiraling inwardly toward monomaniacal doom. Ahab, strutting jauntily on two legs across the fresh-scrubbed deck of his ship. Ahab, sniffing the briny wind that sang of poontang. Ahab, thinking of other things besides the accursed fish—the red night sky, for instance, or his supper of salted beef and stale biscuits, his future dalliances with the brassy lass who talked smack at the Mermaid Tavern.

"Hogzilla," I said. "Do tell."

Hogzilla had been ravaging farmland, destroying rose gardens, goring poodles with his mammoth tusks. And all the while, I'd been farting about in a state of ignorance. When the beast made its first appearances, I was at the Center, intentionally cut off from the outside world.

"They say that SOB weighs over a thousand pounds," said Lee. "That he's a mutant, that his breath will knock a man out. Plus, he can jump twenty feet in the air."

"Bullshit," spat Chip. "Just another urban legend."

"Jarvis Riddle spotted him running through Miles Hammond's soybean field," said Lee. "Looked like the boar was flying."

"Jarvis Riddle has a problem with substance abuse," said Chip, who usually reveled in a good convo about outsize wildlife. But now he had diddly to say on the subject. Now he peeled the label from his beer bottle.

"Don't we all," said Lee.

"Not like Jarvis," said Chip. "I think it's ordinary feral boars doing the damage."

"Jarvis said the hoofprints he saw spanned a good nine inches. What you think, Romie?"

I was staring off at the jungle that seethed in the gulch beyond my house, remembering the expression my father got when he suited up to do battle against scrub brush and vines. Fierceness had tensed in his jaw muscles. His eyes had swum with strange fevers.

I'll be back before supper, he'd always said.

I envisioned Hogzilla, the fire-breathing boar, tearing ass through some blighted strip of industrial farmland. His eyes glowed as he performed a twenty-foot leap over a triple-wheeled tractor with tillage equipment attached.

"Earth to Romie," said Lee. "You still there?"

"Yep." I turned away from the jungle. "Just a little stoned is all. Good stuff, Chip."

We changed the subject, talked about our high school hesher days, those sweet years back at the butt end of another century, before the Human Genome Project geared up and nanotechnology took off, back before the Internet had colonized our minds, back when we all flaunted leonine mullets and the future shimmered bewitchingly in the distance like a fata morgana mirage.

• •

I stayed up all night Googling feral hogs. Whereas domesticated swine were sweet Wilburs bred for docility, all it took was a few weeks in the wild to transform these corn-fed fatsos into snorting, murderous monsters. Their regression to wild beast was almost instantaneous. Bristly black hair burst from their tender skins. Razor-sharp tusks shot from their foaming jaws. Add to this a high IQ and an all-consuming food obsession, and you've got a wily fiend ready to rip up whatever landscape it happens to rage through, ready to tear its cutters into whatever warm body it stumbles upon, nostrils on high alert for the scent of estrous sow.

All across the South, these porcine demons were raising hell. "Thousand-Pound Monster Tusker Bagged near Cartoosa, Georgia," read one headline. "Pig Foot Downed in Asheboro, North Carolina," said another. In Texas the feral hog population was off the charts, well into the range of epidemic. An article titled "Texas Succumbs to Pig Plague" waxed poetic while slyly alluding to a Guns N' Roses LP:

> *Feral hogs spawn like rabbits, producing up to two litters per year. Droves of fierce tuskers not only tear up farmland but also trot boldly through suburbs in groups more than twenty strong. They snuffle through trash, root up sprinkler systems, devour all small animals in their path. Their appetite for destruction is bottomless.*

The Texas Parks and Wildlife Department had declared open season, going so far as to legalize helicopter hunting, allowing

gung-ho Rambos to take out swine from the air. There were doc-
umented cases of people being bitten, a handful of dismember-
ments, a few deaths. "Nine-Year-Old Boy in Roxie, Mississippi,
Torn Apart by Razorback," proclaimed one paper. According to
the article, *the boy's bones were picked clean by a frenzied group of sows.*
The Mullet Rapper described the brutal end of a hunter in the Ev-
erglades *who was pounded to pulp by a herd [sic] of apocalyptic porkers.*

The feral hog population in South Carolina, somewhere around
two hundred thousand, was just beginning to become a nuisance.
According to the Clemson Extension, which had started conducting hog-management workshops, *the worldwide swine menace must
be nipped in the bud.* In addition to declaring open season with no
bag limit, the Department of Natural Resources now sponsored
special hog hunts twice a year. I discovered that my old rival Baines
Botworth had cornered the market on trophy boar heads, featuring
a tusked monster with a mouthful of fake foam on his taxidermy
website. And all this time I'd been oblivious, puttering in a dream
of self-obsession and heartbreak. I hadn't updated my website in
four years.

But no more. Adrenaline gushed through my veins. I sat at my
desk, clutching my grandfather's old Savage rifle, surfing the hinterlands of the Internet, my bloodshot eyes glimmering like Ahab's
when he scanned the sea for a telltale spume. At last, I stumbled
upon the message board of HogWild.com, a regional pig-hunting
website where full-fledged Hogzilla obsession had broken out.
Hiding behind monikers like PigMan and BoaredtoDeath, hunters
voiced their mania. They spread half-truths and trafficked in myth
mongering. They dropped helpful tips and red herrings. Many of
them posted in the wee hours, a dead giveaway of obsessive tendencies. I could see them, dressed in muddy camo, hunched over their
computer screens. I could hear the click of their calloused fingers

on plastic keys. Could smell their whiskey breath, their unwashed hair, the hog-attracting scents they wore like rare perfumes: Swine Wine, Apple Delight, Feral Fire Sow-in-Heat spray.

Though they caught glimpses of the legendary pig all over the county, Hogzilla always managed to elude them just when they crept near—disappearing into brush, melting into mist, leaping into oblivion with a waft of ruttish scent. The creature taunted them with his massive glistening turds, encrusted with seeds and bones. It left tracks deep enough for birds to bathe in. Hogzilla's wallows—those muddy spots where the swine was fond of floundering—always seemed to brim with fresh spicy piss and steaming stools, though the hog himself was almost never in sight.

Hunters obsessively charted Hogzilla's rooting trails and wallows. They studied tree bases ringed with the mud he wiped off his colossal flanks. They posted photos of tracks, spore, trails, wallows, and rubs, and, on rare occasions, the hog himself, always captured in a blur, an out-of-focus streak of greased lightning.

—*Spotted that sumbitch on the edge of the landfill*, HighOnThe Hog posted, *just standing there under the full moon like something from Jurassic Park.*

—*Tracked Hogzilla through Twelve Oaks Mobile Home Park*, said Pigwig. *Saw him swallow a cocker spaniel whole, like it wasn't nothing, a popcorn shrimp or a donut hole.*

—*Got close enough to Hogzilla to blast him twice with my 44 mag Super Redhawk*, said HogHeaven. *My semi-wadcutter points bounced right off his hide. Might as well be shooting an iron tank.*

There was much debate over the methodology of feral-hog killing. Though the DNR had legalized picking them off from pickup trucks, many pig hunters preferred the freewheeling badassery of ATVs. Enthusiasts mounted bow racks and gun mounts onto their quads, hitches to haul kill, exhaust silencers that reduced engine noise up to eighty percent. But there were purists out there who felt that any vehicle was an abomination, men who eschewed technology, primitivists who worked with arrows and spears.

—*Shooting from trucks ain't hog hunting*, said Porkfiend22. *That's what real woodsmen call vermin control.*

—*Took out a 400 lb feral with a boar spear*, boasted HellHog. *Don't mess with a spear unless you got a long handle with a crosspiece to keep that fucker from charging up the blade. My brother found out the hard way: 18 stitches on his forearm and rabies shots into the bargain. Wild hogs take a heap of killing.*

—*Check out my new quad y'all*, bragged HogLoverForever, who'd posted a pic of his Yamaha Big Bear ATV, his toddler son at the wheel, his Hitch Haul nonchalantly loaded up with a half-ton boar carcass.

According to BossHawg, who lived in a lean-to and enjoyed displaying his tusk wounds in high-resolution pics, nothing matched the thrill of chasing down a pig with dogs, leaping upon its hot, reeking body and dispatching it with a knife. To wit, *the adrenaline rush of sinking a custom-built high-chromium blade into the throbbing jugular of a razorback takes you back to the caveman days.*

But there were men who went hog wild over technology too, night hunters who installed remote-operated corn feeders and rifle-mounted target illuminators. These stealthy technicians used magnetic tracking lights to mark blood trails. They kept up with the latest boar hunting software. Calibrated their own digital topo maps.

Scrolling down the message board, I felt overwhelmed. I longed for a BAIT download that would magically impart a lump sum of knowledge into my head: the evolution of *Sus scrofa*, pigs in myth and legend, the history of swine hunting, and the cantankerous dialectic of countless contemporary hog-hunting camps.

Yes, I was intimidated. Right here in Hampton County lived a man who concocted his own hog-attractant scents. He downed sows with tranquilizer darts and siphoned their urine with catheters. Another fellow did his butchery on-site, hauling a portable table, saws, knives, and blood buckets around in a gore-spattered ATV. Others posted recipes, tusk-mounting techniques, instructions on how to tan boar hides for moccasins and Mojave loincloths.

There was a woman called PigSlayer, whom I imagined as a six-foot goddess in Amazonian armor, a babe with a crossbow and flowing hair. She'd slain hogs with pistols, arrows, spears, and knives. Knew her way around a forest. Boldly anointed her wrists with boar urine. She had a flair for adjectives. Liked to describe dusk treks through primeval forest. And she was the first hunter to opine that Hogzilla might be a mutant. That his leaping capacity exceeded the realms of normal. That what we were possibly dealing with was a postnatural species with something freaky going down in its genes. *A kind of ÜberPig*, she actually said, which made my heart wobble.

I swallowed the last of my beer. Dragged my radiation-bathed carcass away from the evil magnetism of the computer screen. It was time to slumber, *perchance to dream*. I brushed my teeth. Stripped down to my BVDs. Crawled into the fake rustic bed that Helen had scored on clearance from the Pottery Barn.

I fell into fitful dreaming.

I was on my grandfather's front porch in McClellanville, staring at the marsh. Out beyond the cordgrass, the ocean shone like pounded brass. A creature came flapping over the horizon, did a few twirls around the sun, and glided down into the atmosphere. *Lucifer*, I thought as the beast flew toward me. It bobbed into view—by all appearances a hog with wings—and belly flopped into my grandmother's okra patch. It was Hogzilla, equipped with buzzard wings. Standing upright, he strolled up to the edge of the porch.

Hogzilla stared into my soul with the hungry, phosphorescent eyes of a fallen angel. "Hogs are demonic beasts," he grunted, his voice deep and thick with wheezes. Hogzilla told me everything I needed to know—wondrous hog lore, sacred ancient hunting rituals, a thousand clever tracking tricks. But when I woke to the bellow of my neighbor's coon dog, the knowledge drained from me. I couldn't remember jack.

FOUR

I tapped at my laptop, Kenny Bickle talking at me, a field-dressed deer carcass heaped at his feet. The shop's old landline, still bearing the ancient number from my father's days, was ringing off the hook—that twenty percent coupon I'd circulated in August was still working its magic one week into October.

But I was keeping up with the work, putting in eight-hour days, sticking to my two-beer policy while toiling away on my Panopticon diorama until midnight each night, cleansing body and mind for the heroic feat of legendary feral-hog slaying—unless I was laid out with a migraine, which was happening about once a week. I could feel one coming on now, raw red pain radiating from the site of my BC transmitters, creeping over my scalp. And the sound of Kenny Bickle's reedy voice plodding on wasn't helping.

"Think I'll go with the Bio-Optix II rotators," said Kenny, a small freckled man with graying red hair and a trace of down for eyebrows. "They'll spook the hell outta my wife."

"Good choice for an animatronic eye," I said, massaging my skull. "Subtle movement. Light-sensitive pupil dilation and intermittent blink mechanism."

"Good." Kenny patted his cell-phone pocket. "That's Tina now. *Robocop* ringtone. Wants to remind me to pick up one of them jumbo dog food bags at Walmart, like I need five reminders in the last hour."

"If I'm gonna do a wet tanning on that buck, I'd best get busy. What kind of tongue you thinking about—licking, relaxed, or chewing?"

Kenny squinted at my laptop screen. "You got something more vicious than that? Like maybe we could put in a boar tongue or something?"

"I can do that. I take it you want the Easy Crank snarling mechanism?"

"Hell yeah."

"I think we're set." I closed my eyes. When I opened them, Kenny's face looked blurred. As he came into focus, sparks shot off his chapped red cheeks.

"Look at this here text message," said Kenny, "*Don't forget to pick up that dog food, low-carb Science Diet with green tea.* Have you ever heard of that? Green tea for dogs?"

I felt a swirl of nausea in my stomach. "Okay, I need your WIN card." I groaned. "Tag number, wildlife certificate number, and credit card."

"Here you go." Kenny slid his hunting license and Visa across the counter. "Tina says she's got depression, even though she takes happy pills."

I stabbed pointedly at the contract with my index finger.

"I tell her we all get depressed. It's part of life."

Kenny finally picked a pen from my cup and scrawled his name.

"Want to help me haul this carcass back to the workshop?" I said.

Kenny hoisted the head while I took care of the butt end, and he talked between grunts as we relocated his kill, rattling on about the time Tina's doctor took her off Xanax and put her on Nepenthe, whereupon she suffered nightmares in which her daddy turned into Freddy Krueger and chased her through abandoned strip malls.

"Thanks," I said, closing my eyes to fight off the spins and leaning against the wall. "Now if you don't mind, I think I'll get down to business."

"All right," said Kenny. "Can't wait to see that buck head. It's gonna freak Tina out."

When he left, the air pulsing with delicious silence in his wake, I flipped my shop sign to CLOSED and took three more Excedrin. Out of habit I clicked on E-Live and saw a flashing notification from Helen. I was surprised to see one of those mass evites for some kind of party, figuring she'd forgotten all about the ex-husband lurking on her friends list, his heart a ball of boiling bile.

Apparently, she and Boykin were throwing a masquerade ball at the Dogwood Gallery, Hampton's hippest avant-garde showroom, on Halloween.

Ha! I am Ironic Man.

The place was basically a twee lunch spot that hung paintings, run by a class-action lawyer's wife who dabbled in the arts. Her name was Annabelle Tewksbury DeBris, a cheerleader from my high school days, though I barely recognized her now. Judging by the E-Live photo streams she was tagged in, her face was an evolving taxidermic masterpiece. Her overprocessed skin stretched over the finest Aryan cheekbones money could buy. Brow Botoxed into eerie blankness, lips puffed up into pornified pillows and glazed with purple lube, she smiled the chimp fear grin of a B-list celeb. She was a postnatural specimen, a fembot Stepford in three-hundred-dollar shoes. And now she'd opened a *musée des beaux arts* with the cutting-edge name of Dogwood Gallery, a salon where Hampton's finest dabblers could indulge in lofty chatter.

This was the hot spot Boykin had invested in. This was the crowd Helen now ran with, my girl who used to rag rabidly on all her faux foes—those high school plastics, debs, and cheerleaders who dwelled in the flossy Candy Land of fakery. Helen used to call Annabelle Tewksbury DeBris the Cuntessa of Cunterberry. Pretending to be a fashion critic, she'd describe Annabelle's idiotic getups, imitate her affected Charleston accent, ridicule the doggerel she wrote for the AP English Poetry Read-a-thon. Helen's riffs used to be so entertaining that I'd pop a beer and groove on her vitriol. But now my feisty girl was sleeping with the enemy. Now my Hell on Wheels was hanging up her flaming skates, and, in an oddly comforting way, this made her seem less appealing.

The invitation was mock genteel, hackishly employing Victorian diction scripted in Corsiva font: *We request your presence on All Hallows' Eve.* Their soiree was a costume ball, which meant that I could attend masked, which meant that I could skulk anonymously like the stranger in "The Masque of the Red Death," infecting the rich revelers with a feeling of nameless dread.

But what to wear? What costume would best convey my jaunty misanthropy?

I dwelled on this as I rough-fleshed Kenny Bickle's buck. As I cut around the eyes and split the nose, I thought about going as the oedipal taxidermist Norman Bates. As I got the deer's ears turned out, I changed my mind, thinking Nosferatu would be creepier. As I scraped just enough fat from the cape so that an overnight salt would wipe out the rest of it, I toyed with the idea of something conceptual: the Imp of the Perverse, British Imperialism, maybe the Black Death.

But then, as I dabbed at gore clots with Rittel's Blood Eater, it came to me in a vision: I saw myself moving through the crowd in a velvet frock coat, a Victorian dandy with the body of a man and the elegant tusked head of a boar—an homage to Hogzilla. It wouldn't be that hard to make a lightweight taxidermied boar head with a hollow interior, eyeholes, and breathable nostrils, a gaping mouth for easy beverage consumption. The main hurdle would be bagging the boar, but I was already gearing up for my first hog hunt. Already planning some preliminary excursions to prepare my wimpy ass for epic battle with Hogzilla.

I'd loaded up my rifles. Ordered my Cold Steel spear as a back-up. Purchased a bottle of fine sow urine.

A hint of smoky nip was in the air. Wild boars would soon be in autumn rut, ready to fly ass-over-teakettle toward the intoxicating aroma of estrous sow. Ready to leap right into the arc of my bullet. Ready to go out in a blaze of glorious, squealing lust.

FIVE

On a dry afternoon in mid-October, I'd been squatting in R.V. Garland's boar blind for fifteen minutes when I spotted the first hog of the day, trotting from a wallow toward Garland's crop of bait corn. It was a sow, alas, followed by three other females with piglets in tow—good eating, as they say. But I wasn't after meat. I had two weeks to bag a boar and fashion its head into a killer mask. I'd already ordered a velvet frock coat from OtherVictorians.com, which'd set me back a pretty penny. I'd bought a ruffled blouse and a paisley ascot. And I'd spent five consecutive afternoons waiting in R.V.'s boar blind after knocking off work early. I'd seen my share of hogs, mostly on the small side (so-called defensives) but hadn't made a kill yet. And I was getting desperate, thinking about buying an infrared feed light and switching to night hunting.

Mr. R.V. had planted corn to attract boars, but now he was laid up at Hampton Regional with a nasty case of bacterial prostatitis. The boar blind had been his last hurrah, a simple square structure nestled in pines and splotched with camo paint. Its plywood walls were already warped from rain. It smelled of mildewed lumber, a tree-house scent, redolent of boyhood adventure.

But I was bored up there, kept checking my phone, scrolling down the guest list for Helen's masquerade ball, recognizing the occasional douche bag or bitch from high school. I was about to flip through my ex's photos for the umpteenth time when I heard a rustling in the bracken. Behold: a decent-size tusker was dashing about in the clearing below, sniffing with all his soul at the spots I'd spritzed with Feral Fire Sow-in-Heat spray.

I put down my gadget and picked up my grandfather's Savage .45. Banished all venomous thoughts from my head. Casting the shroud of self-consciousness, I enveloped my being in Zen-like calm. I had about five seconds to go through the seven coordinations of *shichidō*, melding body and gun into one articulate force of nature. By the time I took aim at the oinker, my target was already nosing down a side trail. But I fired, catching him on the flank, and leapt from the stand to give chase.

My calves tingled from the jump. I needed a motherfucking dog. I doubted that the pig was gravely wounded. But I dashed into the woods anyway, scrambling after what I thought was the crackle of a hog in flight through crisp foliage. And sure enough, I saw him, limping down a creek bed, his right ham dribbling gore. I splashed through the creek and chased the boar through second-growth pine forest, right on into a spooky dome swamp.

A white ibis, poised on a cypress stump, burst into harried flight. Another creature, tucked away in the gloom, moaned. The wind was in my face, casting my scent behind me. The boar, a two-hundred-pounder with greasy black hackles and half-foot tusks, paused to lick his wound. I lifted my rifle, felt the fusion of my arms with weaponry, envisioned the bullet as an emanation of my own being, a flame bursting from my heart chakra, sizzling down the barrel and flying through the singing air. *Bam!* I made a hit near the back of its right shoulder. Felt that surge of guilt-tainted triumph as the animal flinched, shrieked, and lurched forward into brush.

I was about to pop from my cover when a deafening screech rent the air. I heard the *boom, boom, boom* of a great beast bounding. I saw branches and leaves flying into the air beyond the copse where my wounded target had taken cover. Some enormous creature let rip a dragon roar.

Downwind of the animal, I could smell the shit-cheese reek of its musk, ruttish and enraged and doing something funky to my neurochemicals, shrinking my testicles into fetal gerbils. My hair indeed stood on end. My teeth actually chattered. I swear I experienced icy sweat and other clichés. Found myself appealing to a higher power for protection, some nebulous entity beyond my present dimension, part god, part alien, part spiritual essence. I didn't know what it was—whether it lived above the sky or percolated through my own veins—but I begged it to spare my life. My prayer went into overdrive when I heard the puny boar I'd been chasing wail. The pig squealed in agony for a solid five minutes, sending flurries of birds into the apathetic sky.

At last, the racket stopped. I sat there for another thirty minutes, pricking my ears for signs of life. Just as the sun started to sink behind the tree line, I crept, still shivering in a fever of fear, over to the spot where the commotion had gone down. First off, I noticed a chaotic series of enormous hoofprints with three-inch indentations. Secondly, the reek that'd made my hair stand on end was definitely of the male porcine variety. By all appearances, a monstrous hog had devoured the hapless boar I'd lured, shot, and chased through the forest. There wasn't much left beyond a couple of hooves, some intestinal confetti, and scattered splinters of bone. But then I spotted the head, magically unmolested, resting upon sprigs of cypress like some garnished centerpiece at a medieval feast.

When the clouds parted and anointed the boar head with rosy light, I wondered what the universe was trying to tell me.

I wrapped the head up in plastic BI-LO bags, stuffed it into my backpack, and toted it home.

· ·

It was Saturday night, the radio playing dreamy oldies, 1950s lust sublimated into crooning, the music of my parents' repressed and ethereal adolescence. I'd broken code and was sipping beer number three, working on my Lord Tusky mask. I'd made a lightweight form by molding the boar skull with Smooth-Cast 300, a plastic resin. I'd worked the boar cape from the bone without tearing the delicate skin around the eyes and lips. I'd fleshed it, given it two pickle baths, and tanned it with a Rittel's kit. Now, after taking a swig of Miller Lite, I slipped the cape onto my homemade form with little angst. I trimmed the eye skin, pinned the lips, and tucked in the tear ducts. After reinstalling the original tusks with Apoxie Sculpt, I popped in a snarling jaw set. For final touches, I sprayed some QuickSpittle Rabid-Boar Froth around the mouth and enhanced the beast's facial fur with violet highlights.

Just when I stood back to reap the reward of my creation, Miller in hand, beer buzz taking the edges off reality and clouding my brain with smugness, I felt another headache flaring in the vicinity of my BC transmitters, which formed a Devil's Triangle in the seascape of my mind, sucking up thoughts and time. I rushed home, cursing myself for forgetting my headache meds, heaping verbal damnation upon the Center for ignoring my increasingly desperate e-mails.

When I opened my medicine cabinet, I discovered one measly capsule in my Excedrin bottle. Like a cartoon doofus, I slapped my own skull. I clawed through outdated prescriptions, crusted bottles of Pepto-Bismol, and jumbo jars of TUMS, knocking plastic canisters onto the floor. All I came up with was a foil pack of Advil Extra Strength Liqui-Gels, three left, which I gobbled before sinking to the floor. Curling up on a bath mat, I marveled at the hair that had collected over the past few weeks—mostly mine, though with a sick heart I spotted a strand of chestnut from Helen's final days. I vowed to give the bathroom a fierce vacuuming when my brain was once again restored to order.

But now the headache was sending out nervy shoots, vines snaking along axons, dark red blossoms blooming in deeper neural tissues.

I tried to sit up.

"Frack," I hissed, attempting to spit out a decent cuss, but my mouth was not cooperating.

"Frack, frack, frack!" I said. "Wit did frack?"

I thought of Al, lapsing into garbled bleeps at the Center, though he'd seemed to be unconscious of this. I tried speaking slowly—"Wud duf frahck?"—but my tongue was crimped, my mouth insufficiently salivated. While my brain felt enormous, fraught with throbbing nerves and veins, bloated and inflamed as though boiled, my body felt stunted and boneless. I had no strength to crawl to bed or couch. I breathed. I suffered. Through blurred vision, I spotted a prescription bottle of Clomid tucked behind the toilet, a cruel blast from the past. A whirl of memories came flooding back as I lay squirming on the floor.

Six years ago, when Helen was thirty-five and we'd been trying to conceive a child for three years, we went to a fertility specialist. Finding nothing wrong with Helen, no hormonal imbalances, and a decent FSH level, the specialist insisted on a sperm analysis. Much to my relief, Dr. Quick found my swimmers to be well within the range of average in terms of morphology, speed, and count.

Our infertility fell into the category of *unexplained*. Nevertheless, Dr. Quick prescribed Clomid, an ovulatory stimulant pill.

During the years leading up to our foray with the specialist, our sex life had been reduced to carefully timed copulations revolving around Helen's fertility chart, the quality of her cervical mucus, and her fastidiously monitored basal temperatures. My once passionate beloved spent hours web surfing for fertility-enhancement info. She ordered biodynamic vitex extract and blew serious cash on maca root hand-pounded by Peruvian midwives under the full moon.

As my headache intensified, garish visual images from that period flashed through my mind: Helen sitting on the edge of our bed, gagging on flaxseed oil; Helen standing in her bathrobe, stoically swallowing supplements; Helen in yoga garb, guzzling gallons of FertiliTea, a nasty brew that smelled like cheap men's aftershave. Strangely, I could still smell the stuff wafting so palpably in the bathroom that I wondered if I'd upset a box of it during my frenzied pilfering for pills.

And then, with a big whoosh, I found myself descending into a familiar well of darkness, the circle of light above me highlighting the cobwebbed light fixture. Although I saw no faces gazing down from this circle, as I had at the Center, I heard a familiar voice—smarmy and godlike, speaking from somewhere in the vicinity of my sinuses with sleazy confidence: *Subject 48FRD showing spotty connection in area XVF395.* And *boom*—there I was, standing in our bedroom, stoned out of my mind. I'd smoked a joint at Lee's place, forgetting that this night fell within the range of an optimal mounting window. Helen sprawled on our bed. She pulled a thermometer from her mouth and squawked at me. Continued her banshee shrieks as she peeled down her panties and dipped her fingers into her vagina. After stretching a strand of egg-white mucus between thumb and middle finger, she flipped me off with her moist digit and reclined upon the bed with her legs agape. I stood there, stoned and confused, staring at her glistening snatch.

"Just get it over with," Helen hissed.

"What?" I fumbled with my belt buckle.

"Climb aboard and do your thing."

I contemplated the word *stud*, oft bandied about in high school, usually reserved for those players in the jock set who sweated testosterone and strutted the halls like bulls. As Helen rolled her eyes and clinically stroked my flaccid cock, I understood the full meaning of the term. I scrambled upon her with a sad sigh. Pumped like a piston while struggling to summon erotic imagery to my pot-shrouded brain: Helen in our hormone-crazed youth, pulling me into closets and darkrooms; Crystal Flemming frolicking naked in the woodland gloom; my favorite Taco Loco waitress, a tattooed coquette who'd recently upgraded from Goth to pinup girl, stripping off her bombshell dress to reveal, um, breasts.

For the life of me, I couldn't summon a decent image of her breasts. Her chest consisted of two rudimentary mounds, the equivalent of a Barbie doll's blank chest.

I lost my rhythm, felt myself go limp.

"Goddamn it," hissed Helen. "Why did you smoke that weed?"

I rolled over onto my side and sulked.

"Come on," she whimpered. "Now is the perfect time."

How had we come to this? For so many years we'd fucked like maniacs. Each green month, a golden egg had voyaged down one of Helen's fallopian tubes, a space orb packed with mysterious genetic code, and loitered in the void of her uterus as my sperm head-butted walls of latex. We didn't want to rush *the future*, which winked at us from a horizon a thousand miles away, a beautiful sure thing.

After Helen moved back to Hampton, we'd readjusted our goals and cruised on connubial autopilot, *the future* still shimmering in the distance, still lovely, we sensed, despite all we'd gone through. But suddenly *the future* was hot at our backs, panting and leering. Suddenly, Helen was stuffed with Clomid pills, zitty and bloated, tormented with blurred vision and headaches but still reclining upon our bed with her legs open, calling me hither.

"Come here, my darling; my head's killing me. Let's make this a quick one."

How could I not experience a wilting of the dick when I heard her plaintive voice summoning me, her electronic ovulation predictor on the floor beside the bed?

"What's the matter with you?" Helen stared at my member, chafed from overwork and defiantly shrunken, practically retracted into my body.

"Too much pressure, I guess."

"Have you been masturbating?"

"Every now and then, okay? Not enough to—"

"How could you?" Her face collapsed. She rose from the bed, stomped off to the bathroom to slam cabinet doors.

When I came back to consciousness, lying on the bathroom floor, cotton-mouthed with dehydration and aching all over, I still heard cabinet doors slamming, as though poor Helen were trapped in some endless hellish bathroom, mirrored cabinets extending into infinity. She kept slamming doors, her anger inexhaustible, bottomless, eternal.

• •

On a rainy night in late October, atmospheric with thunder and lightning and smelling faintly of pickled eggs, I stood before Helen's old full-length mirror and cackled like a deranged scientist in a horror flick. Lord Tusky the Third, a lean and refined gentleman with the head of a boar, had been born. Lord Tusky wore a frock coat of wine velveteen. The lacy cuffs of his thrift-store blouse flounced elegantly from his slender wrists. His ascot of purple polyester paisley was enriched by the added luster of a faux gold pin. Lord Tusky flaunted shiny boots of ebony pleather. Tight breeches of black spandex highlighted the elegant curve of his thighs. The index finger of his right hand sparkled with a plastic ruby.

Lord Tusky smiled.

Lord Tusky smiled and smiled.

Lord Tusky could not stop smiling, a sneer enhanced by his chic black snout. The two polished tusks that curved from his lower jaw seemed to twitch with a playful hint of erotic cruelty. His black fur gleamed with purplish highlights as though touched with Day-Glo paint. Lord Tusky foamed at the mouth. Lord Tusky had several mistresses.

Lord Tusky felt dizzy, for his mask still smelled of hide paste and resins. He could see pretty well through the eyeholes. He practiced drinking with a straw, inserting it into the barely noticeable aperture he'd drilled into the polymer tongue. And he couldn't stop smiling. He smirked at himself in the mirror until he felt lightheaded. Fearing the onset of a migraine, he removed his mask and hung it on his bedpost.

And there stood Romie Futch, a middle-aged divorcé channeling a cut-rate Robert Plant from the fantasy sequence in *The Song Remains the Same*. There stood Romie Futch, with his receding hairline and stooped shoulders. Romie Futch, with his stubborn potbelly and tormented eyes.

But shit, at least the cut of my frock coat downplayed the poof of my gut. At least my mask project had been a success. I had three days to fret before making my dramatic appearance at Helen's masquerade ball. I had three days to vacillate between Promethean audacity and debilitating insecurity. Three days to imagine Lord Tusky strutting into the Dogwood Gallery with devil-may-care ennui as socialites in hackneyed costumes gasped at his creepy elegance. Three days to imagine Helen frowning with disgust as she reassessed Boykin's pathetic novelty costume, purchased at the last minute at Halloween Express. Three days to envision Helen sweeping into the courtyard to tumble into Lord Tusky's arms.

Helen, burrowing her lustrous head into Lord Tusky's scruffy neck.

Helen, raving of his genius.

Helen, ripping off his mask to feast upon Romie Futch's poor, parched human lips.

Helen saying, "I'm so sorry. Let's try again."

SIX

The day before Halloween, I drove out to Dixie City Fashion Mall to have lunch at the Chuckling Newt Café with Dad and Marlene. Seated in a corner beneath a still shot from Dylan's "Subterranean Homesick Blues," the concrete wall behind it faux-distressed to give it a refurbished warehouse look, I watched inked-up hicksters stroll around with plates of food. They moved slowly, wearing bored expressions of haughty idiocy. The whole operation gave off a sad corporate bohemian vibe. Dad and Marlene were late, and I was scanning the craft beers on the menu, wondering if I ought to indulge in a Rabid Mongrel Pale Ale this early in the day.

I texted Trippy about my dilemma, a habit that'd gotten out of hand. Ever since my last blackout, I'd been shooting verbiage into the void daily, wondering if Trippy's phone was viable or if he just wanted to start afresh and put his experience at the Center behind him. I also feared that the racial boundaries created by years of systematized oppression were, now that we were back in the world, too much to overcome. But I hoped a critical mass of texts might stir his apathy or break down his emotional wall. In addition to the burning desire to confab about my migraines and blackouts, I was itching for some decent conversation, our heady Nano Lounge dialogues already pickled and vacuum-sealed in the green-gold brine of nostalgia. Skeeter was AWOL, I'd lost Irvin's number, and Trippy was my last link to what was starting to seem like a bygone era.

"Well, look at you," a feminine contralto squawked. I turned. There was Marlene, fluttering through the restaurant in a chiffon tunic, her new wave coiffure teased and leftward leaning. She enveloped our table in a cloud of perfume. My father shuffled grimly behind her in indigo Rustlers, a plaid poly-cotton dress shirt, and his best suspenders—his go-to getup for public outings, garb that was, ironically, "hip." Glancing around at the framed vintage photos of cool celebs, he winced at the iconic image of John Lennon, naked and fetally curled, clinging to a smug and clothed Yoko Ono.

"Pathetic." Dad huffed.

"You cut off all your hair!" Marlene plopped into her chair. "Why didn't you call me? I coulda given you a real slick haircut for free."

After wiping a crumb from the vinyl seat of his dinette chair, Dad sat down and took a big sniff. "Smells like bleach in here. Bet you money they clean the floor with it. There's a link between brain tumors and sodium hypochlorite fumes."

"Oh, shut up, Dr. Doom," said Marlene. "Romie and I are trying to have a nice lunch."

As Dad scanned the menu, his frown deepened, forming a sinkhole in his face. "I told you it'd be high." He glared at Marlene. "Sixteen dollars for a chicken potpie."

"It's different." Marlene slipped on her rhinestone-studded bifocals. "Slow food fast. Look, they got pit-cooked heirloom pulled pork. Says right here: the free-range pigs eat grass and chestnuts."

"I don't like my lunch moving around." Dad cracked an abysmal grin.

"Ha, ha," said Marlene, "except that ain't funny."

"I didn't see a barbecue pit outside," said Dad.

"Bet you it's in the kitchen," said Marlene.

"Then it wouldn't be a barbecue pit, would it?"

"Why not?"

"Plus, I wouldn't mess with pork if I were you."

"I love pork," said Marlene. "I'm gonna eat a big plate of fatback just to spite you."

"That's cannibalism." Dad grinned until his gums peeled up from the roots of his teeth.

"Hush," said Marlene. "Side of Thai coleslaw. What's Thai coleslaw, Romie?"

"Probably has peanut butter in it."

"Peanut butter in slaw?" My father yelped and then shook his head like an ancient general surveying a burning city. "I reckon I'll get the heritage chicken potpie, but I don't see why they got to put beets in it."

"'Cause it's different," said Marlene. "Just live and let live."

"I'm not used to gourmet food," said Dad.

"I beg your pardon."

Marlene glared down her nose at Dad, squinting fiercely through her lenses. My father sighed and pushed his menu away. Our waitress, a sorori-punk with a snake tattoo entwining her lovely wrist, trudged over to take our orders. I went with the pickled shrimp and arugula. Marlene stuck to her guns and got the pulled pork. Dad stoically submitted his request for the beet-plagued potpie. When Marlene changed her order from unsweet to sweet tea, Dad started up on diabetes and periodontal disease, highlighting links between gum rot and brain cancer. He wondered if the link was correlational, or if microscopic organisms—parasites, viruses, bacteria—traveled through the sinuses into the brain, where they mutated into carcinogenic life forms.

"The world is full of vicious, enterprising creatures," Dad said, nodding toward Marlene. "They'll eat you alive if you give them half a chance."

"Romie." Marlene patted my hand. "Have you ever thought about getting on one of those dating sites—OkCupid or whatnot?"

"OkStupid's more like it," said Dad, after which he returned to his discourse on parasitic entities. "Identity thieves, computer viruses, brain-eating amoebas that live in warm, stagnant lake water."

"My cousin's nephew did it and he met the nicest dental hygienist on earth. Why don't you just give it a—"

"They get in through the nose," said Dad. "So you ought not to swim in lakes. And the ocean is full of great white sharks these days. I know a man from Tallahassee who died of chlorine poisoning. His blood turned to acid. So pools are off-limits too, son. And AARP says swimming is good exercise."

Dad sat back and snorted at his punch line.

"You don't even have to go on a date if you don't want to," said Marlene. "Just shop around, see what's out there."

"Gold diggers and identity thieves," said Dad. "That's what. I wouldn't put any personal information on the Internet if I were you, son."

"Maybe you could get one of those dating apps for your phone. My ex-niece's cousin has one. Met a guy at the bar and *click*—knew he was into reggae and cocker spaniels, had a degree in computers, her kind of guy. They had a drink and *bam*—now they got a one-year-old."

Like most divorcés, I'd given dating sites a passing thought—had even pulled up questionnaires a few times, overthinking my answers, imagining the kinds of women they'd attract, gaming my responses, visualizing the awkward first date, the first stilted coupling, the postpassion chatter spiked with melancholy, ineffable odors of animals in decline, middle-aged genitals drooping under stale sheets.

"*Post coitum omne animal triste est, sive gallus et mulier,*" I muttered.

"Excuse me?" said Marlene, cocking her head to study me through her tiny twinkling specs.

"Pig Latin," said Dad. "Yada yada yada, as the Yankees say."

"Romie, honey," Marlene murmured, pressing my hand, "sometimes you just got to let go. It's been, what, a year? It's time to forget about Helen and move on."

I sat there for two minutes, waiting for Marlene to remove her hand. She finally did, leaving a sheeny film of scented moisture.

The waitress brought our food. Marlene and I ate while Dad picked through his potpie like a prison guard, pulling out suspicious morsels.

"What the hell is this?" Dad squinted at a small black orb coated with dark pink ooze, a strange gland or organ perhaps, pulled from the steaming mess of his gutted pie.

"An olive, you moron." Marlene rolled her eyes. "Can't you just enjoy yourself?"

The waitstaff moved to and fro, talking of Michael Cera and JLo.

Drizzle spattered against plate glass.

Out in deep space, supernovas collapsed.

"What kind of fool potpie has olives in it?" Dad hissed. But he ate the tidbit anyway. Marlene and I both watched with interest as he chewed, his caution turning into curiosity, swinging back to suspicion, and then veering sharply into disgust. He spat a lump of chewed olive into his napkin and secured the bundle beneath the edge of his plate.

"*Man hands on misery to man,*" I muttered, spearing a pickled arthropod on my fork. "*It deepens like a coastal shelf.*"

188 | JULIA ELLIOTT

"I like to look on the bright side," Marlene said. "I read in *O* magazine that optimism makes you live longer."

"If you're born a pessimist," said Dad, "there's nothing you can do about it. I always knew I'd die early. My father did and his before him. Colon cancer took Daddy while a stroke snatched Granddaddy. Weren't none of us Futches born to last."

"Maybe Romie took after his mama's side," said Marlene.

Dad sniggered grimly. Marlene went red in the face upon realizing her faux pas.

I saw my mother's ghost hovering over our table, summoned to the earthly realm of flesh, mud, and sorrow. She slipped into the extra seat. She sat silently, her face pudgy, a crisp cloud of gray hair above her big empathetic eyes.

Marlene's right, Mom whispered. *It's time to move on. Helen's not your thing anymore, Romie. Just think about that for a minute. You're not the same boy you used to be.*

And then she melted into a cloud of white mist. She floated up into an air-conditioning vent with an eerie *whoosh*.

• •

That night I reached a sorry state, exceeding my beer allotment by two units and popping excessive Excedrins as a preemptive strike against migraines. I e-mailed the Center again, describing my regression, the blackout-flashback combo suspiciously characteristic of a brain download, and I received a form response directing me to a twenty-page PDF explaining the Kafkaesque grievance submission process. I sent a fresh barrage of texts to Trippy conveying my latest trials in dark, breezy bleeps: *Monster migraine last night, man, followed by a doozy of a blackout.* After a couple of hours poring over the HogWild message board, I plunged deep into E-Live voyeurism.

Using the Time Machine feature, I quick-scrolled six years back on Helen's profile to view the unraveling of our marriage. Helen, a private person, hadn't said much. But I could see our decline in the reduced frequency of status updates and the bleakness of the links and pics she'd occasionally posted. For example, during the height of our attempt to get her pregnant, Helen posted nothing for two months, and then, out of nowhere, a lone grotesque photo appeared with no comment, a high-resolution ultrasound of a lemur in utero, its little gargoyle face scrunched in fetal wisdom.

This was during the worst time, when Dr. Quick prescribed gonadotropin injection therapy, which required daily injections of hormones for ten days, with expensive ultrasounds and estrogen monitoring, none of which was covered by the crappy insurance we got from Helen's job at Technomatic Quick Lab.

My recent blackout had made all of these memories raw again, and I'd spent the last week staggering miserably down memory lane. I clearly remembered administering the shots with a pen-like doohickey. When an ultrasound revealed that Helen's largest ovarian follicle had swollen to ideal ripeness and her uterine lining had thickened to a luxurious eight millimeters, Dr. Quick plied her with a human chorionic gonadotropin injection (ensuring ovulation in thirty-six to forty hours) and sent us home to couple.

We went through this cycle three times. Each time, the copulation window loomed before me like a high school exam for which I was dreadfully unprepared. The third time happened at three thirty in the morning. The clock ticked. I suffered difficulties. We bickered. I threatened to leave. Helen begged me through tears to *please forget about everything and just go with the fucking flow.* She reminded me how much money we were spending, citing specific sums with decimal points. I experienced an agonizing leg cramp and leapt from the bed. Paced like a madman, whereupon Helen advised me to sit on the couch and think of pleasant things.

My mind went blank. I dozed off. Woke up. Achieved a viable erection just before dawn. We went at it on the floor. After I released my precious load, Helen dampened my face with kisses and tears.

But still, no dice. Her period came, this time with alarming clots. She suffered stabbing pains in her abdomen and wept at the drop of a hat. She had nightmares about her dead father, kept dreaming he was under our house, crouched behind our furnace. She couldn't get enough water, felt dehydrated no matter how much she guzzled, peed every five minutes. Her little sister was pregnant. Her best friend from high school was pregnant for the third time. The television was haunted with pregnant actresses. They sported their so-called bumps, traipsed in trapeze dresses, displayed their spawn on the covers of magazines.

Helen decided to give it one more go, this time with intrauterine insemination.

"Basically, you whack off into a cup." She said. "And they inject your stuff directly into my uterus. They'll keep some in cryogenic deep freeze. Just in case."

"Just in case what?"

Helen shrugged.

On a drizzly June afternoon, after a week of home-administered shots, we drove to Live Oak Fertility for the insemination. A nurse ushered us from a large waiting room into a parlor-like cube hung with yonic O'Keeffe prints. They fetched Helen first, spirited her off, I imagined, to some nook where, with her legs in stirrups, she waited for the plastic grail of my opalescent spunk. And then they directed me to a small room equipped with a love seat and a wall-mounted plasma screen. The nurse, a short muscular woman with a cap of dyed red hair, said I'd find what I needed on the television. She turned on the lamp. Killed the overhead lights.

"Put your name and social on the cup." She pointed to a stainless-steel basin brimming with plastic vials and slipped discreetly from the room.

The TV menu featured a dozen porn flicks, ranging from vanilla hetero intercourse to light S&M sprinkled with male homoeroticism. I chose *SuicideGirls Do Seattle*, sighed, and unbuckled. I got off to a good start, especially after noting a resemblance between one of the actresses and my beloved Taco Loco waitress. But then I realized that I'd neglected to equip myself with a receptacle. I stumbled, half hog-tied by my own pants, to the bowl of vials, which was inconveniently located on a small table that also held a dispenser of antibacterial towelettes. By the time I sank back down onto the sofa, I'd lost my groove.

The first moment of truth had already occurred on-screen. I struggled with the faulty rewind feature and found myself back at the film's tedious beginning. Again, I watched my favorite SuicideGirl chain her fixed-gear bike to a parking meter and trot down a stairwell that led to a subterranean bar. Again, I watched pinup girls purr in retro lingerie as male hipsters sporting ironic mustaches swilled retro cocktails. Again, I watched the female lead discuss business opportunities with the manager. Watched her strip off her polka-dot frock. Watched her fondle the pointy cups of her vintage bullet bra. Release the tortured flesh of her sweet little bosom, both dainty nipples pierced.

Second time around, the film depressed me. I felt the presence of all the harrowed men who'd sat on this couch before me, shivering in the excessive air-conditioning, breathing in smells of disinfectant as digital vixens sneered and parted the pink mysteries of their anatomy. I wondered if there was another sad couple out in the little parlor with the O'Keeffe paintings, waiting for me to finish up. When I noticed that I'd neglected to lock the door, my penis shriveled. I heard husky laughter trailing along the hallway. What if someone barged in at the height of my quiet frenzy?

I got up to lock the door. Sat back down. Took my shrunken johnson in hand. I couldn't help but imagine Helen, clad in a hospital gown, her legs awkwardly agape. I couldn't help but see Dr. Quick, sucking up my semen with a syringe, jamming his latex-gloved hands into my poor bride.

A melodramatic moan interrupted my train of thought. I glanced up at the screen just in time to catch my favorite SuicideGirl getting double-teamed by two emaciated hipsters with full-sleeve tattoos. She was bent on all fours, displaying the lovely curve of her buttocks. I felt a stirring in my groin and fumbled for my tool, closed my eyes, and imagined myself ramming it to the Taco Loco waitress in my boyhood bedroom. I growled like a baby tiger as I spurted my 10 cc. And that was that. I turned off the TV. Capped my cup. Wiped my hands with a Wet-Nap. I strode out into the blinding fluorescence, where a bespectacled gray-haired nurse smiled maternally as she took my warm sample.

On the way home, drizzle thickened into storm. Rain sluiced down the gutters, and I could barely see the road. Helen rode shotgun, clutching her gut.

"I think the bastard bruised my cervix." She smiled a sickly smile, her chin crusted with a fresh crop of zits. "By the way, I know who you were thinking about in there."

"In where?"

"When you were in the cockpit."

"The cockpit?"

"That's what the nurses call the masturbation room. Isn't that funny? I heard them talking about it."

"Very clever."

"That waitress."

"What waitress?"

"The cheesy Goth bimbo at Taco Loco."

"No way. She *is* a total cheeseball. Dumb as a vat of nacho cheese."

"That doesn't matter, does it? She's young and fertile."

Helen sneered at me, her face pasty, her lips cracked.

And then we were screaming at each other as we drove through a shocking torrent of apocalyptic rain. When I felt the car hydroplane, I pulled into a strip mall, sat idling in front of Future Dragon Chinese Buffet as Helen wept.

"Don't stress out," I said. "Remember what Dr. Quick said."

"Go to hell." She eyed me through tears. "This is the last time. I don't care if it doesn't work."

And it was. We never went back to Dr. Quick. Never discussed in vitro fertilization. Helen tossed her ovulation predictor, her supplements, her copy of *A Spiritual Companion to Infertility* into the trash. We never called to ask the office about the sperm sample they had banked in cryogenic deep freeze.

When she got her period, she posted that pic on E-Live, the hideous lemur in utero, puffy and scrunched before a veiny placental backdrop, its little paws outstretched, reaching toward the mysterious flash of light that had invaded its dark aquatic realm.

Helen didn't say one word about the image, or respond to any of the commentary. She joined a gym. Became a mean lean creature with pumped Amazonian arms who subsisted on fish and spinach. I became a sulky drunk with a swollen gut and spindly limbs. Each day, a new medical bill appeared in our mailbox, always more than we'd expected. We set up a payment plan. Fell behind in our bills. Refinanced our house.

We bickered our way through another festering summer.

I thought autumn would save us. But we two who had once been lonely together now retreated into separate mental dungeons. Each of us stared out from the isolation tank of his/her newly individualized misery, stung by all the beauty—the blazing blue skies, the smog-streaked sunsets, scarlet with particulates, that went down each evening behind a fringe of red and gold trees.

SEVEN

I chugged a Miller in the truck. Idling outside the Dogwood Gallery, my boar head resting on the seat beside me, I watched costumed guests stream into the party. Checking my ascot in the mirror, I recoiled from the sight of my weathered face, jaded eyes that spent too much time eyeing a computer screen. We all become parodies of our former selves. We all end up donning cadaverous masks, withered leering versions of ourselves that fit looser upon the skull. It was All Hallows' Eve, that night when spirits of the dead have one last romp upon the warm planet before sinking into the cold slime of winter soil. Perhaps my mother was out there somewhere, skeletal, impish, dancing in the shadows.

The Japanese maples planted along Main Street wore their blighted autumnal cloaks. The shop fronts displayed quaint harvest themes. But the world was still half green. Mosquitoes still patrolled the humid air. I felt hot and overdressed in my pseudo-velvets. I'd cut myself shaving. My mouth tasted weird, as though I'd swallowed a penny.

But when I slipped the boar mask over my head, I felt calmed by the musky tinge of hide—a cozy animal odor that I associated with childhood. I felt a rascally grin overtake me as Lord Tusky pocketed his keys and exited his vehicle. I had a plan.

Lord Tusky would stroll around creepily, nodding greetings to people but never speaking. Hand on chin, Lord Tusky would consider the art. With impeccable posture, Lord Tusky would pose in various corners, steeped in an otherworldly je ne sais quoi. No one would guess Lord Tusky's true identity, except for perhaps one damsel, a lady of a certain age who'd known him in his youth, who understood his deepest passions, his frailest hopes and darkest fears.

Lord Tusky was unnerved by his lack of peripheral vision as he entered the crowded room. He saw a trio of Lady Gagas giggling over a sumo wrestler's inflated physique. Saw a gorilla putting the moves on a Playboy Bunny. Saw Sarah Palin flirting allegorically with a skeleton and a king. Sensing a whir of whispers in his wake, he strode toward the refreshments and obtained a Sierra Nevada from a young barmaid wearing plastic devil horns. He repaired to a corner, retrieved his straw from an inner pocket of his frock coat, and slurped his beverage as he scoped the room.

Although he did not recognize his old beloved among the throng of revelers, he kept hearing her iconic laugh emerging from the mouth holes of plastic masks: a sexy kitten (no way Helen would dress as a kitten), a zombie pirate (too fat), the Bride of Frankenstein (wrong skin tone). But then he spotted her, dressed as a blue squid in a pointy hat and a skirt of wavering tentacles—a store-bought costume, yes, but at least it was weird. At least it didn't reek of desperate sexiness, of middle-aged flesh jacked up in corsetry and decorated with fluffy animal parts. But his heart sank when he saw Boykin beside her, decked out as a fisherman and holding an expensive spinning rod.

Lord Tusky took several fierce slurps of beer through his straw. He turned toward the art. Relieved to see that it sucked, he snorted. There was some good photography out there—even haughty Lord Tusky, who possessed imaginary galleries of fine oil paintings, would admit that—but this was pretty dreary stuff. The digital photos were displayed on wall-mounted flat-panel computer monitors. The images consisted of hip youths in various states of undress, lolling on rumpled beds and moldy-looking couches while sulkily holding up twee handwritten signs that said shit like WHAT WOULD THE HONEY BADGER DO? or FREE MUSTACHE RIDES! or DREAM CATS FOR SALE. Upon reading the artist's bio on a flier, Lord Tusky discovered that Adam Nicholas Hagman was a recent graduate of Savannah College of Art and Design. Lord Tusky was wondering how such vapid hipster froth had found its way into the backwater of Hampton when he felt a tug upon his velvet sleeve.

There stood Helen, her face scrunched in quizzical bemusement beneath her squid hat. "Romie?" Her frown made it apparent that she had not intended to invite Lord Tusky, but she quickly recovered.

"Oh my God, Romie."

She laughed, a rich snigger that reminded Lord Tusky of better days.

Lord Tusky took the fair lady's hand. Pressed it to his lips. Made a smacking noise.

Helen peered into his eyeholes. "How are you, Romie?"

Lord Tusky bowed, almost sweeping the floor with his fingertips.

"*Oka-a-ay*. Well, then. How do you like the art?"

Rubbing his left tusk noncommittally, Lord Tusky took a slurp of beer through his straw.

"The artist is pretty young," said Helen. "Boykin's nephew, actually. Would you like to meet him?"

Lord Tusky nodded theatrically. And Helen led him to a corner where a slouching dude with meticulously mussed platinum hair and jumbo horn-rims tapped at his phone.

"Adam," said Helen, "I'd like for you to meet an old friend of mine."

"Whoa," said Adam. "That mask is sick. Did you make it yourself?"

Lord Tusky nodded.

"This pig doesn't speak very much," said Helen.

"That's the best costume I've seen all night," said Adam. "Kind of steampunk but still cool."

"Adam isn't wearing a costume," said Helen, "even though it looks like he is."

"We all wear costumes every day." Adam tweaked his oversize yellow bow tie, which matched his pleated, peg-legged pants. The boy reminded Lord Tusky of someone, but he couldn't quite figure out who.

"Adam is crashing with his Uncle Boykin for a while," teased Helen. "Starving artist."

"Only until I figure out where I want to go to film school." The boy pouted.

"He's got his eye on NYU," said Helen.

"Tisch is pretty rad, but New York winters are a bitch. So I'm thinking CalArts."

"We're lucky to display his photographs before he becomes rich and famous." Helen winked coquettishly. "Tell Mr. Pig how you got the idea for this series."

"It's kind of stream of consciousness." Adam fingered his phone. "Postmodern Dada minimalism, you know. I like to push boundaries. Each image captures a spontaneous moment of self-expression, my subjects in states of, like, vulnerability, their deepest desires on display like raw wounds. I'm really into the French new wave."

Lord Tusky snorted. Adam looked up from his gadget and stared into the pig's eyeholes.

"Are you an artist?" he asked.

"Taxidermist," Helen said tightly, her voice lilting into a strange hiccup. "If Mr. Pig is who I think he is, I mean."

And then it came to me: Boykin's pip-squeak nephew reminded me of Adrian, the art student Helen had dated at USC. During our first year of college I'd kept chaste, waiting for her summer return. When April exploded with its riot of azaleas and bees, she called me one warm ruttish night, broke down and confessed that she was "seeing someone." The way she put it sounded self-consciously adult.

"Who?"

"Just this guy. An art student."

I was a wannabe artist studying graphic design at Trident Tech, and her words stung me to the quick. Idiot that I was, I nursed the hope that when Helen came home for summer, she'd look into my eyes with repentant sorrow and forget all about this art student. But she moved into a duplex in Columbia, a ramshackle millhouse in the Olympia neighborhood, with two other girls. Adrian occupied the other half all by his lonesome, courtesy of his banker dad. In their backyard, spray-painted mannequins relaxed in retro wheelchairs and milled about among pokeweeds. When I visited, unannounced, one June Saturday, Helen and I had sat awkwardly in wheelchairs, emotionally crippled, out in the jungle of pokeweeds, while Adrian glared at us from an upstairs window.

"He's really intense," Helen said.

She explained that Adrian spatter-painted found objects and placed them in random public settings. Adrian was into guerrilla

art. Adrian had a spiky Duran Duran hairdo. Adrian wore pointy
Beatle boots. Perpetually sported the same model of black jeans
and always, rain or shine, hot or cold, a vintage leather jacket that
smelled like the corpse of Joey Ramone. I finally met the brilliant
asshole one July night when I ran into Helen and her paramour
at the Hampton Waffle House. Sweating in his skunky leather
jacket, he smirked with superiority at my King Crimson T-shirt. I
walked off into the shrieking summer night. Called Crystal Flemming. Got drunk beside the railroad tracks and wept into her lush
bosom.

Even after Helen's dad died and Adrian "was not there for her,"
even after we got back together, she continued to think of him as
a moody, adorable genius.

Now she was making goo-goo eyes at her boyfriend's fey nephew, gushing over a privileged brat's crappy "art." Why was she so
susceptible to the pretentious conceptual drivel of talentless hacks?
Why did she have such a weak spot for skinny pretty boys in tight
pants? I was almost relieved when I saw old possum-faced Boykin
navigating his way through the sea of people, struggling with his
spinner rod and two plastic cups of red wine, his paunch thrust
forth like the prow of a ship.

"Thanks, hon." Taking her drink, Helen kissed Boykin on his
sagging cheek, probably to reassure him.

And it did look like he needed reassuring. He'd gained weight.
His eye bags looked more voluptuous than usual. His hairline had
crept back.

"Boykin," said Helen, "you remember Romie, don't you?"

"He didn't look so hairy last time." Boykin smiled. "But I do
remember him."

Gamely, Boykin set down his rod and offered me his hand. I felt
a little foolish maintaining my air of lofty silence, but a plan is a

plan. I shook his hand, nodded, cocked my head in what I hoped was an open, friendly manner.

"Apparently, silence is part of his costume," said Helen.

"I like it," said Adam. "Very John Cage."

"Adam," said Boykin, "did you get a chance to talk to Annabelle, the owner?"

"She scares me." The boy shrugged.

"But she was kind enough to give you this show."

"So sue me," quipped Adam. "Mr. Lawyerman."

Helen giggled. As she and Adam exchanged conspiratorial smiles, Boykin took a tense sip of wine.

"If you sell any of your work," said Boykin. "You'll have her to thank."

"Money, money, money," said Adam. "That's all you and my parents ever talk about. The revolution will not be commodified."

I wondered who'd financed Adam's dope outfit, his Oracle6 phone, his expensive-looking clown shoes. I wondered if he dyed his own hair or hired a coiffeur. I knew instinctively that Adam expected to be paid lavishly for a flexible "creative" job in some awesome city, to live in a chicly shabby apartment with out-landish rent, and to purchase whatever tech gadgets, cool duds, and artisanal brunches tickled his fancy—all while identifying with antiestablishment ideologies. I actually felt a little sorry for Boykin (even as I relished his discomfort) and longed to break Adam's delicate jaw.

I wondered, now that the cougar meme had reached its full flower in our culture, if it was possible that Helen could be fuck-ing this little prick. I thought of Colette, who'd begun an affair with her sixteen-year-old stepson at age forty-six. I imagined that Adam, whose feeble, digitized sexuality had sprouted during the golden era of Internet porn, would have plenty of aging-woman presets available in his sorry skull—WILFs, MILFs, GILFs, and cougars—cartoonish vixens preening and duck-facing, catering to his solipsistic pleasures.

"There's Annabelle." Helen pointed at the socialite, who was dressed as the Goddess of Love, complete with a Styrofoam Cupid nestled in her elaborate hairdo. In the throes of some anecdote, she contorted her Frankensteinian face and waved her skinny arms.

"I don't think she's human," said Adam.

"Don't worry. I'll protect you." Helen looped an arm through Adam's and tugged the boy toward Venus. Adam pretended to struggle. Helen scolded him with mock maternal sternness.

I could tell she knew that the boy thought her attractive. Knew that the weasel wanted to get his paws into her pants. And this knowledge made her glow.

"So," said Boykin. His smile was shy, his ears tipped with crimson. "Did you make that mask?"

I nodded.

"Very creative. I'm a big admirer of creativity." Boykin sighed as he watched Helen introduce Adam to Annabelle Tewksbury De-Bris. And then, in a very small voice, my ex-wife's lover unburdened himself of a secret dream: "I always wanted to write a novel."

It was a good thing I was wearing a mask. It was a good thing my outraged sneer was concealed within the humid darkness of my fake head. Why wasn't Boykin content to devote himself to tedium for status and a fat paycheck? Why did he have to dabble in the arts?

"Kafka was a lawyer," Boykin said wistfully.

"He worked in an insurance office," I burbled, breaking my vow of silence. "And he loathed it. Though his career proved to be good fodder for his absurdist novel *The Trial*, which is the best companion piece to Foucault's *Discipline and Punish* I've ever read."

"I haven't read much Kafka," said Boykin. "Just that one story about the cockroach."

"It was a beetle," I snapped. "As Nabokov, who was an entomologist, argued in his lecture on *The Metamorphosis*, the convexity of the insect's back, in combo with its mandibles and antennae, suggest that Kafka's fabled vermin belongs to the order Coleoptera."

As my ex-wife's lover peered into my eyeholes and smiled like a sheep, I felt ashamed of my pedantic outburst.

"You're the taxidermist, right?" Boykin looked confused, exhausted. He looked older than I'd thought him to be, at least fifty-eight. And then I realized that he was extremely drunk. His eyes were vein webbed. His mouth slack, his lower lip glazed with spittle. I realized that the poor man was not worth hating. I lay down my imaginary sword. Feeling the fight draining from my body, I sighed.

We were two aging men standing on the sidelines together, wallflowers with depleted testosterone levels. Shadows of men, we watched a beautiful woman flirt with a downy ephebe.

We looked at each other and shrugged when we saw Annabelle Tewksbury DeBris reach into her gold lamé handbag, snatch a fistful of glitter, and sprinkle it upon the heads of Helen and Adam, anointing their dalliance with magical dust. Helen giggled. As Adam took a sneak peek of her still-marvelous boobs, his young face lit up with a smile of infinite entitlement. The world belonged to him.

I could picture the little turd lolling in the guest room of Boykin's McMansion, looking down his nose at the provincial décor while enjoying bagels in bed. I could see him soaking in Boykin's Jacuzzi, whacking off to a mumblecore montage of erotica, incorporating sly references to *The Graduate* as a parade of mature hotties held their own amid his Solomonic harem of sexbots. I could see him mounting the diving board of Boykin's pool, smooth and pale as a marble statue of Adonis, looking much better with his stupid glasses off.

And I could see Helen inside the house, drawn to the window, feasting her tired eyes on the carefree youth. I could see her world-weary smile, taste the bitterness in the back of her throat, the residue of a thousand disappointments—her derailed career as a marine biologist, her dismal sex life with a rich dullard, her host of lost children, a series of golden eggs dropping into a black void one by one and lapsing into slime.

Why the fuck not? she'd think. Men have been doing this shit for centuries.

As Helen and Adam strode back toward us, enveloped in cozy banter, I imagined myself charging Adam, goring him in his lily-white flank with my right tusk. I imagined purple tears of blood weeping from his wound.

"Did you try the food?" Helen asked me. "The duck empanadas are amazing."

"Not much for vegans on that buffet," said Adam, shaking glitter from his hair.

"Like you need to get any skinnier." Helen poked him in the ribs as though he were a toddler whose smile she wanted to spark. And behold: a grin and a blush broke like dawn upon the boy's wan face. Boykin mumbled something and glanced at me with harrowed eyes.

"Aw shit." Adam fingered his phone. "I've got to take this."

Gadget pressed to ear, Adam pushed through the dowdy crowd.

"Time for me to tank up," said Boykin. "Can I get you something, Romie?"

I waved my half-empty Sierra Nevada. Sometimes it was easier not to speak. Sometimes it was easier to lapse into moody silence, to peer at your ex-wife through the eye slits of an animalistic mask.

"So, Romie," said Helen, her voice suddenly grave. "How *are* you?"

I shrugged.

"Well," she said. "I still worry about you. But I saw Lee last week and he said you're doing great."

I nodded, gave her two thumbs-up, frowning behind my pig mask.

"Did Lee tell you I was going back to school?" she asked. "Just two online courses at USC, but it's a start."

I put down my drink and clapped my hands to show my support.

"Now that I can afford to work part-time, I can manage it."

She didn't say *how* she could afford to work part-time, but I knew. For years she'd fantasized about going back to school, but her forty-hour-a-week serfdom at Technomatic Quick Lab had kept her from her dreams. We used to fight about the relative flexibility of my job, especially during the bad years when, low on customers, I'd crack a beer at work, forget to eat lunch, piddle with the corpses of animals as my buzz came on. Then I'd wash my hands for an Internet fix, skip though YouPorn, Fleshbot, and VenusVille. I'd spend entire afternoons clicking through catalogs of sportive minxes and home-made fuckfests, zipping hither and thither like a frenzied bee until I found just the right flower to plunge into.

Afterward, I'd nurse my fourth beer while fussing with inventory, rearranging boxes of eyes and tongues, but never having the wherewithal to overhaul my supply room. I'd somehow make it to five thirty, when I'd trudge home and find Helen on the sofa, too tired to change out of her medical costume, which smelled of strawberry disinfectant spray.

"What do you want for dinner?" I'd ask, opening the fridge, casually plucking a beer as though it were my first.

"I don't care."

"Monkey jerky?" Perhaps my voice sounded menacing, something vile beneath the false brightness.

"Whatever."

She'd watch me move around the kitchen, opening random drawers, another dusk closing in, one of thousands we'd experienced together. Sometimes the windows were open. Sometimes the windows were closed. Sometimes you could hear a bird going at it, twitting with all its soul.

"Drunk already?" she'd ask. "It's not even six o'clock."

I'd choke out a laugh. "What makes you think I'm drunk?"

"I know you, Romie Futch. I've known you for over twenty years."

She'd look at me with pity and disgust. She could see through my skin. Could see my heart, a shriveled thing with a husk of discolored leather, sagging like a half-deflated football.

And then we'd claw idly at each other, waiting for something to catch. We'd bicker until a jazz of insults blared in the night air and we felt alive again, our dead blood oxygenated, pulsing brightly in our veins.

But now Helen seemed calm yet energized, self-possessed with yogic poise.

I could see her out on a patio with her micropad, brain cells revitalized. I could see her glancing up from her homework to feast her eyes upon optimally fertilized flowers maintained by a landscaping crew, not one weed visible in the perfectly spread cypress mulch. I could see Adam in the background, just out of focus, his platinum hair catching the sun. Boykin was at the office, of course, making three hundred dollars an hour.

"But seriously." Helen put her hand on my arm. "I hope you're doing well, Romie."

"I'm fine," I finally said. "I'm making art again."

"Now we're talking." Helen smiled. "What? Sculptures?"

"Postnatural taxidermic dioramas," I said. "Mounted mutant scenarios; working with my own kill. It's taken me forever to deconstruct the taxidermy-art binary that's always hindered me, but now that I have, I feel a small sense of deceptive liberation."

Helen blinked, peered at me. "I'm not sure what that means exactly—maybe Adam would know—but it sounds really creative." There was that word again. (Was it my imagination, or did she seem less clever than she used to be?) "You are so creative. That's one thing I love about you. And your pig costume. I really like the way you—"

"I doubt Adam would get it," I interrupted, "though he'd no doubt declare it *epic* before clicking on the latest viral YouTube video."

Helen bit her lip, removed her hand from my arm.

"You ought to talk to Annabelle about a show here," she said. "She's into things that are different."

"Like anal bleaching?" I sniggered. "Annabelle Tewksbury De-Bris might be too avant-garde for my stuff."

"Oh no. I think she'd like it."

"I am Ironic Man," I said. "Do you really take that synthetic creature seriously?"

"Believe me, I know," said Helen. "But I'm trying to stay positive, you know?"

In my ex-wife's forced smile, I saw some of the old sadness welling up, which made me feel connected to her again.

"Helen," I whispered.

The word sounded ancient, archetypal, like some tender appellation emerging from a caveman's lips—the name of a newly discovered flower.

"Helen, I . . ."

She waved me off.

Now Boykin was at her elbow with drinks. Adam was moving sulkily through the throng of dowdy revelers, many of whom had reached the staggering, bellowing stages of drunkenness, costumes askew. But I was painfully sober. Painfully alone. Painfully alert to some not-quite-rightness, a general drooping of the spirit.

"I've got to go," I said to Boykin when he offered me a beer.

"It's early," Helen said.

"I'm going hunting tomorrow morning," I said.

"For real?" She raised an eyebrow.

"Totally," I said, imitating Adam.

As I walked away, I saw her turning toward the boy to peer at some trifle he'd pulled up on his little screen.

"Wow," she said. "That's amazing."

And I wondered what magical image he'd bewitched her with— a short art film, an E-Live photo stream, some oft-tweeted meme that offered just the right political commentary in six words or less.

As I strolled toward my truck, I thought of the Calydonian Boar, that beast from antiquity who tore ass through the Greek country-side, snorting Stygian smoke. I thought of old Beowulf, the first drag-on slayer in literature, gray haired with shrunken sinews, slumping into the wilderness in heavy mail. I imagined Hogzilla, asleep in his musky swamp nest, dreaming mysterious hoggish dreams.

I'd rise with the sun. I'd smear my body with sacred mud to de-face my decadent human stink. I'd become an animal, fleet-footed, keen-snouted, my mind in tune with the intricately shifting wind.

EIGHT

I sat in an obscure chamber of Hampton Regional's emergency facility, my right hand resting in a plastic vat of antiseptic fluid pinked with my blood. I'd been waiting for nearly an hour as doctors and nurses bickered over whether or not to stitch up my finger, whether there might be nerve damage, whether or not to send me to an orthopedic surgeon. So I slumped in the freezing room, cursing myself. I'd been a fool.

I should've known not to go galumphing into the woods that morning. Should've stayed in bed. Should've waited for a more auspicious day.

After a night of fitful dreams, I'd woken with a headache—the kind of foggy pain that had a fifty-fifty chance of veering into skull-splitting migraine mode. Overcast mornings seemed to bring the agony on—constipated weather states that refused to erupt into rain. But I took three Excedrin and fingered my acupressure headache zones until the ache retreated to a deeper section of my brain. I cleansed my body with an alcohol bath to eliminate my human stench. Decked myself out in freshly laundered camo. Loaded my grandfather's Savage .45 with safari-grade ammo, bullets that would pierce a rhino's hide.

I drove to the edge of a forest, hiked through second-growth pine until I reached the cypress swamp where I'd salvaged the remains of Hogzilla's cannibalistic frenzy. Wearing a prophylactic latex glove, I spritzed various tree trunks with Feral Fire Sow-in-Heat spray. Upon removing said glove, I noted a hole in its pinkie finger. I'd forgotten my stash of SafeWipe disinfectant towelettes, so I dipped my hand into a stream, sniffed my finger, felt sure that no trace of pheromones lingered.

But the sow musk had tainted my flesh. It whispered beguiling messages to the wind.

Thinking myself odorless, thinking myself invisible, I hid behind a clump of buttonbush and waited. The heavens grumbled, but rain did not come.

Into this tranquility rushed a drift of hogs, some thirty strong, sows and piglets and a handful of horny boars. Squealing, grunting, filling the air with the reek of tainted meat, the boars dashed around sniffing the trees I'd anointed with Feral Fire spray. They snuffled and tore up the ground, devouring roots and insects. And then the whole parcel charged onward into wetter zones of swamp.

One boar and a sow dallied, however, with two piglets in orbit—soft, fuzzy creatures who veered in to nuzzle their mother's flanks. Grunting, the boar sniffed the sow's face. He nosed along her fatty rows of teats. He plunged his snout into her anogenital zone and took a deep, drunken whiff.

Squealing, the sow butted the boar's neck with her modest tusks. The old razorback mounted his lover backward and maneuvered himself clockwise into proper alignment, whereupon the white worm of his penis emerged from its furry sheath. Slithering, the corkscrew phallus lashed at its target. At last, the boar clambered atop his mate and grasped her flanks with his front hooves. Thrusting furiously, he rammed his pale pecker home.

It took him awhile to hit his groove, and then he went strangely still. From my research I knew that his flailing phallus had finally wedged itself into the corkscrew-shaped aperture of the sow's cervix. The lovers stood frozen, expressionless in their bliss, as piglets frolicked around them, dipping in for reassuring sniffs of their mother's musk.

But then the clambering of monstrous hooves shook the air. A deafening mastodon roar echoed as the biggest and freakiest hog I'd ever seen bounded into this idyllic scene: the fabled Hogzilla at last. His pop eyes pulsed in fury, emitting a hellish light. His cutters were at least two feet long. Random tufts of black bristle grew from his bald, hot-pink hide. Despite the overwhelming effect of the razorback's visual presence, smell overpowered image: nose hair curling, supernaturally putrid, a chthonic funk beyond belief. A gray streak of stench flared behind the pig's body like a comet tail. Whatever decadent pheromone receptors I possessed in my feeble human olfactory system worked overtime to process this assault. I understood, at the most primitive neurological level, the metaphoric significance of fiery dragon breath. I can't imagine what the other pigs smelled, keen-snouted as they were.

The piglets fled immediately. The mounted boar, struggling to detach his engorged prick as the sow squealed and squirmed, shrieked when his paramour finally ran off into the bracken. His penis bounced and retracted into its pouch. His hackles shot up. He assumed a stiff-legged fighting posture. But Hogzilla got right down to business. Refusing to engage in the usual shoulder-to-shoulder pushing match, the big beast rushed in and gored his rival in his flank. After plowing the little boar over, Hogzilla made an instant porridge of his belly, after which the monster relaxed, casually plunking down to slurp and smack.

Hogzilla pulled bright red gut strings from the gory cavity. Chewed through the spongy rinds of organs. Crunched cartilage and snapped bones.

I dared not move. I'll admit that I pissed myself. Fretting over the fear message my pee smell was broadcasting into the wind, I clutched my rifle with crimped fingers. I attempted to move my frenetic mind through the seven coordinations of *shichidō* to become one with my heirloom gun. But every nerve in my body was raging. Every hair standing on end, all follicles raised into bumps. I still had the presence of mind to notice a pile of fox scat beside my left boot, its stringy texture studded with berries—strikingly beautiful berries—shining in the sun.

The last berries I will ever lay eyes upon, I thought, as tears rolled down my cheeks.

When Hogzilla finished his lunch, he unleashed a brontosauran bellow and romped around the glade sniffing tree trunks. The poor fool thought a fertile sow was in the area. As he dashed around with increasing desperation, his roaring became mournful, full of plaintive notes. In a small, warm corner of my frozen heart, I understood where he was coming from. There we were, two solitary bachelors, too weird to find mates, plying our frustrations in the empty forest. But then Hogzilla turned, sniffed the air, emitted a queer whinny, and trotted right up to me.

I trembled in the vast shadow of the beast. I gazed into his crazy bulbous eyes. Braced my rifle against my shoulders and fired. The razorback snorted with annoyance as the bullet bounced off his leathery chest, his shield fortified with cartilage and scar tissue, tough as a triple-alloy tank. The monster stepped around my buttonbush cover and grinned at me. The great Hogzilla loomed, blotting out the sun. The animal leered with red, protuberant eyes, his pupils shrunk to pinpricks.

I regarded his mammoth cutters, razor sharp and blood crusted. I beheld his gaping mouth, the teeth jagged and yellow and bedaubed with tidbits of gore. His head was bald, the color of Bazooka gum, adorned with haphazard clumps of black bristle. A crop of whiskers grew about his black, smiling lips.

The monster wheezed into my face, his breath evoking primordial slime, some fertile sludge from which newts might hatch. The creature snorted, and I opened myself up to death. Closed my eyes. Waited for the gouge of Hogzilla's tusks.

Instead, I felt the warm tickle of a hog snout against my belly. I opened my eyes. The pig was sniffing me over, huffing and puffing, snuffling under my shirt. Hogzilla sniffed my armpits. My elbows. The fingers of my left and right hands. The animal licked my right pinkie and emitted a sultry grunt. The sky split open with a thousand red shrieks as the bastard nibbled nearly an inch off the smallest finger of my right hand.

I heard the sick crunch of bone. The air went splotchy. I thought I saw Hogzilla extend a pair of dark, fleshy wings and bound off into the clouds.

I fainted, I suppose—possibly from candy-assed fear, possibly from some neurological dysfunction bequeathed by the Center for Cybernetic Neuroscience—but I woke up five minutes later. I gazed with surprising calm at the carnage, ripped off the hem of my T-shirt, applied a makeshift tourniquet, and drove straight to Hampton Regional.

• •

My finger had been bitten off just between the knuckle and the distal phalanx. The harried authorities at Hampton Regional sent me home with my maimed digit gauze-wrapped and encased in iced plastic. Fearing nerve damage and lawsuits, the emergency room doctors referred me to an orthopedic surgeon. Armed with a Demerol prescription, some free antibiotic samples, and the name of said surgeon scrawled onto my release form, I drove groggily home. When I called the specialist who would supposedly take care of me on the spot, his office informed me that they did not treat uninsured patients. They provided the names of several doctors who might.

I slumped on the couch, cradling my ruined finger in my lap, wondering if I ought to call Dad, expert on the medical industry's dark shenanigans, wise to the horrors awaiting an uninsured man in my condition. But no, I could not bear to hear his grim *I told you so*, could not stand the thought of Marlene flitting around me in a perfumed panic, dispensing advice from women's magazines and self-help blogs.

"Fuck the medical-industrial complex," I hissed.

I popped two Demerol, downed a beer, and slathered my pinkie in antimicrobial goop. I walked over to my shop, retrieved the needle and super-thin nylon taxidermy thread I used for small game animals, and stitched up my own torn flesh. I was pretty handy with a needle—even with my left hand—especially since my final BAIT downloads had endowed me with meticulous fine motor skills. Plus, I'd recently had lots of practice with tiny specimens, which require intricate stitching. So I managed to seal off the wound with a fairly neat seam. I applied a glop of SilvaSorb gel, a swaddling of white gauze, and returned to the house. I downed another Demerol, collapsed onto my bed, and fell into psychedelic dreams.

· ·

The next morning I woke up with a morphine hangover and a raging fingertip, which sent me spiraling into a synthetic opioid binge, fueled with splashes of Jim Beam.

In a lawn chair on my back patio, I lolled in a narcotic haze, gazing down into the gorge, watching the sun creep over the algae-infested roof of my boyhood home. Observing the breathtaking exfoliation of the leaves, *drowsed with the fume of poppies*, I marveled at the paradox of festive festering.

My errant fingertip, a floating signifier detached from its original context, had already dissolved in the burbling cauldron of Hogzilla's belly. I envisioned a small sliver of bone wedged like a splinter in one of the monster's steaming turds. I thought of Ahab in his bitterness, Moby-Dick rising from the watery abyss to chomp off the sea captain's leg. I saw the half-crazed Ahab staring down at his bleeding stump. I pulled out my phone. I surfed the web for fake fingers.

Would I go with a lifelike silicone finger prosthesis? Would I flaunt my disability with a clip-on robotic digit made of steel and futuristic plastic? Or would I simply carry on with a nub? Fake fingers were expensive, especially the high-functioning units with bionic flex joints and nerve-sensitive wiring. Calculating how many deer heads I'd have to stuff to pay for a mock pinkie, I panicked about getting back to work, but I couldn't bring my wounded hand anywhere near an animal carcass, pickle bath, or tanning chemicals anytime soon.

I sighed, popped another pill, enjoyed another swig of bourbon.

When I hit an invincible Demerol groove, I couldn't resist the perverse urge to pull off my stiffened bandage and gaze at the sight of blood-crusted stitches oozing at the seams. I worried about infection. I worried about gangrene and deep bone rot. But I slipped the bandage back on, had another drink, and hoped for the best.

I sent a drunken group e-mail to my clients explaining delays in product turnaround. I lobbed another furious electronic message at the Center regarding my headaches and blackouts. Receiving an instant automatic reply, I vowed to drive to Atlanta right then and there. I even looked around for my keys, planning to burst into Morrow's inner sanctum. I'd slam the asshole against the wall cowboy-style. Punch him in his bland face. See if the mannequin had human blood in his veins or some creepy android fluid like the milky stuff that Ash leaked in *Alien*.

I could barely walk, much less drive, and by the time I got there the business end of the Center would be void of humans, humming on autopilot. So I texted Trippy, again and again, too wasted to be disheartened by the sight of multiple one-sided speech bubbles going on and on, a madman talking to himself.

Just after dark, when I finally stumbled inside, I called my father. He bleated like a cryptic goat before uttering my name. But I couldn't bring myself to speak. When I heard the archetypal sound of his sinus-clearing maneuver, I breathed like a serial killer and hung up. The walls were melting from Demerol and Beam. But I still felt the urge to express myself, to volley some poignant message into the cold, mute universe. And so, minutes before I passed out, I removed my crusted bandage, snapped a pic of my castrated pinkie, and posted the gory, Freudian image on Helen's E-Live Wall.

It sat there for a solid week—outcast as a leper among happier images of birthday parties and karaoke jaunts—inciting no comments whatsoever. At last, Helen private-messaged me.

What the hell's going on, Romie? Are you drinking again? I'm worried about you.

I chose to remain aloof in sulky silence. I chose to retreat deeper into pills and booze, nothing to entertain me but the gratuitous stunts of my own cyborgian brain.

· ·

One week later, I was still in self-medication mode, ignoring impatient customers, trashing late notices sent by the shady mortgage company that owned my house, surfing the hog-hunting message boards, exploring the hinterlands of obsession until my eyeballs throbbed. Ahab-style, I vowed revenge against the stinking monster who had casually nibbled my finger off. Vowed to up my game when my wound healed. Vowed to purchase a gun-mounted kill light and blow that motherfucker to pulled pork while he was sleeping.

According to the fanatics on HogWild.com, Hogzilla was still fading in and out of dimensions, melting into air, flying off into the clouds as bullets ricocheted off his pachydermic hide. According to one anonymous poster, *that hell hog gobbled up a toddler in Yemassee.* SquealinGroovey claimed that the boar *ate off a man's leg and left the rest of him to set there and suffer.* PigglyWiggly69 attested that the evil razorback had *ruint a whole kennel of prize coon pups, biting off pieces and leaving the poor things alive.* Though newspapers never confirmed these suburban legends, I could easily see the nasty pig gulping down babies like tender hors d'oeuvres, torturing innocent fawns, milk-plumped puppies, and downy baby rabbits.

As usual, PigSlayer stepped into the debate and offered a more cynical perspective: *I have reason to believe that Hogzilla is a mutant,* she wrote, *a transgenic monster escaped from GenExcel, that genetics lab on the outskirts of Yemassee that's funded by BioFutures Inc. This would explain Hogzilla's baldness, his weird skin color, his quasi-mythical wings.*

Who was this woman who used words like *quasi-mythical* and knew how to slay a boar with a bow and arrow and field dress it with a T-handle saw? Was she real or was she some cynical nerd, holed up in a big city apartment, chuckling as she created fake identities to toy with yokels on backwoods message boards? For all I knew, PigSlayer could be an adolescent boy, indulging his fantasies with a sexy female avatar.

Nevertheless, I sat there, fingers poised over the keyboard, ready to rattle off a clever message to this mysterious woman, converse about the mutant nature of our beloved Hogzilla, discuss the shenanigans of corporate entities like BioFutures Incorporated, a name that rang a bell but which I couldn't quite place. I felt tongue-tied and dull-witted and was, per usual, wasted. I vowed to write a clever bit the next morning—sometime between my first coffee and my second shot of bourbon. But I didn't even have a username, a fantasy identity that would allow me to cut a witty swath through the dense brush of hog-hunting discourse. I was just a voyeuristic creep spying on a spectral woman.

But then, deep in the night, it came to me: I was PorkDork—badass yet nerdy, cerebral yet self-effacing, playful and language drunk, with an affinity for rhyme, consonance, and alliteration, just the kind of man a woman like PigSlayer would be drawn to. With a pounding heart, I typed in my username. I created a password that I'd probably forget. And then I rested my ravaged head upon my keyboard and fell asleep.

• •

One unseasonably warm night, crickets still screaming in November, I felt a headache blooming in my skull, a blood-dark flower swelling up from the stem of my brain. I was out on my front porch, gawking at the mist-blurred moon, when my cell buzzed. It was an unfamiliar number, but I felt lonely enough to pick up.

"Romie, man, it's me." The familiar voice was nestled in static.

"Trippy? Shit, it's about fucking time. Didn't you get my texts?"

"Shhhhh," he hissed. "They'll hear you."

"Who will?"

"Dr. Jekyll and his evil posse."

"What you talking 'bout, Willis?"

"I think they're watching, listening. *Feels like they're in my motherfucking head.*"

"Where are you, man?"

"Can't say."

"You mean you can't tell me or you don't know?"

"Look, I'll get right to the meat. Have you been suffering any blackouts?"

"Actually, a couple. Didn't you get my texts?"

"Some bastard pinched that phone."

"Well, good. That explains why you—"

"Listen, I don't have much time. You been waking up with a sense of lost time?"

"Once or twice, but I figured it was just a side effect, along with retinal hemorrhaging and elephantiasis of the testicles, all covered by section 3, clause 9.5 of contract 2."

I forced out a laugh, but Trippy didn't join me in my merriment.

"Have you heard any voices, Romie?"

"It depends."

"Depends? What the hell does that mean? You either have or you haven't."

I thought of the time I'd passed out in the bathroom after that monster migraine and bout of garbled speech. Yes, I *had* heard a voice, but it might've been part of the dream I'd lapsed into, the one about Helen. Voices in the head were the signature lunatic trait, and I wasn't ready to fess up yet.

"Trippy"—I forced out a brutal chuckle—"have you, perchance, been indulging in some substance abuse?"

"I don't think the experiment's over, Romie. I think they're still dicking with us."

"Who, exactly?"

"Dr. Jekyll. BioFutures. I don't know."

"BioFutures—that rings a bell. Wait a minute."

"Daddy Warbucks behind the Center. Got a weird e-mail from Skeeter. Think he—"

Trippy's voice fizzled, our connection lost. When I rang him back, I was sent straight to voice mail. I remembered that Bio-Futures Incorporated was also, according to PigSlayer, the dark force behind GenExcel, that laboratory in Yemassee that was supposedly doing some unkosher shit with animal DNA. I wondered what kind of dark corporation was funding both GenExcel and the Center for Cybernetic Neuroscience. I envisioned a Darth Vader-esque CEO sitting at a twenty-thousand-dollar desk carved from a chunk of obsidian. I heard his inhuman laughter echoing down the labyrinthine hallways of his corporate aerie. Heard the *click, click, click* of his secretary's noir stilettos on Italian marble tiles.

Sir, the secretary of defense is on line one.

Sir, the CEO of Eli Lilly will be a few minutes late for lunch.

Sir, your wife called. She wants to know whether she should have the mansion in Costa Rica cleaned, or will you be staying on the yacht?

I'd seen too many movies, as had Trippy. And we lived in the twenty-first century, a time when corporations were recombinant monsters dipping multiple tentacles into the private and public sectors, funding commercial enterprises and academic research, dabbling coercively in legislation. Everything was both evil and innocuous at the same time. And Trippy was a stoner with a taste for exotic hallucinogens.

I remembered a story he'd told about the time his true love, Lady L, hanging with a gaggle of her college girlfriends, pretended he was invisible, kept it up all night no matter how much he carried on—reduced his ass to a bellowing mess. He'd almost lost his mind, found himself in the bathroom of Club Satin, strung out on fireballs and vitamin K, trying to touch his mirror image to reaffirm his existence. He was probably having a similar ontological freak-out this very night, fucked up in his sister's basement.

I went inside and shot him a text. Suggested that we get together soon. Told him he was welcome to crash at my place anytime and gave him my address.

Collapsing onto the couch, I assumed the fetal position, fingering the scars where Josh had lasered the apertures together after my BC transmitters had supposedly been removed. I could no longer feel the edges of the wireless electrodes, but perhaps they'd inserted something less protrusive. Perhaps dark entities were sending messages to the submerged sections of my iceberg-shaped consciousness.

I sighed. Rubbed my cranium. Sat staring at the wall, listening to the squirrels that infested my attic. The fact that I had one last frozen burrito in the freezer brought me a little comfort.

NINE

I heard a woman's voice, warm and liquid, calling from some green place where a thousand bird species flourished. There the air smelled of crushed mint. There lambs and lions snuggled in patches of dappled shade.

"Romie," she crooned, "are you asleep?"

The motherly voice washed over me, accompanied by warm, Big Red–scented breath. A damp palm caressed my brow. I opened my eyes, expecting to see Mom, but the face was too puffy, the hair too sticky and quirky. It was Robert Smith, the Cure's lead singer, his eyes gouged out with dusky shadows. His mouth was a primal smear of purple.

"Son," a voice bleated. "You best wake up. It's five past eleven in the morning."

Now my father's sallow face drooped above me, neck flesh jiggling as he spoke.

Dad. Marlene. In my bedroom. No, not my bedroom. The living room.

I was sprawled on the couch, sunlight slashing through mini blinds. I took stock of the situation. Tried to sit up. Again experienced the sensation of lead balls rolling around in my skull, crushing delicate nerves.

"We tried to call, but you didn't pick up," said Dad.

"When you called the other night and didn't say nothing, we got worried," said Marlene.

"I see you've been drinking." Dad pointed solemnly at the empty pint of Jim Beam that lay on its side on my coffee table as though a lively game of spin the bottle had taken place. "I see you've hurt your hand."

"We thought we'd drop by to check on you," Marlene added. "What in the world did you do to your hand, honey?"

"We were driving down to Charleston anyway," Dad said.

"Fixing to do a little shopping."

"She's the one that wants to go shopping, not me." Dad aimed a gnarled finger at Marlene.

"Shopping's good for the economy," Marlene opined. "I saw that on the *Today* show."

"Son." Dad held up his portable thermohygrometer. "Were you aware that it's almost sixty-five percent humidity in here? You definitely have a mold problem. I told you to run your air conditioner in the summer. I told you not to keep the windows open. We run ours right on up through October, then switch directly to heat. You ought to clear some of that brush around your yard. The jungle's creeping in. It'll be up to your door before you know it, eating you alive."

Dad frowned, his eyes wide with doomful foreboding.

"Your gutters are clogged. You need a new roof. You've got a squirrel infestation in your attic."

"Leave the poor boy alone." Marlene patted my arm.

"Looks like your floors are slanting, son," said Dad. "Once your foundation goes, that's it. Ought to crawl up under the house and see what's going on down there. You could use jacks to prop up the joists for now, but what you might want to do eventually is—"

"He's not in any condition to crawl up under the house," snapped Marlene.

"Looks like you've got water damage in the kitchen," said Dad, "where your linoleum's bubbling up around the sink. Bet you a hundred dollars you've got asbestos under there, but I wouldn't pull it up yourself. That's one case where I'd let professionals handle it, even if you have to pay an arm and a leg. I wouldn't mess with asbestos."

"Why don't we all go out to lunch?" Smiling, Marlene spread her kimono-sleeved arms like wings.

"There's no cure for asbestosis," said Dad. "You might be fine for twenty years, and then *bam*—you wake up one day and you can't breathe. Next thing you know, you've got lung cancer, interstitial fibrosis, your pulmonary sacs ate up with scar tissue."

"Good Lord." Marlene flashed a clenched grin. "You see what I have to live with?"

"I'm a realist is all, and she can't handle it."

"He's a *pest*-imist," said Marlene, her voice lapsing into squawks, "while I like to look on the bright side. Let's go out to lunch. Let's have a picnic in the park. Let's go on a balloon ride."

"Woman," Dad said, "are you out of your mind?"

"What's wrong with having a little adventure? Though it would be pure hell to be trapped in a hot-air balloon with you."

"What?" Dad grinned. "A man would have to be crazy to set foot in a dirigible aircraft with a woman of your proportions; you're liable to capsize it."

"What do you mean by that?" Marlene stood up and waved a fist. "Romie, did you hear what your father said to me?"

"Didn't mean nothing personal," said Dad. "Calm down or your blood pressure will shoot sky-high. You're just not at a healthy weight is all. You need to get more cardiovascular, lay off the sugar and refined carbohydrates."

"He wants to suck all the joy out of life," Marlene cried. Her face sank into her hands. She fled to the porch with watery eyes. The door slammed.

"Sometimes I wonder why I got married again," Dad said. "All she does is spend my money."

"Marlene's not so bad." I forced myself to sit up—to hell with the balls in my head.

"Son." Dad gave me the once-over. "You look like shit."

"Rough patch."

"Let me guess." He sighed. "Money problems."

"That's only part of it. I wasn't going to ask, but now that you bring it up. I was doing well with my clients until I hurt my hand, and now I've fallen behind. Don't want to miss my mortgage. I'll be good as new as soon as my hand heals."

The thought of parting with a chunk of cash sent my father into a five-minute sinus-clearing frenzy. He pinched his glabella, grunted and hawked. His eyes oozed. He fished a yellowed handkerchief from his pocket, unwadded the crunchy rag, and emitted several dark loogies into it: first from his nose, then from his mouth, and then from his nose again. He crumpled the cloth and stuffed it back into the pocket of his Rustlers.

"When I was your age," he said, "my house was paid for. My car was paid for. I'm a pay-as-you-go kind of guy."

"I know it, Dad."

"What did you do to your hand?"

"Lawn mower."

"Vague answer."

"Sliced the tip of my pinkie finger off, okay. Are you happy now?"

Dad's mouth performed a strange hybrid of wince and grin.

"How in the world?"

"The blade was stuck."

"Did you cut the motor?"

"I wasn't thinking."

"I taught you better than that." He shook his head. "Hope you at least had the sense to have it sewn up."

"I did."

"You taking antibiotics?"

"I'm no idiot."

"You could still get an infection."

By the time Marlene breezed back in with a manic twinkle in her eye, Dad was deep into the pathological quirks of infectious organisms. Eyes ablaze, he spoke cryptically of fungal infections, intercellular bacteria, and subperiosteal abscesses. Marlene pulled a compact from her purse and glossed her lips with a goop-laden wand. She puckered at herself. Blew herself a rascally air kiss.

"Don't listen to a word he says." She smooched a Kleenex and set the tissue down on my coffee table. "Or he'll send you over the edge."

"Always expect the worst," Dad said. "And then you might be pleasantly surprised."

"Anybody want to try that new pumpkin cheesecake over at the Olive Garden?" said Marlene.

Dad rolled his eyes. "Hand me the checkbook, woman," he said.

It took my father ten minutes to write a check. During the procedure he hawked and wheezed from sinus torments and compulsively licked his chapped lips. With the stern, ashen face of a war-crimes tribunal judge, he placed the check facedown on my coffee table, securing it under my Jim Beam bottle, perhaps with didactic intent.

"We've got to hit the road." Dad snapped his suspenders. He patted his tweedy newsboy cap. Once again, it struck me how odd it was that my father, the voice of doom, could be such a sharp dresser, even though most of his clothes derived from Walmart.

We walked to the porch, stared out at the damp, milky day. Wet leaves decoupaged the asphalt. Birdcalls sounded muffled and blurred. I felt a knot in my stomach. My belly released a surly groan as I watched my father and stepmother drive away. I tried to recall when I'd last eaten. I wondered if I had any sandwich stuff left in the fridge. I thought I had a pint of Old Crow stashed in a kitchen cabinet behind a box of roach poison. Remembering my Demerol cache, remembering the check under the empty whiskey bottle, I hurried into the house.

· ·

The check was for a thousand dollars. I found the hidden pint of whiskey. The sun rose and melted the dank morning away. There I was again, living from minute to minute like a dog, trying to engineer a decent mood.

I ate my last breakfast burrito. I popped a holy trinity (Advil, Demerol, multivitamin). And I began my afternoon tippling out in the yard beneath the shade of a flame-hued maple tree. The birds were loud, the butterflies plentiful in the blooming gorge. Though I could feel darkness licking at the edges of my sunny yard, I kept my face turned toward the sun.

Just when my headache had melted away, the boys came swaggering over my lawn like a couple of smirking pirates, intent on hijacking my day.

There stood Lee Decker in a windbreaker that matched the sky. There stood Chip Watts, his thinning bangs molded into an optimistic swoop with futuristic styling products. He cranked his smile wide-open, displaying bright white veneers. His paunch had shrunk to a modest mound. But his cheeks sagged. A proto-wattle was developing under his chin. He'd turned a strange color since I'd seen him last, the prosthetic pink of Vienna sausage, and I wondered if he'd been experimenting with tanning creams.

"What's up?" said Lee.

"Gonna keep it real and say up front that we came to kidnap you," said Chip.

"Get you out the house," said Lee.

"I am out of the house," I said.

"Out your yard," said Lee. "Out your neighborhood. Out your comfort zone."

"Out your mind." Chip grinned.

"What happened to your finger?" asked Lee.

"Lawn mower blade nicked it. Nothing serious."

"If the machine was running," said Chip, "you were a fool to fiddle with the blade"

"I know it," I said.

"You're not a fool," said Lee. "Just an absentminded professor."

Chip rolled his eyes. "Thought we'd cruise down to First Baptist to check out the LastCar Rapture Series," he said. "They got an ATV park for the youth group set up down there. Been giving me lots of business of late. Thought I should drop in to see the glory firsthand. Plus, my nephew Hunter will be trying out his new Yamaha Grizzly 660. That boy can drive."

"We got extra incentives." Lee nudged Chip with his elbow.

Chip pulled a monster joint from the pocket of his black leather jacket and waved it in the air like a wizard's wand.

"This stuff will kick your ass up your own butthole," said Chip, lighting the twisted cigarette. "But in a good way." He took a long draw.

I thought I heard sirens calling from the wilder depths of the gorge, down where blackberry brambles tangled. Half locust, half maiden, they stridulated in the blighted leaves. It was one of those days, sun-drenched yet poised on the edge of winter's oblivion, and I couldn't resist the joint. I couldn't resist the pseudo-warmth of male companionship, the surrender to cannabis haze, even though I knew that terror lurked in the deceptive dreaminess of it all.

I took the doobie from Chip, drew skunky smoke deep into the jelly of my lungs. I closed my eyes and felt blood thrumming in my head. I smoked until my brain was hazed in ethereal webbing, a silkworm squirming in an airy cocoon. Childlike, I followed the boys to Chip's giant SUV and climbed up into its high backseat. I pulled my flask from a cargo-pants pocket and sucked at the bottle of golden juice.

• •

Hackneyed as the metaphor was, I kept thinking we were trapped in hell.

Infernal, lung-curdling smoke? Check.

Eardrum-bursting, satanic thunder? Check.

Multitudes of shrieking imps? Check.

I kept inspecting my ears for oozing blood. Kept fingering my sunburned scalp. There was no shade to speak of. The fiberglass bleacher seats were not easy on the ass. I had the gut feeling I was trapped there eternally, back behind First Baptist's aluminum-sided temple, where a vast, chemical-green lawn rolled down to a pasture that'd been converted into a rough-terrain ATV park called the Wilderness.

The heats of the LastCar Rapture Series had been divided by age, and we'd just watched a bunch of six- to eight-year-olds compete on Titan 110 mini quads. Nine-to-elevens were up next.

But the youth minister had to deliver a sermon between heats, in which he compared the young drivers to Christian warriors slaying heathens in the wilderness. Using terms like "kick butt," "awesome," "score," and "sweet," he asked God to protect them on their mission and reminded them that Jesus was their copilot.

Pastor Logan was an athletic thirtysomething with a tatt of Jesus on his right tricep. He had a forward-sweeping flurry of emo hair, plus a greasy feather of a mustache that had yet to reach its manly potential. After his sermon, he walked over to shake our hands. Thanked Chip for the righteous thirty percent discount he'd bestowed upon the church, whereupon it became obvious that Chip had been dabbling in organized religion.

"Wipe that grin off your face," Chip said when the boy of God was out of earshot.

"You actually go to church?" I said.

"Look," he said, "I'm no atheist."

"I'm not either," I said, "more like an agnostic relativist if you want to mince hairs, but organized religion? As the good book sayeth, *The Most High dwelleth not in temples made by human hands.* Christians are some of the most unchristian people I know. And Baptists? Jesus motherfucking Christ."

Chip frowned. "Don't talk shit about Jesus."

"If Jesus is God and God impregnated Mary, then . . ."

"Damn it, Romie. I was raised Baptist. The Baptists in this town do well for themselves. Church is awesome for networking. I'm not going to be crass and mention a number or anything, but do you know how many ATVs I've sold since I started attending services back in May?"

"How many?" said Lee.

"An ass-ton," said Chip. "Put it this way: I've moved more quads in the last few months than I had in the whole ten years before that. I'm not naming any figures or nothing, but if I keep going at this rate, I'll be able to retire when I hit fifty, with a swimming pool and the latest Hummer in the garage of my four-bedroom home, in a neighborhood that's not going black."

"I love the smell of racism in the morning," I said.

"Why in the world would you need four bedrooms?" said Lee.

"Not to mention a gas-guzzling military tank," I added.

"Who knows?" Chip winked. "At this rate, I might score me a sweet young thing to marry, have some rug rats."

Chip followed this boast with a display of conspicuous consumption, swaggering over to the food stand to blow a twenty on a round of corn dogs and Cokes for the three of us. The corn dogs—golden-battered, deep-fried tubes of pure-T gastronomical bliss—smelled like paradise. But after the first bite, my stomach convulsed. I placed my tricked-out wiener onto its paper tray and set it aside on the bleacher. I doused my jumbo Coke with Beam. Gazed out at the inferno where the nine-to-elevens had started whirling around in pointless circles, an apocalyptic smoke cloud forming above the ruckus.

A teen girl came by selling T-shirts that read GODWEISER 300: THIS BLOOD'S FOR YOU KING OF KINGS. The shirt's beer-can logos displayed a poorly drawn crucifixion scene plus a winged ATV flying through comic-book clouds.

Winking creepily at the maiden, Chip bought three tees, gifting me and Lee with showy bonhomie.

The girl puffed out her little sparrow chest and grinned. Her braces twinkled optimistically in the autumn sun.

"This will help pay for our trip to Six Flags!" she yelled, bending forward to place her sweet mouth close to Chip's hoary old ear.

I felt ancient—brittle-boned and covered in malodorous barnacles—surrounded by swarms of shrieking youths. They writhed

like larvae all around us, every cell in their bodies stoked and firing at full potential. They radiated idiocy and nubile promise.
They wore shiny synthetic sports gear, corporate logos emblazoned on their garish caps. They pecked at their phones, tweeted
and bleeped and updated their E-Live statuses a hundred times,
while I slumped, crookbacked and slurping my spiked Coke.

*I was a sick man. I was a spiteful man. An unattractive man. I
thought that my liver hurt.*

Dark and cirrhotic, it festered down in the hollow beneath my
heart.

Did my eyes fail me or was the girl actually winking at Chip,
testing the potency of her blossoming womanhood upon my
bloated friend? Chip smirked like a constipated walrus, his face
on fire with a hypertensive blush. Yes, indeed she was. Winking
and duck-facing. And when she flounced off with a wriggle of her
proto-ass, Chip yelped in triumph.

"Hot damn! Did you see that? Fuckin' jailbait."

"Not very godly of you!" I shouted, struggling to be heard above
the din.

"You wouldn't know godly if it crawled up your ass!" Chip screamed.

"Is that some kind of reverse transubstantiation?" I cried.

"What the hell you babbling about now?"

"Some kind of Eucharistic enema?"

Just as I screeched the words *Eucharistic enema*, the ATV thunder ceased. My strange phrase echoed in the awkward silence. Chip
winced. Random teens snickered and gawked. Lee giggled, muttered, "Romie's a trip," and drew a phantom doobie to his lips.

My bladder was full. My left foot numb. I limped off to relieve myself as a dozen girls in red Godweiser shirts pranced
out onto the field, where they began a lewd dance routine to
a techno version of "Onward, Christian Soldiers." The line to

the porta-potty was insane. So I dipped down to a pine copse behind the bleachers.

The wind howled cryptic messages to my stoned brain as I spattered a stump with piss. Gazing into the heavens, I saw a dragon-shaped cloud slither over the sun. The wind had a nip. A cold front was sweeping in. I heard a bellow behind me, zipped up my pants, and turned.

From the shadowy realm beneath the bleachers, where cigarette butts and soft-drink cans littered the squalid dirt, a creature came creeping. His hair was clumped, his skin ageless in its patina of grime. Exuding scents of bowel and forest, the ancient man-beast lumbered toward me. I recognized his harrowed eyes.

It was Jarvis Riddle, the alcoholic woodsman who'd stumbled upon my LSD-fueled frolic in the woods with Crystal Flemming some twenty years ago. I could still recall Crystal, a naked dryad reclining against a tree, her ivory buttocks cushioned by a bed of moss. I could still see the rictus of her horror as she spotted Jarvis emerging from the forest gloom, trembling with DTs and roaring like a Sasquatch. According to local rumor, his long-suffering sister had finally kicked him out of her shed and he'd pitched a pup tent in the woods. We must've interrupted his afternoon nap.

Now he supposedly lived in a lean-to deep in the swamp—in the spooky limbo between R.V. Garland's land and government property. As he crept toward me, I thought of all the poor misunderstood monsters from myth and legend—the Grendels and yetis, trolls and hunchbacks—gentle, red-eyed ogres with hoarse voices and broken hearts, *each one a rover of the borders . . . who held the moors, fen and fastness.*

"Can you spare a few bucks?" Jarvis stood at the edge of the bleachers' shadow, his leathery right hand emerging into the light to take my cash.

I slipped him a five.

"How did you hurt yourself?" His watery eyes brimmed with concern as he scoped my maimed hand.

"You wouldn't believe me if I told you."

"Try me."

"A giant hog bit the tip of my pinkie finger off." I grinned. "How about that?"

"Ah." Jarvis Riddle shook his head. "I *can* believe you. Hogzilla strikes again."

"How did you know?"

"I've had truck with that beast. The woods haven't been the same since he came. Unnatural monster. Sign of the end-time."

Jarvis Riddle stared off at a dark cluster of clouds that hovered over the fiberglass steeple of Hampton First Baptist.

"Where have you seen him?"

Jarvis smiled cryptically. "Here and there."

"Can you be more specific?"

"Not without compensation." Jarvis shrugged apologetically.

I had no more cash on my person. As I regarded Jarvis's embarrassed smile, I wondered if it was true that he'd scored a full scholarship to Vanderbilt eons ago. That upon flunking out, he'd been drafted to Vietnam. That in the green steamy jungle, he'd become obsessed with the Book of Revelation and lost a few of his marbles.

"Where can I find you?"

"Out and about." Jarvis smirked like Merlin and scratched his hoary head. "Where the albino gators slink."

And then he retreated back into the shadows, his cryptic nature poetry drowned by the surge of revving engines.

"The Ten Commandments," Pastor Logan's voice boomed over the PA, "a set of whoops bound to separate a rider from his quad: five jumps followed by a monster jump and a set of step-up doubles. Are you godly enough to handle it? Onward, Christian soldiers!"

By the time I'd reclaimed my bleacher seat, the twelve-to-fifteens were tearing ass over the Wilderness: swerving around orange construction cones, leaping over sandbags, flying up ramps to monster-jump over picturesque man-made gorges worthy of a dystopian film set.

Youths shrieked like locusts. Teen girls writhed in ecstasy. Chip Watts bellowed like a bull, his face the color of liver pudding. Two of the drivers had been flung into the mud. Three were still lollygagging on the log obstacle. Chip's nephew Hunter was neck and neck with some other lad, flying toward the most monstrous jump of all.

"There they go," Pastor Logan yelled, "a forty-foot whooped-out uphill climb, flattening out for a tabletop, then rounded with a step-down landing for one hundred and fifty feet of I-dare-you-to-try-it obstacle."

Lee clapped politely. Chip Watts roared and waved his meaty fists.

"I told you Hunter could drive," he screamed.

"Looks like Hunter Bledsoe's in the lead again," the youth pastor boomed. "Talk about an adrenaline junky. Watch how he shoots up the side, speed-skates over that tabletop, and just flies over the step-down like a torpedo."

And that was that: Hunter Bledsoe swerved to a halt, killed his engine, hopped from his quad, and strode onto the podium to join the pastor.

"How do you feel right now, Hunter?" Pastor Logan shoved his mic into the boy's face.

"I feel awesome."

"Are you a righteous dude?"

"I am a righteous dude."

"We all know Hunter's got high octane in his blood and a liquid-cooled four-stroke single-cylinder heart with four valves," joked Pastor Logan.

The crowd shrieked. Hunter nodded modestly as three teen girls in cocktail dresses stepped onto the stage in high heels, each gal wielding a two-foot gilded trophy.

"Trophy time," the pastor announced.

We had to sit there for another fifteen minutes as Pastor Logan plied the crowd with inspirational speeches. He reminded us that we were all Christian warriors battling Satan in the wilderness. He urged us not to get discouraged when thrown facedown into the mud pits of life. He advised us to climb back onto our chariots of fire and dart back into the fray.

"Keep on fighting evil." He brandished a fist. "Fast and furious and bold."

Cold wind swept in from the north. Tumultuous clouds hovered. I thought I spotted Jarvis Riddle slinking out to the parking lot, weaving through the glittering desert of SUVs.

"What y'all say we hit Bojangles on the way home?" said Chip. "Unless Professor Romie prefers a salad bar."

"I could go for some chicken 'n' biscuits," said Lee.

"Bojangles is cool," I said. "I'm jonesing for some triglycerides and hydrogenated oil."

"Whatever," said Chip. "I don't care if the chicken's fried by third-world toddlers with third-degree burns. I don't care if I gain twenty pounds with every bite. I don't care if my esophagus dissolves from acid reflux and I get the runs for a year. I'm gonna eat my fucking chicken and biscuits and I'm gonna enjoy it. How 'bout that race, Lee?"

"It was awesome. Your nephew sure can drive."

"Hell yes, he can."

We walked to the parking lot. Chip was about to climb into the pilot's seat when Jarvis Riddle popped up from behind the Escalade's hood like a mangy Muppet. Chip winced, slipped a pair of aviators over his eyes.

"Thought I might have a word with you, Chip," said Jarvis.

"Just a minute, y'all." Chip grinned, shut the door of his SUV, walked off with Jarvis until they were almost out of earshot.

The two men stood negotiating in the shadow of an enormous Ram truck. I thought I saw Chip slip Jarvis some cash. Thought I heard the word *Hogzilla* emerge raspily from the vet's ancient, oracular mouth. After Jarvis Riddle staggered off across the parking lot, Chip came toward us, whistling with ostentatious aloofness.

"What was that all about?" I asked when we'd all climbed into the SUV.

"Oh, nothing." Chip removed his sunglasses and pretended to adjust his rearview mirror. "Just a bum hitting me up for a handout."

But I saw the flicker of fever in his eyes. I saw the veins of obsession. I saw dark pouches gathering beneath the windows to his soul.

Cold, calculating eyes of a hunter.

Crazy, monomaniacal Ahab eyes.

Sleep-deprived and bottomless, sneaky as a chimp's, constantly on the lookout for that mythic beast that existed in some twilight wood, just at the edge of human consciousness.

Hogzilla the mutant, winged and bald, nightmare beast of *the future*.

My Hogzilla.

TEN

A windy storm swept in and stripped the last leaves from the trees, killed the lingering crickets, put those lovely autumnal butterflies out of business. I had a bad cough, sipped from a bottle of Robitussin DM, and fell into the throes of a psychedelic fever. Cocooned in a comforter that still held traces of Helen's waterproof sunscreen (it would not wash out), I lay on the couch, falling in and out of dreams. Sometimes I'd wake convulsed with chills. Other times I'd come to sweating, my skin on fire, figments of dreams still bustling around the room. Dr. Morrow haunted this latest round of dreams, a disembodied presence who occasionally offered commentary in his midnight-radio baritone: *Subject 48FRD only vaguely responding to phase-five stimuli*—whatever the fuck that meant.

Was I hearing voices? Or was this the stuff of dreams? Dream stuff, I decided—definitely dream stuff.

But then one night, after chasing Hogzilla over a barren arctic landscape in an ATV, I woke to find Dr. Morrow seated at the foot of my couch, dressed in a lab coat. When I reached out to touch his strangely puffy left leg, my hand passed through his marshmallow flesh. *Subject 48FRD has responded to an intraneurological stage-five facsimile*, said Dr. Morrow, *though I must say, my legs need work.*

Tittering, he scattered into luminous pixels.

I had to admit that this definitely qualified not only as a voice in the head but also as a bona fide hallucination, though I *did* have a fever. I *had* consumed excessive quantities of dextromethorphan. I sat up. I tried to remember where I'd left my phone. I had to text Trippy immediately. Maybe he'd break his latest round of icy silence if I admitted that okay, I *was* hearing something that might qualify as a *voice. Talking. Inside my lunatic head.* I wondered if Trippy was seeing things too (he'd said nothing about hallucinations during our brief phone conversation). But I couldn't find my phone. Plus, I was distracted by a more pressing problem: my throbbing finger, sharp pain shooting from the tip down into the bone. I didn't peek under my bandage. I dared not gaze upon my maimed digit just yet.

I threw back another shot of Robitussin. I was saving my last few Demerols for some deeper crisis. I'd stashed them in a vitamin bottle, the bottle encased in a balled-up sock, the sock stuffed into an old suitcase, the suitcase buried under a pile of hunting equipment.

I sipped at a medicinal tumbler of bourbon until my finger went numb and the room pulsed with womb-like warmth. Deep in the pocket of my cargo pants, I felt the hopeful vibration of my phone. Ah, there it was, in the most obvious place.

It was Helen.

I pressed the phone to my ear. Waited. Breathed.

"It's me," she finally said. "I'm in the neighborhood. Do you have a minute?"

"I have a fever," I said. "But also a minute. Endless minutes. Not on my phone, but in person. And yes, I'm a little tipsy." I tamped down the bouncing elation in my heart, sent it plummeting to my stomach, where it bobbed hopefully before plunging into nausea.

"That's okay," said Helen. "Do you mind if I stop by? I've got to talk to you about something."

I needed to brush my teeth. I needed to smear some deodorant into the musky hollows of my armpits in case she took me into her arms in a sudden rush of emotion, ready to try again. But I had no time. The room smelled of my sickness, but I couldn't get up from the couch. And then she waltzed right into our old living room as though she still lived here (did she still have a key?). She paced around in a pair of expensive-looking riding boots that gave her the air of a miniseries aristocrat.

My dust would hear her and beat, had I lain for a century dead.

I sat up on the couch, keening toward her.

She would not sit down, kept fidgeting, inspecting various iconic objects from our mutual past.

"Poor Romie," she said. "What did you do to your finger?"

"Lawn mower accident. Just a nick. Nothing serious."

"Well, that's good."

"What brings you to this neck of the woods?"

"Oh, Romie. I hate to come to you like this, but I didn't want you to hear it from somebody else and think that you . . ."

"That I?"

She sat down on the edge of the couch. Her entire body convulsed with emotion. She looked into me with her X-ray eyes, saw my heart, repulsive and swollen as a bullfrog in its lust, and looked away. She whimpered. Nibbled her thumbnail. Shivered. And then finally came out with it.

"I'm pregnant," she said. "Can you believe it after all these . . ." She bit her tongue. She blushed. "And I didn't want you to think . . ."

"Think what?"

"That it was you."

"Me? What the fuck? *How*?"

I'd seen Helen only twice in the last year, had not even touched her, much less . . .

"Your material, I mean."

"My material?"

"Your sample." She released a long, slow hiss of air.

Remembering the sample I'd spurted into a cup at Live Oak Fertility Clinic, I imagined a swarm of my hopeful swimmers frozen, the iced chunk of my genetic legacy stashed in some capsule at the bottom of a cryogenic storage tank with hundreds of others, emblazoned with identification numbers linking it to me, Romie Morrison Futch, 251-87-9087-SC-2348576-DNA-55748FRD.

"Why would I think *that*?"

Helen avoided the intense gaze I'd attempted to muster.

"I don't even know what the legalities would be," she muttered. "Were I to use it," she added hastily, which made me wonder.

"*Use* it?"

"God, not that I would. I mean, not that there's anything wrong with . . . But the thing is, I just didn't want you to hear about this from somebody else and start thinking that, you know."

She turned away so that I could not read her face, could not see what I imagined as a subtly gloating expression letting me know that she was fertile after all, that our childless marriage was not her fault.

"I shouldn't have come here." She stood up. "I'm an idiot. I should go."

She walked over to the stuffed bass that hung over our old television. I'd caught the fish as a boy. Under the micromanaging eye of my father, I'd stuffed it myself. My first project, it looked too cylindrical, like a sausage. And its left eyeball had fallen out.

She touched the fish and turned to look at me.

"I'm sorry, Romie. I made a mistake. I see that now."

I felt like the blood in my body had been replaced with cherry slushie, but it could've been the fever. My fingertips felt numb. All moisture had vacated my mouth. I wanted to burrow deep into my blanket and pupate into some other kind of creature. Something winged and bright that could hightail it out of this shit-hole town, flit down to South America, find some patch of rain forest that hadn't been chainsawed down to a desolate moonscape, and feast on opiate flowers until every last human memory I had was obliterated.

"Boykin?" I managed to say, my voice a hideous croak.

"What?" She turned with a sudden jerk. "That's none of your fucking business."

"But you're the one who came over here. You're the one who . . ."

"Only because, well. I already explained myself."

Of course it was Adam, which explained her defensiveness. My mind already had a stock of paranoid imagery to draw from. For the hundredth time, I pictured them skinny-dipping in Boykin's pool. For the hundredth time, I pictured them fucking under a succulent summer moon. I pictured the boy's hairless Adonis ass dimpling as he plied my spread-eagled ex-wife. But this time I added a new dimension to my torture. I saw a fleet of Adam's sperm churning like fierce barracudas toward Helen's placid egg—thick as a tadpole army, fast as futuristic aquatic missiles, each sperm gleaming with the morphological perfection of youth. I saw the lead swimmer leap into her old egg with an electric crackle and jump-start it into zygotic life. As a thousand flickering cells divided, the egg glowed and swelled. The lump of life sprouted limbs and lungs, nerves and gonads. Its tiny brain ripened like a veiny fruit. In the blink of an eye, a naked hipster with white Warholian hair floated inside Helen's womb.

The fetus waved its little newt hand and smirked at me.

"Adam," I said.

"God, Romie, are you insane? We should not be having this conversation."

Helen smiled tensely, jaw tendons tight, but her body spoke a secret language. As she swished around the room, her hips seemed heavier, the gentle swell of her belly poignant with secret life. And her breasts looked more voluptuous. Her hair lush and wild, streaming behind her like a dark bridal veil.

Her lips, enflamed with estrogen, brought to mind sunlit plums.

I thought of the Demerol stashed in my closet. I would take one tonight and try to hang onto the other two until morning, when acidic light crept through my grubby windows to illuminate the dust bunnies that frolicked across my filthy floor. My buzz was gone. I felt stark sober.

"I should go," Helen said. "I'm so sorry about this. I should've never—I see now what a horrible mistake this was. It's just that I thought you should know given our history, just in case you mis-construed—"

"Thank you so much for sharing."

"Romie, I—"

"Don't sweat it."

"Romie, please forgive me. I'm an idiot."

She actually tried to touch me. On the shoulder.

I shook her off. Turned away from her to gaze into the poly-cotton basket weave of the couch she'd once spent three months shopping for.

"Romie."

"Quit saying my name. It makes me feel insane."

"Okay, then, I'll go."

She puttered around for a few minutes, gathering things—coat, hat, scarf, purse—and finally left. It was still cold outside, I guess. But

I was burning up. I wanted to be back in the sunken den of my old familial ranch house, eating the invalid food my mother fixed when I was sick: Campbell's tomato soup and grilled cheese. But my mother was dead. She'd weighed seventy-five pounds when she took her last breath—a puppet version of her old self, made of dried bones and spotted skin. She'd looked gaunt but eerily girlish at the very end, her skin radiant with a strange sheen as her organs began to shut down. As my dad held her hand like a forlorn lover, I could imagine them as youths, way before I floated in a subaquatic dream in Mom's belly, my first perfect home, transitional holding tank that I couldn't remember but that, according to the hokum of various theorists, I pined for, particularly in times of great need or trauma—like now.

Huge surges of nausea passed through me in greenish waves. My pinkie was throbbing again. For the first time in days, I eased the crusted bandage off. I gazed upon an alien thing, swollen and red as though a half-inflated balloon had been slipped over my digit. The stitches, embedded in the puffy scarlet flesh of my fingertip, seeped an off-white dew.

I thought about calling Helen and summoning her back, asking her to drive me to the emergency room. But the thought of venturing out into the cold night made me shiver. I decided to wait until morning and drive myself.

I crawled from my blanket, a naked, crooked creature, and hobbled toward the closet. With one hand, I clawed through piles of junk, strewing the floor with arrows and knives and camouflage clothes, until I spotted my parents' old avocado-green Samsonite. When I opened it, I smelled a strangely familiar mildew spiked with Mom's lavender talc. I retrieved the treasure I'd tucked under a collection of hideous 1990s jeans. I opened the One A Day Men's multivitamin bottle I'd stuffed into a sock. Shook two Demerol into my sweaty palm and swallowed them dry.

ELEVEN

Lying in the recovery room, I kept looking at my hand and thinking of the three-fingered sloth, making its groggy way through the jungle. The incision from the metatarsal ray resection procedure was very neat. When the scabs healed to scar tissue, the legacy of my pinkie finger would be gone—half of it digested by a feral hog, the other half dropped into a basin and spirited off to some biohazard receptacle full of festering human parts.

Though I was awake for the surgery, drugged with a mild antipsychotic, my hand numbed by a local anesthetic, I remembered only bits and pieces of the ordeal. I recalled the nurse's hiss of surprise as she removed my soggy bandage to inspect my tainted finger. I recalled a hasty round of X-rays. I recalled the neurosurgeon scolding me as he casually mapped incision lines with a special pen. If I'd waited another hour, he said, I would have lost my whole hand. And then he bantered about a boxing match as he selected a dainty, futuristic saw.

The spinning blade whined as it cut through bone. The surgeon's eyes glinted as he sliced into my flesh with the jaunty composure of a television chef quartering a quail. The punch line of his sports-themed joke occurred just as he plucked the severed digit from my hand and made a game of tossing it into a stainless-steel bowl that might have been part of an elegant sushi set. I imagined my lone nub, unrecognizable as a finger or even a piece of finger—a morsel of scarlet meat, an elegant hors d'oeuvre for an ogre.

· ·

By mid-December my hand had healed, the puckered pink scar slowly fading to white. I'd gobbled up my last Demerol refill and gone through a writhing, sweaty withdrawal punctuated by mild blackouts during which Dr. Morrow occasionally offered cryptic commentary: *Subject 48FRD suffering a setback due to bodily trauma, not responding to facsimiles of yours truly; investigating the effects of possible neurological damage on wireless BC transmitters.*

I succumbed to cozy alcoholism, steadily drinking a six-pack each night, wine upon occasion, ignoring the calls of Chip and Lee, warding off visits from Dad and Marlene, shooting a volley of unanswered texts at Trippy as wan winter settled in.

Santa Claus, that sinister glutton and surveillance king, was everywhere, the world strewn with tinselly trash. Demonic elves chanted from the television, urging me to *buy, buy, buy*. And every day I opened my mailbox to find a new medical bill hiding amid glossy Christmas junk mail hawking Oracle9s, fuzzy synthetic sweaters, and diamonds hacked from the dark satanic mines of Botswana.

But at least I was back in my studio, stuffing buck heads and wild turkeys, whatever business I could get. I was back to piddling with my Panopticon diorama, slowly filling each prison cell with mutant squirrels and frogs, trying to get the hang of molding and stitching without the convenience of a right-hand pinkie finger. I was back to e-mailing the Center for Cybernetic Neuroscience, describing my migraines and blackouts, alluding to my awareness of the sinister presence of Dr. Morrow, evoking an imaginary lawyer and threatening lawsuits. When I got really drunk, I found myself trolling Helen's E-Live page, waiting for that moment when she'd announce her pregnancy to the world and her status update would grow like a tapeworm with a thousand congratulatory comments. But she'd been dead quiet. By now her fetus would be about two months old, I calculated, a bean-size neckless alien with gills, a mad scientist's big-ass forehead, those spooky button eyes.

On certain magical holiday nights, lulled by a bourbon buzz and the mellow glow of vintage Christmas cartoons, I'd get this gut feeling that the child was mine. I felt almost certain that Helen had used my sperm sample—why else would she have barged into my house that stormy evening to unburden herself?

When she gazed upon her newborn, she'd see my face blinking up at her. She'd see me, transformed into a helpless infant, snuffling for her teat. Flush with postnatal hormones, her body would soften. Her heart would turn to mush. She'd come slithering back to me like a boneless slug.

• •

One drizzly, gray winter night, back on the hog-hunting message boards, I found my beloved PigSlayer again—I'd forgotten all about my brainy Amazon warrior. There she was on my computer screen, dropping a link about Hogzilla at 10:10 PM. The link was like a steaming pile of animal spoor, evidence of PigSlayer's warm biological existence. I smelled her scent on the wind. I caught flashes of her sleek body, dashing among the vibrant winter pines. I oiled my weaponry. I gave chase.

I stalked PigSlayer through an endless thread of comments (re: the rumor that Hogzilla had bitten off a Little League baseball champion's arm). Right before my eyes, she posted a link to the *Varnville Herald*'s article. My heart raced as I read:

> *The ten-year-old Varnville resident's arm was torn off at the shoulder. The child's thirty-two-year-old father, a refrigerator repairman, frightened the pig with gunshots, salvaged the arm, and rushed the brave boy to Columbia, where neurosurgeons reattached the limb. Despite the success of the operation, the child's future as a professional baseball player is not in the stars.*

The message board was enraged.

A thousand patriotic boar hunters were crawling out of the wirework of cyberspace to declare revenge upon the diabolical beast. Imagining hordes of angry hunters crowding local forests and fields, I felt panicky. I needed to get back out there, bag my beast before somebody else did. I contemplated my maimed hand. Yes, I felt petty vowing revenge over a lost little finger when a young athlete's arm had been ripped off. Nevertheless, recalling the burning words of Ahab, I swore I'd chase that motherfucking hog *over all sides of the earth, till he spouted black blood*. I'd do it for the Little League slugger. I'd do it for me and my pinkie finger. And also for PigSlayer, who'd be mighty impressed.

At 11:55 PM she dropped another link. This time the article was from an obscure permaculture site called CircleofLife.com. It described how corporate genetics laboratories were setting up shop in the backwoods towns of down-and-out Republican states like South Carolina and Alabama. After conducting backroom deals with sleazy governors, the companies performed unregulated, ethically questionable experiments with recombinant DNA, which involved the production of nightmarish farm animals.

It was no coincidence that in a backwater hole of Alabama a poultry farmer woke one night upon hearing a hullaballoo in his chicken house. Therein he found, attempting to rape his hens, *a featherless rooster with enormous pecs, four wings, and greenish skin.* This nightmare beast was part of the Incredible Hulk line produced by GenExcel, a subsidiary of Monsanto and BioFutures Incorporated.

I paused in my reading, stared at the word *BioFutures*, remembering that this was the corporation that had stoked the Center for Cybernetic Neuroscience with cash. Googling *BioFutures*, I located its optimistic website, which featured smiling scientists saving the world: staving off starvation with GM crops, rewiring the brains of stroke victims, enhancing the intelligence of a chimpanzee named Hal, who at this very moment was zooming through space in a satellite called Prometheus 6, its Ku-band transponders pointed toward the darkness of Eastern Europe. On an obscure link I found some whitewashed info on BioFutures' dalliance with Monsanto. According to its own website, it was perfecting a variety of *enhanced* livestock, including Incredible Hulk chickens, which boasted *a spinach gene for high vitamin content, plus a salmon gene for omega-3 oil production and cold tolerance.* The world wanted bigger, healthier chicken breasts, bursting with savory grease. And because chicken wings were all the rage in this land of chain sports bars and alehouses, the more wings per organism the better.

On the HogWild message board, PigSlayer posted another comment, pointing out that it was *no coincidence* that BioFutures had also set up a biotech lab called GenExcel on the outskirts of Yemassee. *In a godforsaken zone between a medical waste dump and a juvenile correctional facility,* she said, *a place that, ironically, was once a sacred hunting ground of the Yemassee Indian tribe.* In PigSlayer's humble opinion, Hogzilla was a GM monster who'd busted out of the GenExcel lab. This explained not only his enormous size but also his half baldness and freaky color, his elusive wings and strangely corrosive saliva. And for all we knew, this genetically engineered beast might be knocking up wild sows all over the county, impregnating them with his demon seed. Our feral-hog problem might soon veer into overdrive as hundreds of little Hogzillas hit puberty and began their own cycles of destruction, humping their way into a twenty-first century that would, quoth PigSlayer, *make The Island of Dr. Moreau look like a petting zoo.*

My heart melted over the *Island of Dr. Moreau* reference. I imagined teaming up with PigSlayer in a postapocalyptic waste-land, some swamp beyond the Thunderdome where monster hogs bounded across the earth like herds of mastodon. In a fox-fur bikini and suede thigh-highs, PigSlayer resembled Raquel Welch in *One Million Years B.C.*

I took a slug of Beam to put some fire into my beer buzz. Heart pounding, I clicked on PigSlayer's profile pic (stock image of an Anza knife) and hit HogWild.com's instant message feature. In the lower left corner of my screen, the little box appeared, pulsing with ominous emptiness, brandishing my dumb username: PorkDork.

—*Hi,* I wrote (a lame beginning). *Thanks for the link on the Little League guy who lost his poor arm.*

My heart beat fast as I eyed the box, rereading my idiotic words with an acute sense of shame.

—*No prob,* she finally replied.

—*You think it's weird that HogZ was frightened by gunshot? Thought that SOB was pretty fearless.*

—*Did cross my mind, esp since ordinary ferals have been known to rip off limbs.*

—*And that stuff on GenExcel—good Gd—I live twenty miles from that shit.*

—I think GenExcel just had that article removed from The V Herald's site, BTW. Trying to keep HogZ hush-hush.

—It's gone?

—Just vanished. You a hunter?

—Amateur. But I've seen the beast. Agree he might be a Frankenhog. Swear the creature has wings, but I think retractable or something, possibly from dorsal cavity.

I felt giddy.

—I'm Romie, BTW.

—Nice to meet you, Romie. Call me Vic.

—Short for Victoria?

—Maybe.

A strange sensation swept over me as I imagined a nerdy adolescent named Victor cowering in his dark bedroom. I could smell his boy cave—the fermented testosterone and greasy Taco Bell wrappers, the stale sadness of his crusty sheets. I could see the gaming posters on his wall, featuring Amazonian babes from the digital world, voluptuous butts and boobs popping out of futuristic body armor. I saw the boy's zitty face grinning with self-congratulatory pleasure as he chose his elusive, gender-ambiguous alias. I sensed the boredom and longing that oozed from his pores, filling his room like a fug.

—Are you from Hampton County? I asked.

—Sorta kinda.

—A hunter, right?

—I dabble in lots of different hobbies.

—Renaissance woman.

I thought of those Renaissance plays in which preadolescent boys played maidens disguised as men. As I recalled, the heroine of *Victor Victoria* was a woman playing a male female impersonator.

—What's your weapon of choice for FHs over 500? I asked.

—We talking poundage or yrs old?

—Ha. How would you go about killing a 500 yr old feral?

—Like if I traveled to the future via wormhole and encountered an escaped lab hog that'd been used in life-extension experiments?

My heart sank. The quirky dorkiness of this hypothetical indicated that I was dealing with a nerdboy.

—Exactly.

I could almost hear the hobbledehoy sniggering. Could see him feeding from a bag of Doritos, smearing his keyboard with grease and crumbs as he launched his snide answer.

—Aw shit, Romie. Got to skedaddle. Nice chatting.

—OK. Later.

What kind of teen boy used words like *skedaddle*? I wondered as I gazed at the box.

Our strange conversation floated there in cyberspace, a small blinking star among endless constellations. I spent the next hour scrolling through it over and over, analyzing my interlocutor's text for telltale signs of age and gender. I popped my sixth beer. I pondered the theory of Judith Butler. Cyberspace was the perfect venue for gender performance, I thought, imagining Victor hobbling though a dystopian cityscape in a pair of broken stripper's heels.

After cornering him in an alley littered with rusty robot parts, I peeled off his flimsy cocktail dress—a scrap of polyester gossamer as thin as a dream—and gazed upon the mystery of his body. I saw a thing of molded plastic, only vaguely flared at the hips, a blank nub between the legs. I saw the incipient swells of nippleless breasts. I saw cheekbones enhanced with swipes of blusher, erotically flaring nostrils, a luxurious '80s hair-band mane. I felt the stirrings of arousal, like an undertow, seething in the silty depths of my unconscious.

. .

I woke up with my pants down, head hanging off the couch, the upside-down view of my laptop screen offering me an unspeakable image from the hinterlands of Internet porn. I did not remember accessing this taboo-busting monstrosity the night before. As I back-scrolled my browsing history, I meandered through at least two hours' worth of freaky shit, none of which looked the slightest bit familiar to me, and some of which had required a credit card number to access.

I had a migraine, as I often did after a night of particularly dense sleep. I wondered if last night's lost time could be classified as a blackout or if it was just old-fashioned drunkenness. I vaguely remembered a night tainted by staticky mirth, some kind of distorted laugh track blaring randomly inside my head. I sat up. Massaged my skull.

"Jebus Chris," I said.

I wriggled my tongue, which felt heavy in my parched mouth.

"Jeshus Chrise," I said again. "Frick."

"Jesus Christ." At last, my tongue found its groove. "Fuck."

I lurched to the cold bathroom, where I splashed my face and vowed, once and for all, to drive to Atlanta to confront Dr. Morrow in person, maybe try to track down Trippy, see how he was holding together.

Instead, I rattled off another fuming e-mail to the Center, a useless gesture that was becoming compulsive. I even dropped Boykin's name, calling him my *ruthless lawyer* and threatening a lawsuit that would *crush your verminous little operation like a cyborgian cockroach.* Again, I received an automated reply, promising to route my inquiry through the proper channels, linking me to the official complaint form, a ten-page PDF with size ten font.

By then it was 10:45. I had to get a move on, splitting skull notwithstanding.

It was Saturday, that day when Hampton's hardworking hunters spent their cold, misty mornings crouched in forests and fields, shaking off the drudgery of office or plant by blowing away woodland creatures. And Noah's Ark Taxidermy was already officially open.

TWELVE

I slipped into the side door of my shop at 11:10, stooping to pick up the crushed beer cans that were scattered over the faux-cobblestone linoleum my father had picked out in 1978. The HVAC system smelled faintly of rats. The fluorescent lights lit up every tear in the vinyl furniture Dad had bought from a liquidated podiatrist's office in 1982. I'd planned to put in oak laminate flooring and purchase a Victorian sofa to go with the marble-topped table on which I displayed my mini dioramas, but, like most of my dreams, this had not come to pass. Lord Tusky the Second stared down at me in disgusted disappointment, his furrowed brow coated in dust. I was about to spruce the old guy up with a feather duster, but there was Scovel Boughknight, tapping on the plate-glass door.

About fifteen years my senior, Scovel ran a U-Haul rental place. Tall, with a gaunt, quixotic face, sallow skin, and a fertile crop of moles that flourished just within the moist depths of his shirt collar, he made the most of these features by seldom cracking a smile. Years ago, when he'd been my family's neighbor, his wife had run off with a Jostens class-ring salesman—the jaunty rep who'd plagued my high school—a man with soap opera hair who sputtered bons mots and spit-cleaned his lustrous shoes. After his wife left, Scovel'd joined my father in his crusade against the underbrush that crept up from the gorge into our yard. Occasionally, while enjoying a glass of tea on our patio, he'd talk solemnly about the enterprising species of vines that'd sprouted in his own yard, how their root systems were unconquerable.

He'd wanted to set up a double-wide on a dry windy hill, far away from town, with woods in view but not close enough to invade his property. And one day he did—moved to the boondocks of Yemassee. My father and I once drove out there to look at a riding mower he was selling. We sat on his back porch, a stark slab of concrete, watching lightning bugs sweep up from the woods.

Now Scovel nodded grimly, stepped into my shop with a wadded-up towel.

"Got a strange specimen for you," he said. "Don't know if you've seen anything like this before."

Scovel set his mysterious bundle on the counter and worked it open with long fingers to reveal, at last, a large bald rat with crinkled skin. He plucked a pen from his shirt pocket and used the instrument to turn the specimen over. Nestled into the creature's back was a large eyeball, human-looking, with a clouded iris and red-veined sclera. The eye, with its long lashes and voluptuous lid, looked vaguely feminine, with a delicate coquettish slant.

"Holy shit," I said, thinking, at first, that the specimen was a mutant, of the same ilk as my one-eyed possum, bald squirrels, and albino frogs, but the humanoid aspects of the eye gave me pause. "Where in hell did you stumble upon this?"

"Down by the river behind my house in Yemassee. Near Jarvis Riddle's campsite. The government finally kicked him out of his last place, and last month he asked me if he could build a wigwam on my property."

"What'd you say?"

"Told him he was welcome to it, so long as he kept the noise and trash level down, and though he did build a lean-to, haven't seen him since that day. Found an empty can of sardines yesterday, though, and a rat like this one lapping up what was left of the oil. Caught this specimen with a one-dollar trap this morning. Nothing to it. Thought I'd bring it over to see what you'd make of it. Wonder if it came from that bionics lab."

"Bionics lab?"

"You know, GenEx or whatnot, which ain't but a few miles from my house. They do animal experiments, from what I hear."

"Right," I said. "Biotech research. Recombinant DNA."

"And look here."

Scovel pointed at the rat's scrunched-up left hind foot, where a bracelet of yellow plastic encircled its ankle. I had to get a magnifying glass to read the cryptic script—3583959T9NIMH6—which prompted a dark chuckle.

"What?" said Scovel.

"Ever heard of the rats of NIMH?"

"Don't reckon I have."

"From a children's book. Probably an inside joke among the GenExcel geneticists. Ever met anybody who worked up there?"

"No. You?"

"Nope. Maybe they commute from someplace more urban—Charleston, Columbia?"

"I don't know."

Scovel's harrowed eyes settled upon my maimed hand, which rested on the counter. "How'd you lose the finger?" Scovel Boughknight did not beat around the bush.

"Double whammy: lawn mower accident combined with a bone infection."

"Could've been worse. If I had to part with a finger, the pinkie would be my pick."

"True. It's the thumb that makes us human."

Scovel nodded grimly.

"So you want to mount this specimen for posterity?" I asked.

"Was thinking along those lines."

"What'd you have in mind?"

"I want him just like I found him: head stuck in a can of sardines, lapping at the oil. You don't have to use real sardine oil. And leave the little tag on his leg."

"That makes sense. What you want here is an ironically unnaturalistic naturalistic diorama: the Frankenrat in its habitat."

"Sounds about right."

When Scovel Boughknight smiled—an uncomfortable twitch that was over in seconds—he seemed twice as grim afterward, as though the effort had drained the last few drops of serotonin that percolated through his nervous system. While filling out his specifications form, he looked extra sallow, the yellow gray of old piano keys and stained teeth.

"I best hit the road." He handed over his form. "Left my shop closed up. Somebody might need them a U-Haul."

"Let me ask you something," I said. "Would you mind if I checked out Jarvis Riddle's lean-to? I've been trying to track him down. Had a few questions for the old woodsman. And I wouldn't mind seeing one of these critters in its natural habitat."

I was after Hogzilla lore but also thinking I might bag me a few GM rats for my Panopticon diorama, the perfect guards for my bald squirrels and albino frogs.

"Be my guest," said Scovel. "If I see you creeping around on my property, I promise I won't shoot."

There it was again, the rare spasm of smile that sucked brightness from the air—which broke the world record for per diem

Scovel Boughknight smiles. When it was gone, Scovel resembled a tortured hero from an Ingmar Bergman film, or maybe Abraham Lincoln in his last photograph, when the war had just ended and he was haunted by a dream of his own funeral, days before Booth shot him in the head.

Scovel wrote me a check and walked out into the winter light. With an air of infinite world-weariness, he climbed into his Toyota truck. He cranked his motor and sat there idling for a minute, staring off at the roof of his old house, where he and his wife had lived for three golden years before she ran off with the Jostens dandy. And then he drove away, leaving me with his monster rat, wondering if I too would find myself alone in my midfifties, my personal misery imploded, condensed, throbbing mysteriously like a pulsar.

• •

I found Jarvis Riddle's campsite with little trouble—a lean-to with a fire wall nestled into a creek bend that ran through Scovel's property, which was set smack-dab between the Combahee River and Gen-Excel, not too far from a medical dump called Prima Pure. The ashes in Jarvis's fire pit were at least a week old. All he'd left behind was an Old Crow bottle, a few sardine tins, a plastic Hello Kitty comb, and a faint whiff of ursine despair. As I unpacked my gear, I wondered if the GM rats had anything to do with his relocation. I wondered where he'd made his new woodland den. I set out two small-mammal cage traps with spring-loaded doors and baited them with rancid turkey bacon. And then I walked an old Indian trail, which, according to Scovel, ran right up to the GenExcel security fence.

When I reached the fence—a ten-foot, we-mean-business electric with warning signs featuring an electrified skull-and-crossbones motif—I couldn't get a glimpse of the GenExcel complex. Scovel claimed it was buffered by about a hundred acres of old-growth forest. So I turned around and took my time on the trail back, pausing to inspect a Skoal tobacco tin that might've been abandoned by Jarvis Riddle.

When I got back to the campsite, I was surprised to see that I'd snared two rats already, one per cage, and that the rodents were indeed of the same bald modified variety that Scovel had brought me the day before. While both had humanesque eyes nestled into their backs (with a trace of downy eyebrow running along the spine), only one of the eyes seemed "alive." The organ gazed unnervingly into space, its white fraught with red veins, its iris the murky gray of a shark's skin. And I could have sworn its lashes were touched with mascara. The other rat's eye looked dead, shrunk down to a scabby knot—hardly recognizable as an eyeball at all.

As cold wind whipped through the trees, I studied the rats. Having given up on finding a way out, each animal sat licking its paws, oblivious, it appeared, to the ocular enhancement wedged into its dorsal physiology.

I toted them to my truck, which was parked in Scovel's driveway. I planned to euthanize them humanely with carbon dioxide to preserve the delicate structural integrity of their oddity. I'd tossed some extra bacon into each cage to make sure they didn't die hungry, and I covered the cages with a tarp so they wouldn't freak on the ride home.

Scovel, who was in his prefab shed sorting screws into empty Metamucil jars, walked out to my truck to check out my specimens.

"Funny," he said. "They're always the exact same size. At least that's what Jarvis Riddle said."

"Jarvis Riddle? When?"

"Gave him a ride to Gators just this morning. He was walking down Strom Thurmond Freeway, heading back from the scrap-metal recycling place, where he'd unloaded a shopping cart of copper wiring."

"Did he mention where he was camping?"

"Nope."

I'd noted Gators on the way in, a cinder-block watering hole with a crude mural of an alligator in a top hat painted on its front wall. I decided to drop in on the way home to see if I might find Jarvis therein, huddled over a glass of lip-loosening spirits and brimming with foresty know-how. Jarvis knew which berries were safe to eat. He could point out the streams that ran foul with pesticide runoff. I bet that plied with enough drink, he'd wax poetic on the ocular rats from GenExcel. And hopefully he'd hold forth on Hogzilla—telling me where the pig ran off his rut rage and bedded down for the night.

• •

I stepped into the dark bar, which smelled of reptiles and cigarette smoke and obscure molds dating back to the Eisenhower administration. The walls, lined with gator pelts, seemed to undulate with slick life. Men hunched like troglodytes in a sacred cave, drinking ceremonial elixirs concocted by a half-alligator shaman so old he could remember that time when the first scaly beasts slid from the waters to creep upon the earth. And sure enough, at a table in the dimmest corner of the bar slumped Jarvis Riddle.

Red bugs crawled in his mossy hair. Mushrooms grew from his skin. His breath smelled of leaf mold and river sludge. It took him a minute to recognize me, and then he cracked an earthy smile.

"Sit down, son," he said, "and buy an old man a drink."

"I'll have two Millers," I said to the lizard proprietor, who leaned over the bar to catch my words in his enormous, gnarled ears.

Beers in hand, I sat down.

"This is Lizzy." Jarvis pointed at a blow-up she-gator that hung over his head, the only feminine presence in the room. "The missing link between humans and reptiles."

A man stumbled by, a bald, fat fellow in a Carhartt onesie who resembled a huge, corroded toddler.

"How's the ticker?" Jarvis asked him.

"Clean as a whistle." The man licked at the foamy head of his beer. "I feel like going jogging."

"This gentleman goes by the name of Ned." Jarvis pointed. "And it's interesting to note that he possesses the heart of a twenty-one-year-old prize athlete."

"After I suffered coronary thrombosis," Ned explained, "doctors cut me open and installed a state-of-the-art prize runner's heart. Boy was twenty-one years of age, healthy as a horse when he crashed his car. Sorry to say that his brain was mashed. But his perfect heart suffered no damage whatsoever. I thank Jesus every day this boy was an organ donor."

"Tell him what you did when you got out of the hospital." Jarvis chuckled.

"Well, after a month of taking it easy and making sure the new heart took, I celebrated by eating a pound of bacon. Went to Winn-Dixie and bought the finest thick-cut pork bacon they had. None of that turkey shit. And know what I did? Fried those suckers up and ate every last one."

A guy turned on his barstool, said his name was Bill, said he had a blood glucose sensor in his pancreas. Stepping from the shadows, a man who introduced himself as Everett piped up about his polyethylene kneecap. A little geezer called Dink described the silicon chip in his once-blind eye and the electrodes wired to his optic nerve. Thereupon it came to light that Jarvis Riddle's entire lower skeleton was bolted together with cannulated surgical screws that gave him hell in humid weather. The lizard shaman working the bar spoke at length about his titanium jawbone, how chaw had rotted half his face away.

Other men had hip replacements and cochlear implants, bones made of hydroxyapatite polymers, polydioxanone blood vessels snaking through their livers and hearts. And I myself was a hybrid creature, my brain rigged up with newfangled thoughts.

I chose not to share this information, however, especially since I'd picked my lot voluntarily, while the men surrounding me had fought battles against tobacco and diabetes, the Southern diet and alcoholism, carcinogenic pollutants and Vietnam-era hand grenades, not to mention the inevitable entropy of the mortal body— *the slow smokeless burning of decay.* Yet we all dragged our cyborgian carcasses across the trashed planet day after day. We all chased various forms of intoxication, hoping to soothe our savage souls. I could see myself some twenty years hence, a gray-haired troll slumped on a barstool, my nose a bulbous mess of clotted capillaries.

"Good brew," said Jarvis as he took the last swig of his watery lager. "But beer tends to produce a bloating effect on me. You think maybe we could switch to something with sharper teeth?"

"Depends," I said. "On what you might be able to tell me about GenExcel."

"So that's what you're after." Jarvis spat out a rasp of laughter and eyed my maimed hand. "Had a funny feeling you had an agenda."

"As do you. Isn't it wonderful how the two happen to coincide? What kind of beverage did you have in mind?"

"Something light and refreshing. How about a gin and tonic?"

I ordered two gin and tonics and decided to start off easy with the subject of genetically modified rats, about which Jarvis had no problem free-associating.

"Plague of frogs, plague of blood, plague of boils," he began grandly, "lice, flies, chiggers, rivers of wormwood. Just your garden-variety plagues, man's stupidity backfiring, hoisted by his own petard."

Jarvis took a slurp of gin. A frown passed over his face.

"Just as God once smote the world with frogs," he said, "the Lord has seen fit to unleash a plague of rats."

Men cut their conversations short, turned upon their stools to listen to Jarvis. Some of them grinned condescendingly, while others hearkened with more somber miens. Jarvis continued, enhancing his tirade with singsongy intonations.

"I have seen them in throngs, gathered at the edges of my campfire, bald as worms, unholy eyes blinking upon their backs." Jarvis paused, took a dramatic glug of drink, and wiped his mouth with a crumpled napkin. "I have awakened to the gaze of one hundred eyes, sightless and staring in pure ignorance. They have devoured my provisions. They have crawled upon my body. Unholy creatures from man's unholy experiments."

Jarvis Riddle went on for five minutes about the sons of God who slept with the daughters of Cain, those creatures who gave men the gift of metalworking and harlotry. At last, he mentioned GenExcel, a subsidiary of BioFutures Incorporated. Called it Satan's laboratory and the crucible of sin. Said multitudes of rats had escaped after God smote the laboratory with fire.

"I smelled burning chemicals," said Jarvis. "Saw toxic smoke billowing over the forest, moving south toward the Piggly Wiggly."

Jarvis polished off his drink and fixed me with a sly grin.

"Would you like another?" I asked.

"Wouldn't mind a whiskey sour," he said.

Like magic, the lizard bartender came creeping through the dim room with our drinks.

"What do you think the rats are for?" I asked.

"Sign of the end-time." Jarvis frowned.

"Practically speaking."

"My best educated guess says product testing: no-tears shampoo, waterproof mascara, that kind of thing."

"Makes sense," I said. We slurped in silence. I waited for Jarvis to finish his drink and then visit the pisser, after which I noticed that he had combed his wild hair into a greasy ducktail. He'd scrubbed filth from his facial creases and washed his grimy hands. Reeking of industrial cherry-scented soap, he sat down.

"How about something healthy this time," he said. "Like a screwdriver. I could use a dose of vitamin C."

"How about you give me the scoop on Hogzilla," I said.

We sat for a few seconds, the meat on the table between us.

"Buy me that drink and we'll see what I can remember."

I bought him the drink. I myself switched back to Miller Lite, for I was starting to feel a bit dizzy.

"In my opinion," said Jarvis. "Hogzilla also hails from the evil labs of GenExcel. They probably put some kind of bird gene in the creature to make a leaner pork—hence the wings on his back, his odd affinity for gliding, his predilection for bearing down from the sky like a wily dragon from days of yore. I can attest from personal experience that his slaver is corrosive, that his breath will literally knock you out. Men ought not dabble with God's work, son, tinkering with the genes and whatnot."

According to Jarvis, the airborne hog once chased him through R.V. Garland's cornfield. After Jarvis tumbled to the ground to avoid the squawking beast, Hogzilla glided over him and treated him to a blast of his breath.

"Passed out immediately," said Jarvis. "And my lungs ached for days after, like I'd spent the day huffing butane. And even weirder, there was a clean strip of red on my left forearm where, I believe, the animal licked me—took the topmost skin right off. Don't know why the pig didn't kill me."

Jarvis paused to crack the knuckles of his right hand, one by one.

"As I recall," he said, "'twas the beast that took your pinkie finger."

"That's right," I said.

"And now you're all fired up with revenge."

I nodded. Jarvis snorted and shook his head.

"Where does the hog sleep?" I whispered.

"Depends," said the old man, "on the state of the moon."

"Meaning?"

Jarvis Riddle jerked his head back and closed his eyes with an affected convulsion, as though receiving a vision from the empyrean.

"When the moon is full"—he opened his eyes—"the animal harkens back toward its diabolical origins."

"GenExcel?"

"Perhaps." Jarvis whistled a haunting, vaguely familiar tune and cracked a yellow grin.

"Would you like another drink?"

"Would love one," he said. "But let me relieve my bladder first."

Jarvis Riddle pulled himself up from his chair, shook the kink from his back, and strode to the restroom. After ten minutes, I went to check on him, but the stalls were empty. A faint odor of leaf mold haunted the air.

• •

By the time I got home, late afternoon light was shining at the bleakest angle upon my rotted roof. Recalling the telepathic rodents from the movie *Willard*, I unloaded my rats, stashing them in my shop garage. And then I went into my shop to check the refrigerator for the two Millers I vaguely remembered secreting there last week.

I heard a contrived cough. I turned from the fridge to see two dark shapes perched on stools behind my counter. I flicked on the overhead lights, expecting a rush of robbers, a bullet blast to the heart, a sinking of vampire teeth into my leathery neck. But the men didn't budge. Dressed in the kind of expensive outdoorsy clothing you find in catalogs catering to would-be country gentlemen, they kept their seats. One was slender and balding, with squinty eyes flickering above a long fox-like nose. The other had the blubbery face of a seal—undefined features, thick dark hair that almost blended with his luxurious eyebrows.

"Roman Futch?" said the plump one.

"And to whom do I owe the honor of this breaking and entering?"

"Don't worry, we've done all the paperwork."

Like smug TV goons, they flashed badges and search warrants.

"FDA," said the thin one, "Department of Bioterrorism and Environmental Protection."

"Let's not beat around the bush," said the plump one. "We're here about the rat in your refrigerator."

"How did you—"

"RFID microchip on its hind leg."

"Duh."

"Where did you find said rat?"

"Not mine. A client's."

"Whose?"

"I signed a confidentiality form."

"Scovel Boughknight." The plump one grinned, revealing thick white donkey teeth.

"We've already read his specification form."

"Then why bother asking?"

"Where was the specimen harvested?" asked the thin guy.

"Near GenExcel, of course," I said, getting it over with, thinking I might save Scovel some hassle, wondering when they were going to ask about the live rats in my garage.

"Can you be more specific, please?"

"Twenty yards and ten millimeters from their security fence, south side."

Both men nodded, the plump one grinning, the thin one frowning.

"How did you lose the finger?" the former asked.

"Lawn mower accident."

"Ouch."

"Mr. Futch," said the thin one, "can you tell us about the experiments you participated in at the Center for Cybernetic Neuroscience in Atlanta?"

"What the hell does that have to do with genetically modified rats?"

"We'll do the questioning here."

"It involved downloading information into my brain. They used some kind of biological computer to implant wet chips and direct nanobots to restructure my neurons. At least that's what the contract said—the confidential contract, I might add. From what I gather, you've already given it a look-see. Otherwise, how would you—"

"Do you have any idea who they're working for?"

"Vague question."

"Ever heard of BioFutures Inc.?"

"Yes, but—"

"Mr. Futch." The skinny one pulled an Oracle9 from his pocket and tapped its screen with long, elegant fingers. "Since the experiments, have you experienced any blackouts or lost time? Have you found yourself waking up in unfamiliar places?"

"No. I mean, I've passed out before. What's this all about?"

"Again, we'll do the questioning here. Where have you suffered blackouts?"

"I've passed out after drinking at home a few times. Once while hunting."

"Can you be more specific? Hunting what?"

"Squirrels."

"Why squirrels?"

"For eating. Well, that and a taxidermy project."

"By which you're referring to the prison."

"So you've been snooping in my workshop."

The agents flashed an official flurry of papers again.

"Mutant squirrels, Mr. Futch. Do you have a license for that?"

"Yes, I do. I mean, not for mutants specifically. SCDNR doesn't make such distinctions."

"Why a prison, Mr. Futch?" asked the thin one.

"Why not a prison? It's just art, a statement on the twenty-first-century predicament, hierarchical surveillance, which is ironic considering our little question-and-answer session, which I hope is drawing to a close."

"Actually, it is, but we're going to have to take your rat."

The thin agent held up a Baggie, cold limp rat encased. He finally rose from his stool.

"It's been surreal," I said, thinking of Kafka as I walked the men to the door.

Of course there was no vehicle outside in the drive, and I imagined a black sedan or some such parked a few blocks away, down where the neighborhood dips into a flood zone. It was dusk by then. As I stood outside my shop, watching the agents disappear down Cypress Street, I felt an ache in my phantom pinkie finger—deep in the spectral bone. I thought about my last blackout, trying to figure out exactly when I'd gone under and how long I'd been out.

I recalled an episode of *In Search of* . . . in which Leonard Nimoy, that game-show host of the occult, probed the mysteries of hypnosis. Remote regions of the brain could be tapped for good or evil designs. With the aid of hypnosis, an old man in Massachusetts had quit smoking after sixty years. Via the same mesmerizing techniques perfected by Nazi scientists, an ordinary Russian plumber had been turned into a robot flunky by the KGB. With the utterance of the word *moonbeam*, delivered via telephone, the plumber would lapse into zombie mode and stop whatever he was doing to report to some odd location in Moscow. Dressed in bathrobe and slippers, mustard stains on his chin, he'd once blown up an American spy's car.

I rubbed the scars on the dome of my skull where the three BC transmitters had once nested. I closed my eyes. Stopping up my ears with my fingers, I listened to the roar inside my head— it sounded like a distant volcano, steadily erupting lava, endless quantities of molten rock drawn from tumultuous depths.

THIRTEEN

Tucked cozily into a tolerable drunk, sitting on my couch, laptop trembling on my knees, I was chatting with PigSlayer, aka "Vic." Despite my darkest suspicions, I kept a flicker of hope alive, envisioning her as a voluptuous Amazon warrior decked out in a bikini of jaguar hide. When I brought up the subject of the FDA and Bio-Futures, she said that these nebulous entities were part of a larger conspiracy involving the corporate takeover of the American food supply. She said that BioFutures, Monsanto, the FDA, and the CIA were probably in cahoots.

—*They want to turn plants and animals into products*, she said.

We shot the shit about Monsanto—terminator seeds and patented animals. Talked about GM rogue crops and cryogenic zoos.

—*Actually*, I found myself bragging, *I'm kind of a postmodern taxidermist, specializing in mutant and postnatural dioramas.*

—*That's pretty sick.*

My heart sank, for Victor had reared his pimply python head again.

—*Do you mean* sick *as in* killer *or sick as in* twisted and gross?

—*Killer, though I use contemporary slang w/ a trace of irony. I teach high school English, so YK, subjected to their infectious jargon.*

I recalled my own high school English teacher, Miss Fripp, a romantic dumpling of a woman who wore Gunne Sax dresses and smelled of dry cat food. Now Victor morphed into Vicky, a plump frump with facial moles and a hundred cats. I could see her lolling upon a frilly bed on a pile of accent pillows, the air hazy with fur. I could see her quivering with excitement as she forged a new identity with PigSlayer, decking her fantastic body in neoprimitive ammo and charging the hog-hunting cyberscene.

—*What you doing teaching English in this godforsaken land?*

PIGSLAYER IS TYPING flashed on the screen and remained there for a suspicious two minutes. "Vic" was probably racking his/ her brains to come up with a convincing answer.

—*Student loan forgiveness. Teach in a backwater for five years, debt gets erased.*

—*Really? Sweet deal.*

—*And housing in these parts is cheap as all get-out.*

—*What parts?*

—*Typical godforsaken low-country swamp hole. Beaufort's not too far away.*

—*How far?*

—*A hop, skip, and a jump, good sir. Tell me more about your taxidermy.*

I told her about my Panopticon diorama, pretentiously paraphrasing Foucault and throwing in some quotes from *Simulacra and Simulation* for good measure. I told her about hunting for squirrels and frogs, about my plan to throw GM rats into the mix, explaining my postmodern critique of naïve naturalism.

—*No shit. That's fascinating. Where do you find such specimens?*

—*Out and about.*

—*Near the GenExcel lab, right?*

—*How did you know?*

—*Duh. No brainer. How close did you get to the lab? I'm just curious.*

—Not that close.

—Did you get past the security fence?

—How would I do that? Pretty serious fence.

—Where there's a will there's a way. You approach from north or south?

—South, toward the Combahee.

—Pretty forested. Could you see much beyond the trees?

—Nothing.

Something about her relentless questioning, despite her casualness, reminded me of my recent interrogation, and my interlocutor morphed into yet another identity. This time I imagined the FDA agent (the tall, thin one) sitting stiffly at a Days Inn desk. But now s/he resembled Tilda Swinton. Dressed in ivory silk pajamas, short hair slicked from the shower, s/he studied my file, latching on to particular quirks and peculiarities. She wore no bra. Small breasts pressed against the silk of her pajama top, her dainty nipples alert like the snouts of minks.

—You still there?

—Yup. Just thinking.

—About what?

—GenExcel.

—No telling what's going on in that lab. I would love to take a look, wouldn't you?

—What do you mean?

—We'll have to talk about that later. Got to scurry off to meet some friends.

As she vanished into cyberspace, I wondered what she meant by that last line, wondered if she wanted to get together or if she meant the usual textual chatter. I spent the rest of the night trolling the websites of regional high schools, searching for English teachers that fit "Vic's" bill, scrolling through a thousand head shots of my state's intrepid educators until my head sank to my desk.

• •

The following morning I woke past eleven. The residue of a few weird dreams lingered. I tasted strange chemicals in my mouth—as though I'd taken a huff of Aqua Net hair spray. And strangest of all, there was mud on my bare feet.

Sitting before a stark cup of black coffee, a vision flashed in my head: I saw an empty kitchen with warped linoleum, a brown-paper package sitting on a Formica counter. The kitchen was familiar yet peculiar: stained floor, smells of pet deodorizer and leaky plumbing accentuated by rain—*uncanny*, as Freud would say—and I shivered. I saw myself reaching to pluck the package from the counter. Saw myself clawing it open. Saw thick bundles of cash spilling out—orange $500 Monopoly bills held together with rubber bands. Husky masculine laughter echoed inside my head (I must have been asleep after all).

And now we will erase the experience by dissolving key synaptic connections in diverse areas of the brain, said a familiar voice, a glib manly voice that blended the growl of a bear with the sultry insinuations of a lounge singer. *Subject 48FRD will not remember transferring the bills from location A to location B, though we're still working out a few kinks.*

And then *poof*—the vision was gone, hopefully a figment of last night's forgotten dreams, served up by my overwrought imagination. But there was mud on my feet. I couldn't ignore the mud, though I *had* gone through sleepwalking phases before: once as a child and once much later, when my mother's dementia took a turn for the worse. The first round had happened when I was nine, right about the time Mom had started suffering from insomnia. I had a vague memory of Mom opening the car door and pulling me out (I'd crawled into the driver's seat and curled up on the Naugahyde).

I remembered standing in pajamas on the freezing driveway, Mom slapping my cheeks with her hands.

"Earth to Romie; Earth to Romie," she'd said, smiling to reassure me, but I could see the worry in her eyes.

Decades later, on one of my visits, Mom sat on the porch, absorbed in an intense round of solitaire. When she looked up at me with a smile of recognition, I knew we'd made a mistake. She was not as bad off as we'd thought. She'd been suffering a temporary setback (she'd recently tried to eat a lightbulb, cutting her mouth), but now she looked like her old self.

"What's up?" she said.

"Hey, Mom. Do you know who I am?"

Her green eyes scanned my face. She frowned. "Walmart?" she said, a triumphant grin erupting.

That night Helen found me outside, making my steady way toward the gorge that swept down toward my childhood home.

"Fuck," she said after she'd roused me. "One more step and you would've fallen in."

. .

I sat in my yard in a lawn chair, pondering the voices I'd been hearing, methodically working through a case of Miller. Eyes fixed on the gibbous moon, I stared as though it might wax full any minute now, washing the planet with magnetic magic, goading the blood of beasts. I could picture Hogzilla, hot pink in moonlight, his eyes lit with bloodlust and pining for home. When he trotted down obscure trails to the locale of his birth, I'd be waiting somewhere in the vicinity, odorless and stealthy as death, a Savage .270 Winchester cradled in my arms.

I felt a prickle in my phantom pinkie finger, a keening of imaginary blood. I felt a pain deep in the bone. As I ached for this lost part of myself, my missing finger became a synecdoche for all lost things in my life—women and mothers, youth and full-scalp coverage, soberness and the bliss of solid sleep. Most of all, I ached for *the future* as a shimmering, distant thing.

The night was quiet. I heard staccato dog barks and wind rattling through the dead gorge. It was not wind, I realized, but some sizable animal, scrambling up through dried wildflowers. I jumped to my feet, ready for whatever rabid thing would charge me—coyote or fox or feral dog. But then a shadowy human head popped up from the dark abyss.

"Romie," a familiar voice hissed. "It's me."

"Who?"

A man scampered up through the weeds, his face shrouded in shadow.

When, at last, my long-lost friend Trippy stepped onto level ground, my heart hammered with a warrior's love. There he stood on the open plain, my fellow trooper, the battlefield strewn with hacked human parts, corpses of horses, bloody bullet slugs. We embraced on the sad field.

"Trippy." I stood back to get a look at him. He wore a dark knitted skullcap pulled down over his ears.

"Shhhh," he whispered, scoping the yard. "Let's go inside."

As he loped toward the porch light, I saw that his left leg dragged from some injury, that his jeans were mud-stained and torn. And I felt a sore place in my heart.

• •

At last, I had Trippy J seated at my kitchen table, a can of Miller in his trembling hand. At Trippy's insistence, we both wore stainless-steel mixing bowls on our heads to scramble the nonstop barrage of wireless signals that, Trippy claimed, pelted our souped-up brains. Trippy's skullcap sat on the table, surrounded by scraps of aluminum foil, the shield he'd concocted in a panic before fleeing his sister's basement.

The dude looked shell-shocked, ghoul-eyed. Ashy-skinned, brittle-haired, dry-lipped, and thin. Bedeviled by voices. Sapped by insomnia.

"What's going on, man?" I said.

"Where to fucking start? First things first, though: the Center for Cybernetic Neuroscience no longer exists."

"What do you mean?"

"Well, I finally hauled my ass over there to see what was up, and the whole place is now Blue Cross Blue Shield."

"An insurance office?"

"Judging by appearances. The building now has this big-ass crucifix on the side, hypocritical signage of the usurious institution in question. I quizzed the robot at the desk. I even snuck around a bit—nothing but straight-up office shit, as far as I could see. The whole interior had been remodeled, though the old Nano Lounge was still there, cubicle moles wolfing down instant noodles in a somnambulistic daze—no test subjects, no labs, no dorms, nothing."

Trippy was troubled but still witty somehow, still rattling off streams of purple verbiage that were wine to my parched ears. We compared notes on blackouts and dreams, hallucinations and synesthetic episodes, uncanny sensations and acute déjà vu. Trippy, too, had suffered bouts of feverish, visionary creativity. He'd spent most of his postexperiment time in his sister's Atlanta basement, sawing at his cello, noodling on a thrift-store Casio, composing experimental pieces that he recorded on an eight-track analog Tascam.

"Started off sober," he said, "sipping home-brewed kombucha, an ancient Chinese elixir concocted from fermented green tea. Then I

upped the ante with bhang tea and goji wine, which had my ass tripping old-school, heat in my flow, game in my tunes. Spent the wee
hours grooving to the likes of Alfred Schnittke, Lindsay Cooper,
and Sun Ra, constellations exploding inside my skull, white dwarves
collapsing into pulsars, black holes evaginating into white-hot uni-
verses, dog. I was on a fucking roll."

"But then the voices."

Trippy sighed. His shoulders sank. The passion leaked from
him.

"That and my stipend scratch was dwindling, even though I had
weekly gigs lined up in this live karaoke band, an outfit that Irvin
hooked me up with."

"You talked to Irvin?"

"Just a few times. Put me in touch with this guy he knows. Solid
work but beyond lame, playing for drunk college brats. Plus, I was
starting to get paranoid about going out."

Trippy described the voices that regularly broke through—a
chorus of shrieking harpies, a flirty feminine giggle, but mostly
this cheesy clinical baritone he presumed was Dr. Morrow, gibbering medical mumbo jumbo, perhaps speaking to some corporate
zombies, maybe reciting notes into a voice recorder.

"Shit got real when I realized I'd left my apartment one night,"
Trippy said. "I could deal with voices, blackouts, lost chunks of time.
But then I woke up covered in dog hair. Now, my sister, a middle-
class prig and a germophile, hates dogs. As you may recall, I myself
am deeply disturbed by the master-slave nuances embedded in the
human-pet power struggle, the sadomasochism and mutual depen-
dence that naturally flowers when a wolf forgoes wildness for the
perks of domesticity. Reminds me too much of the human condition, I guess, but anyway, I digress: in short, I don't dig dogs, dog.
Waking up after what felt like a dream, covered in dog hair, with

Dr. Morrow gibbering away inside my dome made me think they're starting to play around with remote control."

"Remote control?"

"You know, programmable human flunkies. Making us *do* shit."

"Like what, assassinating spies and whatnot?" I forced out a croak of laughter.

"Don't get me wrong," said Trippy. "I don't think there's necessarily any rhyme or reason to these experiments—just the lollygagging medical-industrial complex dicking around with their equipment. But the experiment continues, badly designed as it is."

"Which means?"

"That Dr. Morrow and crew still have access. And they're fucking around with it. Just to see what they can make us do."

"Access?"

"Wireless access. Not as reliable as before, but access for whatever so-called research their punk-ass souls can dream up. Which means that any interested parties could, conceivably, gain access to our commodified minds. And though I'd long suspected that they were checking in on us here and there, I didn't get too freaked out until the dog-hair incident."

"When was that?"

"About a month ago. That's when I started experimenting with signal interruption, shamefully donning the proverbial tinfoil hat. And then, just yesterday, I had what felt like a dream in which I was investigating some kind of underground sewer area. When I discovered fecal matter on my shoes, that was it: I swaddled my skull in tinfoil, hid it discreetly under a hat, and headed straight to the Center."

"To do what?"

"I don't know, check out the scene, see what was up, but my intentions were moot, because, as you know, the whole kit and caboodle has shut down without a trace. So I hopped a Greyhound to Hampton to track down your ass."

"It's about fucking time, man."

"The tinfoil worked pretty well until I was in the bus station. Heard the damn voices again, seeping through the cracks, something that seems to happen in public places, key locales of the grid. What I needed was a stainless-steel bowl, but I still got a shred of dignity. Not gonna go traipsing in public with crockery on my head."

"I hear you," I said, not sharing my own story about the Monopoly money and the mud on my feet, fearing that Trippy's paranoia might be contagious, that I might soon become a member of the fabled tinfoil-hat set myself, a border that I did not wish to cross.

"You talked to Skeeter, perchance?"

"AWOL," said Trippy. "Has been ever since we ditched the Center. Irvin hasn't heard from him either. I'm sure he's laid his hands on some kind of phone by now, and he's got our digits."

"Only on paper, which is easy to misplace."

"True that, but you can find people online—you know that. Even you've got a website. Maybe he just wants to shake the experience. Like getting out of prison—put the bad dream behind and get a fresh start. But still, once inside the prison-industrial complex"—Trippy took a solemn sip of beer—"you're in for life, dog. You got an internalized guard pacing in your brainpan, boots echoing, like, forever."

When I reached for my beer, Trippy eyed my maimed hand, shot me some what-the-fuck bug eyes.

"So, like, I *just noticed* you were one finger shy of a full set."

"Just noticed, huh?"

At last, I unburdened myself. Let it all spill out in drunken convulsive heaves: Helen and her silver-fox paramour; Hogzilla, the monster who'd maimed me for life; Scovel Boughknight and his recombinant rats; Jarvis Riddle's mysterious ravings; and the recent appearance of two FDA agents, who'd invaded my house like TV goons.

Trippy winced and emoted, but he didn't seem surprised by any of it.

"The world is a surreal clusterfuck." He sighed.

And then we hashed it out until well past midnight, soaring into the old high talk again, ascending into the heady altitudes of philosophical abstraction and tumbling into the marshlands of scatological wit. We soon found ourselves talking Art with a capital *A*, plotting an elaborate collaboration, an animatronic Hogzilla diorama with original music composed by Ernest L. Jeffords, aka Trippy J.

"Man," said Trippy, "I can hear the overture now, a slow hog trot thickening into thunderous hooves."

"Killer," I said. "And when that bastard takes flight, some kind of cosmic whoosh, a leap into something interstellar."

"Teleportation to Saturn via Sun Ra." Trippy tapped on the tabletop. "A dash of Harry Partch, all cloud-chamber bowls and harmonic canons. A hint of Miles Davis, *Bitches Brew*."

"And a full range of porcine sounds: grunts, squeals, roars."

"You on it, dog. I'm thinking field recordings," said Trippy. "Combined with eerie electronica, à la Delia Derbyshire. Girl did the theme for *Doctor Who*."

We schemed deep into the night, plotting the collaboration of the century, thinking Trippy could hang at my place while we worked it all out. We switched from beer to liquor and enjoyed a joint, worked our way through three plates of microwave nachos, dished on the literary traditions of epic beast slaying, the epistemology of monsters, the deconstructable polarities of science and sci-fi.

We found ourselves picking at corn-chip crumbs in the wee hours, surrounded by crushed cans—red-eyed, raspy-voiced, clawing at epiphanies that were always an inch out of reach.

"You think we can change the world with art?" Trippy said quietly.

"I don't know," I said, "but at least we can try."

"Always already commodified." Trippy sighed. "And I don't know, maybe art versus action is a false dichotomy, but I still got a mind to track down those motherfuckers and—"

"What? What can we do?"

"I don't know, Romie. Let me sleep on that. My brain will be more functional tomorrow."

My friend stood up. We embraced again, a quick manly pounding of backs, and then I led him back to the old bedroom that Helen and I had once shared, hooked him up with sheets and a blanket, thinking we could get started on our masterpiece the following morning.

Trippy was the closest thing to a brother that I had, both of us mutants with newfangled minds. And as I fell asleep on the couch, I envisioned a golden era of collaboration, evenings spent pursuing our artistic visions, dallying in the kitchen with beers in our fists, our eyes aflame with the feverish speculation of visionaries.

• •

The next morning I made grits and eggs with bacon to vanquish our hangovers, took two Excedrins, opened the blinds, and braved the sun. I tiptoed around in sock feet lest I waken my slumbering friend. My ancient coffeemaker gasped. Thick-cut pork belly crackled cheerily. And dust motes sparkled in the sunny air.

After a few gulps of coffee, I almost felt like singing. Thought I might take Trippy down to the swamp, introduce him to the great pink beast; maybe we could take out the monster together. But when eleven o'clock rolled around, I could no longer ignore the free-fall tug in my gut. I went back to the bedroom and found

Trippy's rumpled nest, proof of a restless night, the window wide open.

I shot him a couple of texts, suspecting that he'd ditched his phone again. But still, I kept at it all day, firing scraps of impotent language, volleying useless signifiers into the void.

• •

I kept texting Trippy over the next week, kept my ears pricked for invading voices, though I refused to cloak my skull in a stainless-steel dome. I distracted myself with HogWild.com and fanatically consulted online lunar charts.

According to the charts, the moon would ripen on Tuesday at 2:36 PM, which meant that Hogzilla would be in homing mode, casting his snout toward GenExcel and rooting his way back toward his origins—unless Jarvis Riddle was full of shit.

My firearm of choice, a Savage .270 Winchester, sat dead center in the gun cabinet, its deep mahogany grain a shade richer than that of its peers. I'd oiled the gun and cleaned its barrel and scope. I'd loaded it up with a four-round stainless magazine. I'd fortified the old Iron Maiden flask I'd bought in a head shop back in high school. It featured the mug of the band's mascot, Eddie—a ripped, futuristic zombie, his skinless muscles pulsing with fury, his rotted face wrenched open with a fuck-you snarl.

FOURTEEN

Tuesday was a milky winter day in the midforties, the sun a wan smear in the sky. My phantom pinkie finger throbbed from the chill. Spectral birds cawed in the forest fog. I'd started my hike from Jarvis Riddle's abandoned campsite. On the lookout for a wallow, I'd meandered down a creek bed and found myself on boggy ground, cold ooze trickling into my leaky left boot. Stooping to inspect it, I caught a flicker of movement in the brush. A gangly human being darted behind a puny clump of fetterbush. I aimed my gun right at him, heard a nervous cough, the brisk click of a handgun safety release. We stood poised, intent on mutual destruction. A woodpecker was going at it somewhere, tapping for a spot of rot.

The hiding man couldn't keep still. His ridiculous hat—a green felt toque with a feather that might be dubbed, by a catalog, *the fairy-tale woodsman's cap*—bobbed above the bracken. When he moved again, I recognized his fox-like mug, his thin, reptilian lips. The FDA agent who'd invaded my home a week ago wore a red plaid shirt, a sweater of bright evergreen. Behind him was his seal-like companion, peering at me through binoculars.

I wondered if they'd been following me or if I'd just happened to stumble upon them out in the bush, where they were chasing recombinant rats and other unholy species from GenExcel. I had the eerie feeling I'd blink and see them melting back into vapor. But they stood their ground, gun hoisted and ready to blast.

When a billow of fog rose from the creek bed, I darted down a side trail and scrambled over a piney hill. At the base of an uprooted tree, I found a hollow to crouch in. I practiced my circular breathing. I swiped creeping things from my neck and shifted my weight from leg to leg to ward off cramps. My ears pricked, catching birdcalls, soughing leaves, and finally, the splash of gauche boots in the creek bed. The buffoons were scampering away from me, north toward Scovel Boughknight's double-wide. I wondered if they'd already questioned the poor man, if they'd break into his house now, looking for me. I wondered if Scovel would find them sitting smugly at the bar in his sad bachelor's kitchenette.

• •

Deep in the swamp, a mile south of GenExcel, I found it, the quintessential hog wallow, a basin of rich red mud swathed in clouds of primeval mist. The clay-and-sand wallow, big enough for a triceratops to roll in, was littered with telltale turds. I felt myself go light with fear—feet and hands numb, a sensation of bodily buoyance—as I picked up something beyond the sense of smell.

I was ominously close to the beast's musky lair, that intimate indentation where the pig lay down to dream his murderous dreams. Not far from the wallow, I found slash pines ringed with mud where the hog had rubbed his mammoth flanks. I saw tusk gashes in tree trunks, vast expanses of rooted ground, huge swathes of forest floor overturned, chunks of chewed wood strewn higgledy-piggledy. I found a scattering of ten-inch hog tracks, cloven hooves pressed deep into the mud. And I thought I could make out a hog trail, tunneling into thicker cover.

Upon closer inspection I discovered, tucked behind a tupelo, an ancient deer stand teetering up in the pine boughs. I couldn't resist the boyish urge to climb the ladder that was nailed to one of the tree trunks.

Pressing the floorboards for signs of rot, I crawled into the stand. A square, rough-plank box with a rectangle of lookout window, the stand overlooked the wallow, offering the perfect shot should Hogzilla come snarling forth in a whirlwind of foam and rage. As a gust of wind blew through the structure, its old wood creaked, and I recalled tree houses from my childhood. Chickadees chittered in the boughs. And then a raw human voice jumped out of the forest texture like a loose thread.

I recognized Chip Watts's nasal whine before I saw Jarvis Riddle staggering across a clearing with a nicotine inhaler in his mouth. Chip was right behind him, toting a .338 Win Mag in a sling, waving a camo hat in one hand while tearing at his hairdo with the other.

"I'm on to your ass, Jarvis. You're leading me on a wild-goose chase 'cause I'm paying you by the hour."

"Takes patience to track a boar, Chip, and how many times I got to tell you to quit yelling?"

"I'm beginning to wonder if Hogzilla's real."

"You are, huh? Then check out these tracks."

Chip squatted to take a look.

"Holy shit. Look at that toe spread. Even a charging five-hundred-pounder ain't gonna leave that kind of impression. Sure you're not scamming me, Jarvis?"

"You think I got the wherewithal to mark up the swamp with fake boar tracks?"

"Maybe. You got lots of time on your hands."

"Smell that hog scat?"

"I don't smell nothing."

"Except your own cologne, insect repellent, and hair spray. How many times did I tell you not to come out here reeking?"

"I put on some cover scent, as you advised."

"That won't do squat if you stink to high heaven of civilization. Better pick your tree."

"What you mean pick my tree?" boomed Chip.

"I mean," rasped Jarvis, "your ass better not hesitate for a millisecond if that bastard comes charging through here. Now, don't say another word. Holy motherfucking Jesus! You smell that?"

"Smell what?"

Straight from hell's latrine, the shit-cheese stench of wild boar hit my nostrils, flushing my brain with corticotropin and jump-starting my rickety heart. Before I could blink, the creature itself materialized: a ton of grunting muscle, jaws popping the biggest cutters in the history of hogdom. The razorback spit enough foam to fill an industrial sink. And there they were: the famed wings, stunted and bald, smooth like the patagia of a bat, and flapping in a useless fit that sure as hell wasn't flight. In a flash, the wings vanished—tucked, I gathered, into some nifty dorsal niche. Two seconds later, the hog was bounding full throttle toward Jarvis and Chip.

I aimed my piece and fired a full clip. Though my bullets did little more than knock some dried mud off Hogzilla's hide, the pig roared and veered leftward into brush.

"What the hell?" shouted Chip, scanning the treetops for hidden assassins.

"Up here!" I yelled.

As Jarvis Riddle tugged him toward the deer stand, Chip dropped his rifle. With a dopey look on his face, he stooped to fetch his Win Mag.

"Fuck the rifle," yelled Jarvis, "climb up this goddamn ladder."

The old forest bum was already halfway up when the sound of pounding hooves once again disturbed the woodland peace. Meanwhile, Chip clawed at a lower ladder rung, smiling his dreamy fool's smile.

"Climb, you idiot!" hissed Jarvis.

Chip mounted the first few rungs. He'd made it a third of the way up when Hogzilla rammed into the tree trunk on which the ladder was nailed, bashing it with his tusks and upsetting Chip's foothold. My old friend dangled by his hands for a few ominous seconds before stepping back onto the ladder. At last, a shudder of realization seized him, and he scooted on up with every ounce of energy his old athlete's body had left in it.

• •

"Let's draw straws to see who gets eaten," I said, and Jarvis laughed—a rich croupous chortle—and then spat a dark loogie out into the abyss below. Jarvis took another suck of his nicotine inhaler, then slipped the device back into the pocket of his grubby raincoat, a coat of many colors—sun-faded in spots, stained in others, tinted with bold streaks of its original royal blue.

We'd been treed for some twenty hours by Hogzilla, who at that very moment was tusk-battering one of the pine trunks supporting our deer stand and foaming like a broken washing machine, snorting and rooting and making a general display of his fierceness. At first, every jolt of the thousand-pound feral striking one of the four trees that upheld our little box made us double over in fright. By now, we'd almost gotten used to Hogzilla's ruckus—but not to his stench, which tainted every molecule of the air we breathed.

Between the three of us, we had two half-empty flasks, three canteens boasting various quantities of water, and a sprinkling of odd pharmaceuticals that Jarvis had scored from a medical-park dumpster. Although I possessed a half-eaten bag of SunChips in my rucksack, I kept this knowledge to myself.

Neither my Oracle3 nor Chip's Oracle6 would pick up a signal, so we turned off our phones to save our batteries. We'd gotten little sleep the night before, enduring a cold, damp stretch of darkness complicated by waste-disposal dilemmas and Jarvis's apocalyptic muttering. Deep in the night I thought I heard a few bleeps in my head: *Looks like he's off-grid*, said a mellifluous manly voice. *Ah, there's a flash. Damn, we're losing it.* The voice lapsed into a purr of static and faded away.

I remembered what Trippy had said about heading out to the boondocks to escape the Center's wireless web, which probably depended on an intricate combo of satellites and cell-phone towers. And we were definitely in the boondocks, way out, with nobody in earshot and a fiendish hog rampaging below.

We hoped he'd lose interest and meander off to devour some hapless rodent or chase a whiff of sow. But no: he'd been up before dawn, bashing and ramming, slowly chipping away at the trunks of the four fat pines that supported the tenuous cube of space we inhabited. If he kept this up for a few days, the monster might just fell us, but we'd probably die of dehydration before then anyway.

At least day two in the stand was warmer. At least the fog had cleared, though I still couldn't scope a decent shot at Hogzilla. Chip and I had removed our jackets and Jarvis had shed his swaddling of rags. Late that morning, from an inner compartment of his raincoat, the old man had pulled forth three pills called Valcar, a drug he said was designed to regulate bile acid metabolism but that also functioned as a stimulant. Like fools, Chip and I had gobbled the capsules. Now it was noon and my hands were trembling. Chip's eyes looked bugged. But Jarvis Riddle was his usual self.

Grinning, Jarvis held out three pieces of pine straw. I took one, though Chip refused to play.

"Even if we do decide who gets eaten," I said, "we'd have to eat our man raw."

"I always wondered why a group of starving people would opt to sacrifice the whole life of a person," said Jarvis, "rather than drawing lots and eating parts: a finger, for example." Jarvis blushed as he eyed my maimed hand.

"That does seem more reasonable," I said, "though the victims might get infected; die slow, agonizing deaths from gangrene or"— I held up my hand and grinned—"a bone infection."

"If they had access to fire, they could cauterize the wounds," said Jarvis.

"And cook the meat," I said. "The Long Pig."

"Raw meat won't hurt you so long as it's fresh," said Jarvis. "I ate a raw squirrel one time."

"What about parasites?" I said.

"It was winter," said Jarvis. "So the squirrel didn't have the wolves."

Jarvis and I were inclined to philosophical speculation, which, we'd discovered within three hours of being treed, annoyed the hell out of Chip Watts. We liked *to take upon us the mystery of things, as if we were God's spies*, while Chip, who possessed the mind of a chimpanzee, became exhausted by our aimless chatter. He'd scoot to a corner of the stand, cross his arms, and pretend to take a nap. But after popping that Valcar, he could hardly sleep. He was amped up, jogging his left leg. He'd already torn his molded hairdo into several crisp wisps.

Chip wondered aloud how it just so happened we'd ended up in the same neck of the woods. He accused Jarvis of playing double agent—taking money from both sides. He glanced bitterly at my gun, sorely lamenting the fact that his piece was rusting in the hog wallow below.

"I never took a dime from Romie," said Jarvis, "though I'll admit he bought me a few drinks the other day. But I would like to remind you, Chip, that ours was a verbal agreement; I never signed a statement of exclusivity, did I?"

"That's right," I said. "Plus, I've been tailing Hogzilla for months. You might even call this a quest."

"'Twas the beast that took his pinkie finger," said Jarvis with a solemn frown. "So Romie's got a score to settle."

"Thought a lawn mower blade nipped you." Chip glared at me.

"That's one narrative," I said. "The other one involves my destiny as a dragon slayer of sorts."

"Whatever," mumbled Chip. "You pay good money, you expect good product. That's what makes America tick. I'm a businessman. I work hard for my money. I put my money where my mouth is. And this scam artist here—"

"Our noble country is run by scam artists," said Jarvis.

"Agreed," I said.

"You hate America," Chip said. "All both of you do. Y'all're just bitter because you haven't tasted success."

"You really think you're gonna keep unloading those ATVs indefinitely?" I said. "Yes, you've had a good spell, but there's only so many quads the Baptist Church can buy. What's gonna happen after you milk that cow?"

This unfortunate foray into ad hominem attack was interrupted by a long, agonized human shriek. We'd been so wrapped up in our bickering that we'd failed to notice a lull between Hogzilla's assaults upon the pine trunks. We dashed to the window just in time to catch the giant razorback ramming his tusks into the chest of some unfortunate human.

As the victim's head whiplashed, he gaped in a grimace of shock.

Holy shit! It was the tall FDA agent—he of the fox face and slender build. When the agent went limp, the hog wedged his ragdoll body into the crook of a pine bole, withdrew his cutters from the chest area, and gored his victim's belly with his left tusk. Then Hogzilla fed upon the agent's bright entrails, slurping them up like spaghetti with big squishy smacks.

We sat in silent shock, bearing witness to this surreal carnage. Blood thrummed behind my ears. I heard the happy twittering of indifferent squirrels and the drone of a distant jet.

At last, Jarvis let seep a slow whistle of surprise.

"*What rough beast,*" he whispered, "*its hour come round at last?*"

"Jesus!" Chip raked his hand through his hairdo. "What an inhuman cannibal."

"That poor bastard's a spook," said Jarvis. "Should've known he'd be tailing me."

"Wait," I said. "You know him?"

"*Knew* him," corrected Jarvis. "Just barely. Came into Gators a few times with his sidekick, asking for info on the freakish fauna in our area. Told him about the rats, but didn't let one word slip on the subject of Hogzilla—I swear, Chip. Claimed he was from Monsanto, product development."

"You don't think he was?"

"How the hell would I know? I called them Mutt and Jeff. Jeff ought not be too far behind, unless he's dead already. Maybe we could get his attention before Hogzilla enjoys his second course."

Come to think of it, they probably were with Monsanto *and* BioFutures *and* the FDA. They probably had trouble understanding where, exactly, their loyalties lay and what, exactly, the grand narrative was and who, exactly, was running the show. Tugged willy-nilly, they went wherever that elusive thing called *power* pulled them, hopping on jets and sitting down in restaurants and sleeping in disinfected hotel sheets, going through these shenanigans again and again, until, at last, they found themselves inside the hot, burbling belly of a monstrous hog.

• •

We spent the rest of the afternoon solemnly scoping the area, taking turns with Chip's binoculars, looking for signs of Jeff. Meanwhile, Hogzilla pursued his mysterious agenda, patrolling the area, his huge hindquarters swaying as he skirted the diameter of his wallow. His jowls were dotted with jellied blood. Every now and then, he'd trot over to Mutt's corpse and take a nibble. Every now and then, he'd gaze up at the deer stand with his strange, bulbous eyes and emit a sphincter-tightening squeal.

At dusk, when the waning gibbous moon popped out, we could see the hog trails etched into the brambles, hieroglyphs written by Hogzilla's body. Jarvis and I pulled out our flasks, took tiny sips to keep our stomachs from consuming their own linings.

"Got some Xanadu if anybody's interested," said Jarvis.

"What the hell's Xanadu?" asked Chip.

"Designed to help people deal with obsessive-compulsive thanotophobia, if I'm not mistaken."

"Speak English," said Chip.

"Fear of death," I said.

"It's a pretty good ride if you don't have the phobia," said Jarvis.

"But isn't everybody thanotophobic to some degree?" I asked.

"I reckon they would be," said Jarvis. "But I'm talking about a debilitating disorder, where you can't leave your bed."

"What about occasional pangs of pure terror as a thousand-pound hog stalks the grounds below the ramshackle tree house you've taken refuge in?" I joked.

Jarvis chuckled. "Ought to put them to rest."

"Quit with the jibber-jabber," said Chip. "I'll try one."

We took the pills—Jarvis a whole tablet, Chip and I a half each.

Soon, the night's black flower blossomed, dripping its Stygian nectar. As wind purled through the dead trees, we sank deeper into our jackets—each man tucked into a corner of the tree house. An owl offered an ominous hoot. We listened to the crunch of hooves in leaves, the squelch of hooves in mud, the *pat, pat, pat* of hooves on solid ground. We heard the creature snort. Heard the creature belch. Heard him sharpening his cutters against various trees.

"*So I will come upon them like a lion,*" whispered Jarvis. "*Like a leopard I will lurk by the path.*"

And then it hit me. Like dragons of yore, Hogzilla had to have a weak spot, a tender zone that bullets and arrowheads, knives and spears, could pierce: the soft zone between belly and groin perhaps, or maybe his pungent armpit, or the clammy nook beneath his freakish wings.

I took stock of my ammo again: one and a half magazines, which equaled six shots.

I closed my eyes, and my father's harrowed face materialized in the black void. *Always expect the worst*, he said, *and then you might be pleasantly surprised.*

Chip Watts emitted an infantile whimper and curled into the fetal pose.

Jarvis Riddle popped another pill.

"*Like a lion I will devour them,*" he muttered. "*A wild animal will tear them apart.*"

And hellish Hogzilla stalked the ground below us, rustling through the dry winter brush, grunting and smacking his blood-crusted lips.

FIFTEEN

Sometime close to morning I heard a crackling noise. Sensing a presence near me, I sat up and lifted my rifle. Saw a black silhouette crouched over my knapsack.

"Jarvis?" I said.

"What?" Jarvis groaned from his corner.

"Chip?" I shone a flashlight on his face. "Back off, you sneaky motherfucker. And drop whatever you've got in your hands."

Chip dropped the bag of SunChips he'd pilfered.

"Romie's stockpiling food," he complained.

"I'd hardly call a half bag of chips a stockpile," I said. "Now get back to your corner and let's forget about this embarrassing episode."

I sat in my corner, munching the most exquisite chips I'd ever tasted, waiting for the sun to pop up over the tree line.

"You gonna eat the whole bag?" said Chip, a plaintive twang in his voice.

"Mind your own business," I said.

I figured I'd better devour the whole bag, stave off the possibility of an assault or murder while fortifying my stomach for the day to come. The SunChips brought on a rabid thirst, a deep-marrow craving that could not be quenched by a few slugs from my canteen, which had less than a quarter of liquid left in it. Even though Chip and Jarvis each had his own water supply (and who knows what else Jarvis had stashed in his magical raincoat), nothing would hold them back once dehydration turned them into liquid-obsessed zombies.

But I was the one who possessed the firearm, the phallic power, the floating signifier par excellence. If I needed to, I could have Jarvis Riddle on his back, rifle snout pressed into the curdy flab of his belly, his pharmaceutical raincoat at my disposal. I could have Chip Watts writhing like a walrus, begging for mercy.

I sat holding my gun as the sun came up. The stark morning light cast the harrowed faces of my companions into high relief. We all had hangovers from the Xanadu—throbbing headaches, mouths full of foul paste, a general feeling that all glands and organs were underjuiced, not working at full capacity, pumping from the deeper reserves.

Jarvis popped another pill upon wakening. Smiling sheepishly, he removed a crumpled Mountain Dew bottle from his raincoat and pissed into it. He screwed the top back on and placed the warm sample back into its special pocket.

"What the fuck?" said Chip.

"Better safe than sorry," said Jarvis. "In Nam we made use of our own liquids to avoid dehydration, and I suggest you get over any squeamishness you might have about such survival techniques."

"Thought the salt in urine made you even more dehydrated," I said.

"Saved my life once," said Jarvis. "I was in the jungle when God spoke to me, said, *Drink thine own nectar, Jarvis, and thou shalt live.* So I pissed into a tin cup, drank the golden liquid, and here I sit before you."

"I'd die first." Chip spat over the window ledge and gave the landscape below a sweep with his binoculars.

"What's the behemoth up to?" asked Jarvis.

"Can't see him," said Chip. "But I hear him over yonder, rustling in the brush."

Within five minutes Hogzilla came trotting from the forest with a sapling in his mouth. Back and forth the great beast sauntered, toting branches and small shrubs, which he deposited in a heap beyond his wallow.

"What the hell's he doing?" said Chip.

"Dear God," said Jarvis. "I do believe he's making a clearing. What on earth for?"

"Maybe he needs another wallow," I offered.

"Why would he need another wallow when he's got a perfectly good one right down there?"

"Maybe that one's too shitty—literally."

"Boars fancy a nasty wallow," said Jarvis. "Like to smear themselves with their own offal."

"Why don't you try shooting him again, Romie?" said Chip.

"Waiting for the right shot," I said.

"How many shells you got left?" Chip's voice rose an octave as he eyed my gun.

"Enough to do the job."

"Which means?"

"Hey, anybody need a little pick-me-up?" Jarvis pulled a dirty, folded envelope from his coat.

"Of what variety?" I inquired.

"Zip-a-Dee-Doo-Dah," he said. "It cures the old malaise: the alcoholic hangover, the quiet despair of January drizzle, the sick mental residue left after hours of Internet shopping."

Chip was already holding out his hand. And, what the hell, I too found myself gobbling another mysterious pill. This one was lilac, the color of summer dusks, with a Zorroesque Z cryptically etched

onto its surface. Right after I swallowed it, sunlight gushed into
the tree house to warm our jaded bones. We all perked up. Forgot
about the mangled corpse in the wallow below. Forgot about the
dystopian hog up to no good in the gloom of the forest. Forgot
about the acidic seethings of our stomachs, our dwindling water
supply, even the buzzards that now circled overhead.

Jarvis and I pulled out our flasks, offered Chip an occasional
warming swig (I had Beam, Jarvis Old Crow). As we finished the
last of our booze, we discussed various subjects close to our hearts:
ATV racing, taxidermic dioramas, the glories of the Rapture.

"When Jesus returns," said Jarvis, "he'll arrive in a crystal-
line spaceship so vast it'll drench seven cities with healing light.
One by one, the chosen will be beamed up and whisked off to
paradise—a green planet with shining skyscrapers and endless
gardens."

Upon finishing his vision, Jarvis Riddle fell into a nap, an infantile smile upon his face.

"Romie," Chip whispered, turning from the window. "Motherfucker's still as a statue. Check it out."

I peered down at the beast, saw him poised in the clearing, glar-
ing at the sun.

In a flurry, I took two shots, aiming at the darkish dorsal section in which his wings were presumably encased. The first shot
bounced off Hogzilla's leathern rump. Though the second one
popped his hide two inches from my intended target and prompted a deafening squawk, it didn't seem to faze the animal much.
Hogzilla jumped and licked his left flank. Then he went right back
to the business of hauling brush.

"Why don't you let me give it a try?" Chip Watts reached for
my gun.

"That's okay," I said.

Chip scowled, shook his head, and went to sulk in his corner. Crossing his arms defensively, he curled up for an afternoon nap.

• •

It was getting on toward four o'clock. Buzzards flitted back and forth from the trees to the ground, pecking at Hogzilla's leftovers, nibbling foul tidbits of Mutt. The day was warm enough to hatch a single mosquito, which kept an orbit around Chip Watts's hypertensive head, dipping in to suck his thick, sluggish blood every time my old friend let down his guard. Chip would start with a glint of fury in his eyes. He'd swat at air, slap his own face, punch the tree house's rain-warped wall. Jarvis, who took small grimacing sips from his urine bottle, was lost in a reverie. Racked with thirst, he could not stop talking about various soft drinks.

"I'd give my left testicle for a Mountain Dew," he said. "What a poetic name for a soda."

"Shut the fuck up," growled Chip.

Chip looked like he was about to excrete his own bloodshot eyes. And I wasn't feeling so hot myself. The back of my throat was swollen from thirst and my stomach had long since resorted to cannibalizing its own tissues.

"Dr. Pepper," said Jarvis. "On ice. In a paper cup so wet it's half-dissolved."

"No more bullshit," said Chip.

"Pepsi-Cola," said Jarvis. "Black cherry Kool-Aid. Sprite."

"I mean it."

"Or how 'bout a goddamn slushie? Half-melted, guzzled while chilling under the cool cascade of a waterfall. Water, water everywhere. A thousand drops to drink."

As Jarvis licked his parched lips for emphasis, Chip leapt from his corner and backhanded the old man across his grizzled jaw. Groaning, Jarvis wormed away from Chip. Cowering in a rickety area of the deer stand where the wood was starting to rot, he held his hurt jaw and sniveled.

I pointed my gun at Chip. "Touch him again, and I'll blow your head off," I said.

"You wouldn't waste your precious last magazine."

"Got two left."

"Bullshit."

"And I won't hesitate to shoot you in the crotch if you mess with him again."

"Speaking of my crotch," said Chip, "there's something I've been meaning to share with you, I mean, for the sake of our friendship."

"What?" I said.

"Oh, nothing. Just that I fucked your ex-wife last October."

Chip Watts grinned like a jackal and licked his chops.

This doozy knocked the wind out of me. But when I saw Chip turn away from me and rub his nose, I knew he was bluffing.

"A lie," I said, lifting my firearm to aim at Chip's belly.

"Didn't know what the fuss was about." Chip sneered. "Thought I'd have a crack at it myself. Still don't know why you've made such a brouhaha over Helen all these years."

"She wouldn't touch you with a ten-foot pole."

"Perhaps not, but I did touch her with my ten-inch pole."

Chip sniggered, his throat rich with pasty mucus. His overripe eyes quivered in his skull like the orbs of a decrepit Chihuahua. He was lying. He had to be. Not only about his dalliance with Helen but also about his penis size. He was, after all, an unctuous reptile of an ATV salesman who displayed his high school football trophies in a fake mahogany case in his living room. Lying was part of his business.

And besides, hadn't Helen expressed contempt for Chip's womanizing on a number of occasions? Hadn't she tittered over his ridiculous hairdo? Hadn't she opined that his cologne smelled like pesticides? That the hair on his chest reminded her of orangutan fur? Was my lady protesting too much? Did she nurse a secret attraction to this troglodyte? And where, exactly, had she seen his chest hair? Spilling coyly from an unbuttoned poly-blend dress shirt? Or had she beheld it in its full glory, a crispy nimbus encasing his naked, sunburned torso, vestigial high school muscles flexing beneath layers of middle-aged flab?

I recalled an article I'd read, which asserted that otherwise reasonable women, upon ovulating, might find themselves suddenly attracted to what Richard Dawkins called *he-men*. Impelled by a genetic compulsion to procreate with a swaggering fool, such a woman might, at her moment of maximum fertility, step out on her kind, sensitive boyfriend or husband, who could be counted on to dote idiotically on any bastard children produced by sexcapades with chest-pounding Neanderthals.

A win-win situation, from a Darwinist perspective.

"I like my women young." Chip made a gross lusty gurgling sound, which was punctuated by a stray whimper of pain from Jarvis. "And hairless, if you get my drift."

It was true that Helen had always expressed contempt for the infantile pudenda of pornified women, the aesthetic of which she described as *pedophiliac* and *pitiful like a plucked chicken*. It was true that she, back when I enjoyed the fruits of her body, kept genital grooming to a minimum—trimming her nether wisps into a neat triangle, which she'd edge with brisk swipes of her plastic Daisy razor. I could see her, soaping up in the shower, chatting with me as I brushed my teeth or, on special days, slipped into the mildewy stall with her.

I imagined, however, that many women of a certain age declined to shave their snatches. This logical assumption was not beyond even Chip's compromised powers of reason, I figured.

But then, as Jarvis Riddle fell into a wheezy doze, Chip described the secret moles on Helen's body. The moist moles that squatted like small brown toads upon her upper back. The twin blemishes that orbited her navel like dark moons. The plump, brown protuberance that nestled within the sweet, sweaty nook of her cleavage. And most sickening of all, he spoke of her birthmark, which resembled a dusky banana slice, and which marked the creamy flesh of her inner thigh. Perhaps he'd seen her in swimwear, innocently napping in the sun as he ogled every square inch of her exposed body.

"Her nipples are too large," said Chip.

"Too large for what?" I gripped the handle of my rifle.

"For my tastes."

When he yawned like a libertine up to his eyeballs in poontang, I released my safety. And who knows, I may have blasted his head off, reveled in the sight of his limited brain matter spurting modestly as his skull shattered. But right at that moment, the unmistakable sound of a rampaging beast filled the afternoon hush.

It was Hogzilla, bounding toward our tree like a fucking T. rex, bounding with the glint of hell in his eyes, a filthy beard of foam dangling from his jaws. His tusks gleamed with gore in the anemic winter light. He spread his wings.

Right before my naked eyes was a thousand-pound pig gliding three feet above the ground on two flimsy pieces of membrane. But what was even scarier, I realized, was that this monster had built himself a runway—I could see that now as I observed the area he'd spent the day clearing—which meant the fucker could reason, which meant he was using his smarts to plot our deaths. Every hair on my body stood stiff as a needle. In silence, we watched Hogzilla bob bee-style above the ground, strike it with his belly, and finally tumble into a mass of blackberry scrub.

"*Before me was another beast,*" Jarvis murmured. "*And on its back it had four wings like those of a bird.*"

The deer stand creaked. Jarvis whimpered and rubbed his chin. Chip settled back into his corner and soberly eyed my gun.

• •

Just after dusk, a cold front swept in from the north. Once again, Jarvis pulled forth a bottle of rattling pills, this time from a pocket so obscure that he had to shed his coat to retrieve it. He called it Moly, said it tamed the raging beast that dwelled within contemporary man, quieting the riotous caveman heart that thumped upon hearing the crack of a twig.

"But it won't knock you out," he said, looking at me and ignoring Chip. "That's the beauty of it."

The capsule—small, black—resembled an insect's egg.

I took my medicine dry, saving my last ounce of water for later. As I listened to Chip grunt in his sleep, I imagined him atop Helen, hairy buttocks dimpling as he plied her with his sluggish sperm. I saw a half-dozen swimmers making their slow way toward her uterus, the leader of the bunch burrowing sleepily into one of her last viable eggs.

A miracle.

Behold: the zygote sprung of aged spunk. Behold: the cells dividing as Chip's cretinous genetics intertwined with Helen's lovely code. Behold: an amphibious jock cutting a caper in her belly. Once again, I imagined Chip's head exploding with a blast of my Savage .270. Once again, I toyed with the idea of forcing him to jump from the safety of the tree house into Hogzilla's wallow. Chip seemed to have no idea of his potential fatherhood, and I wondered if Helen would enlighten him as to the origins of her infant. Or would she let that old cuckold Boykin dote upon her nursling in ignorant tenderness?

A frigid blast of wind shook the tree house. My mind would not quiet down. It raced on, haunted by images of Chip and Helen. And I could not still my trembling hands.

SIXTEEN

I woke to sounds of scuffling and the sick sensation of an empty rifle sling. The mystery was solved when my firearm exploded in the cold night, sending an owl squawking into the sky. It didn't take a genius to figure out that Chip had snatched my gun and Jarvis was trying to wrest it from him.

Now I could see them in the pink light—two worn-out men rolling over each other like lovers, wrestling for the power of a Savage Winchester. Chip had it, then Jarvis. Jarvis dropped it; Chip grabbed it. Jarvis snatched the muzzle; Chip palmed the butt. Chip kicked poor Jarvis and the gun flew south and slid across the floor, right toward the entryway, where it teetered for a nanosecond before Chip secured it with his hairy monkey hand.

He threw his head back and barked like an alpha baboon.

There he stood, smiling his acid-reflux smile, in firm possession of the Lacanian phallus, lording it over Jarvis, who squirmed like a maggot at his feet.

"First of all," said Chip, "I want you both to hand over your canteens and flasks. Place all belongings on the floor in front of you."

"Go ahead and shoot me," said Jarvis.

"I mean it," said Chip.

"Consider it euthanasia," said Jarvis.

"Speak English," said Chip. "Or I'll feed you to Hogzilla."

Chip kicked Jarvis in his soft flank. After the old man stopped howling, I heard Hogzilla grunting below. A ripe waft of hog musk rose from the creature and enveloped us in its nauseating miasma.

"You're an idiot, Chip," I said.

Chip held the gun, butt down, over my head. He raised the weapon a notch higher. His face hardened into a savage sneer, but just when he was about to bash my skull in, the rotted wood beneath his feet gave. Chip dropped my gun as he fell waist-deep into the abyss, catching himself by his arms so that his lower body dangled beneath the deer stand. I grabbed my gun and stepped back.

Chip blinked and pouted. Finally, he screamed, straining every muscle in his arms to keep from falling through. Every time he squirmed, the deer stand creaked.

"Get me out of this fix, goddamn it!" he roared.

"Let the fucker hang." Jarvis grinned.

"You got to be still," I told Chip, "or you're gonna fall through and bring the whole stand down with you."

Dangling a loogie the ominous color of a smoked oyster, Jarvis crouched over Chip. He slurped it back into his ancient mouth and lowered it again. Finally, the old man spat this dark fruit right into Chip's left eye. Chip screamed as though he'd been scalded. A flock of juncos took flight from a live oak, filling the air with whistles. The boiling red sun peeked furiously over the tree line.

Chip's bloodshot eyes oozed and his purple face was splotched white, but he couldn't do shit. His neck tendons bulged. When the sound of a galloping hog thundered in the dawn, he started blubbering.

"You grab one arm; I'll grab the other," I yelled at Jarvis.

"Like fuck I will," said Jarvis. "That bastard tried to kill me."

"Come on, Jarvis," I said, trying to muster a stern look. "He'll bring down the whole stand if we don't pull him back in. You ready to die?"

"I'm not afraid of death." Jarvis laughed. "I have a prescription for that."

I took note of Hogzilla, hurtling toward us with the cool brutal look of a bestial robot. Out popped his wings and the monster was airborne—nine feet, twelve feet, eighteen feet above the ground, almost high enough to graze Chip's foot with his tusk before his crazy-ass descent into brushwood. Roaring like a laryngitic bear, Chip kicked his legs. A loose board tumbled to the ground.

Now Hogzilla was back on his runway, his jog giving way to a full-throttle gallop, and again he was airborne, higher than last time, his tusks pointed right at the puffy target of Chip's beer belly.

Clear as truth, I saw the vulnerable spot beneath the hog's left wing, where the flesh was tender, protected from cold, heat, rain, humidity, sun, snow, frost, and mosquitoes. I took myself through the Instant Calming Sequence, swept a wave of relaxation through my body, and stood breathing deep breaths of hog-scented air. I emptied my mind and focused on that square inch of baby flesh beneath Hogzilla's left wing. My firearm melded with my body as I took the archetypal stance of the warrior. I felt my last bullet surging with life, bursting with energy like a ripening berry. Electricity gushed from my heart chakra, sizzled along the meridians of my right arm, and poured into my trigger finger. I was one with the gun and the bullet and the pulling of the trigger. "Hai!" I shouted at the moment of release, watching the bright red billowing of my visible consciousness.

And then I slumped, happy and sad in my emptiness, awaiting the outcome of this action.

· ·

When my bullet hit Hogzilla in the clammy spot beneath his left wing, wedging itself into the callous tissues of his heart, the stricken hog unleashed a pterodactyl shriek, flapped his wings, and, just before his tusks would've plunged into Chip Watts, veered leftward, glided over a briar patch, and tumbled into a copse of baby pines. The monster flailed and squalled and flattened a dozen saplings.

Meanwhile, Chip Watts squirmed and cussed. He kicked and writhed until several more rotted boards came loose, and the ATV salesman fell like Satan from hubristic heights, roaring as the bloody knob of his left femur protruded from his knee like a newborn baby's head.

Whereas Jarvis scurried down the ladder before Hogzilla had ceased to twitch, muttering scraps of biblical prophecy as he went, I did not descend until I was sure the beast lay still. And even then I feared the crafty animal might be faking it, that just when I ventured near, he'd hop to his feet with a lusty snort and finish me off.

A hush fell upon the forest as I approached the beast. There lay the mountainous corpse, darkening the earth before it with its vast shadow. I stepped into this shade. Squatting, I held a pocket mirror to the animal's blood-crusted mouth. No mist collected upon its surface.

Flies were already frolicking upon Hogzilla's filth-smeared hide. The bored buzzards that had been languidly picking last bits from the FDA agent's cadaver perked up and flapped over to inspect the fallen monster.

There I hunkered, carcass of a mythic beast lolling before me, my ex-wife's one-time lover groaning and cussing up a storm five yards over, my souped-up head addled from sleep deprivation, dehydration, and hunger. I had no idea what to do next.

"See if you can pick up a cell signal twenty yards west or so," said Jarvis, pricking me out of my stupor. "And, son, I'd contact the press if I were you. Whatever it takes to get credit for this. No telling what kind of shit will shake down from the FDA and GenExcel."

"And I suppose we ought to get some medical aid for that asshole." I pointed at Chip.

"I reckon so." Jarvis Riddle sighed.

• •

Before the Food and Drug Administration, the South Carolina Department of Health and Environmental Control, the South Carolina Department of Natural Resources, and GenExcel Incorporated arrived on the scene, before the sheriff and his goons showed up, before paramedics appeared with a stretcher to haul Chip Watts to the emergency room, before I quenched my rabid thirst and appeased my gnawing hunger, I got Jarvis to snap a pic of me, the epic antihero standing upon the gargantuan pig corpse, heirloom rifle held aloft in triumph.

My E-Live status update, the quintessence of sprezzatura, read *Romie Futch just slayed Hogzilla, y'all*. As the old woodsman had uncannily divined, I'd picked up a signal about twenty yards west of the deer stand, and my update received over two hundred comments within thirty minutes, after which a reporter from the *Hampton Herald* arrived to seal the deal.

The reporter, who resembled Bill Gates with a bob, had no time to laugh at my porcine puns. She squatted under a cluster of hemlock, furiously typing on a micropad. Before you could say *jackrabbit*, she'd posted a five-hundred-word article on their website. As I devoured Choco-Chip Energy Bars, courtesy of Hampton County

Emergency Services, the reporter disseminated a YouTube clip of me standing behind Hogzilla's outsize cadaver. I answered brief, burning questions about my quest as winter wind flirted with my filthy hair. Dripping with machismo, I spouted hog lore and hunting tips, played it cool while Chip Watts, drugged up and strapped into a rescue stretcher, bellowed in an envious frenzy.

Now a helicopter roared above the clearing, poised to whisk Chip off to Hampton Regional for repairs.

"You poached my hog," he yelled, flailing at the poor paramedic who was attempting to hitch his litter to a cable. At last, Chip's spew of threats and obscenities was drowned in helicopter thunder. I felt a surge of elation as the chopper lifted the aging athlete up into the clouds.

"Good riddance," hissed Jarvis, who stood in the forest gloom, eating a Fruit Roll-Up.

Before GenExcel showed up for damage control, the YouTube video had five hundred hits. The story had been retweeted eighty-six times. As I watched my E-Live page blow up with notifications, messages, and friendship requests, my blood ran high. At last, I was trending. After forty-three years of virtual nonexistence, I was surfing a zeitgeist wave.

"I know you're tired," said the GenExcel agent, also an eerie variation on the Bill Gates type (Anglo, bespectacled, deceptively innocuous), which made me wonder if I was dreaming again. "But I need you to answer a few questions."

I sat in a folding camp chair and answered questions as the winter day waned. Cold fog oozed out of the darkening woods. Portable halogen lamps popped on, shrouding Hogzilla's corpse in theatrical light. Other agents crept from the darkness into the surreal orb of light: reps from the FDA, SCDHEC, SCDNR, and GenExcel.

Exhausted, I negotiated with various parties as Jarvis stood in the limbo between light and darkness, Merlin-like, his face scrunched with wisdom.

My story was already a viral YouTube clip before the various agencies began to butt heads over what to do with the colossal rotting biohazard of Hogzilla's body. I'd already raised two thousand dollars on Kickstarter.com before Hogzilla was transferred by refrigerated truck to some remote facility arbitrated by the FDA and SCDHEC, which, pushed by the clamor of the masses, signed a contract with me, giving me the funds to stuff the gargantuan beast, which would, thereafter, become state property to be displayed at such illustrious institutions as the South Carolina State Museum for the edification of the taxpaying public. I even managed to negotiate a clause allowing me, upon completion, to display said taxidermic product as an installation piece in various arts venues for a period of up to three years, after which I'd wash the hog stench off my hands for good and the state would take possession of the stuffed marvel.

PART THREE

ONE

It was February already, sunlight deprivation taking its toll, vitamin D reserves low, postholiday malaise thickening into an absurdist indoor drama with no exit, the skeletal trees downright existential. But I was gearing up for my debut show in Columbia, a high-concept taxidermic installation that would be displayed in a gallery called the Bomb, a renovated Confederate ammo warehouse—not the Columbia Museum of Art, alas. But at least I had something lined up, and according to the gallery manager, my show was building a considerable amount of hype.

I was in my studio with the space heater cranked, sipping green tea, toiling Jonah-like inside the huge corpse of Hogzilla, hollowing out his form to make him lighter, prepping the monster for flight. Technically, the creature I tinkered with was not Hogzilla per se but a modified polyurethane rhino form upholstered with Hogzilla's hide. The pig's hot-pink hue had faded to mauve, despite the double oiling I'd applied, but I'd touched it up with some Life Tone paint. And the razorback was coming to life. I stepped out to take another look.

Posed in the charging position, right hoof lifted, Hogzilla roared at me, mouth agape as though caught in a condescending guffaw.

His bug eyes protruded ferociously. I tweaked his left tusk, which I hadn't yet glued into place, and fluffed the whiskers around his maw. I'd had to saw off the rhino head and reattach a form I'd molded from Hogzilla's skull, installing a jaw set I'd sculpted myself, accessorizing with original teeth. When I got the wiring hooked up, his eyes would roll; his slaver-slick tongue would quiver; spumes of foam would spurt from apertures tucked between gum and tongue. Most important, his weird wings would spread and flap as the uncanny beast lurched into clumsy flight.

The monster was currently wingless; however, his patagia hung from a hook on the wall, original bones in place. Just as I'd suspected, the wing bones were light, hollow, aerodynamic like a bat's. I'd tanned the original membranes with a softening oil, and they gave off a fleshy gleam. Pretty soon I'd get down to the intricate business of wiring Hogzilla's wings, a tedious process involving the consultation of electrical manuals and constant Googling. But I was done for the night, ready to crack open a beer and hit up HogWild.com, see if I might, at last, hear a peep out of PigSlayer.

When I'd conquered Hogzilla, the cyber hog-hunting scene had exploded with chatter. Every hunter in the state had put in his or her two cents about my colossal kill—whether it was real or fake, whether it was possible for a taxidermist to preserve an animal that huge, whether the beast was a mutant or a genetically modified creature hatched in a mad scientist's lab. And I, like an emperor disguised as a beggar, had swelled with pride as I crept among the envious mortals whose lives had not been transubstantiated by heroic adventure. Feeling bold and confident, I was itching to pounce upon any e-encounter with PigSlayer, ready to bring it to fruition in the three-dimensional world.

But just after my conquest, PigSlayer mysteriously vanished from the hog-hunting message boards, making me wonder if she was some kind of agent after all—a flesh-and-blood human, maybe, but not a woman keen to solve the masculine mystery of Romie Futch. Nevertheless, I still kept a weak flame guttering in a leathery hollow of my heart. Though I occasionally hit the message boards with a flirty smile, I eventually stopped trying. I tried not to dwell on Helen, avoided the thought of Chip Watts's bloated mug rendered into fetal flesh, and threw myself into my work.

Thinking with a clear head again, I spent my days tinkering with Hogzilla's deconstructed parts as experimental music tootled cerebrally from my iPod speaker, jams recommended by my old friend Trippy, who, alas, was still AWOL, still running from the wireless range of the Center, as far as I knew. Having suffered zero blackouts or phantom voices since my hunting adventure, I theorized that some remote connection had been broken by my three-day dalliance in the boondocks. I hoped against hope that Dr. Morrow would wash his hands of me and leave me to my own devices.

And now, as I took one last look at my masterwork, I felt an old familiar sensation within me, queasily alive with hope: *the future* squirming with larval potential in my chest—a feeling that zipped me back to high school, five days before graduation at Swamp Fox High's awards day ceremony.

After toking up in my Camaro, Helen, Lee, and I sat in the gymnasium, tucked into a corner near the door, poised for an easy exit. We sniggered as geeks, grade grubbers, and the occasional golden jock strolled to the podium to accept some plaque or certificate: the James Marion Sims Biology Award, the Strom Thurmond Ethics Scholarship. The herd around us stamped its hooves and bellowed its approval as Swamp Fox High's elites, bound for fancy state schools and the lesser Ivies, plucked the fruits of their academic toil. I watched with interest as Mrs. Breen approached the podium and adjusted the mic.

"Swamp Fox reynards and vixens," she said, "I congratulate you on your honors. With pride I announce a new award for excellence in the visual arts: the Frida Kahlo Golden Paintbrush Award. This year, I am privileged to present this award to Roman Morrison Futch."

There I sat, blanched of blood, unable to move, suspecting that my stoned mind had hallucinated the whole thing. But there was Helen, kicking me in the leg with her patent-leather pump. There was Lee, his palm raised to receive a high five. I slapped his hand feebly and stumbled from my bleacher seat. Descending the tricky stairs, I almost tripped. The podium looked impossibly distant.

The principal stood there sternly, his iron-gray buzz cut evocative of military and police officers. He sniffed. I wondered if he could smell the pot on me. But there was Mrs. Breen, beaming maternally, trying to hand me some slender, twinkling thing: a gilded paintbrush with my name on it, what appeared to be a check rubber-banded to its shaft.

My heart surged as I accepted the award. I made it back to my chair without incident, catching sight of my mother and father among the crowd. After a covert telephone call from Mrs. Breen, they'd been smoldering with the secret for an entire week—not only the gold-plated fetish object but also the three-hundred-dollar check. At last, they could release their elation. My father slapped his palms together, his lips pulled from their habitual scowl into a smirk. My mother held her clapping hands over her head. And the crowd erupted: thugs and heshers and losers, lurkers and dorky rappers, border rovers and freaks, all the kids, black and white, who didn't fit into the academic or athletic sets. As they howled in unison like some hive-minded monkey species, I felt it too, bursting up from my heart into my throat: the spontaneous desire to ululate.

• •

One day in early March, that florist-shop whiff of early spring in the air, I brushed over PigSlayer's HogWild profile out of mindless compunction, shocked to note that she'd changed her profile pic from an image of an Anza knife to an actual head-and-shoulders shot. A shimmering creature with dark hair partially concealing her face, she radiated a quiet wisdom combined with a delightful mischievousness. I could envision this woman not only in a white cotton frock enjoying a summer picnic but also in bloodstained camo, chasing a feral boar through a biohazardous swamp. And the very same woman might spend her weekdays teaching high school students about queer subtexts in *Moby-Dick*. In a word, she was the only woman who could understand the New and Improved Roman Futch.

But did she exist?

Or was this photo foisted by some imposter who wished to ensnare me? Whoever was behind it had also added a few suspiciously perfect biographical notes: *hog hunter, rabid reader, reluctant educator*.

But what if she did exist? I was out of my chair, pacing scuffed floors, wondering if she'd read the *State* paper's long-ass profile on me. Had she followed HogWild's fanatical chattering about my coronation as King Hoghunter? Most important, did she suspect that PorkDork and Romie Futch were one and the same? And finally, would she perhaps show up at my show in Columbia in April?

In my excitement I clicked on the instant message feature. Inside the little box, all conversations between PigSlayer and PorkDork were recorded for posterity, or at least until some server cluster malfunctioned, leading to widespread data loss, wails of anguish echoing through cyberspace as a zillion baby pics vanished. I reread our previous conversations, finding them much shorter and less intimate than I'd remembered. I tried to think of some elegant way to reveal my identity, slyly, self-effacingly.

—*So how 'bout that dickhead taxidermist who slew Hogzilla?*

Before I could think twice, I clicked send. I spent the rest of the evening agonizing over what I'd written, vacillating between gloating (*fuck yeah, I killed him*) and shame (*grossest humblebrag ever*), trudging from fridge to computer, fetching beers, and then checking for a reply. It had been almost two hours, and the lady, alas, had not yet responded, probably disgusted by my vanity, sniffing a sociopathic narcissist from a mile away. But at least I still had Hogzilla to occupy my trembling hands.

I popped another Miller. Traversed the well-worn path between my house and Noah's Ark Taxidermy. Slipped my old key into its ancient, archetypal lock, the metal keyhole plate scratched and nicked from over a decade of drunken fumbling. I slogged over worn linoleum, flicked on the shop lights, and beheld my embalmed monster for the umpteenth time.

The chortling old bastard was in a charging pose, wings retracted. I plucked a digital remote from a shelf and pressed the touch screen, which featured a diagram of Hogzilla's body. I fingered the remote and Hogzilla's eyes rolled, insane, hungry for carnage. I thumbed the diagram's dorsal section, and out popped Hogzilla's wings, otherworldly, the dusky hue of aged scrota.

Terrific, whispered the ghost of my mother. *But you need to touch up his bright spots with magenta highlights, catch the play of sun on his body.* I could almost feel her standing behind me, lit cigarette concealed inside her cupped palm, a thing she did when I stumbled upon her smoking. I could almost hear her laughing, the deep jolly growl of a storybook mother bear. I picked up my paint set and went back to work.

••

By the time I got home it was past ten and I was starved. So I scrounged up a sandwich, compulsively sat down in front of my laptop, and ate. My screen emitted a swell of light. And behold: there in black and white, throbbing, pulsing, was an IM from my beloved PigSlayer, dropped a mere three minutes ago.

—*Hi Roman.*

My cheeks burned as I gazed into the little box, an intimate three-inch-by-three-inch space, a tiny private room in which we might get to know each other a little better. A nutshell. An infinite space.

—*Hi*, said I. *C'est moi!*

—*Read a preview of your show in the State and thought that's GOT to be PorkDork. Been wanting to tell you how brilliant I think your work sounds, playful yet profound, esp given the naïve predominance of an archaic form of naturalism in the taxidermic arts.*

Be still my beating heart! Who was this woman who used words like *predominance* and held her own on hog-hunting message boards? How sweet the world would be if her claims turned out to be true and she really was a feisty English teacher who hunted swine during her downtime.

—*Ought to come to my opening*, I typed. *It's at this gallery in Columbia called the Bomb, April 9th, if you find yourself in the neighborhood. Come see the infamous Hogzilla firsthand.*

—*You mean the mummified version?*

—*Right.*

—*Speaking of the discrepancy between live game animals and their taxidermic reps, where'd you bag the monster?*

—*In the neighborhood of GenExcel.*

—*Swamp side or pine forest side?*

—*Swamp.*

There it was again, the sudden lapse from friendly banter into interrogation mode, making me think she could be an agent, possibly affiliated with the FDA, or even, in the darkest of dark worlds, BioFutures. Maybe she was a minion of Dr. Morrow. Or perhaps she was an activist of sorts, a vigilante English teacher in search of ecological justice. I wanted to believe the latter, longing as I did for the company of a good woman, the deceptive referentiality of a relationship, the cozy binary of he and she.

—*Why?*

—*Have you been keeping up with the board lately?*

—*Not really.*

—*Fresh crop of sightings. Seems to be at least one, maybe more, other Hogzillas out there. Why would there be just one? It's a lab, right?*

—*Hogs with freaky traits or just big-ass ferals?*

—*Mostly big-ass ferals, but a couple of people have claimed they saw wings.*

—*Could be their imaginations kicking in, with all the hype out about the real Hogzilla.*

The thought of a Hogzilla factory, which belittled my conquest, depressed me.

—*Don't know, Romie, but I'd like to know more. I'd like to take a look sometime but ideally with a guide. Since you know your way around that part of the swamp, I thought . . .*

—*That'd be so cool!*

My renegade hands compulsively typed this adolescent exclamation and then hovered like raptor claws over the keyboard.

—*We'll be in touch. But now I've got to bail. Get some shut-eye.*

—*We?*

—*I meant me; was using the royal "we" again.*

—*Gotcha.*

She left me alone in the little e-room with the residue of our conversation, our spent words dead and lusterless like the skins of snakes. I scanned our exchange again, wondering why she'd been AWOL for months.

I stayed up Googling backwater public schools county by county, poring over the pics of English teachers young and old, male and female, frumpy and smoking hot, all to no avail. And then I pulled up sites on BioFutures, skipping from link to link like a drunken bee, until I found myself in the hinterlands of the Internet on poorly designed websites with flashy fonts and bad grammar, reading about Stalin's 1926 plot to build an army of human-ape hybrids. According to a site called Darkseed.com, BioFutures was resurrecting Stalin's vision with GM war pigs, the CIA and the Department of Defense in cahoots with the plan.

Closing my eyes, I imagined this absurd prospect. I saw a great sounder of swine, some three thousand strong, trotting down an industrial runway and taking flight. The sky darkened as they flapped and soared. The heavens thundered with the beating of myriad wings. I could almost hear the raspy voice of Jarvis Riddle, imbuing this spectacle with apocalyptic profundity: *And in the darkest hours of Man, swine shall take to the air.*

TWO

I was hiding outside the Bomb gallery. On a patio tucked away behind fragrant shrubs, I drained a beer, waiting to make my appearance for the opening night of *When Pigs Fly: Irony and Self-Reflexivity in Postnatural Wildlife Simulacra*, a taxidermic installation by Roman Morrison Futch. Now that the big night had finally come, I longed to be within the boundaries of my comfort zone, in my backyard lounger, downing a six-pack under the stars.

But there stood Brooke Burns, the Bomb's young assistant director, peering at me through her asymmetrical cascade of black new-wave bangs. She was a scrumptious nymph in filmy disco polyester, all jutting clavicles and poppy lips. Her plastic earrings resembled Ruffles potato chips.

She handed me a mason jar full of bourbon. She patted my arm.

"All's cool," she said. "There's just this amazing band playing on the other side of town, and I know we'll get more traffic after their first set. I'm texting my friend Olivia. She says, like, fifty people are about to head over. So we'll just push the unveiling back to 9:30."

Brooke glanced at the chunky men's watch that hung from her spectral wrist. And I felt a damp heat deep in my groin, smoldering like fire under wet leaves. The bourbon was sinking into my gullet. Now I was hitting my groove. Now a beautiful girl who'd called my work *brill* in multiple text messages was stroking my arm. Now she was tugging me toward the door.

Inside, clutches of hip youth brooded in corners of the vast industrial space, sipping artisanal bourbon from mason jars, their subdued convos echoing like the meek mutterings of pigeons in an abandoned cathedral. My smaller pieces were displayed on refurbished lab tables like forlorn science projects: my mutant squirrel wedding diorama (titled *The History of Marriage*), my cyclopean possum (*Old One-Eye*), my squirrel and frog Panopticon, now enhanced with GM rat guards who possessed eyes in their backs (*Be Good*), as well as a dozen other small pieces, including *Electric Solipsism*, which featured an albino coyote playing solitaire on an old Macintosh desktop (a sly allusion to the classic dogs-playing-cards trope), and *The Sultan in His Labyrinth*, which depicted an obese raccoon slumped at a miniature desk eating cheese puffs while watching a loop of mating wild raccoons on a Dell laptop. My coup de grâce Hogzilla diorama, wrapped in black polyethylene, hung from the exposed beams like a thundercloud.

We stood in the shadow of the cloud. Brooke looked up with an ominous wince. Then she smiled and stroked my arm.

Some kind of shuddering electronica, interspersed with ghostly animal bleating, pulsed from a wall of vintage speakers, mostly 1970s monsters in faux woodgrain.

"Cool tunes," I said. "Who is it?"

Brooke squinted at me. "Yeah, totally. It's Narcolepsy, this recluse from Finland." And then she turned back to her little screen.

Buzzing on bourbon, I idled over to the wild-game-themed food table, where venison jerky and trout-and-turnip crudités were coupled with pickled okra and deviled eggs. On my right, a pair of pretties in '50s crinolines were checking out my Panopticon diorama. On my left, a dark dork in a black mohair cardigan grimly examined *The History of Marriage*. And just behind me, tucked behind the antique bourbon barrel, was some kind of rockabilly hipster, his hair swirled up into a glossy ducktail, his skin eerily pallid, his T-shirt and jeans so form-fitting that he looked like an action figure made of molded plastic.

The rockabilly hipster grinned at me, raised his mason jar. And Brooke hurried back over, her smile tense.

"See that guy in the seersucker suit?" She nodded toward a lushly bearded man in his thirties who stood before *The Sultan in His Labyrinth*, squinting, ruminating. "Art writer for *Dead Parrot*," she whispered. "Please remain chill."

I studied him, trying to comprehend the juxtaposition of Grizzly Adams facial fur and old-boy seersucker, thinking a fussy goatee would be more fitting. And he studied me, eyeing me through twinkling nineteenth-century specs, assessing, I feared, my lame haircut and aged hide, trying to peg me culturally, calculating the ratio of naïveté and urbanity that fueled my art. I was the oldest person in the room, and I longed for the cozy obscurity of my Lord Tusky mask.

But the bourbon was working its magic. Brooke Burns was stroking my arm again. At last, fashionable people were streaming in from the summer night, dressed in the clothes of bygone eras, sporting interesting coiffures and curious clusters of facial hair, every species of mustache, beard, and muttonchops represented. And there were older people among them too, frumpier, not as chicly dressed. The bourbon barrel was a hit. Within fifteen minutes, the room filled with a respectable level of festive chatter. A photographer snapped away, sleek as a seal in his all-black ensemble, multiplying my image and sending a hundred Romie

Futches rocketing through cyberspace. Meanwhile, familiar faces materialized among the strangers like dream figments.

Lee Decker shuffled forth to shake my hand. "Totally killer," he said. "I knew you were a genius back in high school."

Marlene teetered tipsily in a midnight-blue muumuu, her coiffure extra-teased for the occasion, and pressed her perfumed plumpness against me.

"Your father's so proud of you," she cooed. "Even if he won't say so."

"She had one too many at dinner," said Dad, who dawdled behind her, looking shrunken and yellow amid the youthful throng. From a remote drawer, he'd dug a pair of ill-fitting dress slacks, which he sported with suspenders and a new plaid shirt.

"We got lost on the way over here," he said, glancing up at the exposed beams. "What kind of fool place is this?"

"It's an old Confederate ammunition warehouse," I said.

"You said it was an art gallery." Dad bugged his eyes at Marlene.

"It is, honey," she said. "It's hip. Urban chic. They *made* it into an art gallery. That's the thing now."

Dad harrumphed and frowned, but his eyes brimmed with emotive moisture, making my heart go soft like a Nerf ball left out in the muck.

"Time for your moment in the sun," said Brooke, coaxing me toward the roped-off corner where a clutch of interns geared up to activate my animatronic Hogzilla installment. The room was getting packed, filled with the churchy fug of warm bodies in close proximity. I looked around for a glimpse of PigSlayer—dark hair, streaks of gray—and saw no one who matched her HogWild profile pic. I drained my bourbon glass. Walking through the mob, I partook of the collective anticipatory mood, breathed in the over-processed air, and felt a delicious dizziness. I walked with my snout practically wedged into Brooke's sweaty nape, which, contrary to the room's general funkiness, smelled miraculously of fresh lemon. I wondered if I, the celebrated artist, ought to cash in on the hype and get myself a hot young babe.

"Rad turnout," said Brooke. "You ready for the big shebang?"

She stroked my arm again and gave one of her interns a little wave.

The lights dimmed. A moody surge of experimental classical—Schnittke's Sonata for Cello and Piano no. 1, inspired by poor Trippy J—swelled from the wall of vintage speakers. As the haunting music played, an enormous sun of molded plastic resin, which hung suspended from the ceiling, grew brighter and brighter. The fake sun actually warmed the room with its fiery blaze. As lights flashed behind this translucent orb, the sun's surface seemed to boil as though molten.

The crowd let out a collective gasp. The music grew more ominous, oozing like black honey as various images flickered upon the walls: pictures of me standing in triumph upon the slain hog; close-ups of my maimed finger; glam shots of yours truly dressed as Lord Tusky. In addition to these personal images, I'd acquired an animated graphic of Hogzilla's sequenced DNA, which featured cryptically upon all four walls, bright double helixes that twirled and pulsed, conveying the essence of the dystopian hog—that Frankensteinian beast born in a laboratory, that futuristic food product dreamed up by academic dorks or, darker still, that flesh-and-blood war machine hatched by the US military.

As Schnittke's sonata lapsed into its frenetic second movement, garish images from Hogzilla's autopsy flashed upon the screen. And behold: a great beast surged forth from a trapdoor, a thousand-pound feral GM hog, stuffed with a hollowed rhinoceros form and held aloft by an elaborate pulley system designed by a graduate student from the USC theater department. The hog soared upon semisheer patagia, wing bones and veins visible in the light of the artificial sun. Hogzilla bobbed sluggishly around the solar orb, circling closer and closer as the cello part grew more frenzied.

The hog's skin glowed. His Bio-Optix II rotator eyes swelled with arrogant light. Tusks curling, the beast seemed to sneer with pride. In sync with a startling piano boom, the boar released a long dragonish squeal (the collective squeal of over a hundred live hog recordings, compiled by a media arts student) as his wings sprouted flames. And then the aspiring boar tumbled to his doom. Performing somersaults in the air, Hogzilla plummeted to the floor, landing roughly within the confines of the roped-off area. He flailed and grunted and spurted purple and red streamers that represented the spectacular explosion of his entrails.

The sun dimmed. Hogzilla lay still as the melancholy coda of Schnittke's sonata plied its ominous notes. After a spell of silence, the crowd erupted into applause.

I felt hot. The track lighting shot sparks into my eyes. The crowd pitched forward, hundreds of drunken red faces, sweating in the tight space. Nervy pain flitted up and down neurovascular paths of my brain.

"More people than I thought," Brooke muttered through her clenched smile. "Fire hazard."

I scanned the audience, looking for PigSlayer. I saw Dad hightailing it toward the exit, Marlene in hasty pursuit, her mouth open in midharangue. I saw Lee in a corner, chatting up a pretty hippie. I saw Helen in the distance, big with child, attempting to waddle toward me. Boykin, the old cuckold, shuffled behind her, looking ten years older than the last time I'd seen him. Right behind Boykin, communing with both his phone and a cute redhead dressed like a 1960s airline stewardess, was Adam.

High on my success, I entertained the notion that Helen would go into labor and announce my paternity that night, disposing of pitiful Boykin. But then I spotted Chip Watts in the crowd, flashing a chimpanzee fear grin as big as the moon. I had not spoken to the idiot since our camping adventure in the deer stand, and I felt my heart pop a valve. But it was not Chip Watts—just another sunburned, hypertensive fool with bright white veneers and a hick-van-dyke.

My blood pressure was almost back to normal when I espied another Chip doppelganger near the EXIT sign—same arrogant grin, same ham-hued face, but with a white fleck of mustache. Yet another Chip Watts stood three feet in front of me, leering.

I saw the sweat drops on his flushed cheeks. I saw every speck of dandruff in his eyebrows. I looked out at the seething sea of people and beheld a multitude of bloated ATV salesmen, gloating in unison. Helen parted the great sea of assholes with her pregnant belly and strode toward me. I could see the child growing within the mysterious brines of her uterus. It, too, had the chapped pink face of Chip Watts. But then I blinked, and the swarm of ATV salesmen vanished. Helen stood before me, looking tired and tense in a peach nylon cocktail dress.

"Good job, Romie," she said. "I'm impressed."

"Thanks for making it out, especially in your, uh, I mean—"

Boykin, the old dupe, smiled proudly. "She's about to pop."

Now I knew that Helen had not told him the truth, and this disappointed me.

"I've got three more months." Helen rolled her eyes. "I was an early shower. And now I'm just huge. Also, exhausted. Just wanted to say hello before we headed out."

She leaned closer. I gave her a clinical hug. After exchanging a high five with Adam, I watched the dysfunctional family make its way through the crowd.

I felt a presence behind me. I turned to find the rockabilly hipster almost pressed against me, so close that I could smell his fruity hair gel. A blue vein pulsed on his temple. His skin looked vaguely amphibious. When I pushed my way to the edge of the crowd, he shifted toward me. When I trudged to the bourbon barrel, he came skulking after. And when I ducked into the unisex bathroom, he sheepishly entered, avoiding eye contact, his bloodless skin shining in the sickly fluorescent light.

Backing away from him, I dropped my mason jar, which bounced on the linoleum tiles without shattering. I hunkered down to pick it up and he did the same. There we squatted, face-to-face, blinking at each other. He picked up my glass.

"Here you go," he smiled, revealing strangely tiny teeth—corn-niblet teeth—a perfect row of seed pearls save for two incisors that twinkled like the fangs of a toddler vampire. When he handed me the jar, his fingers brushed mine, and I swear I felt a prick, a minuscule sting, as though his finger emitted an electric shock. I shuddered. I took the glass. The young man stood up and thrust his hands into the back pockets of his jeans.

• •

I woke with a panic attack in Brooke's kitsch-cluttered apartment and stumbled toward the bathroom, which was decorated with Jesus camp. As I fell into the throes of gastric distress, the handsome blond Messiah gazed down at me from a lacquered oval of pine. The previous night's events flashed through my mind's eye in a headachy montage. I saw Brooke scooting me out of the Bomb, offering maternal sucks of bourbon from a flask as we traversed a dim grid of city streets. I saw Brooke leading me down a staircase into a windowless bar that smelled of leaky plumbing and the ashen residue of the public smoking era. I saw myself drinking more bourbon, tucked into a corner behind a birdcage filled with sparrow skeletons. I radiated a sketchy smugness fueled by bourbon and what I fancied was artistic success. Brooke was more mobile, hopping up and down to fetch drinks, hug hipsters, shimmy her lithe body in the dim, candied light of the vintage jukebox. She kept touching me with her satin fingertips, tickling my skin with the mothy film of her dress, pressing her hip bones frankly against me. I would have succumbed to the pleasure principle had I not spotted, sitting behind a pierced and rainbow-haired gang, alone at a booth and nursing a lager, the rockabilly hipster. He smiled cryptically while fingering his phone.

"Who's that?" I asked Brooke.

"Don't know," she said. "Just some rockabilly guy."

And then I was back at her apartment, slumped in a wicker peacock chair as she cleared her futon of vintage frocks. Next, I was hacking over an enormous bong. Finally, I was naked and crouched over her, lost in the intricate foliage of her sacral tattoo. At last, I found my target (the pudendal configuration floating abstractly beneath the cartoon tree) and burrowed the mauve snout of my phallus. One minute I was pulling mental gymnastics lest I melt in instant pleasure. The next I felt numb, fearful of humping to the rhythm of the chillwave loops that trickled from Brooke's iPod dock. Later, I was staring down at the sea medusa of a spent condom floating in the commode.

Had the lady experienced pleasure? I could not remember my own, much less hers.

But there she was now, stretching sultrily in her sunlit kitchenette, wearing an antiquated red velvet robe that looked like something the Empress Josephine would've moped in when on the rag. She seemed cheerful enough.

"I'm thinking brunch at the Grub," she said, consulting her phone. "They've got these vegan ham biscuits I'm addicted to."

We headed down to the Grub, a retro diner with a smiling neon maggot on its roof.

"The worm is way more awesome at night," said Brooke as we waited in line.

We met Brooke's friends, a scruffy crew of dashing youngsters, on the patio. We were seated one foot from a busy road. Had I stretched out my leg, a car would've mangled it. Partially due to the roaring road, partially due to my failing ears, partially due to my cultural cluelessness, I could barely understand the kids' chatter, most of which revolved around the names of things: apps, turntables, bands, blogs, sneaker brands, vintage cameras. Their jokes were densely referential and impenetrable, their laughter like the cawing of raptors, a dozen little talons pricking my brain tissue.

My jeans were the wrong color. My hair was thin and blighted with gray. I downed several Bloody Marys. I could feel my ghoulish jowls drooping from my jawbone. And there was Brooke Burns, radiant despite last night's endless bacchanalia, consuming faux ham, laughing the summer day away. She glanced at my ravaged face with a businesslike eye that belied her bonhomie. She was not rude to me. But she no longer reached out to touch me with her silky hands.

It would be a relief to be back in my truck, I thought, speeding toward home, but first I had to pick up my stuff from my hotel room. I tried to finish my eggs, but they tasted strangely bitter and my stomach recoiled. I discreetly spat a half-chewed mouthful into my napkin and ordered another Bloody Mary with half the vodka, settled into a semibuzzed groove of exhaustion and resignation, waiting for brunch to be over. *This too shall pass.* But then I saw *him* sitting two tables over, eyes obscured behind Ray-Ban Wayfarers, hackneyed bicep tattoo half protruding from a rolled T-shirt sleeve, his skin cadaverous in the sunlight. It was the rockabilly hipster munching an English muffin.

Was he an obsessed art fan? Did he have the hots for me? Or was this just a coincidence—a cool guy hanging at a cool place?

I fled to the restroom. When I came back, a starling had alighted upon the rockabilly hipster's empty table. It pecked up a crumb, cocked its head, and regarded me with its blank black eye.

• •

On the way to my hotel, I felt a queasy delirium, a psychedelic nausea that reminded me of my old mushroom days, when Lee Decker and I would drop shrooms between third and fourth period. I made it to the Econo Lodge, somehow produced the necessary card, swiped it, and stumbled into my room. I collapsed on one of the beds, lay breathing in odors of synthetic honeysuckle and doom.

I longed to sleep but felt a raging thirst, so I forced my dog-tired body out into the blinding sunlight in search of a vending machine. I watched my shadow skulk along the stucco wall. I paused to consider the sun, lewd and boiling in the blue abyss. I regarded the quiet degradation of an overflowing dumpster, the poignancy of a half-empty motel parking lot.

And then my heart drained of blood, turned to ashy frass, and dissolved in my chest. There, three cars down from my truck, idling in a black Ford Focus and chatting on his phone, was the rockabilly hipster. His windows were open. His ducktail had gone clumpy, but it was definitely the same guy. I ducked behind a Camry, crept around a Jeep, and peered at the apparition.

I was close enough to make out his ironic bicep tattoo, a med-text diagram of a heart, the words OEDIPUS REX flowing along a ventricle in ornate cursive. I recognized the near-iridescent sheen of his pallor, which made me think that he might be some kind of apparition installed by the Center, a shimmering configuration of neurons.

"Don't worry, boss. He's nodding off as we speak." The creature spoke into his phone. "Yes, got a blood sample at the show. He didn't feel a thing, and the girl, Brooke, she saw nothing. Innocent as a lamb. Yes, he's safe, perfectly isolated. In his hotel room. Did a blood scan last night. VSST2. Bumped into his waitress and dusted his eggs with the nano serum at 10:20 or so but didn't activate the Lethe until he checked in. Okay, Doc. I'll install the hardware within the hour, promise."

I watched the young man's lips break open to reveal a cocksure smile—self-congratulatory, infuriating. I reached into his window to grapple with whatever he was. My crimped fingers did not pass through a spectral neck but sank into pliable flesh. My opponent emitted a satisfying shriek, flailed as I applied pressure to his Adam's apple. I withdrew my hand, tensed it into a fist. I was about to break his jaw when the sky receded with a big *whoosh*. My head hit asphalt. I saw multiple red suns popping up from the horizon like bubbles of liquid mercury. I saw clouds condensing into dark clots and breaking apart again. I saw the rockabilly hipster sinking toward me, his throat bruised, his lips pinched into a line as he scrutinized me with trypan-blue eyes.

· ·

When I came to, I was strapped to the hotel bed, the rockabilly creature talking on his phone. He turned to regard me, and I closed my eyes, trying to remain limp.

"That's right. The third BC transmitter. I already tried that. Lemme check."

The young man cradled my skull, poked it with something.

"Now I see it," he said. "Clockwise? Yep. Got it. Yes, boss, he's out cold. I already checked his PCCDs. He'll be back on your network within the hour. And the vis-scanner app is ready to roll. You'll be watching his dreams in living color tonight. Okay. Later."

I couldn't move because I was straitjacketed by an intricate network of straps. But when I opened my eyes and saw the familiar hologram of my brain rotating two feet from my face, its regions mapped in rainbow colors, I panicked. When I saw the asshole typing into his micropad, I squirmed with all my might, writhing like some flying thing in a cocoon. The boy jerked around, eyes wide with shock. But it was too late. I was already sinking into the familiar well that preceded a download, the young man's appalled face above me in the distant circle of light. From the deep dark well of my unconscious, a random memory flooded my mind.

Tucked into the depths of the cavernous Future Dragon Chinese Buffet, Helen sat beside me in the booth, my mother and father across from us. Mom's plate was heaped with sweet things: cookies and banana pudding, deep-fried meats glistening with corn syrup. She was so far gone that Dad had ceased to reason with her. Mom ate fast, like a dog, lipstick smeared around the edges of her mouth. Her eyes sparkled with manic ecstasy, and her irises seemed unmoored, jangling like those plastic googly eyes the Hobby Lobby sold. I felt a deep sickness of the soul, a general cellular entropy.

"You are so beautiful," Mom said, patting Helen's hand. "Everything about you is perfect: your hair, your eyes, your lips."

This was Mom's latest mantra. As language began to fail her, the phenomenal world had emerged in blazing, elemental beauty—all objects etched in psychedelic detail, aglow with miraculous presence. And Mom was no longer afraid of anything. Just the week before, she'd picked up a snake—a harmless garter, but still, it'd startled my father to see her moving over the lawn with a serpent in her hands.

"So beautiful," she kept repeating, and then she dropped the writhing creature, squatted to watch it slither away, calling after it: "Beautiful, beautiful, beautiful."

"What's beautiful?" Dad had asked.

"The long short crawler," Mom had said.

"Where's my keys?" Mom said now, pushing her plate away.

"She's talking about her cigarettes," Dad said. "Every tool is a key now: a fork, a hairbrush, a cigarette."

"Where's my keys?" Mom said sharply.

"You can't smoke in here," said Dad, who had long since ceased to lecture her on the dangers of her cigarette habit, a vice that thrived in the dark, loamy soil of her dementia. My mother had always been a covert smoker, hiding at the edge of our yard where azalea shrubs thickened into jungle. She'd smoked at night when she had insomnia, between sewing projects, out on the carport under the moon. Her smoking had seemed like a mysterious facet of her being, a secret roguishness to her matter-of-fact personality. But now she smoked one after another at home, out in the Florida room at a wicker table while playing solitaire.

"Where's my keys?" Mom cried, frantic for the key that would spike her blood with nicotine.

"We have to pay the bill, leave the tip." Dad frowned and fished for his wallet.

"I want my keys," said Mom.

"The tip, Betsy." Dad waved a fan of cash in the air.

Mom snatched a dollar from his hand, jumped up from the table. She stood, scanning the room like a huntress. She zeroed in on the gangly teen who was swapping out a tub of moo goo gai pan. The boy, caught up in the ghastly metamorphosis of puberty, was a slouching, scrawny lad with acne in full bloom. And when my mother ran over and touched his sleeve, he looked confused. When she stroked his arm, he grinned, terrified.

"I want you to have this," Mom barked, stuffing a dollar into the teen's hand.

Helen and I winced, but my father sighed, his face grim, resolute. He stood up like a jaded, dyspeptic general who'd just lunched on rancid salt pork, and who was about to stroll out onto the battlefield to count his dead.

"Betsy," he said, "your keys are in the car."

Mom turned upon the battered heel of her patent-leather pump. The teen boy fled. Mom darted toward the door, and we hurried after her. We exited the arctic air-conditioning of the restaurant and slumped out into the hothouse mugginess of a July afternoon. Mom skipped around their Buick, checking the doors. When Dad opened the passenger side, she slipped in, retrieved her cancer sticks from the glove compartment, and lit up. She sat puffing in the car like a withered teen hoodlum.

We all got in. When Dad started the car, Billy Joel bellowed from the speakers: "We Didn't Start the Fire" from Mom's *Greatest Hits* cassette. When her dementia had come on, she'd fixated on this cassette, insisted on playing it whenever she was in their car. We'd been listening to the same cassette for two years now, and Mom still knew all the lyrics:

> *Joseph Stalin, Malenkov, Nasser and Prokofiev,*
> *Rockefeller, Campanella, Communist Bloc,*
> *Roy Cohn, Juan Peron, Toscanini, Dacron,*
> *Dien Bien Phu Falls, Rock Around the Clock*

She sang, slurring the words together. In the backseat, Helen took my hand and treated me to a tender gaze. She still loved me then.

"Billy Joel is so beautiful," Mom said, turning toward us, puffing smoke into the backseat. "This song is so beautiful."

Dad, Helen, and I all groaned in unison when "Piano Man" came on, the familiar syrup oozing into our ears. How many times had we driven through the empty Sunday streets of Hampton while listening to "Piano Man," our stomachs leaden with buffet food, queasy from Mom's cigarette smoke? We passed an abandoned tanning salon, its windows boarded up, crude palm trees painted on its walls. A bloated sun smiled demonically from its dead neon sign.

"Everything is beautiful," Mom said.

· ·

That's where the memory left me, "Piano Man" trickling through the circuitry of my brain. I woke in the empty hotel room, no sign of the rockabilly hipster save for the smell of his fruity hair gel. The half-opened aqua curtains revealed a nocturnal parking lot awash with LED light. I lay there testing my brain, running through a series of meandering thoughts, probing for a flash of new insight, some cerebral quirk hitherto missing—the ability to grasp calculus, for instance, or to decipher the precise note, pitch, and tempo of the dripping faucet. When I tried to sit up, I detected a wash of static in my head. I heard a familiar voice, that mellow meld of god and game-show host.

While Subject 48FRD's thought waves may not be as of yet recognizable, the brain-grid app should eventually produce a crude video stream.

The voice faded and I lay there, vowing once and for all to find a lawyer and begin legal proceedings against the Center for Cybernetic Neuroscience.

You'll be watching his dreams in living color tonight, the young man had said, presumably to Dr. Morrow, and I had the odd sensation that my thoughts were being siphoned, bottled, reconfigured. But then again, according to the voice I'd heard, *the brain-grid app should* eventually *produce a crude video stream*, some symbolic representation that had not yet fully materialized and could not provide full access to *me*. I lay in the darkness, listening to the distant roar of the interstate and scanning my inner world for signs of static, odd twists of thought, evidence of an alien presence hiding in the convoluted tissues of my brain.

.   .

Morning came soon. I felt oddly comforted by the imminent need to eat, a concrete goal that propelled me from my rented bed, out of the Econo Lodge, into the windy spring morning. Two yellow butterflies cavorted over flowering weeds that had muscled their way through the asphalt. Salmon clouds shimmered in the bright sky. But I couldn't settle into the simple pleasures of a spring day. I glanced around with the feeling that the world was full of cameras, hidden in the clouds and trees. Every flower contained a miniature electronic eye.

The words of Trippy J popped into my head, giving me a reality check: *The prison guard's inside you, dog*. Perhaps my very cells had been reconfigured into cameras, my identity imploded, rippling through cybernetworks.

I climbed into my truck and drove with the windows down, wondering if *they* could feel the wind on my cheeks. Such an intimate thing became an obscenity when broadcast, yet another form of porn. But I drove. I processed contemporary fast food signage. When I spotted a cinder-block dive called Kuntry Kafé, I imagined smug

young techies ridiculing my lack of gustatory sophistication—or perhaps they applauded my rejection of corporate non-food.

The same self-consciousness plagued me as I scanned the menu
and ordered, but I drowned these thoughts in a delirium of eating. I devoured pancakes and bacon. The pile of industrial meat
product glistened with grease. Remembering Ned, that sportive
codger I'd met at Gators months before who'd celebrated his heart
transplant with a pound of bacon, I chuckled to myself, albeit self-
consciously, with too much volume, wishing that I had someone
to share such yarns with, remembering with a sick jolt that I was
probably sharing this yarn now via some crude form of telepathy.
I tried not to think about anything serious and read the label on a
bottle of imitation maple syrup.

But I could not stop myself from thinking, remembering, even
hoping.

I recalled Brooke, adorable in her infantile romper printed with
ironic kittens, excited about fake pork, skipping to her Peugeot,
ready to turn somersaults on the dewy lawn. I saw her naked, reclined, perky of breast and concave of tummy. Remembered her
frowning as she assessed my face in the cruel sunlight. I thought
of sweet Crystal Flemming, taking a noontide bong hit and laughing raspily. And then there was Helen, ripe with child, ready to
burst. Imagining her crumpling beatifically as the first contractions
shook her, I felt almost nothing—a shiver of obscure feeling, the
residue of love. I turned to PigSlayer, envisioning her in all of her
manifestations: Amazon goddess, frumpy schoolmarm, sniggering
nerdboy, sexy spy. I had no idea who PigSlayer was, but she was
in my brain again, an amorphous presence on display, perhaps, for
them. Or maybe she was in on the evil network that plagued me.
Maybe she was tittering at this very moment, listening, watching,
judging me.

I made my way out into the humid day, where the interstate droned and the sun festered like a boil beneath a bandage of clouds. Out of context, I had no meaning. A floating signifier, I drifted across the parking lot. I climbed into my truck, streaming amorphous sensations: the smell of moldy polyester upholstery, the weight of the carbs I'd consumed, the heaviness of meat in my belly. The weather was turning again, squalls of rain blowing in from the east. And my tank was almost empty: another concrete goal to accomplish. Find a gas station. Tank up. Drive home. And then what?

··

As soon as I pulled into an Exxon station, I saw it, the black Ford Focus parked beside pump number six. And I saw *him*, the rockabilly hipster, strolling out of the store with a Red Bull, a smug expression of mindless cool on his face. His ducktail was gone. He'd shaved off his stupid sideburns. He wore khakis with a nondescript plaid shirt—no longer a cartoonish hipster but clearly the same guy—with the same subaquatic pallor, same jut of forehead and rosebud mouth. He didn't walk to his car. He frowned, swiftly rounded the corner, booked it to the side of the building toward the outdoor restrooms, and hurried into the men's room.

I had to think fast. I would follow him, yes, but I had to get gas. My hand trembled as I slid my credit card in and out, until the machine started thinking, crunching numbers. I punched in my zip code. My heart pounded as I awaited authorization. Perhaps they were already watching, listening. Perhaps they knew my coordinates.

Burning eyes fixed on the restroom, I pumped gas, hoping that a certain person (whom I tried not to visualize) was suffering severe diarrhea, hoping said person was an obsessive hand washer, a compulsive user of multiple paper towels, a narcissist who enjoyed gazing at his reflection in restroom mirrors, grooving on his image in a different kind of light. I concentrated on numbers, calculating the ratio of gallons to cost.

I attempted to remain neutral, philosophical, as I eased my truck into the back parking lot. I hummed Crimson songs: "Cadence and Cascade" as I crept into the store, where I purchased a cup of coffee and a box of aluminum foil; "21st Century Schizoid Man" as I shrouded my skull in heavy-duty Reynolds Wrap, securing my helmet with a camouflage trucker's hat; "Formentera Lady" as I scrounged through the junk piled in the back of my truck, locating a boar spear that I'd never had the pleasure of using: ash handle, feather-shaped blade with twin cutting edges, a cross guard to keep a furious, punctured beast from charging up the five-foot shaft.

THREE

I found myself on that endless stretch of I-20 again, driving through a storm, heading toward my maker, I hoped, that banal, corporate neo-Frankenstein who'd gazed into my soul with cold curiosity while nibbling a toasted bagel. I was a petty monster, alone in the world, my brain tricked out with worthless thoughts, coil upon coil of nonsense folding in on itself. Every now and then, a zigzag of gothic lightning ripped across the horizon. Rain pattered my windshield. Wipers swished at high speed.

Despite the dangerous weather, Morrow's lackey drove ninety, hyped on Red Bull, young enough to feel invincible. I struggled to keep up with him, always at least one car between us, the landscape blurred by rain. The rain that spattered my car, part of the world's water system, was spiked with human contaminants, I knew. And I occupied myself with lists: lead, mercury, fluoride, chlorine. Petroleum products, industrial agricultural nitrates, an endless series of pharmaceuticals. I pictured toxic streams trickling, poisoned rivers roaring into tributaries. Steam rose from overheated oceans and thickened into clouds, swaddling the planet like a dirty gray blanket. Polluted clouds hovered over cities, mixed with emissions, coagulated into hot filthy masses, cooled, and condensed, seeping a zillion dirty drops. Water treatment plants seethed with feces and industrial waste, pumped chlorinated water into underground pipes that fed gigantic water towers. The same water trickled through my bloodstream, kept my organs lubricated in their soft rinds, my cells hydrated. My brain floated in a bone tank of fluid like some kind of fancy jellyfish. I sweated. I salivated. Wastewater trickled from my liver into my swollen bladder, and I needed to piss.

But I kept driving, onward through the storm for two more hours, relieved that the rain kept coming, enveloping me in a shroud of mist, concealing my truck from Morrow's minion, who didn't slow down until he'd reached the outer sprawl of Atlanta. He took the Lithonia exit, and I feared he'd lead me to his apartment, that I'd have to stalk him for days before he guided me to Morrow's lair.

He turned left, right, and then right again, onto a highway flanked with car dealerships. The storm was slacking off, sunlight lasering through clouds, glittering upon armies of rain-slicked cars. At last, the black Ford Focus turned left into a shabby office park—dingy beige three-story structures, the parking lot crumbling to rubble at the edges—and pulled up to a building that looked abandoned. Idling behind a clump of feral boxwood shrubs, I watched the young man exit his vehicle, open his trunk, pull out a large gray plastic suitcase, and lug it inside.

∙ ∙

In the lobby, the teal industrial carpet smelled moldy. No air-conditioning system chugged away to give the illusion of sanitation. There was no furniture arranged into clusters of pseudo-coziness. Two fake ficus trees huddled together in a corner, vestiges of more hospitable times. The peach vertical blinds were sallow from the sun.

Leaning my spear against the wall, I stood beside the elevator, a warrior at rest, scanning the mostly empty office directory: Gray and Brown Dental Financial Strategists (first floor), Prime Hospital Receivable Services, Inc. (second), Clickbait Digital Media Co. (second), and Future Solutions United (third).

Future Solutions United had the penthouse suite to itself.

I snorted at the bland corporate optimism of the title, the cooperative gesture, the vague acknowledgement that there were problems that needed fixing. Was this an outpost of BioFutures, I wondered, or had Dr. Morrow gone rogue, setting up shop in this obscure locale to conduct his research undisturbed, chasing that Promethean flame of pure scientific knowledge?

I gripped my boar spear: the blade cold-forged from high-carbon steel, designed to flex upon penetration, to yield to the flailing fury of a stabbed boar. I didn't take the elevator, but quietly climbed a side stairwell, my brain calm and focused in its tinfoil rind.

I stepped onto the third floor, noting dry, chilly air, a current-model window unit purring efficiently at the end of the hallway. I heard voices, not inside my head but toward the opposite end of the hall—masculine, plodding. I crept halfway down the hall, slipped into a dark office, and listened. I recognized Dr. Morrow's voice.

"Are you sure you recalibrated the third BC transmitter correctly? Because not only is the stream not appearing, but he's off grid *again*."

"Maybe he's hunting," said the rockabilly hipster, "out in the sticks."

"I doubt he'd be up for that, but even if he were, we'd have a trace of something from earlier this morning."

"Dr. Morrow," said a female voice, but it was not Chloe, unless Chloe was intentionally speaking at a lower pitch, without her typical elementary-education smarminess. "62367FRD is still not taking the vis-scanner app."

"Did you erase the last version before reinstalling?"

"Of course." The woman huffed with irritation.

"Try rebooting," said Morrow.

"Should I give him another shot of propofol?"

"Too dangerous."

"But he might wake up."

"He's strapped down, isn't he? We can do a synapse patch after it's over so he won't remember anything."

"Not at the moment, but he's still unconscious so—"

"Please proceed. Now, as for you, I think you're going to have to head back to South Carolina. He might remember something."

"Come on, Doc," said the rockabilly hipster. "I didn't sleep last night. Can't you send Josh?"

"I need Josh here. I need Josh now, in fact. Josh?" Dr. Morrow sounded irked.

"Yo, back here," the lad called out. He was in the room next door. "Trying to tweak that vis-scanner grid for the taxidermist."

"Forget it for now," yelled Dr. Morrow. "Pam needs reinforcement."

"Just a nanosec, dude."

Josh strolled out into the hallway just beyond my dark hiding place. His sideburns had flourished into full-fledged muttonchops. His hair looked shaggier. He'd been fucking with my brain, and there he was, gnawing at an energy bar and shuffling down the hall. I crept after him. He glanced back, saw me, yelped.

I leapt upon him. He squirmed, stronger than I'd predicted, but I managed to stick the blade of my spear just beneath his tender, pulsing throat.

"Please note that I have a very sharp object pointed at your neck," I hissed. "And I will not hesitate to impale you."

"Dude, seriously?" Josh noted my weapon. He relaxed in my arms.

I'd never held a man before—he was warm and bony; he smelled of some essential oil (what the fuck: rosemary?); and the stubble that trailed along his throat felt so velvety that I could not resist stroking it.

"What's going on here?" Dr. Morrow was now moving toward us, tailed by a young Asian woman with a Louise Brooks flapper bob that highlighted her spectacular eyes: amber irises, dark eyeliner, mod-Goth effect. She frowned.

"Stop right there or I'll kill him," I said, wincing at the cliché. There I was, smack-dab in a ridiculous action scene, struggling to impress a femme fatale with a clever line.

"You won't commit murder." Dr. Morrow stood tall, puffed up his chest.

With the tip of my spear, I poked Josh, stabbing at the soft flesh under his chin, failing to break the skin. I jabbed again.

Josh screamed, tensing in my arms. My stomach flinched as a rivulet of blood trickled down his neck, wetting my hand, staining the collar of his yellow polo.

Josh shrieked. Josh whimpered. Josh sweated and trembled.

"Sorry," I whispered.

"What makes you so certain the boy is not dispensable?" said Dr. Morrow in his best Nazi-scientist baritone.

"What?" squawked Josh.

I hated to do it, but I gently sliced into Josh's throat, barely breaking the skin, producing another red trickle, another raw screech. He went limp in my arms. An intimate, humiliating intestinal miasma enveloped us.

Dr. Morrow paused. His new assistant moved closer to him.

"Don't worry, Josh. You'll be fine." Dr. Morrow's tongue flicked repeatedly over his bottom lip, lubricating it with saliva again and again. "Let's be reasonable here."

"Where is the fucking rockabilly hipster?" I said.

"The what?"

"The cool fool you sent to tinker with my skull."

"Right here, right here," said the young man, slipping out into the hallway, waving his arms in a farcical gesture of surrender.

"Now," I said, trying to think, "what I want you all to do is—"

"What?" Dr. Morrow's tongue slipped back into the arcane cave of his mouth. He smirked. "You know that murder is a felony."

Fuck. I needed a roll of duct tape, rope, handcuffs, something. Or maybe I could lock them all in that little office somehow. They were creeping toward me, Dr. Morrow in the fore, his face blank and focused like a slasher in a horror film, in no rush to destroy me but confident of my imminent doom—I would be hacked up into synecdochic parts, my tricked-out brain devoured by zombies, symbolically, metaphorically, ironically. The rockabilly hipster actually chuckled.

And then I saw a familiar figure appear in the doorway behind them—dressed in gray sweatpants and a garnet Atlanta Falcons jersey, black socks, his hair recontextualized—none on his head now, but a bushy beard, as though—*poof*—some magician had shifted his pelt from scalp to chin. Trippy J pointed what looked like a plastic price-tag gun at Dr. Morrow's back, pulled the trigger, unleashing a purple beam evocative of a Pink Floyd laser show—*Dark Side of the Moon*. The gun made a fanciful zinging sound.

Dr. Morrow bellowed, did a spastic funky jig, and crumpled onto the floor. He lay there twitching.

Zing. Zing.

Wincing, as though it hurt his stomach, Trippy shot two more purple rays. Morrow's minions brayed and convulsed, fell and lay quivering.

"Some kind of fancy stun gun," Trippy said. "Used this shit on me yesterday in a Best Buy parking lot. They'll be down about five minutes, so we've got to act fast."

"What about Josh?"

"Don't tase me, bro," Josh said, forcing out a cough of laughter, trying to get control of the situation with irony.

"Hold him. I'll be right back."

Trippy darted into the dark office room and turned on the lights. I saw a steel vintage desk, oddly askew in the middle of the room, cluttered with micropads and empty soda bottles. I heard Trippy opening and closing drawers.

"Eureka!" he shouted, returning with two jumbo rolls of packing tape. "Not the best, but it'll do."

Trippy turned Morrow onto his belly, bound his limp wrists with cellophane tape, and mummy-wrapped his ankles. Pulled the same procedure on the rockabilly hipster. By the time he got to Pam, she was groaning, but her limbs still flopped like dead fish.

"Now get on the floor, Josh," Trippy said. "Prostrate, pronto."

"What?"

"Belly down, you idiot."

"Come on, man . . ."

"You want a jolt from this *Star Trek* pistol?"

I pushed Josh forward. He dropped to all fours, sighed as he assumed the worm position.

"Shouldn't we, like, stuff their mouths with something and tape them up too?" I asked.

A thousand television scenes depicting mundane violence popped into my head, merging into a prototype: dark shapes in chairs, hands bound behind their backs, their profiles elongated into snouts by makeshift muzzles.

"I reckon we have to." Trippy sighed. "Lest they start yelping for help."

· ·

I don't know how they'd moved it, but there it was, stuffed back into the room from which Trippy had escaped, the master biocomputer, that six-by-nine-foot high-tech fish tank with a row of lava lamps pulsing on top. Immersed in electric-blue brine, the familiar organisms bobbed and pulsed. Anemones of neural flesh swelled and contracted. Mollusk-like things glimmered with luminous mucus. Eel parts wavered and tentacles flexed.

"Eerily beautiful," Trippy whispered.

We stood in the dim room, weapons poised, gazing into the uncanny tank, repository of all our new knowledge. The computer seemed both prehistoric and futuristic, both pre- and posthuman, a data network that existed unto itself.

"The mother lode," I said, thinking of Kristeva's archaic mother, phallic, primeval, omnipotent.

The tank emitted a strange smell, an evocative combo of marsh funk and synthetic outgassing, an odor that I didn't recall from the Center, making me think that the move had upset the computer somehow, or that it had fallen into a state of semineglect. The bulletproof glass, which Chloe had once informed me was the same shit NASA used to make rocket windshields, looked scummy.

"Too bad we've got to trash it," said Trippy.

We placed our palms on the unshatterable glass. We exchanged soulful looks and nodded. We pushed against the tank with every ounce of strength our bodies could muster, ready to pour gallons of freaky water and creature components onto the floor, reduce all that complexity to filth and chaos in an instant, creepy flesh bits pining for oxygen on spongy office carpet—the kind of drama we pretty much *required* as a purgative at this point. But the tank wouldn't budge.

"Fuck and alas," said Trippy. "You know they got that mother bolted."

So we climbed up onto office chairs to inspect the top component, discovering that it was held in place by a surprisingly old-school latch mechanism and that we could swing it open like a coffin lid and peep down into the depths. We peered. We breathed the boggy funk. And then we got to work: me with my spear, Trippy with the Taser.

I stabbed mollusk-like mounds of pure muscle, releasing trickles of chartreuse blood. With deft swipes of my blade, I reduced sea-medusan entities to wisps of tissue. I chopped tentacles into sashimi. Hacked up minuscule eels. Punctured puffy peach-colored organisms that exploded into clouds of glowing yellow gore, tiny magenta globules spinning in the spew. Meanwhile, Trippy tased the fuck out of the mess, shot purple beams of radiation into the tank, producing a creepy wet crackle that made the components dance and flimmer, churning my remnants into chum. When we'd finished, the water was a sickly gray green, a few bright shreds afloat in the nastiness, meat chunks settling to the bottom.

Next, we got down to gathering every last micropad we could find and dumping them into the tank, taking repeated trips through the hallway to explore various offices, stepping over the four writhing human grubs, trying to avoid eye contact. We had to hustle. It was only a matter of time before one of our prisoners busted through a cellophane shackle or gnawed through a muzzle.

They were slowly worming their way toward the entryway that led to the elevator, but we'd set up a blockade of office chairs.

Most of the micropads seemed to be stored in the messy office room where Josh had been working. As Trippy busied himself with their death by liquid, giving the aquarium a good tasing after each fresh immersion, I staked out the rest of the place, roaming through empty rooms, most of which had no furniture, only indentations in the carpet where desks and cabinets had once stood, but I gave all the closets a scan just in case.

I was finishing off the last room, kicking through a pile of empty manila files from some defunct orthodontist office, when I heard a scream. I ran out into the hallway, thinking I'd see one of our prisoners braying, having chomped through his mouthpiece of wadded-up toilet paper and tape. But no, all four captives were still muted worms. And now Trippy was hollering.

"Romie, man, get in here!"

I ran into the computer room, but all I saw was Trippy standing baffled beside the dead tank. And then somebody let rip another bellow, coming from somewhere behind the tank—but there was nobody there.

Trippy slipped behind the tank and frisked the wall with his hands.

"Holy shit, Romie, a secret passageway. Are we in a movie or what?"

Sure enough, an unobtrusive door was embedded into the drywall, wallpapered in the same mint flower print. Trippy found a plastic lever-knob and opened the door. A funky scent wafted out: meaty, septic. The room was windowless, but we could make out the familiar ergonomic shape of a medical recliner, the jerking body of an unfortunate subject strapped into it.

"You fucking assholes!" screamed a familiar voice. "You won't get away with this."

I groped along the wall, located a light switch, and filled the room with acidic fluorescence.

There was Skeeter Rabin, looking dangerously skinny, flailing against the straps, his huge tarsier eyes bugging with astonishment. When I noted that he wore bloodstained medical scrubs, my heart sank. They'd probably been cutting him open, removing organs, filling his body with bioengineered animal parts, transforming the real Skeeter into something else. I sniffed, detecting a creepy, waxy animal smell in the room—the smell of guts and flesh and taboo inner fluids, mixed with some sharp chemical, that unmistakable tang of disinfected butchery that emanated from supermarket meat departments. There was a lab table in the corner, cluttered with stainless-steel medical instruments.

"Romie, shit, Trippy." Skeeter was laughing and crying, an astonishing gush of tears dripping over his knobby cheekbones. "Thank you, sweet Jesus. Thank you, sweet God. Get me out of this fucking straitjacket."

• •

There we were, three warriors at rest, tucked into the darkest corner of an Applebee's, huddled around a pitcher of Bass and a plate of flaming hot wings, the walls plastered with mass-produced Americana: segregation-era spirit pennants and sports paraphernalia. A fake-vintage photo of three midcentury cheerleaders hovered behind Skeeter's skull-stark head: *Death and the Maidens*. Their tits stuck out like Cold War missiles, ready to nuke Russia to ash. Shouting into megaphones, they cheered Skeeter on as he sucked radioactive sauce from a deep-fried drumette.

"Fucking delicious," he said, for he hadn't eaten since yesterday afternoon, had been receiving medical downloads all morning:

basic human dissection, gross anatomy, human physiology. He'd changed back into the cutoff jeans and Motorhead tee he'd been wearing when he arrived at Future Solutions United three days ago, five pounds heavier, his brain still bustling with the humanities lore we'd received at the Center.

"Okay," said Trippy, "now that you've got a dozen wings in your gut, give us the full scoop."

"If you'll allow me to begin in media res," said Skeeter.

"Was hoping you'd start with your birth trauma," said Trippy, "from which, according to Otto Rank, you're still trying to recover."

"Well, bo, I was actually doing all right," said Skeeter, "living gratis on my uncle's houseboat in Santee, trying to finish a novel before my stipend ran out, flirting with this divorcée who ran the marina, no Internet, no phone, just me and my laptop—no distractions but these loud-ass Jet Skiers who do stunts out in Cantey Bay every weekend." Skeeter grinned. "That and the increasingly frequent appearances of Kelly Ann Flemming, née Dubard."

"Aw, shit," said Trippy.

"Get this," said Skeeter, "just last Thursday I was chilling in the vastness of Lake Marion, sipping the wine Kelly buys by the crate, classic rock blaring from a half-rusted deck speaker, watching Kelly work her yoga-toned musculature as she reeled in a ten-pound catfish. Blue bikini. Yellow sun. Border collie napping in the shade. Kelly and I couldn't stop smiling at each other. I felt reckless, engulfed by dangerous joy, but goddamn: sometimes you just got to close your eyes and go for it."

"Word," I said, thinking of PigSlayer.

"And there was also the novel," said Skeeter, "tucked deep inside me, a flame guttering in the wreckage of my life—not just the plot and the characters but a bona fide vision."

"What's it about?" I asked.

"Don't want to spoil it by talking about it yet," said Skeeter, though he did reveal that the idea had stormed his brain shortly after he'd settled into the houseboat, two days after he'd first met Kelly, that first misty morning on the lake.

"Coffee cup in hand," said Skeeter, "gazing out into ethereal fog, I half expected a fairy hand to pop out of the water and hand me Excalibur."

"All this time," said Trippy, "and no static from Morrow and his goons?"

"Just the occasional migraine," said Skeeter, "but no voices or anything like that."

"Must've been the water," said Trippy, who'd spent his last month living signal-free with his cousin on Daufuskie Island, in a flood zone notorious for its bad cell reception.

"I was feeling cautiously optimistic for once," said Trippy, "normal enough to take jaunts to Charleston to visit an old flame. But then one day, ten minutes after I left Lorraine's house, as Romie already knows, Dr. Morrow tased me in a Best Buy parking lot."

Skeeter shook his head.

"Same here," he said, "but it was Blue Bay Hardware and Feed. I'd driven over there to buy kibble for Kelly's dog."

According to Skeeter, as he struggled to stuff the jumbo bag into his trunk, a black Ford Focus eased into the space beside him. Seconds later he felt every muscle in his body tighten inexplicably, as though he'd jumped into an arctic lake, and then a pulsing heat penetrated his bones. He twitched. He fell, flailed upon the asphalt, and then he couldn't move. A hoodied hipster squatted over him, pricked him with a jet injector. He woke up in the room we'd found him in, strapped into a medical recliner.

"And there was our old friend Dr. Morrow, examining my brain hologram just like old times, except that I was shrieking to high heaven. But he just sat there, pretending like he couldn't hear me."

Skeeter had kept screaming as he descended into that familiar BAIT-download well and a childhood memory rose from the obscurity of a frontal lobe: the tragic death of Godzilla, his pet iguana, who'd passed away when Skeeter was ten.

"Thirty minutes later," said Skeeter, "they had me shackled to a lab table, dissecting a fetal pig."

"And you were totally knowledgeable about pig anatomy?" asked Trippy.

"Pretty much."

"How'd they make you do it?" I asked.

"Well, let me tell you, bo: Josh stood there holding a Taser the whole time, bored shitless, thumbing his micropad with his free hand, snorting over E-Live posts, looking up every minute to make sure I stayed on task. Ashamed to say that after recovering from the horror, I sort of got into it, wanted to see if the diagrams and techniques in my head jibed with the real world. Plus, what else was I gonna do with the next hour, chained up in an empty room? And the pig was long dead, pickled and shrink-wrapped. But when they amped it up to primates, I couldn't handle it."

"Uh." Trippy took a tense sip of beer. "Dead or alive?"

"The first one was dead, some kind of rhesus monkey, but not pickled. Then they brought in a live one. I could hear it shrieking in the cage in the next room. Course, it was anesthetized when they spread it out on the table, but that didn't make it any easier. I flat out refused to do it, and then that little shit Josh tased me like it was nothing. Next time around, I was more cooperative. Proud to say the monkey successfully recovered from open-heart surgery."

"You Ironic Man?" said Trippy.

"I'm serious. Not the most seamless surgery ever, and there was nothing pathological in the monkey's heart. I didn't have to *do* anything to it, just incise the chest, saw through the sternum, spread the two halves with a retractor, survive the freakishly violent sight of a raw heart beating in open air, wire the sternum back together, and stitch up the incision."

"Fuck," I said. "How you know the monkey survived?"

"Heard it moaning in the next room as it came to, and then they took it away. Just this morning they started up with the human anatomy shit. And I praise the Lord God Almighty—don't laugh at me, you agnostic motherfuckers—that you two arrived before they made me . . ."

Skeeter shuddered, took a big gulp of beer. He gazed at our faces like he could see beneath our skin, scoping those delicate muscles that raised our brows, wriggled our noses, and jerked our lips open. Like he could view tiny valves fluttering inside our eyeballs, ossicles beating within the arcane canals of our ears, mucus-smeared cilia wavering like windswept grass inside our nasal passages.

"But it's all over, dog," said Trippy, a note of forced optimism in his voice.

"Hope so," said Skeeter, shuddering like he was trying to shake a ghost off his back.

"Speaking of that," I said, "who's gonna make the call?"

Skeeter had wanted to leave our prisoners taped and bound, insisting they'd bust free on their own; I was undecided; but Trippy had insisted that we find an archaic pay phone somewhere and report a burglary, just in case they didn't. That way the police would show up and make sure those bastards didn't starve to death, make sure we weren't on par with common murderers, no better than the corporate goons who'd tortured us.

"I'll do it," said Trippy. "Since I know my way around Atlanta. There's an old bowling alley not too far away: still got a functioning pay phone outside if my memory serves."

When our entrées arrived, we dug into mounds of grilled meat and greasy carbs, which took us back to the Center cafeteria, when the whole BAIT crew had hashed it out over tots and chicken tenders. Al and Vernon were still AWOL, though Trippy had talked to Irvin that one time.

"Had his number in the phone I threw into a pond," said Trippy. "Along with yours, Romie. Bet you he's doing fine. Maybe he got out before Morrow installed whatever he's been tracking us with."

"I pray that the connection's now busted," said Skeeter.

"Even if they got our data stored in the cloud," said Trippy, "bet you we set them back so far it'd be hell to get started again."

"Totally," I said. "They appeared to be operating on a low budget, no longer funded by a mega-conglomerate like BioFutures."

"But don't forget what the contract said," said Trippy. "They can sell their research to the highest bidder. Sit on it for years until the market's ripe. Speaking of contracts, must be something in the fine print that covers the shit they've been doing to us. Otherwise, why wouldn't they just get new subjects, nab some homeless people?"

"Also cost to consider," said Skeeter. "We've already got the hardware installed in our skulls, pretty much forever, I reckon."

My cell rang. It was Frisky Fish Marina. I solemnly slid Skeeter the phone. He took the call, spoke to Kelly Ann Flemming in soothing tones as he hurried outside. He had not told her about his stint at the Center, and she was likely freaked by his three-day disappearance, the discovery of his abandoned Corolla at Blue Bay Hardware and Feed.

"What the fuck will he tell her?" I asked Trippy.

"Hey, hon," said Trippy, "I've been receiving anatomical BAIT downloads and performing compulsory surgeries on baboons, what's up with you?" Trippy wheezed out a half-assed laugh and shook his head mournfully. "Shit's convoluted. How to explain it to the woman in your life?"

And then I told Trippy about PigSlayer.

"For all I know," I said, "this woman—if she is a woman—could be in cahoots with BioFutures, keeping tabs on me all this time by worming her way into my heart."

"You'll want to keep an eye on her either way," said Trippy. "Right?"

"True."

He told me he was in a semirelationship with Lady L, who went by Lorraine now and had a master's degree in public health. While delighted by his new smarts, she was also baffled, particularly since he had no diplomas to speak of.

"Told her I was dabbling in online education. Doing free course-work with Academic Earth, knowledge for knowledge's sake."

We both sniggered fiercely at this and then fortified ourselves with fresh gulps of beer.

"Reach rock bottom of your life," I said, "place body and brain at the disposal of a corrupt research organization, get your mind tricked out by a mad scientist, and still, a man wants companionship."

"'Tis the nature of humanity." Trippy sighed. "To seek love. *Love is a word, another kind of open—as a diamond comes into a knot of flame.*"

We sat in silence, watching Skeeter pace along the sidewalk outside the window, his mouth moving, spitting out heaven-knows-what kind of fool narrative. His face looked ashen, etched with new wrinkles, but his eyes shot out rays of hope. You could see it plain as day, beaming out of his skull like an SOS signal from a corroded, sinking battleship.

• •

I'd hit a stretch of woods on I-20, the dark roadside haunted with eerie swaths of fog, glowing like a host of bioluminescent plankton. The sky had cleared. The moon was fat, so maybe the phenomenon was just a trick of vapor and lunar light. But I felt half-asleep, lulled by five beers and the illusion of freedom.

The image of Skeeter and Trippy standing in the Applebee's parking lot already felt like a snapshot, tagged and dated, affixed to the E-Live Wall of my life. We'd exchanged contact info yet again, this time plotting to meet up monthly, pick each other's brains, make sure Morrow wasn't stationed in the Panopticon's central tower. And I hoped that this time the promises would stick. This time we'd track down Irvin and Al, maybe even Vernon, get them in on our game plan, see what our posthuman brothers were up to.

Courtesy of Trippy, I was still on a Delia Derbyshire kick, and '60s electronica purred from my dashboard speakers. Eerie swells of sphärophon rose like some emanation from the fog, slithering through old-school synths and melodic static, the perfect medium for my strange and hopeful mood. I could almost feel my soul expanding, filling the cab of my truck like some kind of ectoplasm, curling out of my partially open windows and floating into the infinity of night.

CODA

I stood, coffee cup in hand, staring down at the old gorge where hydra-headed vines grew so fast I could almost see them slithering like snakes. It was wild berry season, that brief and lovely spell before summer went rancid. A flock of birds had descended into the gulch, and everywhere I looked, some industrious feathered thing was scrabbling through brush to peck at ripe black fruit.

I felt halfway decent, had suffered no blackouts or migraines since the shakedown at Future Solutions United, was communicating regularly with Trippy and occasionally with Skeeter, who sometimes called me from Kelly's phone. Plus, firing across various sections of my tricked-out brain was a new vision. I saw a gallery space painted a shimmering violet. I saw swarms of winged pigs, zipping and whirling in the air. I saw art lovers walking into the hullabaloo, their hearts pounding as demonic swine darted toward them. And better yet, Trippy had agreed to compose a score befitting the majesty of *Hog Hell*.

Better to reign in Hell than serve in Heaven, he'd quipped in a text that morning.

I took another sip of coffee and smiled, for my vision was good and true. I'd head back out into forest and fields to tromp through mist with a rifle in my grip. I'd slay a slew of newfangled swine. I'd stuff them. I'd give them a second life with animatronic parts, smear their tusks with Day-Glo gore, give their skin an unearthly gleam. Rejecting the ironic dead end of snark, I'd draw poetically upon the 1980s head-shop psychedelia that had moved me in my youth.

I'd been cruising HogWild.com for the past few weeks, drinking in the latest rumors about the new fleet of Hogzillas that supposedly teemed in the swamp near GenExcel. So far, no hunter had made a kill of the hogs in question. Hogzilla's brethren still inhabited that hazy realm between rumor and reality—hatchlings of the mind, all smoke and neuron. I'd been communicating with PigSlayer on the board, hashing out the intricacies of for-profit research, postnatural hunting, the clusterfuck corruption of the agri-industrial complex. Each evening we crept toward each other, entangled our ideologies, and then scooted back. I was still suspicious of her, fearing that she wasn't who she claimed to be. And she, too, went hot and cold, sometimes seeming like a flesh-and-blood woman cautious about romantic entanglement, other times transforming into a Machiavellian cynic who gamed me with coy IMs.

My neighbor's yard dog released a long, neurotic whimper that spoke to my depressive tendencies. But my soul floated like a red plastic fishing bob on the polluted pond of my life, because I had a new project to obsess over. The morning felt balmy. It was Saturday. And I had a refrigerator full of beer. I walked inside, planning to spend my morning researching the latest round of feral hog sightings. Perhaps I'd tromp out to the swamp that very afternoon, take a look around, get a feel for the land, sniff the air for signs of musky monsters on the loose.

I sat down at my desk. My message icon flashed. I maximized the little box.

—*Hey*, said PigSlayer. *Attending a conference in Charleston next Friday. Passing through Hampton. Want to meet up to talk GM hogs, possible excursion in the GenExcel area?*

I started to whistle. Serotonin saturated my poor parched brain as my neurons flickered with beautiful thoughts, like the snack bars of my youth and girls at the skating rink in tight Gloria Vanderbilt jeans. I saw rows of bright mallards in my father's freezer. I saw my mother's yellow bandana, which matched the butterflies and the walls of her favorite room. I saw my warrior father hoisting his chain saw and disappearing into the gorge. And O the gurgling of desire, and O the idle creeks of my boyhood and the toxic sunsets and the fig trees and the okra patches, yes, and all the peculiar little streets and the voodoo-blue houses and the azaleas and the magnolias and the Confederate jasmine . . .

—*And yes I said yes I will Yes.*

But then I checked myself. I swallowed my hot-pink euphoria, which went down bitterly, like Pepto-Bismol, and backspaced over my reply. I wanted to sound cool and casual, off the cuff, not saturated with what seemed like light-years of loneliness, a universe of longing howling in some star-spangled void.

—*Yeah. Sure thing. When's a good time for you?*

· ·

We were meeting at Frances Ann's Front Porch for lunch, a strip-mall joint disguised as an antebellum house, its fake columns entwined with plastic wisteria. The waitresses wore gingham frocks. On Fridays, Frances Ann herself appeared, sashaying in a hoop skirt as she replenished the biscuit baskets. She'd just dropped by my table, in fact, telling me to *smile, honey*, and tickling my proto-jowl with her brightly polished nails.

Did I look worried?

PigSlayer was ten minutes late.

Moreover, tucked into a corner, skulking behind sunglasses, taking small rodent-like bites of cornbread was an unfamiliar species of hipster. Like the rockabilly hipster, he was pale. But his dark hair was sheered into a monastic bowl cut, and he sported a thin, clammy mustache. He wore a Dickies jumpsuit with combat boots and some kind of studded tool belt.

Did he seem to be peering over his menu to check me out? Yes, but I was something of a local legend, wasn't I? Perhaps he recognized me from the newspaper.

Did he stand out ridiculously in this greasy spoon? Yes, but I'd seen hip kids popping up all over town, gonzo foodies who photographed their entrées, their style quirks unreadable.

Could he possibly be another Morrow minion sent to monkey with my brain? Perhaps, but while the rockabilly hipster's over-styled costume had made sense (he'd been trying to fit in at an art opening), why would Morrow send another faux eccentric after me? That would be idiotic. And Morrow was no idiot. Unless the jumpsuit and tool belt were tricked out with sinister equipment.

I checked my phone again. Now PigSlayer was twenty minutes late. I'd already devoured several grotesquely fat buttermilk biscuits and downed a cup of coffee. I'd already checked my phone ten times. Just when I started to doubt PigSlayer's existence again, I received a text (we had, at last, exchanged numbers, and a more intimate version of her pulsed within the coordinates of my Oracle6).

—*Running late. Got lost in the boondocks of Allendale. Razorback country. CUMB.*

I too was cussing under my breath. I ordered another coffee. My left knee vibrated.

I was smack-dab in the quintessential twenty-first-century predicament, a man of *the future*, awaiting the incarnation of my elusive cybercrush. I wondered how many other poor souls on the planet were in similar circumstances at this exact moment. I pictured men and women sitting in restaurants, checking their gadgets, assessing, for the umpteenth time, the familiar, almost iconic image of the persona with whom they'd been communicating, wondering if the pic was up to date, wondering if it'd been Photoshopped, looking up from their screens and feeling the undertow of disappointment as the fleshy version of the person they'd envisioned walked into the room, plumper or shorter than expected, wrinkles around the eyes and mouth that placed them in a higher age bracket than professed. Or worse, what if the persona in question was much hotter than anticipated, intimidatingly young, beautiful, radiant, rich, tall, glamorous?

I could picture disappointment flickering in PigSlayer's eyes as she took in the sad sight of me, slumped in my chair with my receding hairline and stained Nikes, a fortysomething man with diseased gums and incipient age spots on his forearms, a taxidermist with hands the color of raw hamburger, an aging hesher with an unsophisticated haircut and drooping buttocks. But I did have nice, expressive eyes (or so I'd been told) that burned like will-o'-the-wisps above my sincere, yellow smile, windows to my fathomless soul, a soul questionably upgraded at the Center for Cybernetic Neuroscience, ready to mingle with the beautiful soul of a mysterious woman with dark hair and obvious intelligence, who perhaps hunted wild hogs as a hobby and taught English to unappreciative teens, or perhaps worked as a spy for some government agency or private research organization, which was still sexy—though Dangerous with a capital *D*.

I gazed down at her profile pic, again glanced up at the door.

There she was at last, standing beneath a trellis decked with fake vines, wearing khaki capris and a sleeveless navy blouse. Her hair was even darker than expected, a skunky streak of gray at the temple. She was small, just as I'd imagined, in her mid to late thirties, I figured. She was a real person walking among tendrils of plastic wisteria, greeting me with a nervous smile and a birdlike way of cocking her head as she stopped at my table to size me up.

Her eyes were hazel, etched with faint crow's-feet. Beautiful. Inscrutable. Perhaps these eyes contained cameras that offered remote viewers a vision of my twitchy smile. Perhaps these warm eyes concealed the cynicism of a seasoned agent. Perhaps these lovely eyes conveyed the guarded curiosity of an intelligent, world-weary English teacher who, miraculously, still believed that love was possible.

"You're Romie Futch," she said, offering her hand.

"Guilty," I said, thinking of my mother as I pressed her soft fingers, not too firmly, not too weakly.

Insecure men always come on too strong, whispered Mom's ghost, which seemed to billow behind me in the fan-blustered air.

When PigSlayer sat down I noticed the hipster in the corner craning forward to gawk. Surely, if he were an agent, he would not be so obvious. He was just a smug asshole with youth to burn, amused by our courtship, tittering over two seasoned people trying to squeeze a drop of nectar from the parched husks of their lives.

"And you're, uh, PigSlayer."

She laughed. "Call me Beth."

"A nice compact name."

"No frills." When she smiled, a small indentation appeared in the tip of her nose. She sat down. We studied our menus, stealing glances over the laminated pages, calculating, assessing.

"Yep," I said, suddenly tongue-tied.

"So congrats, for the umpteenth time, on your exhibition," she said. "Reminds me of Renaissance-era spectacle, a kind of post-modern masque. I thought this instantly when I read the article. Sorry I couldn't make your opening."

Her smooth syntax, her command of the diction spectrum, her obvious intelligence combined with a casual earthiness that deflected pretension. The spark of mischief in her kind eyes. The way she worked her napkin with restless fingers. And something unstated, possibly pheromonal, oozing from her glands and breath, made me feel present in my skin. My blood pulsed with oxygen. Data flowed into my sensory organs: light rays, sound waves, particles of scent. Tiny papillae throbbed as too-sweet coffee trickled over my tongue.

We both ordered the special: country-fried chicken with butter beans and rice, a side of collards for her, okra for me.

We sipped coffee.

We chatted about Renaissance lit as we awaited our food. We both had an affinity for Jacobean drama, a fondness for Aphra Behn. She'd read *The Anatomy of Melancholy*. She had a working knowledge of pre-Copernican cosmology, anatomy theater, the great chain of being that hilariously placed oysters and clams beneath minerals and sand. She zipped back and forth between the sublime and the absurd with ease.

"But our classification systems will probably seem just as ridiculous to generations down the road," she said.

I agreed, nodding my head enthusiastically, not crazily, I hoped.

We discussed *The Archaeology of Knowledge*, Borges's *The Book of Imaginary Beings*, krakens and lizard men and Sasquatches, which naturally brought us around to the subject of quasi-mythic GM hogs—particularly the fresh crop of monsters that had recently been sighted in the Blue Horse swamp area near Yemassee, spawning a whole new swarm of conspiracy theories.

"Gives new resonance to the term 'war pigs,'" said Beth.

"I have a project in mind for these boars," I said. "Well, it's not exactly a project yet."

"Go ahead and call it a vision." Beth winked. "Why the hell not?"

I described *Hog Hell*: the sounder of phosphorescent pigs spinning in the sterile air of a vast gallery space, bewildered art patrons ducking and shrieking as the swine swooped toward them, Trippy's thunderous music assaulting them from multiple speakers.

When the waitress set down steaming plates of food, we both blinked, stunned. Had we forgotten where we were? My giddiness thrummed in the silent space around my ears. Beth's smile seemed suddenly forced.

We ate. I became self-conscious again: about my overstuffed mouth, my bestial chewing, my desire to probe with my tongue to remove a masticated morsel from the hollow between my gum and upper left canine.

This woman was a passionate polymath, too good to be true, the recipient, she claimed, of a postgraduate degree about which she was cynical, and also a compulsive Googler. A shadow of suspicion darkened my mood. What if she'd had BAIT downloads? What if she was a robot flunky, programmed by Dr. Morrow, or some other species of BioFutures affiliate, sent to ensnare me?

I remembered the hipster in the corner, whom I'd forgotten in my excitement. There he was, settling his bill. There he was, standing up. There he was, exiting through the faux-mahogany door with ostentatious aloofness, vanishing into the ether of afternoon. Or perhaps he was posted outside the door, communicating with Dr. Morrow or Beth or other obscure agents who had some stake in my poor overdetermined brain.

"Romie." Beth put down her fork. "I admire your work tremendously. I think it's pretty damn brilliant, in fact. But I was wondering if you've ever thought about taking a more active approach."

My stomach flipped. I glanced toward the window. Thought I saw the jumpsuit-clad cool guy slouching outside in the summer haze. But no, it was something else. A greyhound leashed to a bench. I turned back to Beth.

"A more active approach to what?"

Beth sat stiffly in her chair. She scanned the room. She leaned forward.

"GenExcel," she whispered. "BioFutures. Find out how it all fits together."

"Funny you should say that because . . ."

I was about to tell her about the Center, the BAITs, my recent brush with Future Solutions United. I was about to let it all spill obscenely like a spew of shiny coins from a slot machine, but I caught myself. I studied her face, detecting nothing in the way of mood, tone, intent. She took a cautious sip of coffee, as though it were piping hot—but it had long cooled.

"I'll be frank with you," she said. "I kind of came to recruit you."

"Into what?"

"I don't want to say too much about it here." She glanced around again. "Why don't you take a little trip out to the swamp with us?"

Us. I imagined goons in military garb stationed along the sidewalk outside, buff action-figure types positioned in front of Hobby Horse Craft Hub, Cut-Ups Kids' Salon, and Pal-Med Diabetic Supplies.

"There you go again," I said, "with the sinister royal 'we.'"

"Actually," she said, "there *are* some people I want you to meet. We aren't an official organization, just some like-minded people I've met through the Internet—progressive outdoorsy types, organic farmers, environmentalists with a penchant for meta-drama, writers, filmmakers, the kind of people who could put together a pretty convincing exposé. But I'm saying too much in this particular context."

"Are you really a schoolteacher?"

"Yes."

"A hog hunter?"

"Not as badass as my online profile conveys, I'll admit, but I've bagged my share."

She smiled again, creating that nose dimple, which humanized her. If she had goons waiting in the parking lot, why would she admit it? Wouldn't she just lure me out into the swamp with her feminine wiles and laugh as they crawled from the forest and bonked me in the head? I saw myself getting the business end of a bludgeon and dropping into instant unconsciousness.

"Why me?"

"You're obviously smart," she said. "Politically, ideologically, you get it. You know your way around a forest, know how to use firearms safely, are clearly capable of brave acts, and last but not least, as the slayer of a legendary GM monster of regional fame, your celebrity would make a killer PR tool."

She smiled again. Her flattery went to my head like a hit of nitrous oxide, unmooring logical thought, making my cheeks burn.

The possibility that she was a bona fide revolutionary enhanced her attractiveness by a factor of ten. I pictured us decked out in camo, sneaking through night forests, climbing barbed-wire fences silvered by the light of the moon. I saw us relaxing after an exploit, enjoying a few brews at the secret hideout, which in my imagination resembled some kick-ass Robinson Crusoe–style tree house complex.

If she was telling the truth, if she could be trusted, she would help make sure Dr. Morrow was out of business for life, perhaps ensure a future unmolested by the tinkering of a mad scientist.

"Why don't you at least come outside and meet a couple of my friends," Beth said, "and then see how you feel about it?"

I nodded. I would go out into the parking lot and take a look, but I would be careful, make sure there were plenty of cars around, people out and about.

Beth insisted on splitting the check. We walked outside. I slipped on my aviators and surveyed the parking lot.

Summer was coming into its own—the sky a giddy pilot-light blue, cicadas thrumming in the mammoth pines, the air balmy, smelling of car exhaust and mown grass. Butterflies darted over green hedges. A girl whizzed by on a bike. A toddler sat down on the sidewalk and chortled, evoking the kind of carefree effervescence that often preceded the first appearance of a killer in a horror film, festive carnival music underscored by the dark minor chords that viewers would soon recognize as the psychopath's signature theme.

Now Beth was waving at someone. Now a Subaru Outback with a kayak rack was cruising toward us, a thirtyish shaggy-haired guy at the wheel, a black woman riding shotgun, dreads spilling out of her orange batik head wrap—the kind of people who haunted health-food stores and parks where bright Frisbees whirred through the air.

"Hey." The guy stuck his hand out of the open window. "I'm Andrew, and this is my girlfriend, Althea." We shook.

"Nice to meet you, Romie," said the woman in a Brit accent.

Was Andrew's Patagonia tee a bit much? Was Althea's British accent fake? Did the script read *Enter innocent hippies*? Did they have stun guns in the glove compartment? Did they possess micro-pads bearing my brain's most intimate coordinates, my CC levels, the enigmatic symbology of my genome map? There was a cooler in the backseat, an empty Cheetos bag, a small character lapse that gave me hope.

"What do you think, Romie?" Beth said. "Are you up for a hike today?"

Making a visor of her left hand, Beth shielded her eyes from the sun. She smiled. Her teeth were nice but not blazing white. She had a dimple on her chin that matched the elfin indentation in her nose.

I saw myself walking away from her. Saw myself driving back to my house, making my rounds through the cluttered emptiness, opening windows to let the summer day wash over me as I lounged on the couch, wondering if I'd made the right choice.

"Why not?" I said, already working the door handle. I climbed into the backseat. Beth slid in through the other door. I tried not to stare at her as she leaned forward, instructing Andrew on the best route out of this town.

ACKNOWLEDGMENTS

Although this novel began years ago as a short story that was too big for its britches, I retrieved it from a remote computer file after reading my cousin Carl Elliott's essay "Guinea-Pigging" (originally published in the *New Yorker*), which chronicles the subculture of clinical-trial research subjects. Carl's compassionate and trenchant piece inspired me to invent the fictional Center for Cybernetic Neuroscience, which serves as the engine of transformation for Romie Futch. I'd like to thank my wonderful agent, Denise Shannon, for championing my fiction and also Kelly Malloy, the novel's very first reader, whose boundless enthusiasm gave me the confidence to let Romie and Hogzilla run loose in the world. I'm forever indebted to the kickass crew at *Tin House* magazine and books, some of the most friendly and visionary folks in contemporary publishing, helmed by Rob Spillman and Win McCormack. My brilliant editor, Meg Storey, deserves to have her name and picture on this book, not only for putting up with me but also for whipping my hog-wild narrative into shape, patiently prodding me until I coughed up a beginning and ending that made the book tick. Nanci McCloskey has to be the hardest-working publicity genius in the book biz, performing miracles to get my prose noticed while also answering my numerous annoying e-mails. For the second time, Diane Chonette has designed a stunning cover for my book, but this round, she graciously endured my obsessive-compulsive font-color anxiety, and for that I must apologize. I would like to thank Talal Gedeon Achi, one of the readers at Tin House Books, who gave me invaluable feedback, and also Thomas Ross, Michelle Wildgen, Tony Perez, and Meg Cassidy. I am grateful for the University of South Carolina, which has just granted me a sabbatical, and also the Rona Jaffe Foundation, which generously supported this endeavor. I couldn't function without my in-laws, John and Sybil Dennis, or without all of my friends, particularly the weirdos, arts people, and my colleagues at USC. The Elliott clan has nurtured and inspired me since I began my freakish existence, particularly my father, Joseph Elliott, and my late mother, Francis. Stephen Taylor is not only one of my oldest friends, but he also designed (and continues to redesign) my beautiful website. My honorary sister Libby Furr is always there when I feel a nervous breakdown coming on, willing to endure hours of deranged chatter. Finally, my husband, Steve Dennis, and daughter, Eva, not only bear the burden of my love but also get to see my numerous monster faces. It may seem strange that I dedicated this mock-macho book to my three-year-old daughter, but I wrote most of the first draft when she was in utero, kicking me from the inside, prodding me onward.

JULIA ELLIOTT's fiction has appeared in *Tin House*, the *Georgia Review*, *Conjunctions*, *Fence*, and other publications. She has won a Rona Jaffe Writer's Award, and her stories have been anthologized in *Pushcart Prize: Best of the Small Presses*, *Best American Fantasy*, and *Best American Short Stories*. Her debut story collection, *The Wilds*, was chosen by *Kirkus*, *BuzzFeed*, *Book Riot*, and *Electric Literature* as one of the Best Books of 2014 and was a *New York Times Book Review* Editors' Choice. She is currently working on a novel about hamadryas baboons, a species she has studied as an amateur primatologist. She teaches English and Women's and Gender Studies at the University of South Carolina in Columbia, where she lives with her daughter and husband. She and her spouse, John Dennis, are founding members of the music collective Grey Egg.